(continued from front flap)

Soon after Jack discovers the Chairman has his own designs on him, he is confronted by Dolores's jealous, street-smart husband, Hector. Jack finds his life spinning wildly out of control—until he must fight not just for his job and for Dolores, but quite possibly for his life.

Written with immense authority and insight, *Bodies Electric* is a journey inside the dark quarters of a global corporation, the rotted heart of the ever-harrowing city, and the urges that reside within every man and woman.

BODIES
ELECTRIC

Also by Colin Harrison
Break and Enter

BODIES ELECTRIC

a novel

COLIN HARRISON

Crown Publishers, Inc.
New York

Copyright © 1993 by Colin Harrison

Published by Crown Publishers, Inc., 201 East 50th Street, New York, New York 10022. Member of the Crown Publishing Group.

Random House, Inc. New York, Toronto, London, Sydney, Auckland

CROWN is a trademark of Crown Publishers, Inc.

Manufactured in the United States of America

Library of Congress Cataloging-in-Publication Data

Harrison, Colin
    Bodies electric: a novel / by Colin Harrison.
    I. Title.
    PS3558.A6655B6   1993
    813'.54 — dc20   92-40766
                                               CIP

ISBN 0-517-58491-3

10 9 8 7 6 5 4 3 2 1

First Edition

For my parents, always encouraging

Acknowledgments

A number of individuals kindly helped me with certain points of information during the writing of this novel: my old and good friend, Jay Batley, executive assistant, U.S. Senate; Sidney K. Stein, M.D.; Leo Spellman at Steinway & Sons, Inc.; Jeffrey Turkelson at GE Americom; Steve Gelmis at Public Interest Telecom, Inc.; Timothy Sultan; Earl Shorris, a generous man and gifted writer who also gave wise counsel; in Brooklyn, Michael Daly, John Gallagher, Barry Paikoff, and Dorothy Chandler; Larry Slaughter at J. P. Morgan, Inc.; Jane Ross and Nathaniel Bohrer at Bear, Stearns Co., Inc.; and, finally, two executives at one multinational media-entertainment corporation who preferred not to be acknowledged by name. Any and all errors should be attributed to the author, however.

The epigraph is taken from Walt Whitman's *Specimen Days*, which appears in *The Portable Walt Whitman* (New York: Viking-Penguin, 1986), edited by Mark Van Doren. The Spanish prayer on page 130 is taken directly from a small devotional packet I found in a botanica in Sunset Park, Brooklyn; its origin is unknown. The Spanish prayer on page 292 is from *Colección de Oraciones Escogidas*, published by De Pablo International. The quote from the German philosopher Arthur Schopenhauer that appears on page 348 can be found in *The Will to Live: Selected Writings of Arthur Schopenhauer* (New York: Frederick Ungar Publishing Co.) in Chapter XII, "On the Sufferings of the World." I came across the quote in a brilliant story by Thom Jones, "I Want to Live!", which appeared in the August 1992 issue of *Harper's Magazine*.

Much of this novel was first composed at the VG bar/restaurant at the corner of Broadway and Bleecker in Manhattan, and I wish to acknowledge the waitresses there, past and present, who were unfailingly patient with my sprawl of papers.

I am deeply indebted to Lewis H. Lapham, the editor of *Harper's Magazine*, who understands the difficulty of balancing one's responsibilities as a magazine editor with the compulsion to write one's own books.

Kris Dahl, my agent, provided me with encouragement and smart guidance in this project.

David Groff, my editor at Crown, again amply demonstrated that there are still book editors in Manhattan who actually edit.

Last and most, I am immeasurably grateful to my wife, Kathryn Harrison, who read every draft with the shrewdness of the fellow novelist she is and with the sensitivity of a spouse. And it was she who held our crying newborn son while I completed this book.

. . . as we went a little further we met the woman afoot. I could not see her face, in its great sun-bonnet, but somehow her figure and gait told misery, terror, destitution. She had the rag-bundled, half-starv'd infant still in her arms, and in her hands held two or three baskets, which she had evidently taken to the next house for sale. . . . We stopp'd, asking about the baskets, which we bought. As we paid the money, she kept her face hidden in the recesses of her bonnet. Then as we started, and stopp'd again, Al., (whose sympathies were evidently arous'd,) went back to the camping ground to get another basket. He caught a look of her face, and talk'd with her a little. Eyes, voice and manner were those of a corpse, animated by electricity. She was quite young. . . . Poor woman—what story was it, out of her fortunes, to account for that inexpressibly scared way, those glassy eyes, and that hollow voice?

. . . Tread the bare board floor lightly here, for the pain and panting of death are in this cot. I saw the lieutenant when he was first brought here. . . . He had been getting along pretty well till night before last, when a sudden hemorrhage that could not be stopt came upon him, and to-day it still continues at intervals. Notice that water-pail by the side of the bed, with a quantity of blood and bloody pieces of muslin, nearly full; that tells the story. The poor young man is struggling painfully for breath, his great dark eyes with a glaze already upon them, and the choking faint but audible in his throat. An attendant sits by him, and will not leave him till the last; yet little can be done. He will die here in an hour or two. . . . Meantime the ordinary chat and business of the ward a little way off goes on indifferently. Some of the inmates are laughing and joking, others are playing checkers or cards, others are reading, &c.

—From *Specimen Days*, by Walt Whitman

BODIES
ELECTRIC

ONE

My name is Jack Whitman and I should never have had the first thing to do with her. I shouldn't have indulged myself — my loneliness, my attraction to her — not with what was happening at the Corporation at the time. But I'm as weak hearted for love and greedy for power as the next guy, maybe more so. And I was crazy for the sex — of course that was part of it. If only I'd worked longer at the office that Monday night or gone straight home, if only I hadn't even *seen* her.

Instead I took a cab uptown to eat at a small Cajun place right on Broadway and had a few drinks with dinner. I watched couples lean toward one another, and when I'd been made lonely by their intimacy, I stepped outside. This was just last April, and that night the city felt lifted on a breeze of pollen, a time when you suddenly see that spring has come again and that you missed it all along, missed the little fenced plots of yellow tulips in front of the better apartment houses and the sharp pale shoulders of women out for lunch at midday. At the subway I paused to look up Broadway for a cab but saw none coming and so I ducked down the stairs. That one choice, right there, made all the difference.

In my seat I opened the *Wall Street Journal* and settled into a boozy semiconsciousness in which the entrance and exit of passengers, the rush of the train, and the conductor's scratchy announcements blurred together. Hunched over in my charcoal gray suit, I scanned the paper for news of the Corporation's competitors — quarterly profit information, sneaky little deals meant to eat into our market share, who was in, who was out. And then I turned to the stock pages to check on my own portfolio. Money has a certain intellectual fascination if you have enough of it, and I did, more than necessary for a thirty-five-year-old guy living alone in New York City. How much?

Everyone wants to know once they find out you work for the Corporation. They get that quick squint in their eyes and inspect your suit, they figure inwardly, *He's wired into the big money.* They want to know but are afraid to ask. Well, I'll get this point out of the way right now: my compensation at the time was $395,000 a year, which is, of course, a shitload of money, equal to the salaries of about thirty Mexican busboys at the Bull & Bear, a sum that made my father wince when he heard it—a little less than $33,000 a month gross. Getting killed on the taxes, of course. But it was nothing compared to the sums the Chairman and Morrison, our CEO, were pulling in. Millions. Tens of millions. The whole audacious game was rigged for their benefit. Of course, neither man was worth such sums. No one is. We're all replaceable. Just bodies. Isn't that true?

The subway car, grinding through the dark tunnels, was empty enough that everyone on it was seated, and as I stared at the newsprint, something touched the toe of my shoe. It was a red, well-used Crayola crayon that had rolled at an angle across the floor of the car, and sitting opposite me was a dark-haired girl of about four, holding her hand out for it, wiggling her fingers in anticipation. Her legs swung freely above the floor. On the girl's lap was a coloring book. I picked up the crayon, reached across the car, and handed it to her, smiling at her mother in the polite manner of strangers.

"Oh, I'm sorry," the woman whispered in an obligatory, embarrassed way, pulling a ragged coat around her. I noticed her mouth—she knew what she was doing with lipstick. "Thank you."

I nodded and returned to the paper, but like most men, single or otherwise, I don't miss a good-looking woman. I glanced into her face and saw her exhausted eyes quickly look down, avoiding mine. It was then I suffered that first jolt of appetite for her, that gripping in the stomach that is sexual and maybe something else, too. Did I love her immediately? No, of course not. Yes, in that sudden, helpless way, such that I stared. She had the same coloring as the little girl. I couldn't have said what her race was, not exactly, but it wasn't white. Dark hair held up with barrettes. Eyes the color of Coca-Cola. Skin that velvety brown. You could put this woman in an ankle-length black mink, I thought to myself, set her in a polished lobby with a doorman on the Upper East Side, and you'd be convinced she was a

Venezuelan or Brazilian heiress with some black or mestizo blood—
something different, something to my whitebread taste *exotic*—trained
in the best international boarding schools and underwritten in her
glass palace over Park Avenue by a multilingual father reselling oil or
computer chips or Eurodollars. And it was equally clear that if the
woman had been dressed in a pair of tight jeans and cheap red pumps,
she might be a New York–born Puerto Rican whore addicted to
self-destruction, carrying a purse filled with rubbers and wrinkled bills
and selling herself to all comers at the entrance to the Lincoln Tunnel,
a woman who, despite providence's gift of fine bones and large, deep
eyes, was forced to live life faster and harder than was ever meant.

But the woman sitting across from me in the subway car belonged
to neither such group—she possessed some other story, and I felt that
immediate compulsion to study and know the face of a stranger. Was
this wrong? Can I at least be forgiven *this*? Don't we all memorize the
faces of strangers? Her cheeks rose sharply and her lips were full.
Slightly too much so, suggesting imprudence and passion. On dark
women, red lips have a certain lurid appeal. She was a beauty, a tired
beauty.

Yet New York City is full of beautiful women, thousands upon
thousands of them, and most are understandably wary of the sudden
attentions of strange men. So I looked away. I *am* polite, after all, not
the type to make an aggressive compliment. I don't have the glib
confidence. And I've never insulted a woman, said the things men say
aloud. Of course I *think* those brutal thoughts. Men are full of brutal
thoughts.

I peered blindly at the *Journal*, but after a minute or two looked
up a second time, wondering how such a magnificent woman was so
obviously riding the edge of homelessness. The women one meets in
the Corporation and at its social rituals possess a certain high gloss,
with small fortunes spent on clothing and jewelry. Quite charming
with a wineglass in their hands, they are able to tinkle polite laughter,
and underneath their sleek dresses they wear silk panties the color of
jade. They are very smart about the guests on "Nightline" and up-to-
date on their mammograms, and so on. At times such women had
interested me, other times not. They and I had been through it.

Now, I saw that the child continued to color in her book, choosing each crayon carefully, after happy consultation with her mother. The girl was clean, with brushed hair; if she had no older sister she was dressed in what I suspected was clothing given out by a church or bought in a secondhand shop. Her mother was dressed no better, or even a bit worse, but it was hard to tell, as she remained wrapped within her old coat, which was large for her and spotted. I took the woman to be in her late twenties, and among the last things I noticed was a narrow gold wedding ring on her left hand.

That the woman was married struck me as a great waste, for it appeared she lived nearly hand to mouth; perhaps her husband was unemployed, perhaps he was a drug addict, perhaps he was any of the kinds of men upon whom so many women desperately depend. I knew, of course, that beauty was neither qualification nor guarantee for the receipt of love and happiness, but it pained me that the woman was obviously uncared for, even as she lifted her daughter into her lap and lightly kissed the child's head. I sort of suddenly loved the little girl as well. (I was drunk, I was sentimental, I was nostalgic for something that had been taken from me. Those of us who have known horror never forget it — one is forever changed.) The woman held her daughter with both arms and gently rocked her. She didn't know I watched. Her face tipped forward in fatigue and, by habit, I supposed, she kissed the small dark head again. I wondered if she lived in the outer neighborhoods of Brooklyn, the final destination of our train, where the rents are lower, as are the social classes. And her apparently married condition didn't disappoint me, for I had already made the usual half-conscious assumptions about her race and background and education — married or not, she wasn't the kind of woman I ever got involved with.

Still, I watched them (*of course*, I tell myself now, *of course* you watched them like you had not watched anyone in a long time, you watched the mother in your horny bastard's mind as she lowered herself down upon you, the lips red and huge and her eyes wet smoke). Sitting beneath advertisements for cockroach poison and AIDS hotlines, mother and child appeared to live only for each other, and I saw that the daughter desired to please her mother as much as her mother sought to shield her from the harshness of the subway. She held her daughter tightly, as if drawing strength from the wriggling young body in her arms.

"I can draw," the girl declared as she scribbled energetically over a page of the coloring book.

"Yes, you can," the mother whispered into the small ear next to her lips. It was then that a rhythmic hollering could be heard through the door at the far end of the car, coming from an advancing black woman of about sixty, who was dressed immaculately in white. "I am here in the name of the Lord!" she announced in a ruined voice that admitted no fear of the opinion of her listeners. She had a squat muscularity to her carriage and gripped a small Bible in one hand. "You must ask sal-*va*-tion of the Lord! He does not love the sin, but He loves the sinnah!" She spat these words at the riders, most of whom had already bent their heads back into their papers and books. ". . . I'm not here to talk about no *nice* stuff! I'm here to talk about the lies and corruption of the body of Christ. About the crack and the drinkin' and the killin'! And the greed for the golden calf! And infidelity! About all you men who say you been out with the boys when you been out with the *girls*—"

"Some *womens* want some that good stuff, too!" came a man's voice toward the other end of the car, followed by sniggering and smiles all around.

"That's right!" the gospelizing woman answered. "Sure they do! They want *that* because they think it going to make them happy. But the body is a weak vessel, it will rot and *putrefah!* The man's penis, it putrefah! And the vagina, it putrefah! And the hand what got the golden calf in it! And all the rest of the body! Anybody here gone to live forever?" She looked around accusingly. "Anybody here three hundred year old? The body is nothin' but rotting *meat!* while the *soul*—the soul is *divine*. Anybody one hundred and *two?* I didn't *think* so! Anybody here *not* a sinner?" The woman looked around menacingly, her teeth bared. "I didn't *think* so! And the soul will putrefah without salvation! And those of you who sin and sin again, shall be *snatch-ed* into eternal fire!" The woman swiveled on her thick hips, blasting one end of the car and then the other. "The Lord is watchin' . . ."

The train slowed as it neared the Forty-second Street stop and I turned my attention back to the mother and daughter across the aisle. The mother put away the crayons with the care of someone who knows to the penny what they cost and then stood up. The coloring book, I saw, featured cartoon figures known to all children and licensed by the animated entertainment subdivision of the film division of the Corporation. The mother pulled her coat around her shoulders, still talking in a low voice to her daughter, while down the car the old woman raved: ". . . children around the world bin killed ever-day and nobody care ex-*cept* the Lord! *You!* And *you!*" She pointed a fat gloved finger at several commuters reading their papers or staring out the windows at the dark tunnel blurring past. "You be standin' *by* while the little children of God are being killed by sin and wickedness!"

"Shut yo mouth, old woman!" came the same heckling voice again, this time angry and fast.

"If your momma had shut her *legs* when you was being *born*," the woman responded, "then you would have *died*, sinner!" She resumed her transit toward my end of the car, muttering damnation and putrefaction under her breath. She passed the young woman and her daughter without incident; perhaps they did not appear as sinners in her eyes. But before heading out the door to the next car, she let her manic, accusatory attention rest on me. Her eyes boiled with crazed dark righteousness—*You 'specially wicked and don't you think I don't know it* they seemed to shoot, and I felt an odd fear, staring into the bright black face furrowed in judgment.

The train cleared the subway tunnel and slowed past the many waiting people on the platform. The woman gathered her daughter's hand and I felt a sudden, inexplicable anxiety that I was never going to see them again. I jumped up. "Excuse me," I blurted. "I noticed—" The subway car lurched and I did a broken dance step. "I noticed that you might need something—"

"Yes?" the woman answered in a clear, self-possessed voice. "What do you think I need?"

"Well—a job, maybe?" I stayed several feet away, in order that she not smell the drink on my breath. The woman's eyes moved over me appraisingly, as if despite my suit and overcoat and fine leather shoes, I might be yet another urban madman, pressing specious friendship upon her. Other than that, I was merely some white guy going soft in the belly. "I thought maybe you might need work," I stumbled on, "and I wondered if I could be of help. I work for a large company . . ." I fished into my wallet and found an embossed business card, with the famous logo of the Corporation most prominent. "Here." By now, people were staring at me with the guarded, what-now interest New Yorkers reserve for beggars, con men, and incompetent subway musicians. Meanwhile the brakes of the train screamed and the conductor's voice, dismantled by static into a protohuman chatter, blasted over the intercom: *Forty-second Street change hereforthenumber onelocal, numbernine, RandNtrains, steplively whenexiting the train, watch your step letthemoff please, letthemoff.*

"Here, take it." I leaned forward as the subway car doors opened and pressed the crisp, heavy-stock card into the woman's hand, careful that our fingers not touch. "I'm not a nut, you understand? Not crazy. Call me if you need a job."

The woman and her daughter stepped off the train. The doors jolted shut and I felt strangely exhausted. The other riders stared at me. The woman turned back, safe now on the other side of the glass—still beautiful in the harsh fluorescent light of the platform—and glanced down at the card in her hand. Her daughter waited for her mother's reaction. Then the woman looked up at me, lifting her chin, her pressed-lipped expression admitting nothing.

♦ ♦ ♦

Brooklyn is, still, a great and romantic place. I lived in the Victorian brownstone neighborhood of Park Slope, not far from Grand Army Plaza, the entrance to Prospect Park. An immense arch honoring the thousands of Union men who died in the Civil War stands in the plaza, and is decorated with generals and soldiers and freed slaves massed in the heat of struggle. At the top of the arch thunders a giant bronze monument of winged Victory driving her chariot of horses. The figures have tarnished to a bright, marbleized blue, and their frenzied, death-rapturous eyes have blind dominion over the plaza, where black nannies clucking in various Caribbean dialects wheel an army of white babies into the park each day. The neighborhood attracts upper-middle-class families and abounds with Montessori schools, video stores, automatic banking machines, real estate offices, good bookshops, cafés, and bakeries selling croissants and expensive coffee. On weekends, beneath the old maples and oaks that canopy the streets, children can be found scribbling in colored chalks on the massive slabs of slate that front the grand nineteenth-century buildings while their mothers or fathers sit out on the stoops with a fat Sunday *Times*. I lived there because of the quiet atmosphere, because the train that ran past my office in Manhattan deposited me only a few blocks away, and because it had once seemed an ideal place in the city to have a family.

My house, a four-story brownstone that needed a couple of hundred more hours of my labor, had been owned by a Mrs. Cronister, the last remaining heir of the man who invented the pneumatic tire and manufactured them in Brooklyn. In the small front yard a flowering pear tree arched over the cast-iron fence and the stone steps that lifted sharply up to the first floor. I lived on the parlor floor and the two floors above it, slowly renovating room by room, and from time to time rented out the garden apartment to help pay the mortgage. Within the triple set of parlor doors, the walls were original horsehair plaster, smooth as glass, the inlaid parquet floors firm, the rooms quiet and large, and the mahogany woodwork ornate and magnificent. Weekends I sat reading in the small, sunny backyard and each spring I worked the soil, finding old marbles, bits of broken free-blown bottles, bent spoons made of pewter, and, once, an 1893 Morgan silver dollar. By July I would begin to harvest several varieties of tomatoes, as well as scores of cucumbers that exploded in a happy riot of vines and yellow blooms over the fence. At night, when I was feeling melancholy, in a mood to drink, I sat on the roof in a pink beach chair and gazed past the dark silhouettes of Brooklyn's rooftops and church spires toward the awesome, ever-blazing Manhattan sky-line—the twin towers of the World Trade Center jutting into the sky on the tip of the island, and farther north, the calm grandeur of the Empire State Building, the soft curves of the Chrysler Building, the sharp Citicorp spike. I loved this house, the beveled surfaces of dark stone, the old windows, the stair banisters that rattled faintly when the subway passed beneath. Like the sprawling borough of Brooklyn, it had once seemed a great and romantic place to raise children. Now, however, the house was my dark, silent partner, a vault of solitude.

That April evening, my head still light, I closed the front door behind me and, as I did six days a week, removed and discarded the pieces of mail that had my dead wife's name on it. Her name continued to exist and multiply in the unending generation of computer mailing lists despite my efforts to put a stop to it, spawning CAR-RT-SORT permutations of catalogs for clothes, housewares, charities, and so forth. I have found that it helps to be drunk when throwing away mail addressed to one's murdered wife, and I could not stand to see her name printed plainly above the address of the house she cherished and where she had never lived.

Liz and I met after college, lived together a couple of years, then married. She'd come from an unhappy childhood and later — when she had traveled far enough from that upbringing, and she had even been able to laugh about what horrible people her parents had been — she would tease me that I'd married her because I was a sucker for women in distress. We were both children of divorced parents and I think there was something broken in each of us that the other more or less fixed. Or maybe it was something else — the reasons didn't matter to me; I was happily domesticated, not terribly mindful that we lived in a cramped Upper West Side apartment, thankful — in the shallow, confident way that I was back then, the way we all were, back in the eighties — that I had been lucky enough to find someone. I was just starting out at the Corporation, not yet in the big money. Hell, I didn't even have my acid trouble yet, not even the first light wheeze in my throat. Not even the first small, useless cough.

How was it back then? Good — better than I realized. For four years we lived an unremarkable, largely satisfying life. Jack and Liz Whitman, young married couple. Sex, work, food, friends and related gossip, exercise, books, arguments, movies, enough money — the stuff of days. I don't pretend that our love was spectacular or unique, and I suppose that later in this account I must explain certain of my own transgressions against Liz, but for the most part we were happy. Our hopes were high, and when Liz became pregnant, we decided to look around for a house, using money her father had left her when he died.

Her belly was swelling week by week and we had seen the flickering blob on the ultrasound machine that our obstetrician identified as life, and at five months Liz could feel a tiny nascent kicking inside her— "kicking field goals," I would tell her—and friends began to give us lilliputian cotton outfits with duckies or rabbits or clowns floating dreamily across the tiny chest and bottom, and Liz held these up before me, marveling at how absolutely *cute* the little feet were, and how funny was the amount of space in the tiny pants, large enough to accommodate the chubby legs and fat diapers. I began, of course, to think of Liz as a mother and not only as my wife, as possessing the independent power of maternity that men can only observe, and I became interested in such things as baby strollers and changing tables. My one moment of panic came when Liz fainted in the summer heat of Grand Central Station. Sprawled on the gum-stained platform, she was revived by a retired fireman. But she became stronger, and after the first three months exhibited remarkable energy—the energy of hope, I concluded. Our apartment was awash in books about pregnancy nutrition and childbirth and breast-feeding. We knew that the baby's heart beat about 130 times a minute, and every day that Liz's pregnancy progressed normally, the fetus gaining precious ounces at an increasing rate, I gave silent thanks and (though not a religious man like my father) appealed to God to deliver to us a healthy baby. We found the brownstone in Park Slope. Childless Mrs. Cronister, spurning the rapacious real estate brokers, knew she was moving to a nursing home and soon onward to the grave. When she saw my pregnant wife, her eyes watered and she dropped her price seventy-five thousand dollars. Life was good.

Three days after closing on our house, signing the mortgage papers at the bank; three days after we put the change-of-address forms in the mail, after we walked up the stoop, drank a couple of glasses of Mumm's in the empty living room, and awkwardly made love on a flimsy mattress I'd dragged into the house for that very purpose—with me making the necessary compensations for the marvelous warm swell of Liz's belly (two hearts beating against my skin —one large and the other the size of a thimble); three days from that glorious and hopeful moment, and thirty-four weeks after Liz had conceived, the whole fat happy dream went straight to hell.

This is what happened: Liz traveled way uptown after work to Columbia-Presbyterian Medical Center to visit a friend who'd just had a double mastectomy, and on the way back from the echoing hallways of the hospital to the subway she paused in front of a storefront Korean grocery to wait for the light. I now know every foot of pavement between the hospital and that street corner, and how Liz stood back from the curb near the stands of bright fruit. The Korean owners, ever industriously self-improving, polished tomatoes and yellow peppers and apples while an English-language instruction tape played with monotonous solemnity—"I agree to buy the television . . . *you* agree . . . *he* agrees . . . *we* agree . . . *they* agree. *They* agree to buy the television. I *have* agreed to buy the television . . ." Around Liz swirled the lights and sounds of Harlem; across the street was the Audubon Theater and Ballroom, where more than twenty years prior Malcolm X preached his message of black revolution and was assassinated. Behind her, as the NYPD detective told me later, stood a group of "young black males"—the ubiquitous handful of postliterate homeboys in acid-washed jeans, gold chains, big jackets—the kind of young bloods who scare the hell out of the white middle class, who scare the hell out of *me*, all angry voices and stylized for violence. I was always telling Liz not to come home too late. She stood on the corner inconspicuously in her wool coat, perhaps a bit short of breath and feeling the ever-greater heaviness in her belly; perhaps, too—rather likely, given Liz's charitable temperament—she considered the condition of her friend, who that very moment lay staring at the ceiling of her hospital room, wondering if she was fated for a slow, agonizing death from cancer. What is certain is that as Liz waited for the light, a silver BMW with tinted windows—in my nightmares, it is a sleek, fantastic vehicle of death, gliding noiselessly through wet, empty streets, colored lights sliding up the dark windshield—pulled over and someone poked the short metal barrel of a nine-millimeter semiautomatic pistol over the electric window and started shooting. The scene itself is no longer remarkable in our society—kids scrambling for cover, screams, the clipping pop of gunfire, glass shattering, sirens arriving. Liz was right in the way of it.

I have wondered, at least a million times, about the sudden expression on Liz's face. I have imagined myself stepping bravely in front of her, I have imagined every permutation of chance, including the version in which she bends her head forward to look in her purse for something—a subway token—tipping it forward just enough that the slugs whiz harmlessly a quarter inch above her temple, and I have imagined the version in which she suddenly crouches in a successful attempt to protect the baby, and the version in which she realized she is wounded but is still able to gesticulate with quick practicality to another bystander that she is pregnant and that the baby must be saved above all.

But none of these things happened. The ambulance took Liz directly back to Columbia-Presbyterian. The proximity of the hospital made no difference, ultimately, and I do not like to think of what those bullets did to her or to the fetus, which at nearly eight months could have lived outside the womb. I asked to see my baby. Two nurses and then a doctor refused me. I begged. I wept and snarled and threatened hysterically. No, they said, absolutely not. I invoked one of the Corporation's law firms. That scared the doctor. He asked me to wait a few minutes. Then one of the hospital administrators, a tired little man, appeared and sat me down in his office, holding a slip of paper in his hand.

"You're in shock, Mr. Whitman, you must understand that."

This didn't impress me. "I want to see my child," I said.

"I can't allow that."

"Why?"

He studied me.

"Why?" I repeated.

"We just can't allow it."

"Why?" I insisted. "You must have some reason."

The hospital administrator heard this and nodded. "It is"—he sighed with detached exhaustion—"it is the *seasoned* opinion of my emergency room surgeon that exploding bullets were used. These are very popular among certain populations." The baby was a girl, he added, reading now from the slip of paper, perfectly formed, utterly healthy, and an estimated six ounces heavier than average for thirty-four weeks' gestation. She had turned head down early—as if eager to be born, I thought. Had she not, it was possible that the bullet would have passed by or through her feet. But, the administrator told me, his eyes locked on mine, with the baby inverted in Liz's womb, the bullet had hit her head. Almost nothing of it was left.

"I'm sorry," he concluded.

Meanwhile, Liz lingered, her body trying to recover both from its wounds and from the unsuccessful emergency cesarean. She never regained consciousness and I counted that a good thing, for though I was unable to say good-bye to her, neither did I have to tell her that her baby had perished. She died two days after the shooting, late at night, while I was asleep in the waiting room. The nurses forgot to wake me, and in the morning I found an empty, stripped bed in Liz's room. The momentousness of it rushed at me when I stood before her corpse in the hospital morgue, the white-coated attendants standing idly near. I remember that a radio played from the other side of the room. Something hard and angry by the Rolling Stones. Liz's face was lifted upward in the squinting grimace of death, her eyes filmily half-open, unseeing, not tracking my face as I looked at her. *I'm so tired, Jack*, her expression seemed to say. The air around me roared. In her pregnancy, Liz's skin had flared with demure little pimples, a badge of fertility, and she had dutifully covered them with whatever skin-colored gunk she used, and there in the morgue I noticed that the oxygen mask had smeared this stuff away. And seeing this, I suffered a great affection for those pimples and for the first wrinkles and cellulite and drop of flesh that Liz, a woman only thirty-one, already had. I pulled back the white plastic bag far enough to see one of the star-shaped exit wounds, hatched with sutures of thick black thread. Her nudity before the morgue attendants seemed a gratuitous violation and I pulled the bag back up. The tip of Liz's nose was cold. Her lips, when I bent to kiss her the last time, were set like stone. This, then, was the first great deviation from my plans and desires. This is where, I see now, it all began.

♦ ♦ ♦

I was monstrous with the grief of it, homicidal for revenge. Of course I'd believed that this was the kind of thing that happened to *other people*: gang members, crackheads, the foolish, the unworthy. And now it seemed that any ten coked-out dudes lounging around the street corners abusing the English language or begging change in the subway stations were not worth the life of my lovely, blue-eyed Liz. I looked at every strutting teenager with a gold chain around his neck as if he were the one who had killed my wife. *That guy could be the guy.* I thought about buying a gun and just driving up to Harlem and picking off someone, some poor bastard, as retribution. Why the fuck not? In the great balance sheets of justice, it seemed reasonable. I was demented, of course, a man whose grief had ignited his smoldering racist beliefs. These were the ugliest of thoughts, but I had them, I fed them, I believed in them—they seemed fair and true. I hounded the detectives, but every witness said all he or she remembered was the silver BMW—"with that fucking smoky glass, man," said one—and inside it several young black men, the pounding stereo speakers and an absurd moment of laughter after the gun appeared above the power window and fired.

To be fair, to be sure to spread the grief, mine was not the only loss. One of the gunman's bullets had crashed through the store window, ricocheted off a cash register, and, tumbling through the air, destroyed the windpipe of an old black woman inspecting the grocery's green onions. She survived. Another bullet also passed through the length of the store into a back room, and entered the perfect heart of a thirteen-year-old Korean boy standing on an overturned vegetable crate, instantly killing him.

The *New York Times* ran a couple of stories on the double homicide because one of the victims was a pregnant, white, professional woman, and what happened to her is what the demographically select population that reads the *Times* fears most—constantly weighing the opportunity of New York against the notion that the longer you stay, the more likely the odds that the city will call your bluff. The reporter, a guy named Weber, listened dutifully to my grief. The tabloids grabbed the story too, and if you lived in New York then and read the *New York Post*, you might have paged past a picture of a man in a raincoat clutching a briefcase and gazing down toward something just out of the frame of the photo. The flash of the camera illuminates a jaw frozen tight but not the hollows of his eyes, which remain darkly hidden. PREG WIFE MURDERED IN DRIVE-BY, the headline says. One isn't sure whether the man is gazing into the grave of his wife or the depth of his own hatred for her killer. I hated everybody then, including myself, for not somehow saving Liz. And I hated the newspapers for converting my torment into a minor entertainment for the masses.

Without a suspect, and with the next horrific crime a few days later (that was the one in which the skull and soupy features of a ballerina were found in a long-steaming cookpot in an apartment in the East Village), public memory quickly forgot Liz's murder. The carnage in New York is continuous, of course. It was just as well, because the nuts had begun to call, excitedly telling me they were sorry—"Oh, what a tragedy!"—that they knew who did it and would tell me for a certain amount of money, or that Liz was *still alive* and, misidentified by the hospital bureaucracy, lingered in a coma in an obscure wing of the hospital. One desperate woman sent me a perfumed note asking if I wanted to remarry and included her photograph, which I studied and then returned.

So I moved into Mrs. Cronister's crumbling, unkempt brownstone for refuge. The empty house, which of course I legally owned and was still obligated to pay for, offered the haunting comfort that came with knowing Liz had wanted us to live there. All I wanted was to be as tired as possible, too tired to think or feel, or remember. Later, when the police started to hear rumors from the street about the killings, and they developed a suspect, I was denied any chance at seeing Liz's killer or understanding the motivations of those who took her life with such sporting dispatch. The suspected triggerman was one Roynell Wilkes, a twenty-year-old unremarkable in all ways, including his record of violence and the two gold teeth brightening his mouth. I chose to hate him in the easiest way possible—by imagining him as a ninth-grade drop-out, a bubble-headed jigaboo in an outsized L.A. Raiders jacket who bought the violent rap videos that the Corporation was selling by the millions, a kid without a conscience, a bad customer, a coward in baggy pants and Air Jordans. But it wasn't nearly so simple as that. Later I learned that as a child Wilkes had been repeatedly beaten by his father to within an inch of his life, causing certain learning disabilities and year upon year of frustration in school. And whereas Liz was not killed on purpose, young Wilkes was. He was found at dawn handcuffed to the steering wheel of that same BMW, parked in front of a Harlem flower shop, two bullets in the back of his closely cropped skull, and ten new, carefully folded hundred-dollar bills stuffed deep into his throat. The *Post* ran a photo of that too, and one could see that Wilkes had a lightning bolt shaved onto his skull and, incongruously, a face that in the repose of death was soft and even sweet. My heart was not large enough to forgive him, yet I never could be happy that he had died. No, despite myself, his death saddened me—ultimately, I realized, Wilkes was killed by the same thing that killed Liz. They were both killed by the city.

So my vengeance was expired, though not my grief, and I withdrew deep into myself, burrowing into the work at the Corporation, churning the paper and phone calls and meetings with the fervor of one who must never think too much. Friends suggested I see a "grief therapist" for a few months, that I date or travel. Instead, after the funeral, I returned to work. I could not do anything but work. My propensity to remember was obliterated under the stamping machine of work. Bush came into the White House, the great golden decade crashed and burned, yet the Corporation thrived. The country fell into a shuddering recession and the United States Air Force incinerated thousands of Iraqi soldiers. The Corporation sent five thousand VCR cassettes of our movies to the troops. They watched them in the tents. It was my idea. We were heavily leveraged but we kept making money. The Corporation—America's largest media and entertainment company—is very, very good at making money. In my department on the twentieth floor I became known for my odd, emotionless ambition. In a perverse sort of way, my luck turned upon Liz's murder; her death freed me to become my own worst efficient self. Morrison, second in command in the Corporation, the man everyone feared, started paying attention when my subdivision turned a $49 million profit as a result of my marketing plan. Morrison had lost half a leg and most of a hand as a Navy SEAL in Vietnam; having survived, he had the confidence of five men. Combat had shown him that we are all merely walking bags of meat, and once a man has decided that, all manner of brilliant scheming becomes possible. Morrison also had a mean, opportunistic streak—I knew that, even then—and he figured that my loss created his advantage. I had possibilities.

He brusquely promoted me up to the thirty-ninth floor, where the air-conditioning was cooler and the toilet paper softer, and where twenty-five people ran the whole damn operation, managed the forty-six thousand employees of the Corporation. My new title was one of those meaningless strings of words that begin with "vice president for." The special assignments came, then the access, the dinner parties, the raises, the stock options. I didn't screw up, I quit worrying about the mortgage payments each month. I started having my shirts picked up by the laundry and delivered back. It happened over just a few years. My name did not appear in the annual report, with the color photographs of the Chairman and Morrison and four or five other key executives in stiff poses. But I rode in the cars and saw all the budgets and went to the small meetings. Morrison didn't like me much as a man, but he saw my usefulness to him. That is what bosses look for, even at my level—usefulness.

♦ ♦ ♦

I was thinking about the woman on the train as I stepped inside the parlor floor of my house, recalling her full lips and dark eyes, when Morrison found me again. His voice boomed from my answering machine: "Got the call from Bonn this evening, Jack. Don't know what took them so long. They're ready to start negotiating. They have problems, of course—the succession thing, and the stock numbers look pretty far apart, but now we're going to—" He went on about a meeting the next day. We were speeding up now. Acceleration and deceleration are two of the skills of a CEO. A few months earlier, Morrison had secretly gathered his loyal people in and told them that he was proposing a merger between the Corporation and Volkman-Sakura, the world's other immense communications corporation, itself the product of the 1991 buy-out by the German media conglomerate of the Japanese electronics manufacturer. The Chairman did not know of the deal, Morrison had said, but that was only one of the difficulties we would face. Legally, a merger would be extremely complicated but possible. The lawyers would find a way to skirt the FCC limitations on foreign ownership of American media. Various shareholders would be shocked and would immediately file suit, but he was counting on the arbitrageurs to buy up the big blocks of stock in a desire to diversify their holdings into deutschemarks, a currency at the time far stronger than the American dollar. The administration in Washington would be sympathetic. Certain assurances had been made, certain friendships maintained. Those of us in Morrison's team would work out a proposal to integrate the two companies' markets and products. A huge task. The deal was far bigger than Matsushita's $6.1 billion acquisition of MCA in 1990. We were shocked and then excited, and began to dream about how we were all going to make our careers on this. Our plan was unknown outside the thirty-ninth floor. "Deutsche Bank okayed the financing, in theory, so as long as our share price stays with three points of the thirty-day moving average," Morrison went on. "So that's good." He paused. "And one more thing, Jack, why don't you and I have a little private talk in my office after lunch? A small item. Real fast. See you tomorrow."

Everyone knows the name of the Corporation. Everyone watches the movies that the film entertainment division pumps out—forty a year, now—the big movies, with the names we all know, at any one time playing on approximately nine thousand first-run movie theater screens nationally. And everyone reads the stuff that comes out of the magazine division—news, sports, money; and watches the cable television division's stations; and buys the publishing division's cookbooks, self-help books, celebrity biographies, novels, and even the cartoon coloring books such as the one held by the little girl on the train; and purchases the compact discs and cassettes created in the fiefdoms of the music entertainment division. The Corporation is the world's largest distributor of TV programming, licensing over eighteen thousand hours of shows in more than one hundred countries and in fifteen languages. The levers are pulled and the great trembling colossus of popular culture walks. The only question is whether the product will move, whether it will play, whether the people will buy. The average person doesn't care where it comes from, wants only the product—the news, the music, the comedies, the game shows, the soaps, the movies, the grotesquely spotless theme parks (the Corporation owns sixteen now), the fanzines, the best-sellers, the spinoffs, the next hit of information, the buzz of the buzz. The Corporation is even quietly getting into late-night infomercial programming and 900-number companies. The Corporation is sewn into all of us, it has informed who we are and how we see the world. Even now, as you breathe, it grows bigger, buying subsidiaries—anything under $100 million not even worthy of a blink—independent music companies, megaplex movie theaters in Russia, strange new computer research outfits in small offices in California, Brazilian television studios, hot new comic book publishers, fledgling film production companies. It grows like a fat woman gorging recklessly on chocolates while others shrink back in horrified amazement at her appetite. If she were to fall, the earth would shudder; only by her great weight does she remain on her feet. This is *the* big American media-entertainment corporation, many times larger than Disney and Paramount and all the others, the one whose stock is considered a blue-chip growth equity into the next century and is thus owned by the Japanese and German banks, by all the universities and other institutions with huge endowments—my undergraduate alma mater, Columbia University, and by Harvard, the Ford Foundation, all the giant pension fund operations—the California Public Employees, New York State, the Texas Teachers Union—the huge equity mutual funds, by all of them. I'll give you the Corporation's numbers: 1992 annual revenues, $32.6 billion; annual profits, before interest, taxes, depreciation, and amortization, $4.6 billion. Ranked by market value, the fifty-sixth largest publicly traded company in the world. Way up high on the thirty-ninth floor, I lived in its heart.

♦ ♦ ♦

The woman with the memorable lips and her lovely, innocent child had looked at me and seen nothing except some guy with a thinning hairline in a good suit who stank of booze and loneliness. This seemed the only reasonable conclusion. She had waited for the subway car to move away, then smiled at her daughter, smiling the funny man and his funny business card out of her child's worried face. They had walked toward the exit stairway, the card left in the trash. A minute later the woman had forgotten the entire affair. Forget it, I thought, you'll never see her again. I brushed my teeth and took my nizatidine pills, three hundred milligrams. My kind of acid is serious, requires medication. It's not an ulcer, which is down low in the stomach, it's high in the throat—*erosive gastroesophageal reflux disease* is the term. You get to be an expert about just how it works, whether it's just ticking quietly in your chest, little matchheads flaring brightly for a second, or the real lava jetting up through the sphincter at the top of the stomach into the esophagus, making you cough a quick, useless cough every fifteen seconds. Vomiting is occasional. You take the pills every night but that doesn't do it completely, so you lay down a cup of Di-Gel or Maalox like a buffer. Chalky goop, Maalox. Either that or Mylanta. I used them all. I've swallowed barrels of the shit. And eaten the tablets—Tums, Rolaids, half a dozen at a pop minimum. But the acid always comes back—it burns, it sticks in the throat.

That April night, so far away now, I set the alarm for 4:00 A.M. and went to bed as I always went to bed, knowing that the morning would be an agonizing rise from the grave of sleep, the tide of the day pulling at me from my bed. The smoking, clamorous earth would grind forward on its axis, and after a shower I'd again stand naked at my dresser bureau, staring into the mess of my underwear drawer, the bottom of which was littered with coins and unused condoms and tickets from my Chinese laundry, trying to find a matching pair of socks, thinking about what needed to be accomplished that day—get numbers on a joint-venture deal to build fifty multiscreen complexes in Japan, plan a schmooze lunch with the South American syndicators of the Corporation's films, whatever momentarily important task it was—pulling one blue sock out and comparing it with another, tired of working and shopping and laundry and solitude. What a stupid life. As children, we never imagine the tedium and suffering of adulthood, the grinding grimness of it all. The cups of coffee. The way years disappear. I worried that I might be slowly becoming my neighbor, Bob somebody, a twice-divorced hospital-supply salesman in his early forties who quietly squired various long-single women in and out of his house next door. These women had the grimace of suppressed expectation on their faces—*Perhaps! Perhaps he is the one!*—but inevitably, the next week, the next month, Bob was with someone else. He had a stooped, hangdog look about him, yet sported a thin mustache and walked with an oily swagger. On weekend mornings when I sat in the garden, I sometimes caught an accidental glimpse of Bob through his kitchen window as he stood in his black bikini briefs making coffee. He looked ridiculous in the tight underpants, twenty years past his prime, his fleshy ass dimpled and low and sad, a cigarillo hanging from his lips; he reminded me that men who don't marry successfully, ever, are often doomed to a slow, obvious wasting.

I did not want to be one of those men. Many of the couples Liz and I had known together now had children, and I was shocked by the frank physical love that they had for their kids and which was re-turned — two-year-old boys squirming against their mothers' thighs, tiny girls lustily digging their teeth into their fathers' chests. I missed this, the arc of a natural life that had been robbed from me. Every day that I did not find a woman and make a family was a day lived in deepening loneliness. I think that if we can imagine ourselves dying alone, without benefit of loved ones around us, that it sets life into a certain perspective; the implications of a solitary, unloved death run backward through time, backward to the moment of that death's imagining. All around me at the Corporation were very smart men and women who were going to die alone. Some knew it, but most did not.

I lay in the dark, staring at the liquid shadows on the ceiling. Only now do I understand that things were already in motion. Only now do I see that I should have heard the odd rattle in Morrison's voice when he mentioned a "small item." He was lying fearlessly and I should have heard it. And what I should *not* have done, ever, even as lonely as I was, was to be so recklessly charitable as I'd been on the subway that evening, casually offering my business card to a beautiful, unknown woman.

TWO

Dawn arrives unwanted, snatches you forward. I waited at the corner of Sixth Avenue and Forty-ninth Street the next morning, sun brightening the meager designer trees of Rockefeller Center. Across the street, the Corporation's uniformed maintenance crew had rousted the homeless off the sheltered benches in the building plaza and was steam-blasting away the piss and garbage deposited there the night before. The men moved slowly, hourly wage workers in no hurry. I crossed with the light. Inside the lobby, another man pushed a polishing machine slowly across the gleaming marble floor, as pink as an expanse of frozen salmon mousse. I passed the computerized building directories and nodded to Frankie, the sleepy old night guard ending his shift, and he slipped off his stool and summoned the reserved elevator, which stopped only at floors thirty-eight through forty-one. When I got on, the bell chimed softly and the doors slid toward one another.

"Hold it!" commanded a woman's voice. "I'm here!" A hand chopped through the two-inch slit between the elevator doors—five red fingernails on five long fingers and the cuff of a business suit. The doors reopened automatically and there stood the tall blond presence of Samantha Pipes.

"Good morning, Jack!" Samantha gave me her usual moist smile, which suggested great pleasure but promised only misery, and entered the elevator in a gust of perfume and makeup and coffee breath. "Oh, they're going to fight us on *everything!* All the market overlap! About the stock price, and the management succession, just *all* of it, don't you think? But we have to do it! And they do, too!" she cried happily. "It's the most logical thing!" She turned and savagely jabbed the door button. "I hate waiting for everybody! We'll ride up together."

We rose in a continuous glide. Samantha's soft, almost babyish features obscured the intensity and intelligence of her thought. One might never suspect that she was an expert in corporate law as practiced by the chancery court in Delaware, which is where most large American companies are legally incorporated. We had come up through the ranks together, along with my rival, Ed Beales. When not wearing a formal business suit, Samantha was given to clinging silk dresses, usually a deep blue or green, and except for one detail — or perhaps because of it — she was an unusually striking woman. The defect was her left eye. The fine blue iris turned inward, cross-eyed.

"I reread your joint operating plan last night," Samantha said, glancing at her makeup in the brass button panel. "It's *good, so* good. I *forgot* they have four satellites over *Africa*, over all the big markets. Nigeria is *big*, a hundred and twenty million people. And Asia! Indonesia, one hundred and ninety-five million! Those population curve estimates are shocking! In twenty years the markets will be *huge*, Jack."

"As far as I see it, Samantha, either we grab this deal or somebody else will, five minutes from now."

"I know!" she exclaimed, her eyebrows lifting. "It's the *future!* And when did they buy all those movie theaters in southeast China? The Chinese are becoming better capitalists than *anybody*. And they have the exclusive cellular contract for Poland! Have you had your *coffee?* I think I had too much this morning. I got up and ran around Central Park *twice*."

"Twelve miles?" I asked.

"I wasn't even thinking of anything! I just kept going! They have that rat poison all over the park right now. Of course our famous *Chairman* is not exactly going to be *happy* when we tell him what we're up to," Samantha went on, her voice harder now, "but there comes a time . . . he *suspects*, I know it. Only a *fool* wouldn't suspect! Now we have to get the poor old guy up to speed, *somehow*." She studied me. And with Samantha, that was a strange thing, even though we had an old affection for one another, which I'll explain at some point. When I'd first met her, the crooked eye was barely out of kilter, even slightly fetching, for she seemed to be concentrating intently on whomever she looked at, but she had gone to an expensive Swiss eye surgeon on the East Side, and instead of perfecting that one wandering blue eye, he botched the job, so that now, when Samantha became agitated or argumentative, the iris wandered closer to the bridge of her nose. Samantha's successful malpractice suit, which relied on a chorus of expert medical testimony and alleged that the good doctor had enjoyed a glass of wine at lunch two hours before the operation, had reduced the surgeon to ashes and was written up in the law journals. That the eye was permanently unmoored served, strangely enough, to Samantha's advantage, for in the heat of discussion she suddenly appropriated the qualities of a Picasso portrait done during his Cubist phase—it made people *uncomfortable*. The juxtaposition of her passionate, airtight arguments with her wandering eyeball disconcerted experienced consultants and weighty attorneys of counsel who suddenly lost the conviction of their opinions. They paused, they worried about which of Samantha's eyes to look at, they babbled, she interjected, they were lost. Samantha was playing a game of higher stakes; if she could not have two perfectly aligned eyes, then she would have any and everything else.

When the elevator whispered to a stop at the thirty-ninth floor, Samantha and I bypassed, as usual, the large formal lobby with its teak paneling and glass security walls and took a shortcut through an unmarked door near the elevator. As always, a fresh tray of assorted fruits and pastries lay on the inner reception desk. "Hmmm!" Samantha cried as she snatched a large strawberry and plunged it into her mouth. I followed her high heels and fine legs down the hall, past framed moments of the Corporation's history. As usual we were the first ones onto the floor. We both worked in smaller vice presidents' offices on the back corridor that ran along the northern face of the building. The Chairman's huge northeast corner office suite was flanked by the office belonging to Mrs. Marsh, the only secretary in the entire building who had a window. The offices of the chief executive officer—Morrison—lay at the other end of the corridor on the northwest corner. All of our windows faced toward Central Park nine blocks away, and I often stood at the glass, gazing at the miniature maple and beech trees in the distance, the softball teams, and the figures sitting on the park benches; and in these moments of contemplation I almost always thought of Liz. We had walked and bicycled in the park. Eaten turkey sandwiches. I'd proposed to her there, too. Musing at the window, I'd test myself to see if I remembered her face. Sometimes I didn't.

Now, through the office wall, I heard Samantha listening to voice-mail messages on her speaker phone.

"Samantha," I called out my door, "how many dates do you have lined up this week?"

"Not enough!" she called back.

"Let's have lunch."

"Can't, sorry. I'm booked."

"A young prospect?"

"Yes," she called. "Untested as yet."

After a string of the usual affairs, Samantha now scorned the attentions of professional men in their forties, who attempted to replace waning sexual ability with the vigors of wealth — new cars, ski lodges, exotic travel. She had decided, I think, that her career would not allow for marriage and children. But there could be compensations. Samantha now favored the long arms and wide backs of the twenty-year-olds who rowed on Columbia University's heavyweight crew, even watching home regattas from her own inboard forty-foot powerboat. Every year or two she would pick out a new young man and seduce him with a hungry forthrightness that younger women didn't yet possess. The junior or senior in question was inevitably from a small town in Ohio or Connecticut and would be shyly present at Samantha's annual Christmas party. "My friend," Samantha would casually introduce him. Mike or Tom or Larry was clearly flattered by Samantha's expensive attentions — a dozen shirts from Bloomingdale's, gold cuff links, whatever — and probably saw in her lust a challenge largely athletic. No doubt, too, the young stalwart was reassured by Samantha's declaration that he was not to feel committed to her in any way. She liberally abused the Corporation's car service account to bring her boys down from Morningside Heights to the East Side. She came to work with the cold clarity of a woman who has successfully commodified sex for maximum pleasure and minimum bother. When it came time to discard her young man, she was irritable until he was replaced. We all knew these things about Samantha Pipes, and it scared us a little. She understood that to be to her advantage.

♦ ♦ ♦

That day, just before noon, Helen Botstein, my executive assistant, came in to my office, shut my door, and sat down in the chair across my desk. "Security had some people asking for you downstairs in the lobby," she said.

I was involved with several reports in preparation for the meeting that afternoon. "People?" I asked. "Don't we always have people around here? Some pretty pathetic characters, too."

Helen managed a smile. "I didn't want to bother you so I went down. It's a woman," she said. "And her child."

"A woman and a child? What do they—" It came to me, then, just who Helen meant.

"She says she knows you."

I remembered the woman's face.

"She says you gave her your card. Jack, the woman has a terribly bruised eye. I brought them upstairs and got the little girl some milk," Helen explained. "She's just beautiful, like her mother."

"Right outside the door?"

"Yes," Helen whispered.

"The woman probably is dressed in pretty dirty—"

Helen nodded her head fiercely, almost in tears. She wanted children almost as much as she wanted to breathe and had been trying to get pregnant for three years, and now was taking fertility drugs. "The little girl has this *head* of curls."

"Yes."

"Send them in?" she asked.

"Please."

Helen got up and quietly opened the door.

The woman entered slowly, with the same proud composure I had seen on the subway, stepping across the Persian rug in badly scuffed heels, holding her daughter's hand firmly and not looking back. Helen left and closed the door. The woman was wrapped in the soiled coat I'd seen before. Same marvelous lips, same body. But what

I noticed with sudden alarm was the bruise around her left eye—it was puffy and tender, a shiny asymmetrical swelling; in the fifteen hours or so since I'd seen her the evening before, someone had really whacked that eye. The little girl shook free of her mother's hand and rushed to my office window, where she pressed her tiny hands against the glass and looked down at the yellow taxis moving on the street below. Her mother stood in the middle of the room with her arms at her side, ignoring her daughter for the moment, and stared at me. She did not move close enough to shake hands and appeared worried that she had made a great mistake.

"Please," I said. "Sit."

"Thank you." I could smell the woman's perfume—something cheap, yet floral and pleasing. Despite her attire and even her battered eye, she was immensely attractive. Disheveled, yes, without clean clothes and with the barest amount of makeup—only a touch of lipstick perhaps, a cherry red that set off the dark coloring of her eyes and hair, but *vigorous*, a firm body beneath the stained coat. She perched on the edge of the chair and clutched her purse. It seemed only right that she speak first, since she had sought me out.

"Your—uh, Miss Botstein said I could come in and talk. You gave me your card."

Her voice had the usual inflection of a native New Yorker, but there was also something softly musical about it, as if she'd grown up hearing others speak quite differently. I knew it wasn't the clippity Haitian vowels one hears in taxis or a harsh Puerto Rican accent; it was something else. "Absolutely," I answered. "I meant what I said on the subway."

She took a deep breath. "My name's Dolores Salcines, Mr. Whit-man. And this is Maria. When you gave me your card I didn't really think—I mean, I don't usually talk to men on the subway, but I just decided to call and see if you really worked here, because, I mean"—she paused—"I recognized the name of the company, so I thought I'd come see you." She smiled with polite guardedness, and I wondered if doing so made the bruise hurt. "I know somebody who installs the wires for the cable company."

"Big Apple Cable, you mean?" I asked.

She nodded. "You own that, right?"

"The Corporation does, yes." It was the local New York City cable franchise held in large part by our cable television division, constituting a minute fraction of the Corporation's empire. The white vans with the Big Apple logo on the side were everywhere in the five boroughs, driven by men in striped uniforms.

"Well, I heard of the company, so I kind of thought—I was pretty sure . . ." Dolores Salcines looked nervously at me. "I guess I *figured* that because I don't have any clothes, any *decent* clothes, and I know I look like some kind of *homeless* person. The guards downstairs looked at me pretty bad, but I guess they let me go, on account of I had your card to show them." She glanced at her daughter, whose head was still pressed against the glass. "You don't mind if she just stands there?"

"Not at all." I watched her dark fingers clutch one another. "Not a bit. How old is she?"

"She'll be four in two months."

"What a beautiful child."

"She won't mess anything up."

"It's okay," I assured her. "Dolores," I began, unable to avoid saying it, "somebody has *hit*—"

"I know." She quickly nodded in shame, her fingers flying up to touch her eye. "*Please*, don't ask me about it—it's not important right now. It's really not your problem, Mr. Whitman, believe me, I know that. I see you're busy, I can see that from where they put your office up here—I mean, are people like me even allowed up here?"

"Generally? No."

She was quiet a moment, unsure of how to proceed. "I thought, you know, maybe you really *could* help me. I'm not going to give you a whole long story, Mr. Whitman. I need money, I need work. You could've seen that last night, I guess."

"You looked like you needed help," I agreed. "But before we talk about a job, first can I order you a little something to eat, coffee?"

"No, I'm fine—" Yet she glanced toward Maria, who'd discovered a glossy stack of the Corporation's magazines on a low, lacquered Chinese table chosen for my office by the Corporation's "furnishings consultant" and was paging through them, looking at the advertisements for diamonds and wristwatches and ninety-thousand-dollar cars. I buzzed Helen and explained we needed sandwiches and coffee and juice — anything she could have the food service send immediately.

"I'm not here for charity," Dolores told me when I put the phone down, pulling her coat tight around her. "I know I look terrible, but this isn't my normal situation, I don't usually look so bad . . . I just need a job."

"And you're living here in Manhattan?"

She gave a vague nod, meanwhile unconsciously twisting the wedding ring on her finger. "They stole my suitcase and money at the place where I'm staying — it's a hotel, sort of, a place to stay. I looked at apartments but they're so expensive."

I nearly asked then about her husband, but didn't, for each personal question seemed only an affront to her powerlessness. I assumed that she had little education and wondered about the un-skilled and semiskilled jobs in the building. All the janitorial and kitchen jobs were contracted out to service companies. "Dolores, what kind of qualifications do you have?"

"I graduated Catholic school in Brooklyn," she said. "I wanted to be a nurse but things got messed up. I haven't worked much the last few years, I was taking care of Maria." Her hand drifted toward her bruise but she pulled it back into her lap. "I'm looking for a night job so I can work while Maria is asleep."

"You don't have anyone to take care of her, then."

"No."

"Can you type? Because if you can, that changes everything."

"Yes," said Dolores, with some hope in her voice. "At least I *used* to be able to type."

"Good." I looked through the Corporation directory and phoned Mrs. Triscott, a battle-ax whose meanness was her only marketable commodity; she used it to drive the sixty pressured souls of the word processing department. I'd been down there once in my early days. It was a huge, low-ceilinged room on the fifth floor, a brightly lit dungeon of cubicles of women clacking away at computer screens. The department operated every minute of the year, processing truck-loads of memoranda, reports, sales kits, handbooks, whatever. Yes, Mrs. Triscott told me in gruff disgust, people kept quitting and there were a couple of openings.

"I have a friend here who I think would do a good job."

"What programs?"

I covered the phone. "Know any word processing programs?"

Dolores shook her head. "I never did a computer before . . ."

She was unskilled for office work.

"But I can learn," she said fiercely, perhaps seeing my reaction. "I can learn anything."

I returned to the phone. "Mrs. Triscott, she knows WordStar, Xywrite, WordPerfect, a couple others less well."

"Words?" Mrs. Triscott requested grumpily.

"Words?" I repeated.

"Per minute."

I asked Dolores this.

"Maybe . . . thirty? It's been so long."

"One-oh-five a minute," I told Mrs. Triscott.

"She'll go through personnel," she answered skeptically. "They actually hire."

Helen arrived with a plate of sandwiches brought down from the executive dining room on the fortieth floor. She smiled nervously, her eyes watering, and while Dolores and Maria helped themselves, I called the personnel office and leaned on a young assistant manager who sounded new. I wanted, I said, for him to give Dolores Salcines, the applicant, all due consideration for the next word processing job that came open and to take into her account my strong support for a job in the company.

"We have certain procedures," he squeaked, apparently not recognizing my name. "First, it's mandatory, really, that we do a work history. That way we can match the skill level of the applicant with the—"

"I'm requesting that you hire her."

"Wait a sec," he said with less certainty in his voice, "you can't just call *up*—"

"Yes," I interrupted, "I can."

"And what floor might you be on?" he asked bluntly.

I told him. Each floor of the Corporation is identified by a certain degree of fear. The thirty-ninth floor is the most terrifying. It is seen

as the floor of giants. The personnel manager began babbling promises and accommodations, a certain hysteria now in his voice.

"Eight-thirty tomorrow, floor five, room five-forty-two," I told
Dolores after I hung up. "You begin work at nine."

Her eyes widened. "Just like that?"

"It's not great but it pays enough to live on, maybe eighteen or
nineteen thousand, and I assume it has some kind of decent health
insurance. Maybe after a few months a secretarial position could come
open and you would have polished up your skills and—"

"It's *fine*, Mr. Whitman," Dolores responded, gathering her
things as if to stay a minute longer jeopardized her new job. "I really,
really appreciate this, I don't know why you did this for someone you
don't know."

"Don't worry about it." I shrugged, but I let my eyes linger on
hers, and so even in those first minutes after Dolores and I had met,
perhaps we both knew that things were more complicated than they
appeared. Dolores hovered for a moment in the middle of my office,
appearing to indulge a desire to pass her gaze around it one last time.
Maria wandered over to me and inspected my watch, which Liz had
given me.

"Can I see it?" Maria asked.

"Maria!" Dolores said crossly. "That's so rude."

I slipped the watch from my wrist and handed it to her.

"Maria, you give that back right now."

The girl pouted her lip, handed me the watch, and slinked
playfully toward the window again, pressing her stubby fingers against
the glass and looking down fearlessly. I wanted to kneel down next to
her ear and point out the horses and carriages in Central Park. I
wanted to go and buy this little girl new clothes and an ice cream cone
and a college education and a million other things. "So high up!" she
cried happily. "The cars are little yellow buggies!"

"Yes. Come on, Maria, we've bothered Mr. Whitman too much."
Dolores took the child's hand. "Thank you," she repeated. We stood
awkwardly, not shaking hands.

"I'll walk you out to the elevator."

Which I did. Samantha happened by, and she looked with undisguised fascination at Dolores and Maria, then remembered to smile brightly and continued past without saying anything. We reached the reception area.

"You'll get that eye looked at?" I asked, wondering if Dolores needed money.

"We're fine, Mr. Whitman. You've been very nice and we don't need any more help," Dolores Salcines said decisively. "Thank you. Good-bye."

She entered the elevator then, the palm of her tight hand guiding Maria's head of curls, and the other touching the brass plate of elevator buttons. I felt a great pressure to say something to her, but no words came. I looked directly into her large dark eyes but she glanced away nervously. "All right, then . . ." I stammered. We gave each other a last polite nod. I tried to reassure myself that Dolores and Maria's circumstances were going to improve. But reassurances were not forthcoming. The elevator doors closed.

I returned to my office. Not a bad way to start the day, I thought to myself; high-salaried young executive on the thirty-ninth floor does a kind turn toward a sexy, beat-up Hispanic woman. I would have liked to talk to her longer. But she and her daughter were gone now, and I assumed that we would not communicate further. From the window I looked down at the streets. It was lunchtime. Below me, workers drained by the thousands from the buildings to the sidewalks, specks of color moving in the great stone grid. In a minute Dolores Salcines and her daughter, Maria, would be among the many, hurrying, battling for space and light and air. What happened to them was not my affair, I tried to convince myself, not my responsibility.

◆ ◆ ◆

An hour later, we filed into the conference room. On the side table was a large box of doughnuts. I found my usual seat to Morrison's left, while the others came in, Samantha, the bankers and consultants, a few of Morrison's finance people, and of course Beales, who had a sort of cold jauntiness that I had always disliked.

"Afternoon, Jack." He smiled, the prince of congeniality.

"Ed." I gave him a dead nod.

Beales was all fine features and squinty handsomeness, nearly six feet four, much given to wearing thousand-dollar suits, and I'd hated him from the moment we'd first worked together years back. He had something I didn't—he had grace. He appeared unconcerned; he seemed always to have time for pleasures and enjoyments. Morrison used Beales for ambassadorial purposes—visits to subsidiaries, investor relations, emceeing annual sales meetings, glad-handing at the professional tennis tournaments the Corporation underwrote, including the U.S. Open, where he handed the big check to the winner in front of the cameras. His voice was deep and pleasing and lent him unearned authority. He was physically always gazing down at me. (I'm a grinder, I never look rested, my face gets pinched and distressed when the acid swirls around down there—I'm a mess.) Beales was paid for his manner, not for his mind, which is the way it often goes. After Liz died, he had come up to me to say how sorry he was, and for a moment I had believed him and then I looked straight into his unblinking eyes and could see he was—that very second—studying me to determine if my grief presented him with some advantage that he should know about. It gets narrower at the top. Looking back now, I see I could have been smarter about Ed Beales.

We sat waiting for Morrison, ten tired, irritable people. The chitchat of our earlier meetings had run dry. For months we had lived on Corporation time, in which a week may be an eternity and an epoch may change with a phone call. There were others on the floor, including Campbell, the vice chairman of the executive committee. But he was out of the loop and never coming back. His wife had lung cancer and had been dying for eighteen months. And on the east corridor lay the offices of the executive vice president and general counsel, and the senior vice president and controller—older guys with a certain wincing softness to their step, five or eight years too young to be forcibly retired, too gray and beaten to be considered for further promotion. They understood their future absence; the Corporation is a world in which it is better for young men to look older and for old men to look younger. These men were also out of the picture, even though their stock option plans were in the Corporation's Series D 12% Convertible Exchangeable Preferred Stock, which is the limited, powerful stock shares. I no longer worried about them. Of the Corporation's seventeen vice presidents, only three (Beales, Samantha, and I) had offices on the thirty-ninth floor, with the rest on the floors below. The three of us were the comers, the prospects, and if anyone didn't know that, it was to their own peril. We pushed the deals through, made the hard phone calls that Morrison wanted to avoid. I did not instruct the older men, but I controlled their access to Morrison and I could look them in the eye without fear. This is an important thing, fear—in addition to the formal lines of power, fear courses through the unpredictable web of human relationships. In every organization there is the inner group of those who make the market in fear.

"Okay, everybody, here we go." Morrison stumped his way in, holding a briefcase to his side with his bad hand, the one that was missing three fingers. We straightened in our seats, became attentive. Morrison slid into his regular chair. I'd always felt sorry for his war injuries, because he was a proud man, with that thickened thorax and attractive belly armor that men get in their fifties.

"Sorry we had to start so late, I wanted to wait to be sure the Chairman was gone for the day," he said. "Jack, you can start smiling. I get worried when you don't smile. I'm going to smoke a frickin' cigar even though it bothers some of you guys. Ed, if you want good Cuban cigars, you have to buy them in Switzerland. I was talking to the guy in the cigar store. Castro could go anytime now. Anytime. You guys should read the international news first instead of the sports page. Cuba goes into civil war and we get boat people everywhere, in the pool at the Miami Hilton, in the moat at Disney World, everywhere. Soon as Castro goes I want us ready to move in there. Buy a couple hundred movie theaters, the next day. I mean it. Jesus, we should buy some hotels, too, right on the beach. Tear them down and put up new ones. Jack, you'll make a note of it? Get somebody to run some numbers?"

I nodded dutifully.

"Just let me have my cigar and we'll do this fast. Everybody get the doughnuts and stuff? I ordered them up. I figured if you guys get doughnuts I get my cigar. Samantha? If it's okay with you then I know I'm okay."

"We're ready." She smiled from down the table.

"Good. I got the call last night from the guy who's running the deal for them, Otto Waldhausen. Number-two guy. We seem to have a good rapport. He's all green light. But he also understands the delicacy of the thing." Morrison set the cigar in his mouth and then took it out. "He says Volkman-Sakura is ready to talk. They know our situation, they know the Chairman is not going to be happy about the idea of a merger, and they know we don't yet have the board of directors with us. In other words, they know how frickin' crazy we are." Morrison lit the cigar. "But Waldhausen also knows that the markets match so well. I said the situation is dynamic, that we've got a group of people here committed to this thing. We've been working on it for months, I told him. I got reports a mile high, I know everything about your company, I know how much money you made last quarter in your pay-per-view rugby matches in Australia, I know how many light bulbs you got in the ladies' room. Right? He was very impressed. I said we can pitch or we can catch. Better to do it over here, though. Your people speak English and ours don't speak German, except for Jack, of course, our intellectual. But we need to get going, I said. Also we need some kind of basic understanding on how the deal might be structured so we can convince everybody in the back of the bus. I said quite honestly we have an absentee Chairman, and we try to tell the directors as little as possible. He said he knows we have a passive board. He asked if the power has shifted downward one notch. I said yes. Everything important, everything *new*, gets done by the people in this room. We have idea people, we have deal people. The whole team. They get that. Waldhausen said he'll fly over with his people. Lot of talk and handshakes. Maybe tennis. Germans love tennis, even though Boris Becker is finished. Can't play on clay—*Ed* could beat him on clay." Morrison grinned affectionately at Beales and I felt a familiar bitter twist in my gut. "We'll feel each other out. Broadway shows, whatever. The whole thing is people. Fun and games and good deals. I think we can talk to them, not like the Japanese guys. They got some big Japanese guys in their computer division but we don't worry about that, that's internal on their side. I told Waldhausen, quite frankly, we don't know how to talk to the Japanese guys. We sort of hate them and fear them and we don't want to talk to them. They get that. So, we're going to start talking and see how it goes, maybe you guys'll get to do a dog-and-pony show. Now, they're probably trying to get a fix on how far along we are with the Chairman and the outside board. They understand everybody in this place doesn't see it all the same way. They understand that if this thing blows up on the runway we're gonna be dead men in trees—"

"Men?" Samantha complained mockingly. "What about me?"

Morrison relit his cigar, sucking hard against the wet end. "Samantha, I got a feeling you're gonna be okay. Don't ask me why. If I told you, you'd sue me for sexual harassment and then I couldn't promote you, right? You'd sue me and I'd be forced to live in a railroad shack the rest of my life. Catch some trout." Morrison's eyebrows shot up in thought. "Sounds good, actually. Now, anyway, they'll be very interested in why our Chairman hasn't shaken a couple of their hands. I'll be working on that angle. They'll want to know who the players are. Waldhausen says he understands it could get messy over here."

"Who would head up the new merged corporation?" Beales asked. "Have you talked about that?"

"Maybe their guy, maybe not," Morrison said vaguely. "Me, you, anyone. Madonna. I don't know. A lot could happen." Of course Morrison assumed he was in the line of succession at the Corporation. No overt successor was being groomed and the Chairman planned on ruling the Corporation until he dropped. Morrison was well liked by the Corporation's board of directors but that guaranteed nothing; despite their passivity, they retained absolute legal power at the Corporation, and anybody, even a number-two guy, can be forced out tomorrow if his smell goes bad. Several of the directors had been chief executive officers of Fortune 100 companies that had been gutted in the frenzy of junk-bond buy-outs in the eighties; they hated unsecured debt; they hated raiders and management coups; and even more, they might well hate the idea that a German-Japanese company might mingle management with the Corporation. So the trick for us was to convince them that the deal was good for the Corporation and the stockholders. This might be nearly impossible, for the directors were extremely loyal to the Chairman. They still believed, at this late date, that he had the magic. He was one of the thirty-odd men who sat in the pantheon of corporate gods. His tanned face was seen at all the black-tie galas, with his most recent wife in tow, a correctly attractive woman twenty-five years his junior, not much older than his children by his first marriage, a woman with slim ankles who, it was rumored, received estrogen shots to keep her face soft. The Chairman had, of course, once been a fine, prescient businessman. Prior to 1985, he had given final approval on nine of the twenty-one highest-grossing Hollywood films of all time. He had initiated the start-up of the Corporation's three most profitable magazines. And in the dinosaur days of cable TV, the Chairman had taken on the networks by starting a cable network from scratch. Now, the Corporation's cable television division offered subscribers eighteen different national channels — news, sports, movies, children's programming, business news, science, Spanish-language programming, you name it — and owned distributorships in most of the country's large markets. The Corporation's total share of all television audiences was a remarkable 19 percent. Gross profits from this division alone were now over $600 million a year. The Chairman was the sole, iron-fisted architect of this stranglehold, and in the years of its construction he had ruthlessly fired anyone who did not share his vision. He had been brutal and he had been right.

But now the Chairman needed to be deposed, we all believed, in order that the Corporation expand and prosper. Tremendous new multimedia technologies were coming, driven by advances in microchip technology, making the usual entertainments pale in comparison. Eastern Europe was like the Wild West, huge, open for the taking, though Germany had the lead. Our international expansion was substantial but as yet consisted only of a patchwork of alliances and marketing deals. We wanted a bigger presence — "Napoleonic," Morrison had prescribed. "We must seek transformative victories." We had the chance to implant our products into cultures and populations wholly unfamiliar with them — people without checking accounts or credit cards. It was, as everyone knew, an unstable global market. With that great click into the twenty-first century, we believed the Corporation would have found its future. The inhabitants of what used to be the Soviet Union and the Eastern Bloc constituted a population larger than that of Europe, Japan, or the United States. The new entertainment market easily reached the hundreds of billions of dollars. Black market and pirated products were giving way to established Western-style market controls. Southeastern China was opening up, too. And South America was becoming more stable politically; those markets were opening. The Corporation could be there and everywhere, ready with the product. So could our tradition-al competition — Disney, Bertelsmann, Paramount — as well as the new players who had the size, cash, and expertise to mix computers, consumer electronics, and communications — AT&T, Sony, Mat-sushita, Microsoft. It was a chaos of creative destruction. Whatever outfit triumphed would become one of the most important companies in the twenty-first century.

"They'll be arriving at the Plaza Hotel early next week," Morri-son continued. "The first meeting will be the day or two after that. When we have a stock valuation and a market organization proposal worked out, we can go to the Chairman and the directors with it, get them all gassed up on the idea—"

And so on. We went on talking. The details turned on figures and formulas and the interpretation of great sums of money, that week's stock market climate, the Corporation's debt levels and projected profits, the direction that interest rates were moving and the Federal Reserve Board's behavior and what the volatile Japanese stock market might do in the short term and at least twenty other factors. I glanced from time to time at Ed Beales, whose expression indicated he was up in the box seats and not on the field. When he met my gaze his handsome eyes crinkled, as if he knew the joke and I didn't.

◆ ◆ ◆

My meeting with Morrison was pushed to 5:00 P.M., and at the appointed time I waited in the western corridor outside his office. The hall was lined with oil paintings of the founder, now dead twenty years (who missed a chance to buy CBS on the cheap in 1957 and Para-mount Pictures in 1964), former chairmen of the Corporation, and the handful of the venerable magazine editors and publishers who had made the Corporation what it was. Those same men, lucky or brilliant or natural salesmen, were now irrelevant. The big profits were no longer in the printed word. Our top five rap music videos yielded greater net profits than our famous eighty-one-year-old news maga-zine, but that's the slope of the culture now. The Corporation was one hundred times larger than it had been in 1950, twenty-five times larger than in 1970. Our overseas sales accounted for 40 percent of gross revenues, which wasn't surprising, given that America's largest export is pop culture and the Corporation its greatest exporter. The Chairman's portrait was also among those that Morrison passed each day, a large, purposefully virile painting full of bright blues and whites and yellows, showing the Chairman many years prior at the age of about fifty-five.

"You can't learn anything from dead men, Jack," Morrison announced, limping down the hall. "They don't even know they're dead, for starters. Trust me on that." He walked past me, yanked off his overcoat, and I followed him into his office, where a gaudy de Kooning brightened the shiny cherry-wood walls. Mrs. Comber, his secretary, came in and poured tea for us.

"I'm supposed to go hear the vice president talk tonight." He absentmindedly examined his spoon. "Want to go?"

I tended to drink too much at these things.

"There's a dinner beforehand. We need somebody to go. It's the vice president of the United States, for God's sake."

"I've seen him talk. I'm not crazy about it."

"Neither am I." Morrison smiled. "The jokes are bad and I never understand what the appetizer is. It's sitting on my plate and it could be a clam or a cucumber or the nuts of a pig, for all I know." Morrison's good hand, large and meaty from overuse, flipped through some papers. "But it'd look good to have somebody there. We paid something like five grand for a plate and said we would be there."

I shrugged. "You want someone to go, I'll go."

"I saw the other names. It's a good table. There'll be a State Department guy who could talk to us about China. And maybe what we could do in Cuba when it goes off, how to get in there fast."

"Right."

"So, you'll go?"

I nodded. Morrison had known I would agree to go.

"Mrs. Comber will call and change the reservation."

"Right."

"So these Volkman-Sakura guys arrive next week. It's crucial we have him on board with this thing," Morrison said, meaning the

Chairman. "He's got his shares and controls the ones owned by his foundation—"

The phone issued a soft plaint and Morrison took the call. I watched. His war wounds had not been the end of his bad luck; Morrison and his wife had suffered the stupendously horrible fortune to have two retarded children, both boys now in their late teens. I had often wondered if he lay awake at night wondering about the odds of having two sons such as his, or if there was something wrong with him or his wife. I'd never asked, of course. He had not put either of his sons into an institution, and both lived at home in Scarsdale with full-time attendants. I admired this. He kept the boys' pictures on his desk; both *looked* retarded. It had been a tortuous twenty-five-year climb for Morrison—stints in sales, planning, finance, and other departments, licking each step of the ladder. Of course, now he made four million dollars a year, before bonuses and stock options.

"Right, as I was going to say, I think we got enough people on this," Morrison began again, not quite sure where he'd left off. "The numbers take care of themselves, one way or another. It all comes down to people. We can get Volkman-Sakura all oiled up but nothing happens if he doesn't tell the board it's okay. Or, nothing will happen *easily*. If he doesn't agree, then the board has to be forced to make a decision, which of course it is very uncomfortable doing." Morrison shook his head in disgust. "I'd have to lobby each member beforehand and then give some kind of speech and then we'd have a big fight. The only way for this whole thing to happen *easily* is for someone to make the case to him, someone he isn't expecting. He can't stand me, so I can't do it. It has to be someone who understands the whole complicated plan, the *idea* of it and all the aspects, *and* can talk about it. Samantha tells me he probably has a drift. But someone's got to bring it up overtly, feel him out on the question. So, Jack, that's why you're here. I want to pull you out of the negotiating group—now, *wait*"— he'd seen my expression change—"before you interrupt me, just let me *finish*—Beales and Samantha can cover the marketing aspects—we have your whole thing on paper, so we'll refer to it. You'll come back into the deal later—"

"No chance," I told Morrison. "No way I'm going to just walk away from all the—*the thousands*—of hours—"

"For Christ's sake, Jack, just listen," Morrison went on, "okay? Now, the Chairman's guy—what's his name—"

"Fricker."

"The guy with the headaches. He's not going to be coming back anytime soon." We'd all been told that Fricker had developed a syndrome of dizziness and headaches, so acute he woke from his sleep with heart-stopping vertigo. He'd disappeared from the floor two months back. "Mrs. Marsh told me the Chairman doesn't have time to interview anyone. But he needs somebody in there with him in the meetings, somebody who can carry his briefcase, the whole deal."

"I didn't know the Chairman even *went* to meetings anymore."

"A few. Just to get around," Morrison said dismissively. "Little stuff. Just to feel good."

"He doesn't know me," I argued. "He's going to want somebody who—"

"He doesn't care who it is so long as the guy's smart."

"I worked *months* on this stuff." Volkman-Sakura dominated portions of the European, Japanese, South American, and African markets. The two corporations had great intersecting mechanisms of production and distribution and marketing. "It's the best work of my career, like try to wire two brains together, every synapse and capillary and whatever the hell else no longer works in Fricker's head, all the marketing information—"

Morrison nodded as he fiddled with an antique mallard duck decoy on his desk. He claimed he could aim and shoot a shotgun with one hand. "Everybody knows that. That's why we're at this point. You saw how it could be done."

Beales would take credit for everything, slip in there, offering sage banalities. "You'd be handing it off—"

Morrison put his palms up in front of his chest, as if pushing on a wall. "But you, more than anyone around here, are qualified to argue with the Chairman. And you *like* to argue, Jack. You're doing it *now*, for Christ's sake. I haven't talked with him in weeks. The man is some old guy in a golf hat, so far as I'm concerned. He said nothing last month in the board meeting. I carried the whole thing. I mean it. Nothing! Things change. Cuba is going to blow and the Chairman's going to ride off into the sunset. You're part of this, Jack. We all have a role, a job. We can do it, we can run up the wall with this thing. I don't know what he even reads anymore, the memos and reports. He's always going somewhere in the helicopter. Where, I don't know. Mrs. Marsh won't tell anybody. So you got to get in there. Talk. I only know the overview, the others know the pieces. You're the only guy around here with a good enough memory to have the whole deal in your head—"

I could feel the disgust on my face. "Beales could do it. He's *perfect* for it."

"No he isn't. And I need him for other stuff, showing Wald-hausen and these guys around. And, dammit, you haven't even heard what I want you to do, Jack."

"Okay."

"The thing is that we can't get the board all whipped up. The merger idea has to be presented in such a way that they can overrule the Chairman's objections, if necessary, and feel they are brilliant and terrific and smart. A bunch of wise men. They have to see the logic of it for themselves."

"Look themselves in the mirror the next day, not feel guilty," I said.

"Right. But if the board finds out we did this behind the Chairman's back, they'll clean my clock with a pipe cleaner." This was true. The average age of the board of directors was about sixty-two; men with multiple houses, wives and former wives, and expensive hobbies such as fly-fishing with their mistresses in Alaska by guide. Their faces revealed that they knew, with a visceral certainty that a younger man like myself could only conjecture, that in five or ten years there would be a new game for them to play and it was called cancer of the prostate or heart disease or Alzheimer's. They were in no mood for cheap turmoil on the thirty-ninth floor. "So I'm going to try to avoid that," Morrison said. "I going to try to do this the easier way, by assigning you to stick with the Chairman. Go to whatever meetings he still—"

"I *really* don't want to do this."

"—he's got something in Washington next Monday," Morrison went on. "Go with him. Find his head. The mood. The *deep* mood. It requires a certain touch. How aggressive we should be. Should we force a confrontation in front of the board or flatter him into thinking he should present them with the deal? Maybe he's looking for a swan song, a chance to hit a home run in the ninth inning of the World Series and then retire. Feel him out on the question, Jack. Go to the parties. He tends to throw down the sauce. See what he says *then*. Remind him what decade it is. Okay? This is just a couple of weeks, tops."

I glimpsed the Chairman only now and then, for he had his own elevator from the parking garage below street level and spent much of his time away from the office, content to let Morrison run the day-to-day operations. On rare occasions he decided against his limo or even a taxi and took himself to work in an old Mercedes. But he drove so infrequently now that the Corporation's parking garage attendants kept a small can of custom apricot-colored paint that matched the tint of the car. After he arrived, they could be seen dabbing their brushes on the new dings and scratches. Occasionally I passed Mrs. Marsh's office as she typed using a foot-operated Dictaphone, and the Chairman's voice, disemboweled, started and stopped, started and stopped, over and over and over. His absence created a presence. It suggested his power. The Chairman was certain to resist the merger plan. Even if I could jimmy my way into his schedule, there was no reason that he would necessarily listen to me; he had seen dozens of Jack Whitmans. Meanwhile Beales would be glad-handing on the inside with the V-S executives. I didn't like it. In fact, I hated it.

But what could I say? Outside Morrison's window, a piece of paper floated on an updraft in the perfect blue, a white sheet lazily lifting and tumbling, over and over. Above the buildings and cars and noise, the clouds inched across the horizon, mocking the petty strivings of men such as me. And men such as Morrison, who pushed people around on a board in his head.

"You know I don't want to do this," I said finally, the acid rasping my throat.

Morrison looked at me, then skipped his gaze toward the rest of the day's schedule. I was dismissed.

"I mean, I really *don't* want to do this," I said firmly.

"Yes." Morrison raised his eyes. He had seen the heads of men explode. "But I don't care."

Fuck him, I thought, fuck his certainty that I will do what he tells me. And fuck me for doing it.

THREE

And over the next few days, while we waited for the Volkman-
Sakura team to arrive, what happened that would winch tragedy
in my direction? Well, nothing — nothing *apparent*. The Chairman was out of the city, having skin cancers removed, so I would have
to wait for him to return, too. The hours were mundane in a lulling
sort of way; they suggested constancy and security and order. One
would never have known that events were ripening from mere un-
likeliness. My pharmacy raised the price of a twelve-ounce-size bottle
of Extra Strength Maalox Plus, mint creme flavor, to $4.99. I thought
about Dolores Salcines while lying in bed. My stockbroker called to
pitch a company that makes little television cameras that goggle
around like an eyeball on the end of a wire. Surgeons send the device
through the rectum up into the lower gastrointestinal tract. "America's getting old!" my stockbroker exclaimed. "Everybody is going to
need it!" I bought two hundred shares. Samantha and I put together a
little fifty-million-dollar deal for the Corporation. Someone pawed
through the garbage cans outside my house, leaving a chicken carcass
sucked clean of every shred of meat. Beales spent a lot of time in
Morrison's office, which worried me. It rained, I read the newspapers.
The Norway maple in my garden leafed out. Morrison stumped past
my office door from time to time, barking orders. At lunch one day, I
spied an attractive woman and followed her for a block, for the hell of
it. She changed sides of the street. I read more newspapers. The circus
came to town. Then, on that Friday, I was standing at my big office
window talking on the phone to one of our marketing people when I
noticed several tiny handprints smeared faintly on the glass —
crisscrossed, translucent streaks like a single character of an unknown
alphabet. The janitor, unaccustomed to looking for the messes of

children, had missed them. There was a ghostliness to the marks; I felt beckoned. I cut the conversation short and called Mrs. Triscott.

"How's Dolores Salcines doing on the job?" I asked.

"Fired her," came a voice of irritation. "Can't concentrate. I had to get her work rekeyed. She's too tired to work under pressure. I told her to go home this morning. Can't worry about one person, got a thousand pages have to be input today—"

"You fired her?"

"That's what I said."

Mrs. Triscott was fearless. "This woman has a child," I said.

"So do a lot of people, Mr. Whitman."

"You should have called me first before firing her. This woman doesn't have any resources, any money—"

"Look, Mr. Whitman, you gotta understand something, okay?" It was the nasally, exasperated voice of a woman who survives in the lower bowels of corporate bureaucracy hating every minute of work. "I'm just doing my *job*. You're up there on thirty-nine and it's all the same to you. These gals have to be fast. Fast and no mistakes. I get a memo every week on productivity. Efficiency. You wouldn't hire a lousy person, why should I?"

She gave me a number for Dolores Salcines and hung up. I wasn't sure I should call. She might feel embarrassed at being fired, but it seemed I'd set her up in a job she couldn't handle and therefore owed her an apology. I dialed. On the fifth ring a male voice answered and I asked for Dolores.

"Well, she might be here and then again she might not be," the man's voice echoed strangely.

"What do you mean?"

"I don't know who all's livin' here, bud. I hain't been here two weeks myself."

"What place is this?" I asked.

"This a hotel, bud." The voice coughed out a laugh. "At least that's what they call it."

"What's the name?"

"I don't know. 'The something.' "

"Where is it?"

"Uh, lemme think about that—" I heard the gurgle of the man putting a bottle to his lips. "Ahh, uh, all right, I'm pretty sure we's exactly and precisely approximately near the corner of Forty-third and Eighth Avenue."

Not far from Times Square—no doubt one of the aging buildings catering to the transient population of drifters, drunks, runaways, enlisted men on leave, and so on. Big waxed Cadillacs and limos nose their way through these streets in the off hours, and two or three avenues to the west the prostitutes do a stupendous business at night—where the morning light falls across certain paved-over lots to reveal a great littering of used rubbers, flattened and translucent, many of them ringed with lipstick halfway down from the tip. "Listen," I said, "you'd remember this woman if you saw her. She's got a child with her."

"She black?"

"She looks Hispanic, maybe a little black as well. I don't know, exactly."

"Well, is she *hot*, man?" the voice cackled. "Lot of fuckin' *hot* babes around here, man. See them titties bouncin' around, an' I want to touch them nippies . . ." The voice devolved into garrulous, hacking laughter. I listened as Helen came in and placed several letters to be signed in front of me.

"I'm just asking you if you think you've seen her."

The laughter stopped abruptly. "Who the fuck knows?"

"Could you just look around, maybe? Ask around?"

Helen stared at me and then left.

"You want somebody around *here*, you gotta come go knockin' yo'self. I can't just go fuckin' banging on some people's door—you can get yo'self *shot*." The voice disappeared and the line went dead. I called back. No answer. I stood up and took my coat out of the closet. On the way out I told Helen I'd be gone for a while.

"Where're you headed?" she asked.

"Just out. Walk around, talk to God."

She looked at me with patience, which was one of the reasons I'd hired her. "Mrs. Marsh sent over all this stuff for you to read for your trip to Washington on Monday."

"I'll get to it," I promised.

"Jack, do you *really* have the time—"

"Hell, how much is it?"

She handed me a folder five inches thick, a good six or seven hundred pages of memos, letters, reports.

"Who does Morrison expect I am?" I asked her.

Helen looked at me, her eyes watering slightly, as if she knew things I did not. She was smart, she saw things coming, and she ate lunch with other executive assistants; they had their own grapevine of gossip and back-door information, they typed the confidential letters and important documents, they knew who was calling whom.

"Mrs. Marsh said his car will meet you. She said that you should by no means expect him to have read the file."

"I'm covering his ass?"

"She just said that this was the complete file and that—"

"Yes, fine," I interrupted. "You know Morrison yanked me off the negotiating team?"

She nodded. I put the folder in my briefcase. "Helen, you have any theories about what they're doing with me?"

"No." She looked up at me. "I'm sorry."

"Let me know if you do," I told her. "I need some interesting theories."

In the hallway I spied Asad Ru Adoo, the in-house investment consultant, who was occasionally seen scuttling fatly into a back office on thirty-nine carrying two double-wide lizard-skin briefcases with digital locks and his name embossed in swirling script. He wore a dark blue turban and sported a tremendous paunch that he pushed ahead of him like a wheelbarrow full of gold, and his self-importance meant that he spoke to almost no one.

"Hello, Asad," I said as he passed.

"Yes, yes," he muttered darkly behind his beard, without looking at me. "Thank you."

He was paid something like a million dollars a year to play the Corporation's cash against the dollar by moving into and out of deutsche marks, yen, Hong Kong dollars, pounds, Eurodollars, Swiss francs—whatever currency would give the best return. But no one seemed to know *exactly* what he did, except sit in his office late into the night, consulting Tokyo, New Delhi, Kuwait City, Hong Kong,

Seoul. There were rumors that he had virtually assaulted a quiet secretary on the floor below when she refused to date him; the secretaries down there, some of whom were from the streets of Harlem and knew a thing or two about men's egos, had nicknamed him Boo-Boo, and after he had paraded past them trailing the stink of French cologne, they had been seen to go wobbly on their high heels and weep with laughter. I had no doubt that Adoo was involved in Morrison's machinations in some way, finding ways to hide a couple of hundred million in cash from Volkman-Sakura if necessary in all sorts of low-to-the-ground deals, and I wondered frankly if Morrison attached too much importance to Adoo's swagger and thickly mysterious accent, the Kissinger of the Corporation. Like the others, like me I suppose, there was something wrong with him — that was the only way he could work on thirty-nine. Another freak. The floor was full of them, myself included.

◆ ◆ ◆

I walked straight toward Times Square, past the lurking porn palaces where good, useful men in suits and wedding rings were whacking off in the peep booths, past all the splendid squalor, the religious nuts and racial instigators with sound systems harassing crowds of white tourists, the coal-skinned Nigerians selling counterfeit watches and mass-produced fragments of African culture. Past the Peruvians in traditional black hats and bright homespun colors, just in from the cloud-wreathed mountains, still looking innocent. God knows why *they* would come to Manhattan. Above Forty-fourth Street hung the gigantic television screen playing some shirtless black guy in a pair of torn-up jeans dancing wildly, his girl's ass and sinewy back undulating in opposite directions. I think he was on one of the Corporation's eight music labels. Half of our pop music talent can't sing a regular studio session, and a few are nothing but lip-sync artists. But they look good. There're so many and they change so quickly I can't keep them straight. They score platinum on the first album, a zillion dollars, a house in Bel Air, maybe spin off a TV show for a season, surf the notoriety, and tomorrow no one remembers their names. The Corporation is smart about this, gets the talent on the way up, cuts it loose before the fall. I think the music entertainment division had even quantified the growth-and-decay cycle in American pop music using a formula that could estimate where an artist was along the career curve. Its works, too. The music division earns about $250 million each year. The guy who runs it, Italian from New Jersey by way of Hollywood, knows nothing about music, but is very good at flipping over the talent. Very smart about personalities, knows all the L.A. people. Very ruthless. We were glad now that we didn't sign Michael Jackson a few years back; the big money years are behind him and the freak years are ahead. Someday they'll laugh at him like they laugh now at John Travolta. Same with Madonna. Pretty soon she'll be a pathetic old tart in her forties and when she claws at her crotch it won't be pretty.

I stopped at the corner of Eighth Avenue and Forty-third Street, not far from the New York Times building, in front of a crouching six-story wreck of a hotel whose brickwork needed repointing. The Victorian flourishes above the entrance were eroded by acid rain, and judging from the ornate tile floor and Ionic columns, the lobby had once been grand—a place of cool drinks and potted palms and ladies with cigarette holders—but whatever had been the hotel's charms were dulled now by coat after coat of paint, the last a bilious yellow that hung in flakes from the ceiling like leaves about to fall, and one understood in this small fact part of the great tragic sweep of New York's history. Luxury is always in decay. Several unattended black children sat playing on the steps inside the doors, flicking lighted matches at each other. The kids were dirty in the way that only poor children are, their clothes filthy, noses running, one of them coughing with unmindful hoarseness. I hate seeing children suffer. It makes me sick. It makes me feel guilty, too, because I'm doing nothing to help them. I'm an asshole. A real bastard. The kids noticed me and stopped the game. Perhaps Maria played with them, I thought, perhaps they knew her.

"Any of you kids know a little girl named Maria?" I asked breezily. No one answered. They stared up at me in curiosity and fear. White man in a suit, maybe trouble. One little boy thrust three dirty fingers into his mouth and started to suck on them anxiously.

"I don't know nobody like that," a little boy said.

"No, I think she that one got killed by the police," another boy volunteered in a high voice, and the children laughed.

The check-in desk was a reinforced box with a locked door and bulletproof glass with a small slit through which to pass money, keys, or anything else. Inside was a small engraved brass nameplate: Martin Clammers, Manager. A wizened man shrunken inside a polyester suit sat perched like a monkey on a stool, holding a minute nub of pencil and figuring in the margins of a racing form, while a radio called out one of the early races at Belmont. His hands were unusually big, as if enlarged by the daily handling of cash. I knocked lightly against the glass.

"What can I do for ya?" He eased off the stool and stepped forward to have a better look at me, perhaps mistaking my suit and tie as that of some city official come to badger him.

"I'm looking for a woman and child. The woman's name is Dolores Salcines."

"Yes?" he said.

"Are they here?"

"You like the last guy who came looking for her?"

I watched his face for a clue as to who he meant. He had leaky eyes. "No," I answered.

"You here to pay her bill?" He examined me expectantly.

"No. I'm only a visitor."

"She's gotta pay her bill today or it's out."

I nodded my comprehension.

"I mean, fellah, if you're a friend of hers, you better help her pay up. This ain't no welfare hotel," the old man said, turning down the radio. "I been in business a long time—a *long* time—and it's because I keep the level of the clientele up. Can't have the ones who won't pay." He found a handkerchief and wiped his eyes. "I ain't nasty about it, I'm just telling you in case you think you might be helping this Salcines woman out."

"You rent by the week?"

"If they look okay, it's one-sixty-two. That's twenty-three dollars and fourteen cents a night, cheap as you can get."

"She owes for a week?"

"Yep. And if she doesn't pay, she's out tonight."

I handed him a credit card. "Put it on this. Mind telling me which room?"

He shook his head. "I don't let anyone up."

"You afraid I'll burn the place down?"

"I can't go letting people up and down."

"Can you make an exception?" I said, signing the receipt.

He handed my card back and stared dutifully at his racing form; he had all his bets figured. "No, sir, I can't."

"Can you make an exception for fifty dollars cash?"

"Yes, sir, I think I can."

I handed him the money—a couple of more bets. He pulled out a clipboard and ran his knobby fingers down a long list of names and then across the sheet to find the room number.

"She know you're coming?"

"No," I answered. "Not really."

Mr. Clammers dialed a number on a telephone, waited a moment, mumbled something into the handset, listened, and then looked at me.

"She wants to know what you want."

"Tell her I came to visit for just a few minutes."

This he did, looking back furtively with increasing distrust, so it seemed.

"She says it wasn't her fault she was fired."

"Okay. I know that."

The hotel manager hung up the phone. "Four-sixty-six."

A shaky wooden banister led me up four flights to a long, windowless hall, along which ran corroded sprinkler pipes on the ceiling and a stained strip of magenta carpeting on the floor pocked by gum stains. The hallway smelled of insecticide and stale cigarette smoke. It occurred to me that Dolores's husband might be with her and Maria in the room, in which case—in which case, I wasn't quite sure what I'd do. The doors were solid and wooden, some with many holes from previous lock fixtures and each with a neatly painted gold number. I followed these numbers, passing a garbage can stuffed with whiskey and wine bottles. Except for some faint weeping behind one of the doors, the dark hallway was as quiet as a tomb. The hotel was, if not quite the bottom, then one of its lower rungs, where lives ended in anonymous silence, the sort of place where a few days pass before the bodies are discovered.

I heard a door open behind me. "Are you *new* around here?" came a strangely high voice.

I turned back to see a gaunt, elongated figure in a robe and stockings, hair a jolting orange tint, and face a lurid mask of makeup. It was a man. A lacy black bra pushed the meager dough of his chest into the semblance of breasts. His torso was shaved of all body hair.

"I asked if you're *new*, honey." He pulled his robe back to reveal, above his gartered stockings, a shaved groin and a penis pierced by half a dozen small gold rings. I looked at his face. His tongue, skewered by a closed safety pin, lolled wetly on his bottom lip.

I shook my head. "You got the wrong kind of guy."

"Are you *sure?*" he purred. "Taster's choice."

I didn't know what this meant but it didn't sound good. "No chance," I told him.

"Then have a *very* nice day." He smiled and shut the door.

There was a pay phone farther down the hall. I stopped and checked the phone number I'd called earlier — it was the same. A few doors on, I came to Dolores's room and stopped. Inside a radio played salsa, the song lush and passionate and full of soaring trumpet blasts. I knocked. The radio quieted.

"It's unlocked."

I pushed the door open. Dolores sat in a ratty armchair, dressed in a torn-off Knicks T-shirt, her hair tied up above her head in a dark mess of curls, arms folded in front of her. Her eye was less swollen, but the bruise had darkened and drained like running mascara beneath her skin.

"The old guy at the desk said I could come up."

"What do you want?" Her face was hard.

I looked for a place to sit. The room was insufferably hot and cramped, with enough space for a chair, a small basin, and the bed. A radiator hissed in the corner despite the warm April day. The wastebasket was full of take-out cartons and the room smelled of beans and garlic.

"Careful," Dolores said sharply, pointing.

Maria lay at the top of the bed, nearly hidden under a blanket. She was asleep and wheezed as she breathed.

"Is she sick?"

"She has chills," Dolores said. "A little fever."

"Sounds sort of congested."

"She's okay. She just needs to sleep." Dolores watched the slow rise and fall of her daughter's back. "This place is so noisy, she can't sleep. Quiet all day, loud at night."

"It's hot as hell in here."

"The heat is on. Won't go off." She looked at me suspiciously. "So, why're you here?"

We were strangers, of course. "I called Mrs. Triscott and she said she'd fired you."

"Yes?" Dolores said testily. "So?"

"She said you were too tired to work."

"Well, I'm tired, but I was also thinking about Maria. I had to leave her here and I didn't like doing that. Listen, I appreciate you checking on me but—" Dolores flashed her dark eyes at me. "But I don't need your help."

The radiator hissed erratically. I nodded my agreement. "Your eye looks better."

"I kept ice on it a long time. Plus I'm a fast healer," she added sarcastically.

"Where's your husband?

"Who the hell are you to ask?"

"You wear a wedding ring, Dolores. Where is the guy? Why isn't he around?"

"These are pretty personal questions, you know?"

True. I was out of my mind. I didn't know the woman, she didn't know me. But there I was, looking into the dark smoothness of her face. And her daughter lay sprawled on the bed asleep.

"I'm not asking *you* who you're married to, and what's her name, and is she pretty, right?" Dolores asked angrily. She crossed her legs. "I mean, where's *your* wife?"

"That's a long story, actually."

"Oh, *right.*" She laughed in disgust, and her reaction, so sudden and clean, was a lovely thing. It meant she was strong. There was something about the way she was so certain of herself that I admired.

She knew herself, she liked herself. Liz had been like this. Strong women are the most attractive women. "It's *always* a long story," Dolores went on. "You come here and then tell me it's—"

"I was married," I interrupted. "My wife was killed. A guy drove by the corner where she was standing and shot at some other guys and she was in the way."

"Oh Jesus, I'm sorry," Dolores said quickly, eyes wide. "I mean, I had no idea. I just said that because—"

She didn't finish her sentence. She leaned over and rubbed Maria's back.

"I understand why you said it," I answered. "You don't know why I'm here and I don't really know why either."

Dolores considered this. "I just think you should know that I'm not free, I mean, I'm still, like, *involved.*"

I said nothing, instead wondering what sleep and better food and new clothes might do for Dolores. She stood up to check Maria's forehead. Her T-shirt, lifted by her breasts, ended at the navel and I glimpsed her stomach and imagined running my thumb down the curve of her waist. The smoothness of the skin. It would be interesting to see my white hand against the dark flesh of her belly, or thigh, or anywhere. Or my penis in her mouth. I thought that, too. These things come into my head.

Now Dolores bent over and adjusted her daughter's pajama top. "It's all screwed up between me and my husband, okay? And he's *incredibly* jealous—" She glanced up at me, expecting a reaction. "I'm trying to keep away from him, you understand?" She looked at her watch. "He wants me back home. Also he knows I'm here in this place. I got to get another place to sleep tonight—"

"How does he know?"

"I got too many girlfriends in my old neighborhood who, like, feel sorry for him. I got to move me and Maria."

"Is he the one who hit you?"

Dolores shut her eyes and tipped back her head, expelling a breath. Her throat was smooth. Then she lowered her chin and opened her dark eyes. "You know, except for where you work, I don't know who you are or what you want, though I got a pretty good idea of what *that* might be. Maybe it's *good* I got myself fired from your big company where a computer keeps track of how many keystrokes you type each hour — did you know that? It tells you when you can take a break and how many minutes you got to go to the bathroom. And Mrs. Biscuit — "

"Mrs. Triscott."

"Yeah, well, she treats everybody like they're stupid, right? She made one of the other girls, this very sweet Chinese girl, cry in front of everybody, yelling at her about how to spell 'fiduciary extrapolations.' " Dolores went to the closet and pulled out the coat she had been wearing the night I first saw her on the subway. "I want you to get out of here."

I stood to leave. "From all I can see, you're at the end of the line, Dolores."

She pulled the coat tight around her in spite of the radiator's oppressive heat. "Oh?"

"The guy downstairs was hoping I'd pay your rent."

She shut her eyes and exhaled in frustration. "All right, yeah, I don't have any money. You were very nice and gave me your card. Then I came to your office and you got me a job. Then I got fired. I feel pretty stupid about that, you know? What am I supposed to *do*, ask you for another job?"

"I'd try to help you get it," I said. "It's a big company. I'm sure there are other — "

"Look," Dolores interrupted, "you seem like a really *nice* guy. A dumb, nice guy, you know? My life right now is very fucked up. I appreciate the trouble you've gone to. But I'm in a situation, okay?" Dolores's dark eyes burned at me, warning me, it seemed, to leave for my own good.

"If I can find a safe place for you and Maria to stay, would you take it, to stay for free for a while?"

She smiled ever so slightly at my brazen willingness to press her; it was not quite an expression of pity but something more elusive.

"Not where *I* live," I went on, "but another place, here in Manhattan. Totally free, for a week or two."

Dolores glanced at Maria. I realized that every question ran through Maria. "I'll have to think about it. Actually, no thanks."

"Why?"

"Just no thanks, all right? *Jesus.*"

"All right."

She stared at me indecisively, not yet ready to close the topic. "You're just looking for an easy fuck."

I should have let it go, right then. But I couldn't. Dolores and I were already locked into something. She was challenging me, seeing how serious I was about helping her.

"Yes or no, Dolores," I said. "A place to stay, free. *Safe.* I could check on it and give you a call here at five o'clock. At that pay phone down the hall. Keep your radio down and you can hear it. I paid your bill here, incidentally. Take it or leave it. If you leave it, fine. Have a nice life. And good luck dealing with the shelters. You'll be in one huge room with five or six hundred other people. Half will be mentally ill or violent or fucked-up. They'll steal every last thing you have and they'll have every kind of infectious disease you can imagine—AIDS, TB, hepatitis, everything—and you're going to be worrying about Maria every second. I mean that. I don't like to think of Maria in a place like that. I really meant that, too, much as you think I'm some kind of crazy asshole. So have a nice life, Dolores. I hope it gets better."

She anxiously looked at Maria and then, strangely, she stared at a small glass jar set in the middle of the dresser. It was half-full of water. Dolores examined the jar, as if expecting to see something inside it. Then she turned back to me. "You're not some weirdo?" She cocked her head, her expression doubting, fearful, wanting to trust. "You're not some sick guy who's gonna hurt me and my daughter?"

"Do I look like that?" I asked, my hands open—a salesman's trick, incidentally.

"You *look* like a nice guy." She frowned. "That's what I don't get."

"I *am* a nice guy, dammit," I protested. "I'm a nice boring guy with a good job. I wear a suit, I go to work, I pay my bills, I'm a nice guy, okay? My father's a retired *minister*, for Christ's sake."

"Those are the worst kind." She smiled. "With the fathers like that."

I knew we were past the hard part now.

"You're worried about us, really?" she asked.

"I heard you were fired and I got the number from that old bitch and thought, I'll call and see what happens. Okay? I didn't know if your husband was going to be here or what, you know, maybe beat the crap out of me."

Her lips curled suggestively. "You're not looking for a little easy something?"

"If I were, then you would tell me to go to hell and that would be the end of it, right?"

"Oh sure."

"So it's a deal?" I pressed her.

Dolores said nothing. But she shrugged, and I took this to be a yes.

♦ ♦ ♦

On the way out of the hotel, I rapped on old man Clammers's window.

"She's going to have to be here a few minutes after five o'clock," I told him. "Got that?"

He ignored me and continued to finger his racing form.

"She's going to get a call upstairs," I continued. "She's paid up now, so I don't want you to kick her out or anything before she gets my call about five o'clock."

He shook his head. "Spare yourself the trouble, fellah."

"What do you mean?"

"I mean it always turns out exactly how you didn't expect it." His old eyes contemplated my face. "You're lookin' for this and you get that. Ain't worth it. I seen too many cases."

♦ ♦ ♦

Ahmed Nejad was going to help me but he didn't know it yet. We'd both played on the Columbia soccer team, traveling around the Ivy League, to the University of Pennsylvania to play in Franklin Field, to Harvard's field, to Yale to play in the Yale Bowl. Ahmed's family escaped Iran not long after the Shah fell, and they'd reorganized their clan and millions of dollars in New York. The family were all moderate, internationalized Muslims, and had foreseen that the rise of the Ayatollah Khomeini would be bad for a family that did business in the West. Ahmed was a fiery player and temperamentally suited only for the striker position, which requires one to cut through defenses and deliver the ball into the goal. Ahmed's play depended on a skilled recklessness and an almost cutthroat desire to get past the obstruction of players on the other team. His thick, hairy legs threshed and damaged those of opponents. Ivy League decorum meant nothing to him and his one great weakness was a violent temper; invariably three-quarters into the game, Ahmed would receive a yellow card for his tantrums. On the ride to New Haven or Cambridge or Philadelphia he would play poker with those who were stupid enough to challenge him. No one sufficiently understood the nuance of his accent to know when he was lying. And since then, he had done quite well—the city's ever-shifting patterns of commerce were the opponent he played against now. In college, we had both shared an interest in restoring old houses, but he had decided to do it for a living. He renovated buildings with the forcible intention of a man planning to score well when reselling, even into a bottomed-out real estate market. At the present, I knew, he was at work on a six-story brick manufacturing building a block west of Broadway in Soho. Ahmed had big plans to turn the abandoned, soot-stained edifice into a modern urban confection, with an exterior color scheme and bright new offices on the top five floors, trendy shops and galleries below. The plans included a penthouse apartment on the top floor, which I knew was nearly complete. This is where I hoped Dolores and Maria could stay temporarily.

But the only way to contact Ahmed was to find him at the site, so I hopped a cab and directed the driver downtown toward Ahmed's building. We pulled up in front of a huge freight doorway, from which blew a gritty dust that spiraled upward in the air. Workers wheeled refrigerator-sized waste canisters out of the building, each bin stuffed with wood and iron and plaster and cement. They emerged dusty and blinking from the deep gloom of the building, within which hung long strings of work lamps, much like the entrance to a mine. I found Ahmed, who, as usual, was dressed in a close-fitting European suit. He stood with a small wizened Pakistani or Indian man around the other side of the building. They were peering at half a dozen Mexican men who dangled from scaffolding about sixty feet up. Ahmed and the man conferred and then the man hollered a warped, Pakistani version of Spanish to the Mexican men, one of whom drawled a response with an explanatory bobbing of the head, whereupon the man on the ground translated to Ahmed, who responded in Farsi. Then the man hollered in a clipped musical British accent to a two-man crew from Bangladesh who, I saw, were higher up, closer to the roof, waiting for instructions—their perfectly black hair shining in the sun, their shy voices echoing down the wall. They were working the facade of the building, sandblasting the sooted brickwork to a fresh and prosperous rose. Ahmed saw me then.

"My friend!" He walked over and held out his hand.

"Ahmed," I said. Then I pointed to his companion. "A translator?"

"Sanjay is my foreman. He knows six languages, not including the Romance languages. He is the most brilliant man I have ever employed." Ahmed waved back at Sanjay, who continued to relay instructions between the two crews.

"And you pay him very well?"

Ahmed turned back to me. "He thinks so, yes."

"You only hire people off the boat?"

Ahmed frowned. "These men are the only men who know how to work. They don't want health insurance. Or the pension plan—they don't expect it. All they want is work and the cash I pay for it." As he spoke a fine silt of brick dust floated down on us. Inside the building we could hear the shrill pitch of grinders and drills. "And, Jack, that is true of you. All you know how to do is work." He grinned wickedly. "You work—but *I* make money." His smile showed his teeth, which he knew were very fine. "And now you want something from me, am I right? Americans only come to Iranians when something is wanted."

I described the favor I was requesting of him as we walked around to the entrance of the building, explaining that it was only for a little while and that Dolores and Maria absolutely had no other place to stay.

"This woman and her daughter, they are without any money, yes?" Ahmed asked. "They are not going to pay me?"

I nodded.

"What are they doing?"

"Trying to get away, trying to change their lives," I said.

"But this is not the place to do that."

"Didn't your family come here trying to change their lives?" I asked. "And what about these guys?" I gestured toward his workers.

"I assume that she is very attractive." Ahmed smiled his fine teeth. "This is not in doubt."

He looked directly at me then, having hassled me enough to be sure that I didn't take him for granted. But it wasn't that simple, either; what neither of us had mentioned was that I had found a job in our movie division's Hollywood studio office for his cousin, the one member of Ahmed's far-flung and talented family who was most assimilated into American culture. Her desire to give good phone for a third-tier studio executive was perceived as a betrayal by the family, Ahmed had told me, and the young woman seemed to have become a generic American, happily shorn of her Iranian heritage. But that was a family matter; what was important between us was that he had come to me and I had delivered, which he was obligated now to do. "I don't have a lot of lights up there yet, but there is electricity," Ahmed said. "She's got hot water but there's no washing machine or dishwasher hooked up."

"That's okay," I assured him. "She just needs to stay for a week, two at most."

"That is all? You are sure?"

I was not sure, but I nodded anyway. We crossed the street to an old-time restaurant that had pictures of the boxing greats going back seventy years, and sat up at the long bar. Muhammad Ali, back when he was Cassius Clay, stood over us, fist cocked, fierce and sweaty and magnificent.

"*You* have a big house," Ahmed remarked. "Why doesn't she stay with you?"

"She won't do that."

"She is very choosy for a woman who has nowhere to go."

"You're right," I said. "But we don't have the kind of relationship where I could just invite her to stay. Some guy, a boyfriend or husband or somebody, is after her and—"

"Please my friend, no more." Ahmed waved both palms in the

air, unwilling to hear about such sordid affairs. "Just so long as she pays for any calls she makes and is out in ten days. I have got painters and finish carpenters coming."

"You have a phone up there?"

"Sure." Ahmed found a pack of French cigarettes in his breast pocket. "We put it in last week."

I took down the phone number. "Any furniture?"

"There's some chairs and a bed, but no stove. There is a refrigerator. We cannot yet burn oil down in the power plant," Ahmed went on. "But we have some electric space heaters for the men who do fine handiwork. I will see that two heaters are put in the apartment in case the nights get cold."

"That's great, Ahmed, really."

"Once she comes in, she can't leave until six o'clock in the morning. That's when the canine service comes for the dogs."

"Dogs?"

"I have got two dogs that stay on the inside. A German shepherd and a rottweiler." Ahmed looked at me. "Every morning we find a homeless person and cut him up and feed him to the dogs, who are very hungry by then." He laughed menacingly. "Okay, not funny to you. We have got about a half a million dollars in equipment and tools and completed work in there. This morning I had an elevator circuit panel delivered. That was seventeen thousand dollars. These things cost a lot of money. So she is going to have to go by my rules."

I nodded. "That's only fair."

"And there is a guard whom we have hired to stay around outside. She will not bother him."

"Right."

He stood from the bar, ready to leave. "I'll have Sanjay get the place ready."

"Thanks, Ahmed," I said.

"I trust she is worth all of this trouble."

"Maybe," I said.

"Are you trying to get her for yourself?"

"I don't know," I told him. And that was the truth.

♦ ♦ ♦

I called Dolores at five o'clock. She picked up the phone after one ring. I explained what the place was like and Ahmed's conditions for her staying there.

"This is a free place?" Her voice was guarded again. "Totally free?"

"Yes."

"Uh, you're not paying my rent for me by any chance?"

"No."

"It's a favor from the guy who owns the place?"

"Right."

"What does *he* want?"

"Nothing. He owes me a favor."

"And nobody else lives there?" she asked suspiciously.

"Nobody."

"That's sort of weird."

"I agree."

"It's safe, though," she said. "Right?"

"Nobody knows that anybody *could* live there, right now."

"Where do *you* live?"

"In Brooklyn."

"Where?"

"In Park Slope."

"Where the rich people live."

"A lot of different kinds of people live there."

"Me and Maria would be the only ones in the building?"

"The only ones."

"Will you have keys to the building?"

"No."

It went like this for a few more minutes, which seemed reasonable to me, since Dolores had to think of Maria and was trusting herself not just to me but to other strangers as well. But she agreed to come, finally, and I gave her the address. Then I called Helen. Mrs. Marsh had confirmed Monday's schedule in Washington with the Chairman. I started to read the thick file Helen had given me. It was more technical than I realized, dense with detail. I'd have to memorize as much of it as possible. The bartender came over wiping a glass and I ordered two complete steak dinners, packed and boxed.

♦ ♦ ♦

When the taxi pulled up, Dolores got out with Maria and one very large suitcase. I paid the fare. Sanjay, who seemed to suffer from sore feet, hobbled over and dragged the suitcase toward the building as the cab pulled away.

Maria pointed. "The man's taking it, Mommy."

"It's okay." Dolores bent down and checked that Maria's coat was done up near her neck. "He's taking it to our room." She pulled a tissue from her purse and put it to Maria's nose. "Blow."

"No!"

Dolores pressed the tissue into Maria's face and the girl obeyed. Dolores looked at me. The afternoon sun was in her face and brought out the richness of her coloring, the light dazzling the dark mass of unruly long hair and brightening her eyes. I handed her the warm boxed dinners.

"You didn't have to do this for us." Her fingers grazed the sleeve of my suit, ever so lightly. "Thank you."

Sanjay came back and nodded deferentially toward me.

"We are ready, sir."

"There's a phone up there," I said before leaving. "I'd like to call you, all right?"

"Sure," Dolores replied with ever so slight a smile — a smile that understood that my casualness was hardly casual. Then she and Maria disappeared through the dusty haze into the gloom of Ahmed's building, and I felt a sort of cheap, cunning satisfaction.

♦ ♦ ♦

I sawed away at the thick file for a few hours that night, knowing that I was responsible for everything in it, every small ridiculous fact, such as the transponder wattage of one of the Corporation's satellites. Men like the Chairman no longer read anything closely, for they expect to have younger men know the answers to the little questions. Then I climbed up onto my roof in Park Slope with the portable phone in one hand and Dolores's number in the other. I dialed, waited. The line was busy. The wind whispered maple blossoms across the roof and far away rose the blue and red lights of the Empire State Building. In the faded pink beach chair, I wondered why I felt so drawn to Dolores Salcines when I'd been acculturated in childhood and adolescence to meet and know a particular kind of girl and then a particular kind of woman. They wore Shetland wool sweaters and had been bright students. They had gone to one of the twenty or thirty name-brand colleges or universities in this country. They were good girls, or if they had not been good, exactly, then they had never been *bad*. Maybe they had shoplifted a few times as teenagers, maybe they had slept around or done speed. Redial: busy. They had always been destined for a life of marriage and career and children. You could draw a line through the points of these women's lives: they had been to Europe, they were dependable, they were up-to-date, they had too many shoes in their closets, they took vitamins, they could have plenty of orgasms, they didn't watch much television usually, they liked to read, they were *attractive*, they knew a lot about coffees. They were white. I loved these women, many of them. My mother was one, in the way of her generation, and Liz had most certainly been one. Dolores Salcines was not.

Sirens sprinted down one of the nearby avenues, echoed by and interspersed with other sirens, now near, now wailing far, conveying always in the night an unending urgency in all corners of the city. Only rarely do we cross over to the other side of ourselves, to the other side of possibility. I hit the redial on the phone again. I let it ring twenty times before I hung up. Dolores should not have been out, but she was out.

FOUR

L ike a great ominous insect, one of the Corporation's shiny black cars glided through the gloom and up my block the next Monday morning. It waited there, red parking lights bright. Inside, briefcase on my knees, I continued to cram the file into my head: now I was learning about satellite uplink frequencies and transmission footprints. The car threaded through Brooklyn toward LaGuardia Airport, past the little black boys selling roses and air-fresheners and hernia belts at the intersections. A pack of ten-year-olds sucking car exhaust all day long. I've seen the same thing in the Zona Rosa in Mexico City and near the Grand Eastern Hotel in Calcutta. At the red light they pressed their faces excitedly against the dark glass of the car, hoping to see a celebrity. The driver slid down his window three inches and said something brutal to them. Their faces were already marked by struggle and privation. You see the doom of their predicament. I looked and then I looked away.

On the shuttle I chewed antacids and kept reading about satellites. Called Helen from the plane and went over a few things. There was no message from Dolores, so I dialed her number directly. One of Ahmed's workmen answered and said Dolores was out. I hoped that she was looking for a job, I hoped she wasn't looking for trouble. I glanced at the newspaper. Then I gazed out the plane's window and tested myself to see if I remembered Liz's face. Yes.

Before landing, I checked my smile in the restroom, grimacing close to the mirror to see if any stray bits of breakfast clung to my teeth, had become jammed up high where the gumline was receding. These things matter. People make decisions about you. People are happily vicious. We once decided not to hire an assistant vice president of information systems because he wasn't in control of his saliva. Very smart guy, every credential in the world, well spoken of, nice silk tie, every possible business connection, but an excess of spitty shine on his bottom lip. It bothered a few too many people, Samantha especially. I opened my mouth wider in front of the mirror and stared into my throat. A chronic acid condition in the esophagus can cause "abnormal" cells. My internist told me this when insisting that I cut back on the coffee and drinking, both of which relax the sphincter at the base of the esophagus and let the contents of the stomach rise upward into it. He was urging me to change my lifestyle, reduce the stress. What does abnormal mean? I asked. Precancerous, he answered. We do an endoscopy, get some cells to look at. I could move you up to metaclorepropamide or omeprazole, he went on, but that's not a first-line therapy; there are serious side effects. And if it gets worse? I asked anxiously. You might develop what's called "Barrett's esophagus," he answered, which means that the lining of the esophagus is becoming similar to the lining of the stomach. Generally we then have to do a surgical procedure called "Nissen's plication." A specialist makes an incision in your stomach. Then he sews part of the stomach around the base of the esophagus to tighten it up. That doesn't sound very nice, I said. No, he answered, it's not.

♦ ♦ ♦

The car met me at National Airport, and as the driver held my door, I sat down inside expecting to meet the Chairman somewhere in the District of Columbia, but there he was, turning his tanned face toward me.

"Good morning," came the voice. I'd never been so close to the bright blue eyes, the skin mottled by age. "Have we met?"

"Just briefly," I answered. The car was moving.

"Mr. Morrison assures me you're the fellow I need," he ventured, placing a cigarette in his mouth.

"I'm read up."

"Good—I'm not. You're doing the talking. I'll fill in here and there." He adjusted a brass knob on the side of the car and our small space was filled by the haunting sounds of a Gregorian chant. "Now then . . ." His gaze drifted out the window. He was done talking. The marble monuments hung against the blue sky as we crossed the

Potomac into the District. The Chairman retrieved a book from his briefcase—it was a novel by Trollope, *The Way We Live Now*—and primly set a pair of bifocals on his nose. A hundred men sung mournfully to us in Latin. The Chairman flipped a page. This was a man who held a fortune of about nine hundred million dollars. I was gone from his mind.

◆ ◆ ◆

We spent the day driving around the capital, pulling into the reserved lots beneath and behind the government buildings. A staffer was dutifully waiting each time, took us to the particular office. Different issues, short appointments, each an attempt to get the government to rule or act in the interest of the Corporation. I regurgitated the appropriate sections of the file while the Chairman listened and inspected a small Band-Aid on the top of his hand. Skin cancers. There was much respectful nodding. I couldn't tell if he was pleased with the job I was doing or not, for in the car we said almost nothing to each other. He didn't appear to want to be jollied up as some bosses do. He took several calls. A few words. Then he would softly put down the phone. He smoked two cigarettes an hour and ignored the briefing papers and reports provided by his office, as well as the day's newspapers. While he read he pursed and munched his lips, swallowing now and then as if the information on the page was not passing to him through his eyes but being ingested in soupy chunks through an invisible straw. Disappointment spread through me; the Chairman seemed merely a well-dressed Mr. Peepers, not the mysterious titan who had Morrison grinding his teeth down to the gumline. Across from me sat a retired mailman, a polite apple-cheeked codger in a cardigan at the public library perhaps, somebody's grandfather who liked to go fly-fishing. This was some kind of setup, no? Now I was sure Beales had convinced Morrison to yank me out of the negotiating team. People do this, they plot, they wait years for the right opportunity. Beales figured that with me out of the picture during negotiations with Volkman-Sakura he'd have a chance to build relationships with the Germans that would later prove useful. He knew, of course, that I spoke a little German. I could schmooze the V-S execs in their own language. That bothered him. And why was I in a position to bother him? In 1974, my mother read in the *Wall Street Journal* that Spanish, Japanese, Chinese, and German were the languages of the future. But Spanish was the language of cleaning ladies so far as my mother was concerned. Japanese and Chinese impossible, languages of noodles. That left German. Her firstborn son would learn German. He had a tin ear but a good memory and actually learned the thick-tongued language. It had an unmusical brutality to it that I came to appreciate. In college I even worked my way through Thomas Mann's *The Magic Mountain* in the original. Now Beales was punishing me for it.

More appointments. At the end of the day, we spoke with the chairman of the Senate Foreign Relations Committee and my counterpart, his chief of staff. The aide led us down the waxed hallways to one of the paneled hideaway offices in the Russell Senate Office Building. As we waited for the senator to arrive, my eyes wandered over the accoutrements of the office: the framed pens used by past presidents to sign legislation sponsored by the senator; the unbuggable secure phone direct to the White House and Senate majority leader; the leather-bound copies of the *Congressional Record;* and the legislative clock on the wall, which indicated by way of some sort of special system of lights and buzzers whether the Senate was in recess, about to vote, or in a quorum call.

"The senator needs to be on the floor in twenty minutes," the aide noted as soon as the senator had shaken hands.

We sat down in four chairs. I knew the routine by now. "As you remember," I began, "we received final approval last June from BRA-ZILSAT to establish one of our television satellites over Brazil."

"Yes."

"This is fast becoming an important market for American-produced entertainment."

"*Yes.*"

"This one uses the new nickel-hydrogen-battery technology which prolongs the life of the satellite. It has smaller and lighter batteries," I said, sounding like I was reading a brochure. The senator's man looked at me; we both knew I didn't know a damn thing about satellites. "We wanted to test transmission patterns over a specified footprint in Brazil, and we went to considerable planning to launch a satellite into geostationary orbit just due north of Brasilia. I don't need to mention that this is extremely expensive technology." The satellite was a big shiny bug with fragile solar-panel wings that faced the sun. It cost, said a memo in the file, $289 million to build and launch to its altitude of 22,300 miles above earth. This sum was paid by smiling investors who in 1986 bought the Corporation's bonds during the capitalization phase of the satellite project. Most communications companies don't own their own satellites, instead buying time from the satellite companies themselves. But it's often better to be the landlord than the tenant, so we'd bought a few for ourselves. The time was coming when only so many satellites will fill up the sky. The price to transmit will go up and our competitors will have to pay that, while the Corporation will have its own capacity.

"Now then," I went on, "the Brazilian Air Force complained almost immediately that the Corporation's satellite signal interfered with their communications. But our antenna pattern was authorized. See, every satellite is built with a customized transmitting capacity based on its orbital position and the transmission footprint on the ground that is desired. When we refused to adjust the position of the satellite, their air force jammed its signals."

"All this seems very familiar," said the senator's man.

"I appreciate that, but I'm just running through the key points of our situation." We smiled poisonously at each other. I glanced at the senator. His face was slack, dreaming of something: Sunday church sermons, blowjobs, his lost boyhood—anything but this. "The jamming affected what is known as the downlink frequency. Let me explain that. To avoid signal interference, satellite transponders translate uplink frequencies into different downlink frequencies, and the change in the downlink frequency caused the satellite to stop directing the Corporation's test commun—"

"Was it *true?*" the senator asked, his mind running thirty seconds behind the conversation. "The satellite signal interfered?"

Yes. The satellite's actual transmission footprint was 30 percent larger than was authorized, in order to cover a greater possible market, according to the file. But this had never been admitted, even to the Corporation's ten full-time lobbyists, who had communicated "concern" about the satellite problem to various representatives of the administration, the National Telecommunications and Information Administration, the FCC, and the State Department.

"No," I said. "Their information is wrong. We're within fifteen miles of the transmission boundaries that we agreed on."

"What *is* true, then?"

We believed that BRAZILSAT, the Brazilian satellite agency, had reversed itself, I said. Perhaps an investor down there had bought off one of the BRAZILSAT officials.

"Surely, if the Brazilians do not *want* one of your satellites over their capital city, they do not *have* to have it," the senator's man said, folding his arms in obvious patience.

"This represents a very large market for us," I told him. "We want access to this market. One hundred and sixty million people. And we could have bought that satellite from someone else . . ." I didn't need to add that the satellite had been assembled in the senator's own state. Big defense contractor, big PAC money. "And we'll be putting bids out on two new satellites in the next year."

The Chairman and senator listened with abstracted looks.

"We need something done in the next few weeks," I continued. "It would be very advantageous if—"

"No, no, it's premature to promise anything," the senator's man said. "I mean, the *channels* take time, you have to call people, see what their position is—" He hummed on about drafting a cable to the American embassy in Brasilia to inquire on an informal basis— protecting his boss from commitment while implying that action would be taken. I did not like him. He was the type who gets his hair cut every other Monday: a spittle-licking drone, a loyal flack, an ambitious, coffee-sipping brain-for-hire. The national political edifice is choked with men and women like this. " . . . or, if there were more time," the senator's man continued, "we might consider making an inquiry to—"

"We don't need an inquiry," the Chairman interrupted politely, leaning forward as if to catch some elusive note with his ear. "We need *pressure*."

The room was quiet. Then the senator and the Chairman looked at each other and nodded, each understanding the proper proportions of talk, power, and insinuation. They stood up and shook each other's liver-spotted hands.

"Give me a call if you're up on the island this summer." The Chairman winked amiably to the senator. "We'll get a round in."

In the hallway on the way out, the Chairman turned to me. "You were too contentious. These things are done subtly."

"I should have been more careful."

"You have a certain fervor to make a point," he observed.

"I suppose I do."

He looked at me calmly. "Is this why you were assigned to me?"

I considered my answer.

"Did you *want* to be assigned to me?" the Chairman asked before I could answer.

"No," I said. "I did not."

I expected that he might say something then, yet we walked on toward the car with no further talk. But I did glance at his face. The Chairman stared ahead, but caught in the crow's feet around his eyes was the unmistakable wrinkle of amusement.

◆ ◆ ◆

We weren't taking the shuttle back to New York. Corporate lore had it that years prior, on a business flight, Morrison and the Chairman had been sitting in the regular-class compartment of the airplane when the wing engine outside the Chariman's window had fallen off. Just like that. The Chairman, looking out the window, had seen it happen, Morrison had reported, and watched as the giant shiny turbojet dropped away, tearing a strip of metal skin from the wing, leaving only the ruined engine mount below the wing. The Chairman looked at his watch, coolly marked the time, turned to Morrison, and said, "If it's more than thirty seconds before the captain informs us, I'm never flying again."

That nameless captain had taken, in fact, four minutes to announce the emergency landing, and so now the Chairman's car took us to the Metroliner, through a mysterious side entrance in the back of Union Station, bypassing all the other passengers standing behind the glass doors, right onto the platform. It occurred to me that of course Amtrak had built secret entrances for use with presidents, heads of state, the big players. We were seated by the time the others began to board.

"Why not the helicopter?" I asked. "You use that sometimes."

"Don't like them at night," the Chairman explained with a wince on his face. "A bad bet. Look what happened to Senator Heinz and all those fellows who worked for Trump." We settled in the half-empty club car and the Chairman lit a cigarette and poured himself two minature bottles of scotch, neat. He'd been waiting for this all day and his face sagged in contentment after the first swallow. Around us sat others, mostly men in suits, some drinking and laughing with their fellow workers, others talking quietly into their telephones and a few gazing into laptop computers. In each group I could pick out the dominant one immediately. Usually he was the oldest, of course, and often one of the younger men was watching with a special deep attention. It's something that can happen between men. So many of us are silently desperate for fathers, even as we pass into middle age. Often we find them at work.

"Can we really get those Brazilian colonels to stop messing around with our damn satellite?" the Chairman asked. Then he shrugged before I could answer. It didn't matter. Others would grind out solutions to the Corporation's problems—me, Beales, Samantha, the lobbyists, the corporate relations office, somebody on down the line. All the Chairman had needed to do was to mention a round of golf to the chairman of the Senate Foreign Relations Committee. This was essentially now his job.

"So, Jack, tell me about yourself," the Chairman said, loosening his tie and looking out the window. "Who the hell are you, anyway?"

"Well," I began, flattered by the question, "you may know my title is vice president for—"

"No! *Please* no. Tell me something *interesting*, for Christ's sake," the Chairman said with an agreeably dismissive wave. "Tell me why a fine fellow like you hasn't remarried."

I turned to face him. "You know about—?"

He nodded. "Of course."

"You know about Liz, what happened?"

"Yes. I was told the next day."

"The next day?" I said incredulously.

"I still know a few things about what's happening in my company." He smiled suggestively. "Now, as I was saying, tell me why a fine fellow like you hasn't remarried."

"I haven't found the right woman."

"Then you must have dalliances," he concluded. "A fine old word, 'dalliances.' A girl, a hotel room, a cigarette at the window, room service afterwards."

I wandered what Dolores was doing that very moment. Perhaps putting Maria to bed. Perhaps anything. "I've got too much work these days," I answered warily.

"Ah, that won't do!" the Chairman exclaimed. "Life is short. Sometime I'll give you my theory of dalliances." He chuckled. "Sometime. Anyway, I'm not getting much out of you. Tell me about your father. Men like to talk about their fathers."

"It's not a happy topic."

He held up his glass and swished the liquid around in the light. "Few topics are, I think."

The drink had put him in an amiable mood now and he wanted to be entertained. Diverted. So I described to him my father, who for more than twenty-five years had lived in the same small, run-down clapboard house in upstate New York, a miserable, overly introspective man. It was not that he purposefully drew attention to his loneliness and isolation, but it nonetheless hung on him like an oversized jacket. At twenty, the neat part of his hair had fooled my mother into thinking that here was a man with a future. That's how she told it. When I was four years old, she asked my father for a divorce.

"Did she remarry?" the Chairman asked.

"Instantly."

My mother, I told him, had been young enough to replant her life, and took me along with her to the ample house of the man she was having her affair with, her new husband, Harry McCaw, a big-bellied fellow who loved me fully and without reservation. My father, a seminary student at the time, consented to the divorce on one condition: that his son's last name remain the same. "My father, Charles Whitman, is a direct descendant of an uncle of Walt Whitman," I said. "He named me after the first known Whitman in America, John Whitman, who lived from 1602 to 1692 and came over

from England in 1640 on a ship called the *True Love.*" The great
bearded poet was, of course, a homosexual and left no progeny—or at
least none who carried the Whitman name. And that name is all my
father ever possessed that might suggest greatness. And it was all he
could give me. When I was about seven he showed me his shelf where
he kept copies of editions of *Leaves of Grass*, the major biographies,
and the fat *Portable Whitman*. Later he read to me the poet's moving
description of the ancient Whitman family graveyard in Long Island
("This is where you come from, Jack," my father told me, "and you
must never forget this, ever.") and Walt Whitman's accounts of nursing Union soldiers injured in the Civil War. Later still, my father
insisted I read the long poems. Only then did I understand why my
father had demanded that I retain the name of my ancestors: although
Walt Whitman was, in my opinion, a better reporter than he was a
poet, he had a great and true heart and my father understood this.
Walt Whitman understood the yearning and vitality of the unknown
masses. My mother wanted *out* and the satisfaction of my father's
pride was a small price to pay for her deliverance. So I remained a
Whitman. It's just a name, of course, and means little, except perhaps,
if you want to get fancy about it, that I am implicated by blood in
something inextricably American.

"How marvelous," the Chairman said. "Remarkable, really."

"What?"

"That a long-descended relative of Walt Whitman would come
to be an executive in America's largest media-entertainment company.
It's too perfectly ironic."

"My father said something like that too. He said, and I quote, that
it 'confirmed the death of the venerable republic.' "

"Well, don't be too angry with him," the Chairman responded.
"As you get older you see these things, you see how history made the
present, the way things twist into the future. After age fifty, you feel
time moving all the time, across your hands, so to speak."

I didn't answer.

"So your mother knew your father would fail," the Chairman
mused, returning to my background.

"Yes."

"Despite the glory of his name."

"Despite that, yes." I fell silent. My mother saved the two of us, I know, from a narrowing, ever-sadder existence with my father, who subsequently eked out a living as a minister of a small Methodist church upstate where rhetorical delivery on Sundays was not as important as endless patience to listen to the miseries of the church members during the rest of the week. Harry McCaw was by contrast a man without misery of any sort, and if that meant that his character had never been tempered by self-doubt, then that did not bother my mother, who had listened to too many of my father's anguished soliloquies. My earliest memory of Harry is when he rubbed an inflated balloon on his sweater and miraculously stuck it to the ceiling. Big-bellied, big-dicked Harry made my mother laugh, earned good money in his insurance office at Seventeenth and Market in downtown Philadelphia, and sent me and my younger half brother and half sister to good Quaker private schools. I easily accepted Harry's largess – the piano lessons, the big backyard where we played catch in the spring when he came home from work, the many months of summer camp in Pennsylvania's Endless Mountains, the news articles neatly scissored from the *New York Times* and placed upon my bedside table for me to read if I wanted, the new school clothes each fall, picked out at John Wanamaker's department store in downtown Philadelphia by my mother, the annual pair of soccer cleats that I cherished, the ten-speed bicycle on my thirteenth birthday, the school band trip to Europe, the braces, the kindly but firm lecture to please not get a girl pregnant and *never* to drive with anyone who was drunk, the first arranged summer jobs, the tuition to Columbia, all of it. I have no complaints: it was a reasonably happy childhood, better than most, better than Liz's. Or Dolores's, for that matter. My mother would always comment she had made "the deal of a lifetime." Her luck continued, even to this day. Harry possessed the amiable shrewdness useful to an insurance man, and he had foreseen that the Reagan era could be very good to him, and for five years he tossed every nickel he could find into the stock market, finally pulling out a gigantic wad in August of 1987, and sticking it back in the following November to make another wad, then out a year later, and again back in November 1991 – thus one of the few men in America who timed the Reagan-Bush bull market perfectly. Just as the real estate market topped in 1988, he and my mother sold the big house on the Main Line and made the American elephant graveyard migration—to a Florida retirement community that faced the Gulf of Mexico. They were unthinkingly content, wealthy enough to live within a compound patrolled by a force of private police where golf and the lack of rain were the urgent topics of conversation. My mother had never liked Liz that much—she felt Liz had "married up," and hadn't been properly grateful. I rarely called my mother now.

"Need another round here." The Chairman suddenly stood. He looked flushed and took off his coat. His shoulders were naturally squared off; even at his age, he had a certain physical confidence in his carriage. One wouldn't be surprised to learn that he cut a decent step on the ballroom floor. A few minutes later he made his way back along the aisle, another drink in his hand, meeting the eyes of no one, and sat down. The train rattled on, and in a few minutes I saw that the Chairman had shut his eyes and rolled his head heavily toward the window, where the Maryland countryside rushed past in the twilight—the small towns and heaps of rusted cars and washing machines and deep woods standing mute. The wind of the train turned up the undersides of the new leaves. Rain was beginning to fall. I glimpsed a boy sitting on the hood of his pickup, the kind of boy I would have been if I had stayed with my natural father. His shadowy presence throughout my childhood—I occasionally visited him by bus, never in the company of my mother—reminded me always that a parallel fate followed my days, the fate of another Jack Whitman who, except for being skinnier and with longer hair, looked just like me and lived in a small New York town, smoking pot and working afternoons at one of the gas stations out on the interstate, grease on his KISS T-shirt. Cigarette breath, interested in motorbikes, of little prospect. For when I visited my father, this is what the boys my age seemed to be doing. That is what would have happened to me. At fourteen they already had an edge of bitter toughness in them, and they understood everything about me from the way I talked and the expensive sneakers I wore. I got into a few fights, just a few, and won almost as many as I lost. There is a narrow, hard vein of meanness and expediency in me and this is where it comes from. I knew my fate had been changed forever.

My mother did not trust fate, however, and did what she could to see that I would not become my father. I would have braces, I'd be instructed how to read the stock pages, I'd be practical. I would have a certain large mole removed from the lobe of my ear when I was about twelve, "because it will matter how people see you," she explained matter-of-factly. Anything to further distance me from my father. Perhaps this was why I still looked for a father, because my real one hardly seemed to fulfill the possibilities. His personality, for instance, seemed to be expressed most clearly through his toenail. That sounds strange, admittedly. But when my father was a boy, the large toenail of his left foot was somehow mangled, in a car door, or crushed by a dropped sledgehammer—I don't remember the cause. What remained was a shrunken, brown, thickened nail that my father cut each month with wincing exactitude. It looked like a stamp-sized piece of rhinoceros horn and I can remember, growing up, seeing my father stooped over his toe in the bathroom with an expensive stainless-steel Swiss nail clipper—perhaps the only item of luxury he owned. To say that he *clipped* the nail would be wrong, with its connotations of quick, careless energy, the spring of little shards everywhere. He sculpted and shaved that piece of horn meticulously, accounting for the shape of his shoes and mysterious "tender spots" only he could locate. He didn't like for me to watch—as if looking at the nail *made* it hurt—and certainly I was not allowed to touch it, so painful were the compacted nerve endings underneath. The toe had hurt him every day of his life. He had never remarried or even, I think, had sex after my mother left him. It was as if that toe accounted for my father's hesitant footfalls through a diminished, unhappy life.

Thus, marrying Liz, I'd believed, made me forever different from my father. He loved Liz as the daughter he had never had. He took me aside on our wedding day to congratulate me for not letting his disastrous marriage to my mother ruin my own feelings. I hadn't the heart to tell him that, beyond not even remembering his marriage to my mother, it was, instead, her faithful happiness with Harry McCaw that formed my optimistic expectations about the relations between men and women.

As my father's only child, it was up to me to keep an eye on him, especially after the church's conference bishop called me one day to ask how my father's mental health seemed, *to me*. They asked him to retire early, for his sermons brought little comfort or inspiration to the members of his church, and the bishop was only able to guarantee a genuinely paltry pension; members of the clergy usually die poor. I would take care of all his money needs of course; this had been understood for at least ten years. Doing so gave me little satisfaction, for it only implied that my father had so mismanaged his finances that now he lived out of his son's wallet. When Liz was murdered, my father seemed to deflate even further, for now he suspected that he would not have grandchildren, that his branch of the great Whitman name would now disappear, and that, aside from me, no one would ever be around to take care of him. It hardly mattered to me what my father's selfish motivations for grief were. I barely spoke to him at the funeral. The occasion gave him license to practice his profession again for an afternoon and he hovered about in ministerial fashion, pestering Liz's and my friends with his condolences. I didn't hate him. I hated what had become of him.

Now the rain slashed against the train's windows. The slack skin of the Chairman's neck fell over his shirt collar as he dozed. I considered calling Morrison from one of the phones at the end of the car but thought better of it, in case the Chairman woke and guessed who I'd called. The two men had danced in a hateful, silent embrace for years. The Chairman was an aging seventy-one and Morrison a fit and steaming fifty-three. The Chairman needed Morrison's energy and market savvy to push into new ventures, while Morrison needed the Chairman to get the board's approval for new projects. The Chairman had stacked the outside membership of the board with old friends and had shrewdly blocked the election of any of the representatives from the big pension funds who were now fighting their way into the boardroom and causing hell for company managements by demanding that they remember the stockholders before themselves. If the Chairman went down in a bloody fight, Wall Street would know that the Corporation was in flux and the share price might begin to tank. The man had stayed on top a long time — there had been Morrisons of one type or another all along the way, the statistical whiz kids, the generals, the world-class salesmen, the palace Rasputins. He'd used them, brought them along, sucked out their talents and energy, then scrapped them when they became powerful enough that there was talk of succession. Back in the late seventies, he had forced a majority of the board to resign after they had secretly courted another executive who inconveniently dropped dead of a heart attack before being hired. He had made and then broken half a dozen Morrisons. And if Morrison lost this battle, then the thirty-ninth floor would be gutted, me included.

Sitting there, I studied the Chairman, as men do their corporate fathers. All faces, especially those of old men, have a sort of grotesque quality. The Chairman's eyeballs rolled demonlike beneath their lids. Capillaries ran like crazed red wires under the skin of his nostrils, under the age-slackened cheeks. His mouth hung open slightly. Tobacco stains were etched into the cracked enamel of his teeth. I felt a strange affection for him.

◆ ◆ ◆

Later, after the train shot through the slums of North Philadelphia, the Chairman lifted his eyelids into a boozy consciousness. "Finished, hmm? Right?" He waited for me to answer and I didn't. "Those who are liquid and can move their assets out will be all right . . . the smart money is in Hong Kong for the next two years . . . but the rest of them . . . ahhm . . ." He gazed out the rain-streaked windows into the nickel light of New Jersey's industrial parks. "So many . . . who'll never have, or even *know* what happened . . . why are the blacks such a tortured people? I've asked myself that for thirty years . . . why, societally, do we hate them so much? So much anxiety . . . it's—hmm . . . I myself have grandchildren . . . it's going to be much worse than anyone ever imagined." He swiveled his head and stared at me. I saw the years in the skin around his eyes. "The government is *dead*, you realize that—all those men we spoke to today? They're floating belly up in the river, not to be trusted . . . these people, ahhmmm—excuse me, happens when I drink . . . the forces are too big, why the British pound used to be the currency of the trading nations. Aahem." Odd shards of light drifted over the sagging folds of his cheeks. "People said the pound would reign supreme for five hundred years. It lasted fifty. Then the dollar. No one thinks about the Chinese, what they could do . . ."

He lapsed back into silence and the minutes passed. Finally the train slid undergound into Manhattan and we exited. The escalator from the platform was broken, so the crowd trudged in group exhaustion up the paralyzed steps, flowing with unconscious precision around a stinking woman in her fifties with several scabs on her cheek who lay across the concrete, her mismatched skirts lifted in gruesome display. "This is America now," the Chairman muttered. I slowed my pace for him. We found his personal car waiting for us outside the station, and once inside its dark softness the Chairman picked up the remote and flicked on the screen. He scrolled through an alphabetized list of companies to the Corporation to check the day's closing price. It was up three points, from 107 a share, a sizable jiggle. Anyone holding a thousand shares of the Corporation's stock, say, would go to bed tonight three thousand dollars richer than he had woken up, having done nothing. Perhaps somebody out there was buying in anticipation of the Volkman-Sakura deal. Or perhaps one of the big institutional investors had merely decided it was a good time to make a play on the Corporation's stock. The Chairman, however, seemed uninterested and he switched off the screen and leaned forward to give the driver a few words.

"Be right there, sir," the man replied with an efficient nod, and the big car turned uptown on one of the avenues and gathered speed, caught in a bright river of taxis, blowing past Korean groceries, past a pet shop window full of puppies pawing frantically at the glass and office workers straggling home late and a long line of moviegoers standing under the bright lights of a marquee — "That one's ours," the Chairman murmured, pointing at the movie being featured — and we pulled to a stop at a private club and got out, the Chairman leaving his coat behind. The chauffeur would pull up the street, lock the doors, and doze.

"Lackley is giving a party," the Chairman said, referring to our man at Citibank, to which the Corporation owed eight hundred million dollars. "Certain rituals have to be observed."

Once inside the marble foyer, he shed his sleepy fatigue and came back to life, crinkling sex-amused eyes at the hostess, a striking woman of about sixty who, it was said, had slept with John F. Kennedy. The Chairman barged agreeably inside, handshakes and smiles all around. The women wore brilliant stones and the men expensive shoes, but the money was quieter than it had been five years prior. As always, people were drinking hard, against the direction of time. I missed Liz. If she had been there she would have slipped her hand into mine, Liz a woman who spent teenage summers handling live lobsters at her father's restaurant, and whispered, *Jack, let's get out of here before it gets desperate*, and we would have gone to thank the host. And then gossiped in the taxi on the way home, with my hand in her crotch under her coat. I got a glass at the bar and by the time I had turned around, the Chairman was already sitting within a circle of guests on a sixty-thousand-dollar Empire sofa, the scrolled arms thick as tree trunks and cushions soft as the puff of crab something being served on silver trays. I composed my face into the proper degree of geniality and had the usual conversations. The women were beautiful and strangely uninteresting, and I slipped away to find a phone, hoping that Dolores might have called and left a message. I dialed my own number and punched in the playback code, and heard nothing, wanting to hear Dolores's voice, wanting—I wanted to fuck her. I guess that's true.

When a polite hour had passed, the Chairman signaled me that he was ready to leave, and after we retreated to the limousine, he instructed the driver so quickly and casually that I understood he had referred to an address the chauffeur knew well. Five minutes later we pulled to a stop in front of an apartment building in the East Eighties and got out.

"Ever been here?" he asked, plunging ahead of me.

"No."

"You recognize the address, though."

I looked up at the number on the striped awning.

"No."

"You really don't know about this place?"

"No."

He seemed pleased by this. "Well, you better let an old man show you a thing or two."

Inside, the doorman nodded at the Chariman and we ascended to the tenth floor, and when the elevator doors opened, we emerged to a small, rather plain foyer. We waited in front of a closed door.

"It's usually a minute or two," the Chairman said.

"Before what?" I said anxiously.

He looked at me. Don't say stupid things, I thought. "Before they let us in."

"How do they know we're here? The guy downstairs call up?"

His eyes were amused. "They know."

At that moment the door opened and we were met by an attractive redheaded woman in a silk robe. She ushered us into a small lounge, which by the quality and taste of the decor might very well have been the waiting room of one of the suites of private banking offices on Park Avenue. An antique English mantel clock was striking eleven. The Chairman swayed ever so slightly, boozy on his feet, and I could see from his face that he was impatiently eager. He lit a cigarette, not bothering to worry about an ashtray.

"I like your tie tonight," the woman said with a British accent. They smiled at each other and then she punched several digits on the phone, whispered into it, listened, and then said to us, "Would you like Miss Najibullah or Miss Choonhavan to join you tonight?"

"Miss Choonhavan."

"And the gentleman, sir?"

"I would surmise that Miss Najibullah would be a very fine addition to his evening."

"Does he have any . . . requests?"

The Chairman turned to me. "Any proclivities you want indulged, Jack?"

I was still figuring it out. "No," I said, to be safe.

"On your account?" the woman asked.

"Absolutely, he's my guest."

"He is a new guest?"

"I'm sure he'll be fine."

"We'll follow the usual procedures, of course." She smiled warmly at me, then turned to the Chairman. "The usual envelope in the room?"

"Aaaah, yes," the Chairman said. "And I switched to rum about an hour ago, so you better have that in there, too."

The woman disappeared. I understood now.

"Everyone new is tested," the Chairman explained. "And the girls are tested every single week. But they're fine."

His attitude irritated me. I doubted that he knew anyone who'd died of AIDS; it was an abstraction to him. But not to me. I'd lost half a dozen college classmates. And people with AIDS were everywhere in the subways, begging. "How can I be sure?" I asked. "I mean, prostitutes are notoriously—"

"You can be sure."

"How?"

"*Because*," he answered with a rich man's pride, "this is probably the most expensive whorehouse in America."

We were led to a carpeted locker room that had about thirty cubicles, each double wide and semiprivate like the ones professional athletes have in their locker rooms. Each had a small brass plate engraved with initials and contained, in addition to a personal assortment of colognes and toiletries and combs and brushes, a laundered terry cloth robe and several towels, all maroon. A leather easy chair fronted each cubicle. Several of the lockers had business suits neatly hanging in them. An attendant in a white coat appeared. The Chairman gave me a reassuring nod. The attendant guided me to a small office, where he asked me to roll up my left shirtsleeve. He swabbed the crease at my elbow joint with alcohol and expertly took a small blood sample and had me sign a small release form.

"How long does the test result take?" I asked him.

"Ten minutes. We have a lab on the premises."

I barely believed it. Back when Liz was still alive, I'd bought a life insurance policy and thus had an AIDS test. The results had taken a few days at the least. "I've never heard of a test that's so fast—"

"The common test is the ELISA test and then, if that tests out positive, the retest is done with the Western blot," the technician said. "But we're way ahead. We're using the SUDS. Only a few private practice doctors are using it yet."

"Who *actually* tests the blood? Looks under the microscope, or whatever?"

"I do."

"What's your training?" I asked suspiciously.

"Well, after my Ph.D.," he said, looking up from the blood sample, "I worked with the CDC in Atlanta for five years—I can describe that, if you'd like."

While we waited for the results, the Chairman showed me

the steam room and sauna. "A lot of fellows don't have time for mistresses," the Chairman explained, "and they . . . hhrrrmmm, and they really don't need the trouble. Oh, the trouble they can be! I had a girl once who . . . well, it's a long story. But a mistress can be a hell of a lot of trouble. Geez, I need that rum. We keep the membership here at twenty-five, see. It's very quiet that way. Ahhhhrrrm-*ahh*. Excuse me. The rule is that you have to be fifty years old to join, though guests may be younger. A few fellows wanted to let their sons come here so we wrote that into the rules. The annual dues are up to about a hundred thousand. That doesn't include usage fees. Only a couple of new spots open up each year, usually when somebody dies. Membership is by invitation only. We all know each other."

He showed me a small lap pool and exercise area. A few men sat at the far end with drinks. The Chairman gave them a regular nod when they looked in our direction. Every surface was as clean as an operating room. Then he pointed to a hall of doorways.

"The rooms are back there. I've been happy with the club's management, actually. They bring in ten new girls a year. Each girl works a few nights a week. They don't get run down. They get paid quite well, so that there's no reason to do any other work. They get to know us, know what we want. Sometimes it's only a rubdown or a swim . . . some of the older fellows just want a little help getting into the sauna." He chuckled, indicating he was different from them. "That's all they're up to at their age. We've got one fellow who's almost ninety. Remarkable."

The attendant found us and nodded at me.

"You're all set, sir," he said, like a valet parking cars at a restaurant.

The Chairman and I returned to the locker room and he showed me where the guests' cubicles were. I was given to understand that I should change into the laundered robe. This I did, though not without the usual misgivings and modesty. I was embarrassed by appearing before some strange woman. And, as if we were at a public beach house somewhere on Long Island, the Hamptons say, I worriedly stuffed my watch and wallet into my smelly socks, thinking as I always did that a prospective thief might think twice before rooting through them.

A minute later the Chairman emerged wearing a towel. His tan was current and a number of small Band-Aids were adhered to his shoulders and chest—more skin cancers removed, no doubt. His back sprouted a thicket of gray hair and his legs were bandy in the way of older men.

At that moment a surprisingly beautiful Asian woman in a white robe appeared and took the Chairman's hand. Her matter-of-fact manner shocked me. She possessed a slender body, almost like a child's, and could have been Thai or Filipina or some rarer mixture of races. She whispered coyly in the Chairman's ear. They were not strangers, not at all, and she led him down the hall.

And, while I stood there awkwardly, Miss Najibullah appeared, also unusually attractive, with dark skin and very long black hair and a strong nose and forehead. I guessed that she was twenty-two, at most. She led me to one of the doors in the hallway and shut the door. The room contained a wet bar and an oversized massage table whose height could be varied.

"Where're you from?" I said, to break the silence.

"I come from Afghanistan."

Her accent was very thick. She'd probably been in the United States only a few months, her looks creating a new destiny.

"I am tired of the fighting so I come here. Please." She gave a graceful flourish of her small hand, "You lie down here first."

I lay down on my stomach, letting her rub my shoulders.

"Very tight," she said. "You are very tight."

"Yes."

"Now, here," the woman whispered, her hair falling across my neck. She turned me onto my back. I passed inspection. At first I figured I wouldn't do it. She was ever so slightly aloof. This was business. No doubt the Chairman had chosen the other woman for a reason. But I changed my mind. She was *available* to me. This is a word with wide possibilities. She did as I instructed, one thing and then another. I was not a pig, but I made use of the opportunity. Liz would have been disgusted yet also understanding. The woman's muscle tone in her buttocks and stomach was superb. Quite marvelous.

◆ ◆ ◆

Later. Miss Najibullah asked me if there was anything more she could do for me and I thanked her and said no. She left. No doubt the tip was built into the fee. I put on my robe and floated out the door into the hallway. I listened at the other doors. The chrome handles were nonlocking, I noted, probably to protect the women from being trapped inside with one of their clients. In the hallway I approached a naked man in his fifties wearing sandals and a fogged pair of glasses. I recognized him as the youngest son of the city's wealthiest real estate mogul, now a senile man in his nineties. He was rather short and fat, and his skin was the color of broiled ham, with a froth of reddish gray pubic hair. Beneath the tiny button of his penis, a set of bull's testicles flopped from one corpulent thigh to the other in the dropped, loose way of older men.

"Miss Pearl?" he cried out in a lost, boyish voice, barely seeing me as we passed each other. "Miss Pearl?"

I moved down the corridor.

"Send that down here, honey," came the Chairman's voice from behind one of the doors, the sound of it weighted by the throaty, indulgent quality of a man lying on his back. " — uh, thank you, honey, that feels nice. Send that right down here. Yes, there . . . that's very — *very* good, don't want to spill my rum, yes there, bring that down here to daddy." He laughed deliriously. "Here . . . mmmn, *mmmn!* — there's a hundred for you. All right then . . . let me put another — aah . . . *yes*, that's mmm, mmmn. That's another hundred. Two hundred in ten seconds, you can get some nice shoes."

She answered murmurously, too softly for me to understand.

"Now, this one," the Chairman grunted. "I'm — hey, I'm going to hold it — a little tight, sweetie, bring that down to daddy, bring that down! . . . very tight! . . . a little . . . mmmmmn, mmmnn, ha, mmmn, very *very* nice, what's that come to? Eighteen hundred? We can—*uh!* that's good . . . my drink there, thank you . . . it's a fine, fine night, quite an evening, quite a pleasure . . . now come get this one . . ."

They were doing something with one-hundred-dollar bills. I tiptoed in my towel toward the locker room and took a long, hot shower. A few minutes later I was nearly dressed when the Chairman came back into the locker room. I looked up to see him at the urinal, wearing the maroon robe. He stood in front of the white procelain, waiting patiently for the urine to arrive, with yet another new drink set on the top of the urinal, a cigarette stuck in his mouth, thinking that he was alone. His back was to me and he spoke to himself and hummed, with no variation in tone, no attempt at music, instead making an odd vibration as if someone had hooked up a low current to the fillings in his old ruined teeth. ". . . aah, the bastards, the frolicking bastards, hhrrrmmmmmm . . . noncallable bonds will kill all of us, hmmmn and the mummhermmhum . . ." I could see from his eyes that he was inspecting his penis, evaluating it with interest, as if hoping it might do a trick for him. Or perhaps he looked at it with gratitude for recent accomplishments. A vein of blue smoke spiraled upward from his cigarette as the crack of his mouth kept moving. " . . . ah hmmmum, she's a woman who likes a nice pair of shoes, a pair of shmmmn . . . the Greeks were geniuses, they sent messengers to bring the news of the war . . . hummmrrmmm . . . geniuses, tactical — " Then he lifted his head instinctively, as if a cool draft had reached him, and he turned around. There I was, the young man, already knotting my tie.

"What? *You?*" he asked with sudden vulnerability, as if he had seen a terror, his voice echoing loudly in the marble bathroom. "What? Done so fast, are you?"

I said nothing. He must have had ten or fifteen drinks since we'd gotten on the train hours earlier. I didn't see how he could be standing.

"Ahh, *of course*, it's all quite . . . they *picked* you, they decided you're the messenger," the Chairman exclaimed boozily, his eyes bloodshot and glassy, " — I can see that, aaahhmmm . . . they think you can tell me something the others can't . . . don't think I don't know that, knew it the minute — saw the danger immediately . . ." He rocked forward on his feet, perhaps in danger of falling over. "Well that's very good . . . hmmmn . . . I know the news, I mean, I *know* it, right? . . . you *seem* like a decent fellow, you spoke to the senator quite . . . but I expected that . . . such . . . they can send a *hundred* fellows! It'll never work. It's too big, never been done . . . the language differences, the computers, the debt load. Terrible. Full of terrors. I've put in almost fifty years . . . young fellows like you don't *know* terror. They might be fooling with you fellows, ever think of that?" He paused. His eyes drilled into me as hard as he could. "What if they have the Japanese banks waiting in the wings? Dai-Ichi Kangyo Bank? With assets of half a *trillion* dollars? Or Sumitomo Bank or Sanwa Bank? Did you know that the seven largest banks in the world are all Japanese? Don't believe they don't have any money . . . the smart fellows pulled out before the markets in Tokyo crashed . . . sitting on *billions*, they'll *buy* this company, Mr. Jack Whitman, man of no terrors . . . those suckers will come up with fifty billion . . . they'll simply buy us, me, and . . . so—" He lurched crazily, caught himself. "So go get your winged sandals because I'm—no . . ." The Chairman stumbled, grabbed the urinal for support. "Don't try even . . . don't even *try* to talk me into anything . . . I can be a nasty son of a—I'll fuck up you, I'll fuck up Morrison, I'll—*there!*—" He looked down into the urinal again and realized he had been pissing. "There it is!"

The Chairman cinched his robe, spat his cigarette butt on the floor as if he imagined himself to be a young tough, and weaved heavily out the door back the way he had come. I stood on the wet, marble floor trying to remember his angry, drunken words of warning and noticed that he hadn't bothered to flush the urinal, as if his golden liquid were a mark of himself too valuable to ever be flushed away.

FIVE

I cannot think without coffee and early the next morning I stood in front of my house in a blue suit and green tie drinking my third cup of it, trying unsuccessfully to wrap my mind around what had happened the previous evening with the Chairman. My head hurt from lack of sleep and I stood there dazed and vaguely anxious. The tulips had only just bloomed victoriously—red as blood. A couple of scrubbed fifth-graders skipped by on their way to Berkeley-Carroll, the neighborhood private school where my daughter would have gone, about ten thousand bucks a year. It occurred to me that the Chairman had deliberately taken me to his club. But why? To demonstrate his virility? To intimidate me? I was going to have to start anticipating his manipulations. A trio of homeless men advanced down the street, one pushing a shopping cart loaded down with cans and scraps and any number of things. They knew the garbage truck schedules and did their best scavenging on streets due to be collected. Then the phone rang inside.

"Who is this woman?" Ahmed yelled when I picked up. "No! I don't want to know, there is no time for talk. I just want you to get here as fast as you can. Somebody tore all the hell out of my building! My foreman has called me two minutes ago and said the door to the building was open—"

"Wait, wait, where are Dolores and Maria?" I interrupted in confusion.

"I do not know! Something has happened. They might be here! It is a very big building—"

"You can't find them?"

There was a pause. "If there is a problem, my friend," Ahmed answered slowly, menace in his voice, "you are going to solve it, not me."

"Wait a minute, Ahmed—"

"Just get here as fast—" And he hung up on himself.

When I arrived, Ahmed stood in front of the building in all his sleek brutishness, pacing about in a shimmery Italian suit and holding a woman's shoe. Dolores's shoe. His workmen stood off to one side; clearly no labor had begun and the men dared not penetrate his agitated rage. He looked up and saw me. "Finally!" he growled, and in that moment I knew our friendship of more than fifteen years was over, for despite the fact that Ahmed and I used to carry each other piggyback in the grueling soccer drills our coaches devised for us, suddenly we were again and forever strangers to each other.

He took me by the collar of my coat and threw me up against the wall. "Listen, you motherfucker! I have just found out that the door to my building was open for *five hours* last night! Anybody and his crackhead motherfucker brother could have stolen my equipment! I have got millions of dollars of other people's money involved here." Flecks of spit hit my face. "Something has gone wrong and it is your fault! I do not know where that woman is and if she is even *alive*. But she better not be in my building! If she is dead in there now, that is not where her body is going to be *found*. Understand that, Jack? Got that?" His face was in mine and I could see the fine lacework of pink veins in his eyes. "So what you and I are going to do, right now, and *fuck* your big-time corporate meetings, is we are going up *there*, up to find out what it is has happened, just you and me."

And with that he shoved me inside the iron doorway to the building, pulled a gate shut, and fiddled a key. I was locked in. He turned toward his men. "Sanjay and Boktu, come here."

The small dark man with coal-black eyes and hair whom I had seen before—the translator, and one of the other men, a skinny stoop-shouldered man of about forty whose entire facial expression was distilled in wrinkled worry about his eyes, stepped forward from the group of men. I watched from inside the gate.

"We need to look for Dolores and Maria," I called anxiously. "Let's go!"

But Ahmed was running the show. With Sanjay translating, apparently in a Hindu dialect, he interrogated the older man.

"What happened?" he demanded.

"Mr. Ahmed, Boktu say he is just doing his job checking every hour on every floor and he was standing outside to smoke and he had locked the gate and some man came up to him and started to talk—" The other man interrupted in his worried voice, waving his dry brown hands. "And he say that they went across the street to have just one gin drink. The man was buying the drinks—"

Ahmed hurled a piece of lumber against the wall. "You will ask him why a poor man will drink gin in a bar while he is being paid to protect my property!"

There was some more insistent explanation and clarification and translating but here the chronology was somewhat lost to the watchman, because the next thing he knew, he said, he was lying in an alleyway nearby, his arms tied around his back, his keys gone, a bread delivery truck on its morning rounds honking in the dawn light for him to move. The man stuttered something more.

"He is very sorry," Sanjay explained, "he gives his word—"

"You will tell him he is fired and that I will not pay his last paycheck," Ahmed replied with dispatch, waving his hands in disgust. The translator relayed this message and the older man immediately fell to his feet and began to beg Ahmed, putting his hands around his legs in a death grip of terror. He took handfuls of dirt and put them in his mouth. He wept.

I felt nothing but fury. "Ahmed!" I screamed. "We need to look for Dolores and Maria—they could be hurt, they could be—"

Sanjay continued translating for Ahmed in a lilting Indian accent. "Boktu say he does not have any money and that he has five little children. He begs for your mercy upon him. He say he did not know there was the madam in the building."

Ahmed scuffed his feet from the man's grasp. "You will tell him that his begging disgraces him as a father and as a man."

"You are the boss," Sanjay said, "but I believe that this is too much punishment."

"You will tell him my last words or you will be fired too."

The translation was made and Boktu stiffened—his dignity now no longer a liability to him—and stood and strode quickly away. Meanwhile Ahmed had grabbed the iron gate that kept me in.

"Lock this behind me and nobody comes in or out of here until we come back down," Ahmed ordered his other men. "If the police come, tell them you don't have the key and have to call me to get it. Then you call my house and I won't be there and you say you don't know what to do. Sanjay, you come."

Then, pushing me toward the dusty gloom of the interior, he continued. "You are responsible for this man who loses his job, Jack, not me! He has never had a bad night. I am firing him because I must, as a message to the other men, but it is something you have caused." We plunged down a narrow corridor. Immense iron steam pipes ran along one side, their jackets of asbestos insulation torn and damaged, the dangerous fibers piled in drifts on the floor. "Do you know how big my building is?" Ahmed glared at me.

"What the fuck does that matter *now*, Ahmed?" I answered angrily. "We're looking for—"

"*No*, of course you don't know, Jack, all *you* fucking do is push around tiny pieces of paper in your office. Tiny pieces of toilet paper. You guys do not have any idea of what the real world is. This is not one of your magazines with a woman prostituting herself on the cover. This is ninety-five thousand square feet and we are going to check every single foot, if necessary. You do not understand how hard I have worked." He stared at me, his anger done for at least a moment, almost haggard in exhaustion. "I have got three Japanese bankers and they are very hard, only agree to a revocable mortgage. They want to take their money back to Tokyo, buy land while it is cheap now. Better investment, maybe. I have to kiss their asses every week. Nice kisses. I cannot lose time, I cannot lose money."

Inside, Ahmed opened a huge electrical panel and began switching on power and lights throughout the building, and as we paced over the first floor, looking hurriedly under tarps and within unfinished closets and air vents, it became apparent from the watchman's story that the intruder had entered from the rear of the building. He had encountered the smaller of the two dogs on the second-floor landing of the interior fire stairs. The rottweiler had stuck her head between the steel stair railings, Ahmed surmised, barking at the intruder. From below, on the way up the steps, the intruder had clubbed the dog with one or more blows—with a motion like a tennis overhead smash. A section of pipe was nearby, one end sticky with blood. The dog had collapsed, paws and nose hanging over the edge of the stair, blood dripping from its muzzle to a small, sticky pool below. Her open eyes, clouded now, stared at me like a gargoyle's, seemingly apologizing for failing to halt the man's attack on Dolores. What kind of man, I agonized, could kill a trained rottweiler?

"She was a very good watchdog and she was worth at least a thousand dollars," Ahmed said. "So do you know who this man is? This man that wants this woman? He must want this woman very badly," he goaded me. "All my men say she is very beautiful. Oh yes, she must be very beautiful. A great lover. With a cunt like butter, a cunt as hot as—" He spun toward me and spoke with bitter sarcasm. "You have at least *fucked her*, have you not, Jack?"

He didn't wait for an answer, and with the translator leading the way, we raced up each set of stairs, hurriedly checking every room and wall space, past veins of joint compound on the walls and electrical wires snaking through ceilings. We found nothing, only open doors. Ahmed grabbed my biceps like a demented schoolmaster, intent that I witness the destruction done to his precious renovation, but I shook free and ran ahead, calling Dolores's name. There was no response. Then, on the top floor, the stairs ended and I stood facing a bank of arched ten-foot-high windows framing a view north, past Washington Square and up toward the Empire State building, ever imposing and magnificent. Each window had been shattered.

"Oh no," Ahmed said from behind me. "Every one a thousand dollars!"

Then we rushed to the penthouse apartment where Dolores and Maria had been staying. The door was open, the wall next to it hacked and broken open with a hole the size of a pumpkin. Just large enough for a man to wriggle through. Broken plaster was sprinkled whitely over the rug.

"He couldn't get the fucking Medeco lock open so he has busted through the wall to get in," Ahmed analyzed aloud. "That is five hundred dollars of damage, that hole alone." We pushed open the door. I was sick with apprehension that we were about to come upon a body. A woman's hairbrush lay in the middle of the floor, next to a pair of pink, cotton bikini underwear, inside out, with the usual stains. Where were they? I glanced past a mattress in one corner, a phone, and a few other rudimentary items. A dozen or so crayons lay scattered across the carpeting, bright sticks of color, a few broken and crushed underfoot. Then I saw something that made me stop: the same jar of water as had been in Dolores's crummy hotel room, half-full, set out purposefully atop an overturned box. I didn't understand.

"The apartment's empty," Ahmed said, pushing me along.

Then we heard Sanjay calling us.

"Mr. Ah-med! Mr. Ah-med!"

"He's on the roof ladder," Ahmed instructed.

We hurried up the ladder to the tarpaper roof, plunging outside into a brilliant morning sky. Ahmed picked up a woman's shoe that was missing its heel; it matched the one he had found earlier on the street below.

"I don't get it," I said. "Where are they?"

We quickly scanned the large roof. Ahmed's men were in the midst of tearing up perhaps half a dozen layers of ancient tarpaper, crackly underfoot, and replacing it with new firm asphalt paper that they cemented into place with hot tar. Amid the big metal cans and flapping rolls of supplies, brushes, tar trowels, work gloves, shovels, and canisters of material, there stood an immense wheeled cauldron, thickly dripped over the sides with dried tar.

"Here!" Sanjay cried, showing us that the huge cauldron leaked whiffs of sulfurous smoke. "The big pot is very little bit hot. Very little bit," he said excitedly. "See, there is no fuel, Mr. Ahmed. No fuel is left." He pointed at the rippled surface of the tar inside the cauldron. My fingers started to shake. "Look! It is the madam. Or her daughter."

We saw hair thickly clotted with tar on the surface of the oily black stuff.

"Pull her out!" Ahmed commanded.

Sanjay immediately cowered in fright, as if he were being accused of the act himself.

"No!" I argued, not willing to see what was inside. "The police should do this."

"Get her out! Sanjay! Pull her out of the tar!" Ahmed screamed. "We must get her out of this building."

The small man was shaking his head, terrified. Ahmed pointed at me.

"You do it!" he said. "You must do it."

Sanjay ventured a finger against the black surface, then pulled it back. "The tar is too cold, Mr. Ahmed," Sanjay cried. "Too cold."

"Then get the gas, Sanjay."

He hurried to the side of the roof, whistling down the face of the building to the street below. Then he threw a heavy rope over the side and ran it through a pulley. Ahmed walked the perimeter of the roof in agitation, inspecting for further damage. I stared at the clotted black hair at the surface of the hardened tar; the cauldron was just big enough to hold a woman and a child.

I couldn't bear it. "Ahmed, you can't do this," I screamed at him. "It's wrong."

He paced back toward me. "Japanese bankers are very cautious. They have many little clauses. If there is a body found, every dollar in my account goes back to Tokyo. They make one call and ten minutes—"

"I have it!" came Sanjay's voice and we both turned our heads. Yanking the rope hand over hand, Sanjay secured a canister of propane. He set it beneath the burner, fiddled with a knob, lit a match in a small tube, fiddled with the knob some more, and then the burner jetted to life, the blue flame burning loudly. I stared, fascinated with the process but unable to stop it. The tar warmed quickly, the dull skin on top exuding swirling steam until it liquefied into a glossy liquid black. The mass of oily hair eased below the surface.

"Are you going to get this woman out?" Ahmed demanded of me.

"No. I'm calling the police. Don't touch her."

Sanjay looked back and forth at us.

"I cannot have anybody here, we have business to do."

"That's your problem, Ahmed," I said firmly. "The police should do everything." I wasn't going to help him but neither was I foolish enough to try to stop him. He saw this.

"Fuck!" Ahmed hollered, pushing me back. "All right!" And then, in his Armani suit and leather shoes, he leapt angrily upon the machine and balanced each foot on the two-inch edge of the cauldron. He took off an immense gold Rolex and thrust it into his pants pocket.

"Give me those," he ordered Sanjay, and he put on the thick leather gloves that went halfway to the elbow. He squatted carefully, ready to use his powerful legs. Then he thrust his hands into the viscous black mass up to his forearms, grasping blindly until his fingers found something. His eyebrows arched in realization. His arms tensed and he pulled against the thick resistance of the tar. In one great, groaning effort, Ahmed slowly straightened his legs and back and yanked from the tar the long-haired hindquarters of the missing female German shepherd and then the rest of the dog high into the air, the head turned upward in grotesque stiffness, its eyes tarred over and dead, mouth locked in a dripping, black grin.

The three of us stared for several shocked seconds.

"Look at this, Jack! Look at this!" Ahmed screamed, furious and demented. He swung the dog out and she dropped with gruesome heaviness onto the roof. He jumped down and thrust the sticky, blackened gloves to my throat. "Look at me, Jack, *you will face me!* You do not know who you are dealing with, right? No fucking idea!" The black tar stung against my throat and I saw that he was terrorized by the sudden mystery of what had happened. "This woman has not told you some things! You do not know many things! Is that not right?"

SIX

The next two days were a torment. Dolores did not call. I anxiously remembered the bright crayons scattered and crushed on the floor of Ahmed's apartment. My stomach was particularly bad and I spent too many hours watching the sun move across my desk, edges of paper cutting shadows. At lunch I loitered in the newsstand in the lobby of the Corporation building and flipped through the grimy pages of the *Daily News* for a story of an assault or murder involving a woman and her small daughter, but there were no stories like that, though just about every other possible mayhem occurred in the city, including a child who was thrown out of a window and impaled on a fence. I could not tell anyone about my worry, not even Helen. If it was discovered that I was intimately connected to the demise of some unfortunate homeless woman; if, say, Dolores turned up dead with my business card in her purse, then I'd have a lot of explaining to do inside the Corporation. Yet although whatever had happened to Dolores and Maria was not my burden, it seemed likely that only I knew they were in trouble. And this made me uneasy. I considered going to the police and insisting that a young woman and her small daughter were missing, but what would I be able to tell them? In New York City, the threshold for disaster is higher. I couldn't *prove* that Dolores and Maria were missing. But I did call the hotel manager, old Mr. Clammers, who remembered me from the fifty dollars I'd given him. She hadn't returned, he said. No, he didn't have a forwarding number. "Hey, fellah, take it from an old man who seen a lot of things," he told me. "I *seen* things. You're a clean young fellah and you gave me fifty bucks, so here's fifty bucks' worth of advice. Steer clear of this woman. She ain't your kind, you know? Not for you." I did not like his presumptuousness but, nonetheless, it seemed emotionally prudent to try to forget Dolores Salcines and her daughter. *Forget it*, I told myself, *you never knew them*. Maybe I was luckier to be done with her, maybe the past week had only amounted to a deviant splice in the quiet life of Jack Whitman.

Meanwhile, the Volkman-Sakura executives arrived from Bonn in the warm rain of early May—five Germans in five cuffed and tailored suits who spoke impeccable English and set themselves up in a fifth-floor business suite at the Plaza Hotel. The Chairman had disappeared again, this time to his compound in the Caribbean, according to Mrs. Marsh, so I insisted to Morrison that I should attend the first meeting that Thursday morning.

"What's he doing down there, working on his tan?" Morrison said irritably. "You should be spending time with him every day now, if possible. I don't care how you get in there. You need to work the relationship around to the point that you can really *press*."

"I think you have to assume he knows what's going on. All the signals the other night were that he'd gotten wind of the deal and wasn't having any."

"He'd do that even if he *did* like the idea. As soon as he's back, you escalate."

"Fine." I was surprised at Morrison's view that the Chairman was utterly hapless. "But the Volkman-Sakura guys are here now and I want in to that meeting."

Morrison contemplated the question.

"There's no reason I can't be in that meeting."

"Jack—"

"No *good* reason," I told him. "Unless—"

"Today," Morrison broke in. "Just today. The Chairman is back tomorrow, so that will be it."

So later that morning I traveled to the Plaza, listening to the rain slash against the windows of my taxi. The Corporation team arrived in twos and threes, just to be sure that the business media didn't pick up on the negotiations too quickly. We gathered and waited on the fifth floor outside suite 565—the bankers, the lawyers, Samantha, Beales, Morrison, a few others. A secretary greeted us and led us into the suite. The Volkman-Sakura team had a whole office set up—phones, faxes, copier machines. She led us into a plush conference room with a big table and Otto Waldhausen stood at the door and greeted each one of us with remote politeness. He was surprisingly short, maybe five feet four. Very unusual to be that short and have such power. His hair was sparse and brushed flat against the sides of his head, as if flattened down by the velocity with which he moved. And then we sat down, and the rest of the V-S team was introduced. Nodding and nervous smiles.

"We are very glad to be in this room," Morrison suddenly announced in his cheesiest ambassadorial voice, trying to get the energy of the talks started, "and it occurs to me that perhaps the best place to start, Otto, is to express our genuine admiration for your company. We have spent many months studying your operations and markets and products and I must say that we are full of admiration. Full of it." He smiled his smoothest smile all around. Morrison was in that false second youth that rich men often come into after having worked hard for twenty or thirty years—fit, barbered, in a new suit; he looked more youthful than ever, though not, of course, young. "I think I said this to you on the phone the other day, that we're very much looking forward to these talks. My sense of the way we might proceed is based on a recognition that your company does many things very, very well, as does ours, and that these elements have value." He was beginning to impose a format of negotiation. "Your cable operations in Australia, for example. Or our music division. Whatever. We have some values we've calculated for each of these elements—"

"Perhaps we should discuss an operating structure first," Waldhausen broke in. He sucked in his lips, and I knew that Morrison's hearty jocularity annoyed him. "It is a question of philosophy of management, no? We should begin with this very important question. Let us work out the values of divisions later. Now I would like to discuss our viewpoint, our way of thinking. Yes? Americans and Germans think differently in many respects." He paused to indicate his firmness. "This will need to be discussed first, because without this in discussion, there can be no agreement on details. I am suggesting that we attempt a meeting of the minds, that is an American expression, no?"

"It absolutely is, Otto," Morrison said. "And I certainly respect your sense that a philosophy of management is crucial. It *is* crucial. But—"

It went badly from there on. We tried to get started. Others chimed in. The five V-S officials had that British inflection and European reserve that Americans suspect as haughtiness. Morrison struggled to inject items that we might agree on. Waldhausen asked for a detailed joint operating plan to consider. This was too fast; we weren't ready to give it to them until we sized up their intent, since the plan contained valuable marketing information—the keys to the Corporation's kingdom. The Germans seemed aloof, contemptuous, uninterested in seeking common ground. I wondered if Morrison had seduced them across the Atlantic without understanding the degree of their interest; I wondered if we'd been fooling ourselves.

And by the end of the morning it was clear that the two companies were starting from scratch. Waldhausen appeared more interested in making plans to attend the current Broadway shows than in listening to a bunch of investment bankers babbling about second-quarter profits and independent syndication values of old TV sitcoms, the debt-reduction schedule, and so on. When we all sat down for lunch, I noticed Morrison stabbing his tiny shrimp with a heavy silver fork. "You get the picture," he said to me, his small teeth grinding the pink pieces of shrimp efficiently. "They sent us a bunch of killers."

"They're stalling."

"Of course," Morrison said, "he's not here"—meaning the Chairman—"and they don't know if we're the guys who catch the whales or dig the worms." He glanced around the room. "You have to start banging harder on the Chairman's door, Jack."

Waldhausen had been sitting next to Samantha during lunch, and after the coffee was served, he unexpectedly called for an early break in the talks, apologizing and saying his group was tired from the travel and they would prefer to reconvene the next morning. Morrison responded with endless generosity. "Of course," he said, "we will be more than pleased to do that." But he nodded ever so subtly to Samantha.

So, three useless hours after we'd arrived, the entire Corporation negotiating team left the Plaza, again in twos and threes, leaving Samantha still talking with Waldhausen, leaning forward with her legs crossed as he sat in an overstuffed armchair. The rain had stopped, with the sun cutting through a heavy, clouded sky. I wanted to walk back to the office but Morrison found it painful to struggle on his prosthesis more than about a few blocks. So Beales and I took the cab with Morrison.

"You shouldn't have let her go off with him," Beales complained from the front seat, shooting his cuffs in irritation. "It's an insult to the other guys. It puts the whole thing on a different footing from the start! It makes it unstable by definition. We're set for what, ten days, two weeks of negotiation, right? It takes a couple of days to warm up, to get used to the accents and everything. This is supposed to be all of us sitting down, not Samantha and—"

"If Waldhausen is happy, the other V-S guys will be too," I broke in.

"Yeah, but what is she *doing?*" Beales argued. The taxi was stuck in traffic now and the driver was getting nervous.

"You're acting like they're in a hotel room fucking this very minute," I said with disgust.

"They very well *could* be, that's my point."

"Wrong," I told him, reaching for the roll of antacids in my pocket. "Samantha knows *exactly* what she's doing. I know her better than you do. She's about a million times more interested in seeing this deal go through than in being humped by some short German guy. She's looking for an avenue of conversation, Ed. Isn't that *obvious?* She realized quickly that the chemistry wasn't so great. Maybe there are too many people in the room. Nobody else seems to have hit it off with any of them. We need to find that sympathetic relationship, Ed. So, if there's any advantage that—"

"I completely disagree," Beales interrupted, his craggy face reddening. "It makes us look small time, uncoordinated—"

"Driver!" hollered Morrison, slapping his good hand on the seat. "Stop the cab!"

The car lurched to a halt next to the curb.

"Ed," Morrison spat hotly over the front seat, "if *you* had an ass like Samantha's you'd do the same thing, and we all know it, so long as I approved. So don't get high and mighty. And *you*—" He turned to me. "You're supposed to be whispering in the Chairman's ear that we have to do this deal, not riding in taxis arguing with Ed." He looked back and forth between us. "Now, both of you get out of my fucking cab and give me some peace."

And we did, right there, without speaking to one another. Morrison threw my umbrella out the window after me and the taxi sped off. Beales and I looked at each other. I popped a couple of antacids in my mouth.

"Too much tension, Jack?" Beales grinned.

When one's enemies think they can insult you without danger, that is when they're after you.

"Yes, Ed," I replied. "I have tension. *People* cause me tension. But at least I know where it is — in my stomach. It's not in my head, it's not in my chest, it's not in my lower back, and, luckily, Ed — don't you think? — it's not in my *asshole*."

He started to say something, thought better of it, and turned on his heel toward the Corporation building. I picked up my umbrella and felt a kind of righteous pleasure as I watched Beales walk away. But, I see now, I was only making mistakes, confusing enemies. Beales wasn't going to be my problem.

♦ ♦ ♦

Later that afternoon, as I wrote a memo to the research department requesting some numbers on what it might cost to build fifty movie theaters in Cuba, Helen told me a Mrs. Rosenbluth was on the phone, insisting she speak with me.

"I don't know anyone named Mrs. Rosenbluth."

"She says — oh, I don't know *what* she says, really."

"Put her on."

"Are you a Mr. John Whitman?" came an older voice, after Helen made the transfer.

"Yes."

"And this is your place of business, Mr. Whitman? This is where you work?"

"Yes. May I ask why you wish to know?"

"Can you tell me the address of your place of work?" she continued suspiciously.

I told her.

"Yes, that's right. Now, Mr. John Whitman, may I ask how old are you?"

"I'm thirty-five," I said.

"May I ask if you are married? Have any children, Mr. Whitman?"

"These are personal questions."

"Well," she sang through her nose, an aging Jewish mother who was secure in her place in the universe, "I have a good reason to ask them."

"My wife was killed about four years ago," I answered, hearing my own voice from far away. Whenever I said the words, I saw Liz's gray face in the morgue and remembered the plain truth of her body laid out in the steel cadaver drawer. "We didn't have any children," I added. The phone was silent for several seconds. "Mrs. Rosenbluth, I don't understand why you've called. What can I do for you?"

"I have a young woman and her daughter here and—"

"Dolores and Maria?"

"Yes, those are their names."

"Are they all right?" I demanded anxiously.

"For the moment."

"Where are they?"

"Why would you want to know?" she asked, her voice guarded again.

I quickly told her that I first met Dolores and Maria on the subway, then mentioned my effort to get Dolores a job and a place to live. I explained what had apparently happened at Ahmed's building, to the best of my understanding, and how that was the last place I had known Dolores and Maria to be.

"So I am to understand that you are not the *cause* of their problems?"

"Absolutely not. Did Dolores tell you to call me?"

"No."

I thought a moment. "Then that means she still has my business card."

With this, Mrs. Rosenbluth seemed greatly relieved that she could trust me. "Yes, that's right. She, Dolores, the mother, is very tired, I think. She said almost nothing when I told her she could lie down on the spare bed. So I was looking around for some sort of information about her and I found your card. The little girl has a cough but otherwise looks healthy. Oh, but they can't stay, you see. I'm very sorry I can't keep them. I'm due to go see my sister today. But I can't just send them back onto the street. I'm a Socialist, I believe in involving myself in society's problems. These two aren't street people, if you know what I mean." Her voice was accelerating into an emotional rush. "I found the poor child this morning in Washington Square, where I walk each day at eight o'clock. She came up to me. Her mother was asleep on the next bench. I just took them home with me, I just decided that I would do it. But I need to know the name of the responsible party. And Dolores didn't say anything about a family or friends. She didn't say anything about you, either—"

"Mrs. Rosenbluth—"

"—they're both asleep now. They ate and then fell asleep by nine o'clock this morning." Her voice was rising toward hysteria. "I can't be the responsible party in this situation. It breaks my heart. I was in the park and the little one came up to me. She's adorable. Children need love. I don't know what to do, I took them in because . . . but I can't keep them, you see, I'm living alone, I—"

"Mrs. Rosenbluth," I interrupted firmly. "Now you must give me your address."

♦ ♦ ♦

The choice was to wait until the end of the day, when I would not have any office work to worry about, or to go immediately. Morrison wanted to see me later during the afternoon, but I figured I could slip away for an hour with no trouble. If I waited too long, perhaps Dolores and Maria would again disappear into the maw of the city. The subway dropped me near a prewar building a few blocks from NYU. When I rang the apartment doorbell, there was some scrabbling at a chain and a woman whom I guessed to be in her late seventies opened the door and peered at me fiercely.

"Mrs. Rosenbluth?"

She put a bony finger to her lips. "Both still asleep. I just had to give the little girl a bath. She was very quiet and cooperative . . ."

I followed the woman into the living room of an urban in-

tellectual's apartment, decorated circa 1958, with several framed di-
plomas on the walls and a number of outdated leftist treatises on
American politics and early hardcover editions of Roth, Mailer, and
Bellow on the bookshelves. Junk mail was piled everywhere, from
every liberal cause imaginable. On the mantel stood yellowed high
school pictures of three sons and a daughter, all pimples and braces
and high school graduation gowns, no doubt adults now and successful
in everything they did, and newer photos of high school–age children,
grandchildren, most likely. On the wall was a framed black-and-white
photograph of a tall, bespectacled man shaking hands with a young
Dr. Martin Luther King.

"Yes," she said, "that's my husband."

We headed into a kitchen. "I inspected every single *inch* of her
body, I looked for scratches or bruises or lice or" —Mrs. Rosenbluth's
old eyes looked at me meaningfully— "or any *mistreatment*, if you
know what I mean." She waved an arthritic hand. "There, please sit
down here in the kitchen, would you like a cup of coffee? The little
one was hungry, but we fixed that up. She does have a cold, congestion, but steam and soup and plenty of sleep should do the trick. Now,
I have been wondering—there, I had the water boiling already, cream
and sugar?"

"Yes," I said, settling back in a wooden chair in Mrs. Rosenbluth's
fusty kitchen, which featured a battalion of cat magnets on the refrigerator, a wall clock in the shape of a rooster, well-thumbed *Good
Housekeeping* cookbooks, and a cookie jar on the counter. Children had
grown up in this apartment. On the refrigerator was a volunteers'
schedule at a soup kitchen run by a local synagogue. Socialism may
have faded away along with the old American left, but here was Mrs.
Rosenbluth, still making her contribution. I felt a sudden rush of
gladness that Dolores and Maria had landed so safely. Mrs. Rosenbluth bustled about on the ancient yellowed linoleum on swollen
ankles, putting coffee and cookies on a plate before me.

"Good," she went on, "that's real cream. Fresh. So, where was I?
Now—yes, this poor child is terribly polite, but she seems to know
that her world is upside down. I can't blame the mother, because I
don't know the particulars. These things can be very touchy . . .
certain *family* situations, but when children are involved . . . these

situations are heartbreaking, just heartbreaking! I saw that dirty, beautiful child and I was ready to cry. I raised four children, Mr. Whitman. My husband was a very eminent professor of sociology here at the university. Now I'm alone and haven't—"

At that moment we heard the padding of feet in the hallway and Maria peeked her curly dark head into the kitchen doorway, dressed only in underpants and carrying a pillow with both hands, her hair mussed from sleeping.

"Maria?" I suffered a stab of love for the sleepy, innocent child.

She was silent and looked from Mrs. Rosenbluth to me and back again.

"Maria, I'm glad you and your mother are okay. Can you tell me what happened?"

The child looked at me and said nothing.

"Remember the big building where you were sleeping with your mother? Did somebody find you there?"

Mrs. Rosenbluth stepped over and absentmindedly smoothed the child's hair. "I think they must have slept in the park or a shelter or somewhere dreadful."

Then Dolores appeared in the doorway, wrapped in a bathrobe too small for her, her face haggard and discouraged. She had lost weight in the days since I'd seen her. But even without makeup, even in her exhaustion, there was that ripe something about her, that *heat.* "C'mon, Maria." She reached out her hand. "Mrs. Rosenbluth, excuse me, do you have the wash now?"

"Yes, of course," Mrs Rosenbluth said. "Your clothes."

"Dolores?"

She looked up at me in confusion. "Why—wait, why are *you* here?"

"I found his card, in all of your things when I was washing them," Mrs. Rosenbluth said quickly, "and I didn't know *who*, you understand, I had to call *someone* who might be able to help you—"

"But I don't even *know* him. He's just—"

"Dear, he seems to care about you and your daughter. He left his office immediately when I called."

Dolores looked at me indecisively, her expression glazed. "You found out about the apartment?"

I nodded. "Your husband do that?"

Her eyes seemed to replay the danger. "Hector, yes."

"He killed two watchdogs, you know."

"The poor things!" Mrs. Rosenbluth said.

"Did you hear them?" I continued. "I mean, Jesus, I saw the dogs, I saw what—"

"They were barking!" Maria said with sudden breathless excitement. "And we ran up the stairs and we ran on the roof."

"You went down the fire escape?" I asked Dolores.

She nodded tiredly. "The barking woke me up in the middle of the night. He came up the stairs and I took some stuff and Maria and went up to the roof. We got out before he got too close. I could hear him smashing the windows in the apartment below us and everything. It was dark. I was lucky, I got to the fire escape. That bigger dog slowed him down. I think it was attacking him. He was on the roof with the dog after him and that's the last I saw."

Dolores looked at me intently, with great vulnerability in her face. Her toughness was gone; now she was simply scared and exhausted and trying to figure out who the hell I was.

"We should get the two of you dressed," Mrs. Rosenbluth prompted her.

While the three of them disappeared into the laundry room, I called Helen at the office. Morrison wanted to meet me in thirty-five minutes.

"Can you put the meeting off?" I asked. "A half hour perhaps?"

"No, he's got a flight at six. It seemed important, that's all. I'd really try to make it on time," Helen added. "He seems pretty tense, actually."

"Tell him he's an asshole, would you do that for me, Helen?"

"C'mon, Jack. You're just—"

"Tell him I don't want any more of his shitball assignments, would you do *that* for me? I've worked loyally for years and years and he does this to me?"

"*Jack.*"

"Tell him I quit," I said. "I'll quit and drive around the country for a couple of months, Helen. I'll send you a postcard from Wall Drug, South Dakota."

"Jack."

"That's a real place, Helen."

She laughed. "See you here at four, okay?"

I hung up.

"You have to leave, right?" I said to Mrs. Rosenbluth.

"I told my sister I'd get there by dinnertime."

Dolores and Maria appeared in the doorway, dressed now.

"Listen," I told Dolores, "I have to be in my office in about half an hour uptown and it's a good sixty blocks. I have to leave really soon. So we need to get this resolved. Now, Dolores, am I right that you have no money?"

"I got maybe a few dollars. I was saving that for food. But I can't go back to my old neighborhood. Hector, my husband—" She looked at Maria. "It's no good, he knows all my friends there, too. It's a neighborhood, you know, and everybody knows everybody in the building. He knows where to look."

"Family?"

She shook her head. "I don't have any family."

"Mr. Whitman," said Mrs. Rosenbluth, "as I told you and as I told Dolores, I just can't be the responsible party. I have to leave now. My sister lives out on Long Island in Manhasset and I'm too old to try to get the train at rush hour. They step on me."

"Maybe if I could just get a ride to one of the good shelters," Dolores said. "We got to sleep, Maria is gonna get sick."

"Absolutely not," Mrs. Rosenbluth said. "The shelter is no place for a child."

The old woman looked accusingly at me, her old, red-rimmed eyes unflinching in their silent expectation.

"All right." I pulled out my house keys. "Dolores, you don't have anywhere to go and I have to get out of here. I know you too well now to tell you to go to the shelters or back out on the street. But I *don't* know who the hell you are, I don't know if you're a crack addict or a drunk or if your husband is waiting around the corner to kill me or what. I mean, he really messed up my friend's building. Right? Your whole situation is more desperate this time around. So I'm going to send you to my own home. I'm not saying you can stay there indefi-nitely, but just for the time being, for *now*, at least."

She was watching me carefully.

"If I give you this key to my house and cab fare to get there, will I regret it?"

Dolores shook her head. "I promise."

I wrote down my Park Slope address in Brooklyn and handed it to her. "If I come home and find my house burned down or something—"

"No, no. We'll just sit. Won't touch a thing."

I found a twenty in my wallet and handed it to her for the taxi ride over the bridge. She took the bill politely. "How did your husband find you, by the way?" I asked. "I thought you were trying to avoid him."

"I called my friend Tina a couple of days ago and she came in from Brooklyn to see me," Dolores explained. "Hector must have heard about it and asked Tina's husband to find out from her. That's the only way I can think of."

"Well, I don't want Hector to find out where you're going this time."

"You can be sure of that."

"I don't need any trouble," I said firmly. "You got that?"

"You already got trouble with me. You shouldn't have given me your card."

I had to smile. "You're right," I told her. "You're nothing but trouble."

A minute later, after Dolores had gathered her few remaining belongings, Mrs. Rosenbluth clicked the three locks on her door and we all rode the little caged elevator down to the sidewalk. I hailed a cab for Mrs. Rosenbluth and she climbed in. Then, luckily, another came along. "I'm going to take this one, because I'm late," I told Dolores, searching her face for some indication that we were no longer strangers, that I was trusting her. "You get the next one. But you understand that this is my own home?"

"Please," Dolores said wearily, nodding her head and reaching for Maria's hand. "I'll promise anything."

◆ ◆ ◆

Sixty blocks north, twenty-five minutes later, Morrison followed me into his office and shut the door with his good hand. Two men stood there, one older and lean as a stick, the other with an unruly black beard and hugely fat, a kid almost, who looked uncomfortable in his suit.

"Jack, this is Mr. Shevesky and Mr. DiFrancesco."

We shook their hands and sat down. I was wondering what Dolores and Maria were doing that very moment, whether they had actually taken a cab to my house. The fact of it seemed fantastic, and it excited and frightened me both. More than anything, I wanted to go immediately home and be with Dolores and Maria. But I was obliged to pay attention now. "What outfit you guys from?" I asked.

Shevesky, the older one, leaned forward, a quick grin lighting his face. "CAS—Corporate Assessment Services."

"I've brought these two here today in order that we may have a little discussion." Morrison inspected the mallard decoy on his desk. "I think it'd be useful to know what"—he paused—"certain companies are doing, what they're thinking." He eyed me to be sure I wouldn't ask some ridiculous question, such as the legality of whatever he had planned. "These men tell me that they know how to get information sent out by fax."

"You guys can steal faxes?" I said in surprise.

"We can *retrieve* them," corrected Mr. Shevesky.

"That's amazing."

"We do other work, too. Background checks and so on."

"I got to leave for a plane in twenty-five minutes," Morrison announced. "So you guys got to hurry it up. The scenario is this: a group is now in a business suite on the fifth floor at the Plaza Hotel. Their faxes are coming and going from Germany. Can you get us copies of those faxes as they appear? If so, how? What are the risks?"

"I'll turn it over to Mike."

DiFrancesco was already slouched in his chair like a kid bored in class. He looked disdainfully at me, then out the window. Shevesky was clearly the handler, whereas Mike DiFrancesco was the talent. He retained an aloof composure, knowing that everything went through him. "Well, for your basic fax suck," DiFrancesco began, gazing at the ceiling, his mouth open, "there's two levels to the problem." He put his hands together, as if to pray, his eyes still upward. "The first is getting access to the fax signal, meaning—well, the quantumbogo-dynamics of operation—"

"Mike," Shevesky interrupted. "English, regular English."

"The *theory* of operation behind faxes is that they scan a document and turn a very small strip of the piece of paper into a description of it in ones and zeros—"

"The machine digitizes the strip," I said.

"Yes, it digitizes light and dark spaces in a very small grid into ones and zeros that get coded into a format and translated into tones. The tones are compatible with the voice transmission capabilities of a phone system. Now if you're going to tap that signal we need to get access to the sound of those tones and for that we need some sort of access to the wires over which those tones travel. So, given it's an execudroid hotel suite, there're a couple of complications. I'll come back to—"

"Do we have to get the MIT dissertation?" Morrison asked. "I mean, give me a break."

"This is the way he works," Shevesky assured us, flashing a rabbity smile. "He hears the problem, talks it out *once*, and then never forgets a step."

DiFrancesco combed through his thick black beard with both hands, as if looking for lice. "The first necessity is access to the tones themselves, the second is the ability to capture that transmission and decode it. There's going to be two vendors in that hotel, there's going to be New York Telephone, which has access to the building for adding and deleting phone lines, and then there'll be the vendor company for the switching system that the hotel uses, say Northern Telecom or whoever the vendor is, and the problem is that the fax signal is being generated and being received on an *extension* of the phone system, just like all phones in an office are generally extensions of one main number."

DiFrancesco was now opening and shutting his legs unconsciously, as if receiving physical pleasure. His pants were badly worn where the insides of his legs rubbed together. "Now, that extension will appear in a riser box in some sort of telephone closet where the main cable arrives onto the fifth floor before it fans out laterally and arrives in various rooms as a phone jack, which the wire from the fax machine in question is plugged into. But that extension doesn't exist in the New York Telephone region of the territory and the reason being that when a fax call gets made, the number dialed on the fax machine goes to the PBX and—"

"PBX?" Morrison asked. He cleaned his teeth with his tongue, irritated at the jargon.

"That's the local switch or exchange—"

"The damn box of phone wires on every floor?" Morrison asked. "Is that what you're talking about?"

"Yes," DiFrancesco answered, eyes still up, seeming to be reading flyspecks on the ceiling, the great hams of his thighs vibrating. "When the number is dialed on the fax machine, the call goes through the extension to the PBX on the floor. The PBX looks at the phone number being dialed and decides what circuit the phone number should go out on. It usually has a group of lines that local calls go out on and a group that long-distance or international calls go out on. The whole thing takes about a microfortnight."

"What's a microfortnight?" I asked.

"About one-point-two seconds," DiFrancesco answered, as if I were the stupidest man alive. "Now, my feeling is that physical access is the least detectable method, least potentially pessimal. I'd book a room on the same floor and try to get access to the riser box and—"

"No, *no!*" Morrison shook his head. "I don't want you or some guy in there in the hotel pretending to be a guest or a phoneman or Donald Trump or somebody fiddling around with the equipment box." He turned to Shevesky. "You told me this could be done *remotely*, that your guy could sit in front of a screen and just magically get the faxes that way. This isn't—"

"Wait, it *can* be done. He's just running through the options."

"The PBX will also have a modem attached to it," DiFrancesco continued, as if he hadn't heard anyone speak. "So that maintenance personnel for the service organization can dial in and get access to it, and program remotely to change instructions. When you play around with programming on the PBX you get the additional delay of passwords. Different PBX's have different passwords programmed by the service personnel. That would *seem* to be a problem." His eyes brightened with devilish delight; he was a master of secrets. "Now it just so happens that there's a *factory* password that the factory engineers use and that overrides the programmed password no matter what. I have a bunch of these factory passwords. I can probably dial into whatever PBX is on the fifth floor at the Plaza Hotel. It'll be a major manufacturer. Now, in a big hotel, changes that you make in one terminal turn up in other places. Normally there's a set of routings so that when an extension like ours, the one hooked to our fax machine, makes a call, its digits are analyzed and then put through a filter called class of service, which determines whether this extension has the right to make such a call. If it does, then it gets moved on to another thing called automatic route selection, which determines how the call should be processed, which trunk to pick, is a trunk available, if it's not available does it overflow to another group of trunks, does it wait for a trunk—what happens? And then it processes beyond that to dial rules, which say that now that we have picked a particular line, we may need to modify the digits, let's say we got a lot of traffic to New Jersey and the organization has put in a direct line over to New Jersey. But the caller has put a 201 in the front of the number and so now that the call is switched onto a direct line to New Jersey, the 201 has to be taken off. The dial rules say do this, do that, keep first three digits, pause, cut the caller through, terminate procedure when call is connected, and so on. Now, let me figure the next . . ."

There was a beautiful, ravaged woman in my home now who needed nothing more than the physical comforts I could provide. But I was sentenced to listen to the fantasies of some fat computer wonk. I looked at Morrison, gave a half shake of my head. *Let's not get involved with these nuts.*

". . . so what we have to do for your situation is create a whole parallel body of routing instructions. When this fax machine makes a call, we want it to—wait, let me ask you this—are the faxes you're trying to intercept going to one particular country or company or going to one particular area code?"

"Why?" Morrison asked suspiciously.

"Because we have to create routing instructions that filter for the faxes you want to capture, unless you want to capture *all* of them, which adds a lot of extra work."

"Most of the faxes will be going back and forth between here and Germany," Morrison said casually. "Those are the ones we want."

"Good." DiFrancesco was now twiddling his beard into a greasy black spike that protruded from his chin. "That makes it easier. We're gonna take that call and say, route it as follows and we pick a local line, and instead of going to Germany, the call will be dialed to a seven-digit number, which will be one of *my* lines here in the city. Because I don't want to be detected, it goes to a number that is set to call forward to another number, and *that* other number is set to call forward to my operation. It goes through a couple of call-forwarding legs, just to make it harder to detect. So now the call goes through and my equipment connects. Then the call rules say *now* send the original number that was dialed, the 011 international code, then the Germany country code, and then the number in Germany—exactly the number originally dialed."

"This is too complicated," I said to Morrison. "I think that—"

"You've lost us," Morrison said to DiFrancesco.

"He's a genius." Shevesky nodded to me. "A genius."

". . . so then my equipment makes a bridged connection. Now in the process of setting this up, I have to be very careful setting up digit filters, because the hotel is going to *bill* this room for these calls and I have to make sure that none of these local-dial digits end up as part of the call record. It can't bill out as a local call. It's got to *look* like an international call on the bill. Okay, so the fax comes through my equipment and meantime, I've tape-recorded all the tones, for backup . . . now we've *trapped* the call. Then we have to decode the fax, but it's not simply a matter of attaching a fax machine and playing the recording into it."

"I don't get it," Morrison said.

"When you send a fax there's a little song and dance between the faxes where they ask each other are you a group-one or a group-two or a group-three fax machine, which are all different protocols. Then it might say, 'Are you a Sharp machine?' 'No, I'm a Ricoh or a Toshiba.' You know, each brand has its own rules. That complicates the decoding process."

DiFrancesco took a heavy-chested breath.

Shevesky looked at me. "A genius," he said.

"This is crazy," I told Morrison.

"So we need something that *listens* to the fax," DiFrancesco went on. "I take a PC-fax card, which is basically a specialized modem, and instead of running the fax card manufacturer's software on my PC, I can go in and write direct code to control the fax-modem chips actually on the board so that I can instruct it to *listen*, not transmit, and, based on that, I decode the tones back into digital representations of dark and light spaces in one strip of the document. Then all those strips become the document on my screen. Those strips won't be perfect. Line-feed information, page setup, and page-cut information won't be perfect. A couple of bagbiters will be in there somewhere. But you'll get the text. It might be exploded a little bit, the dots spread apart, and I might have to fool around with it on my screen, but you'll get the text."

"Okay," I interjected. "I think we know enough to—"

"*Now*," he continued, "that being said, there are two things that could foul this whole rig up. If the two faxes are speaking a *very* special dialect, then we're sunk. Chances are that won't be happening because the hotel will provide the fax machine, chances are we'll have two different brands and they'll have to talk the most common fax language, called universal group three. The other problem is what if they're sending back and forth more than text, if it's pictures, if it's pixel-oriented, then the degree of distortion—"

"Oh no, just text," Morrison said quietly, his tone different now, that of a man seeing a beautiful sunrise.

"Okay."

"We'll be able to read the text and translate it from the German?" he asked.

"Yes."

Morrison looked at me; we both knew who would be doing the translating.

"Now, what about incoming fax calls from Germany?"

DiFrancesco's massive face froze, his brain seemingly spinning inside its cavity. "You have to trap the incoming call *before* it gets to the fax machine in the room and starts kicking out information. So you create an extension. When a fax call from Germany comes into the PBX on that floor in the hotel, it gets discovered and bounced to a *new extension* and becomes a speed-dial number routed outbound through the automated routing service to my operation, just like we did with the calls originating from the hotel. I pass the call through my system and have my system dial back out, calling the original number that the fax came in on, but locally. Because it's a local call, the programming in the PBX now allows it to go through, just as it was supposed to when coming from Germany."

"*Yes,*" Morrison exclaimed. "I'm starting to get it."

"But I haven't told you the things that can go wrong."

"Tell us," I said unhappily.

"The maintenance company could find the reconfiguration and report it to the hotel. Also, the international transmission rate for faxes is ninety-six hundred baud a second, and even though the links to Germany are pretty good, by sending the calls downtown and through additional lines and everything, you're decreasing the volume of the connection. You're reducing the *quality* of that connection, so now you run the risk that you'll cause the fax machine to default to a fallback mode, because, see, if ninety-six hundred isn't working right, the fax machine will fall back to forty-eight hundred baud and the machines would be very slow. They might not notice it as important. They might think that the fax machine prints out so slowly or takes the page in so slowly because of the international transmission or bad New York Tel lines, or whatever. But there's another problem, too. All this rerouting of calls downtown and through my system and everything will probably add about fifteen seconds of setup time to both types of calls. *Maybe* it won't be noticed because these are international calls and people expect there to be a little slowness making them . . . but it's a perceptible issue, it's a weak link . . ."

"Fifteen seconds?" Morrison asked.

"About. But what I'm saying is that with each one of these things you're creating an *atmosphere* in which if someone decided to get suspicious they've got all kinds of evidence."

"We're not going to worry about these things," Morrison said. Now I knew why I was in this meeting. I was to be Morrison's dirty tricks bagman. He turned to me. "I want you to set Mike up somewhere and just get him going," he said.

"I only work out of my own location," Mike said quickly.

"How do we get in touch?"

"Here." Shevesky jumped forward and spread around a couple of business cards. "Get in touch with me."

"Okay," Morrison went on. "We'll get Mike to work."

"It's too risky," I said. "It could blow up in our faces. It's stupid as hell. We don't need it."

Morrison sat there, thinking. The framed photos of his retarded sons looked toward him, two scrubbed and smiling faces. If he'd had two normal sons, would he be who he was now? I knew he believed that the right sheet of paper could tell us what information the V-S negotiating team was sending their bosses back home. And if Samantha got anything out of Waldhausen, then it would be a way of checking the veracity of whatever he told her.

"How fast can you set up?" Morrison asked.

"Couple of days," DiFrancesco said.

Morrison glanced meaningfully at Shevesky and nodded. "You and I have worked out the billing—so that's it. We'll be in touch and you'll let Jack know what you have for us on a daily basis."

At the elevator, DiFrancesco asked me about the men's room.

"I'll show you," I said, leaving Shevesky at the receptionist's desk. In the back hallway, I said, "Listen, can you give me a real phone number, your actual number?"

He wrote it down on the business card Shevesky had given me.

"So what are your qualifications?"

He stroked his thick beard in sleepy contemplation. "I'm out on appeal pending a conviction in federal court last month for computer hacking. Class E felony."

"So who is this Shevesky?"

He loosened his tie with a yank. "Ah, he's just a suit who sets me up with jobs." He laughed into the mirror. He hadn't brushed his teeth in quite some time. When we returned, Shevesky was picking nervously at the mahogany framing around the elevator door. I gave him the smile.

"We'll be in touch."

I went back to Morrison's office. "I know what you're going to say, Jack," he exclaimed. "But it's not worth saying. If the deal goes through before they find out then it's an internal matter at most. If not, then a trivial suit we'll settle out of court."

I had to challenge him. "You want my opinion, which I'm sure you don't? This is totally fucking ridiculous. We have the best lawyers and bankers in New York running around trying to justify their fees and we have a floor of research departments and we don't need this rinky-dink shit."

"We might. It could help us."

"It's worth the risk? If they somehow found out, and reported it? The Corporation would suffer terrible public humiliation. Federal investigations, bad press here and internationally. Op-ed writers would moralize until the cows came home. Other companies we did business with would investigate if their communications had been compromised. The shareholder groups would attack. The SEC would immediately investigate. The stock price would crash. Anyone publicly connected with stealing V-S's faxes would be finished."

I didn't add that it was usually the detail guys like me who took the fall. Morrison was protected. He had an ironclad contract. He could be fired, he could quit, he could rape a ten-year-old boy on national television, and the Corporation *still* had to pay him two million dollars a year until he was ninety years old. I was just some guy in a business suit.

"This is wrong," I said.

Morrison drew invisible boxes on his desk with the index finger of his good hand. "You know what stockbrokers say when they try to get little old ladies to trade in their safe, little U.S. savings bonds for new stocks?" he asked.

"Tell me."

"No risk is a big risk."

I shook my head. "I won't do it. I'm already fondling the Chairman's brain for you. You get a look at DiFrancesco? This kid is a *kid*. He'll fuck it up somehow—"

From his desk drawer, Morrison pulled out a small pocketknife with handles of inlaid turquoise and picked at the remaining fingernails on his bad hand with the blade. On the other side of the world lay the scattered bones of Vietcong boys he had killed a quarter century prior. "They tell me he's the best there is."

"I won't do it."

"I want you to. I'll be very disappointed if you don't."

He picked with the knife quietly, intently, as if I weren't there. Perhaps he knew things I didn't. V-S might be screwing with the Corporation's negotiating team. Perhaps there were other players, the feared Japanese banks, as the Chairman had predicted.

Now Morrison looked up. "Well?"

"I predict that this will eventually be understood to be a stupid, costly mistake."

His irritation was unmistakable. "Hey, Jack," he grunted. "Don't you realize I don't give a fuck about your predictions?"

♦ ♦ ♦

When do we suddenly know we are on a steep and dangerous slope? I found my way to my office and shut the door, wondering what Morrison was doing with me. He was freezing me out, marginalizing me, setting me up. This was just the kind of tension that my internist had told me to avoid. And it didn't help that a homeless woman and her child were probably now in my house that very moment, doing God knew what. I got out one of my little plastic bags and the can of aerosol air freshener. None of them knew I did this, not even Samantha. I waited, wanting it to happen. Then I felt the burning in my throat, the dragon, and vomited in bitter, methodical silence into the bag. And again. It always hurts; I've never gotten used to it. I sprayed the oily bile with the aerosol before tying off the bag and dropping it into the trash. Above me the air-conditioning duct vibrated and droned, resonant of boilers and miles of pipes, as if the Corporation were a fat ocean liner under way, where the party was up on the top deck under the stars and where sooner or later a few of the revelers would be thrown overboard.

SEVEN

aybe she had taken my twenty-dollar bill and hit the streets. I
rode the subway home that evening and lingered under the leaves
of the Japanese maple in front of my house in the last long light of
the day, nervously wondering if Dolores and her daughter would be
inside, and whether I wanted them to be there or not. Old Mrs.
Cronister, now dead, had shown me where she'd kept a spare house
key hidden wedged in a joint between the slabs of brownstone, and I
retrieved it and pushed through the front door.

Dolores and Maria were sitting on the couch in the living room,
facing the high windows fronting the street. Their belongings were set
next to the stairs. Nothing in the room had been touched or moved or
changed, but as soon as I saw them everything was different. They
were *in my house*. I wasn't sure how to greet them. It seemed stupid to
shake hands. Somehow we were already beyond formalities.

"You made it all right, then?" My words echoed loudly. I wasn't
used to hearing my voice at home.

"Yes. I locked the door soon as we came in and we just been
sitting here. I gave her a little milk from the refrigerator—"

"That's fine . . ." Maria wriggled close to her mother and watched
me. ". . . of course." I pulled off my coat and loosened my tie, stalling
for time to think. "So—" The question hung in the space between us.
Dolores lifted her dark eyes toward me and they seemed to peer into
me and yet beyond; I learned nothing from looking directly in them
except that I was experiencing again that same weakness that I'd felt
first seeing Dolores on the subway; she was incomprehensibly beautiful. How could she not realize how I felt? And then, seeing that same
gruesome bruise next to her brow, now healing, I realized that it was
only survival that Dolores cared about at the moment. The falling
light from the windows showed the shadows of exhaustion and worry

in her face. Her lips were apart, as if she was about to say something. "So," I began again, "you don't have any place to stay tonight, I'm assuming."

"No, Mr. Whitman."

"Jack," I corrected her.

"Okay."

Our words were bouncing off the high ornate plaster ceilings. "You're welcome to stay here . . . stay for a couple of days," I stammered, trying to sound casual, "or whatever . . ."

She let out a tense little breath of relief. "I really appreciate this . . . I don't know how everything got so messed up. Me, I can take anything, but she's just a little girl, you know."

I nodded silently. The brass heat register rattled quietly as a train passed beneath. Maria took her mother's hand and played with several of the fingers, counting them softly to herself, and in the sweetness of this, I saw that no matter what happened next, at least I was that moment providing this child with a place to sleep.

Dolores looked around the room, her eyes resting on the sliding French doors leading into the dining room. "I never saw a house like this."

"Well, they used to make them with all the mahogany woodwork and everything."

"I always lived in apartments," Dolores went on. "I lived in little apartments my whole life."

I was looking at her eyes and nose and lips. I didn't respond.

"And this furniture?" she asked.

"My wife bought a lot of it."

Maria hopped off her mother's lap. "I like it!"

"We kind of peeked into the other rooms, you know, to look," Dolores admitted, with a hint of a smile. "Just on this floor. It's so big. You could put three or four apartments in this house, *easy*."

I realized that it was late and they had probably not eaten any dinner. I ordered some Chinese food for the three of us and then led Dolores and Maria down the stairs to the apartment on the garden floor, feeling her eyes on the back of my shirt. The apartment still needed work, but the paint was reasonably fresh, and the bedroom backed onto the small brick patio and flower beds, where the summer jungle of morning glories was getting started. "I used to rent it out," I told Dolores. "When my last tenant lost his job and left town, I never got around to renting it again. Here, there's a bed and table and stuff. I don't actually need the room. It was going to waste, no one was here."

Dolores looked at me as if I'd protested too much. The light had faded from the sky but we went out to the back and stood intimately under the dark maple trees. Maria set about the garden, touching the flowers, luminous in the dusk.

"I just need to ask you a few questions," I said to Dolores quietly. "I would have asked this afternoon, but I didn't have any time. I need to ask about your husband, what the story is with him."

She nodded. "Hector is very angry I left him, you know? We were a family but I left him with Maria—things got too crazy."

"What happened?" I asked instinctively.

"Nothing happened," Dolores responded. "I just—things got too crazy and we kept fighting and everything." She looked away from me. "We didn't have any money, things were always hard, you know."

"Could he come here, looking for you?"

"No, because he doesn't know we're here," she said. "He won't hurt anybody, not really."

This about a man who had butchered two dogs. I felt a need to know this Hector, know who I might be dealing with. So I pressed the issue. "What does he do for a living?" I asked.

"How many questions you got?" Dolores said irritably.

I reminded myself that she was probably exhausted and just as scared as grateful to have a place to sleep.

"Look, Dolores," I said gently, "your husband—Hector is his name?—he tore the hell out of my friend Ahmed's place. He smashed windows and broke a hole in a wall and killed two dogs looking for you. I have a right to know this. Just tell me, I mean, is Hector jealous, or—"

"He's not going to hurt anybody."

"Just tell me something about the guy, okay? So I know what I'm getting myself into."

Dolores watched Maria touch the flowers. "Hector's always done a lot a different jobs," she answered dully, as if trying only to convey information, without consciously acknowledging any memories. "You know, anything to make money. He used to clean rich people's apartments. Vacuum and wax and everything. And he used to have a store that sold linoleum and stuff, maybe like four years ago. Now he installs cable. And he sells cars on the weekends. He works hard."

"Installs cable?" I asked.

"Cable TV. They put in the cable all over Queens and Brooklyn. He brings in the little wire from the trunk cable into the house. They also put the satellite dish on the roof."

"So he's the one who works for Big Apple Cable?" I concluded.

Dolores nodded. "That was why when you gave me your card, I knew about the company you work at. Remember, in your office? I told you I knew somebody who worked at the cable company and that was Hector."

"You said he sells cars too?"

"On the weekends, there's a lot down on Fifth Avenue near where we used to live."

"Where's that?"

"Sunset Park."

I was vaguely familiar with the area—a working-class Brooklyn neighborhood of apartment buildings and modest row homes many blocks to the south, heavily Hispanic and Chinese, bordered by the sprawling Greenwood Cemetery to the north, where something like a half a million souls were buried. I'd become lost in Sunset Park once, after getting off the Brooklyn-Queens Expressway at the wrong exit.

"New cars?"

"Used," Dolores said. "They don't give him much time, only the shifts the regular salesmen don't want, like Friday night and Sunday morning."

"Does he make any money from it?"

She shrugged, watching Maria. "Maybe once every couple of months he sells a little bit to make a decent commission, you know."

"What's the name of the place?" I asked casually.

"The name?"

"Yes—"

"Why?"

"I don't know. No particular reason."

"Waitaminute. I'm done talking about him."

"Okay." It didn't matter. How many secondhand car places could there be near Sunset Park? Three or four at most. I knew enough to find Dolores's husband if I ever needed to, without going through the Corporation.

"Okay, there's something *I* need to talk about." Dolores's dark eyes watched mine for signs of disapproval. "I hate to ask for more charity, but I don't have enough money for things like food."

"Eat whatever I have," I told her. "Of course. Anything in the house."

"Thank you. Also, I need to get some stuff for Maria, you know, very cheap, like a plastic hairbrush, maybe two dollars—"

"You can get it for her tomorrow. I'll make sure you have some money. Whatever she needs. Clothes, whatever."

"I guess—I guess I don't know what our *arrangement* is," Dolores said, looking hard at me.

"Anything reasonable Maria needs I'm happy to pay for," I explained. "And for you too."

"But no one *asked* you to pay." Dolores frowned.

"That's right."

"I mean, this wasn't exactly what you had in mind when you gave me your card on the train, right?"

I shrugged. "I never expected this, no. I didn't expect anything, actually. Did I want this to happen? Probably not. Do I mind? No. Is it weird? Yes."

"Is this called moss?" came Maria's voice. She was stooped down on the bricks.

Dolores looked over at her daughter. "Yes, *mi'ja.*" She turned back to me. "I'm not some homeless person, okay? I always lived in an apartment and we had food in the refrigerator and things. We paid our bills, okay? You know what I'm saying? My father worked until the day he died and that's what kind of background I got. I'm not some kind of some lazy ass—"

"Dolores, you don't need to say this—"

"Yes, I do gotta say it. I want you to know that I'm not somebody just off the street, like. It's just . . . things got messed up with my husband. And I don't have any money."

"Okay, I understand." I heard the front doorbell. "That's our food."

"I mean, what am I supposed to *do?*" Dolores continued as we went inside. "Come on, Maria, we're going to eat. Just ask for the money? I don't like doing that."

I looked into her anxious, lovely eyes. The small sum that Dolores and Maria might cost was infinitely more meaningful to me than the piles of cash and debt and profit we tossed around at the Corporation. But I could see that Dolores and I needed to begin with some sort of formal understanding. She wanted to know where she stood. She had pride.

"Basically, Dolores, you and Maria don't have a place to go, right? Against my better judgment, perhaps, I've taken you in. If you want to leave, you're free to do that at any time." I walked to the front door under the stoop and paid the delivery man. He'd come on a bicycle. "But while the two of you are here, I'll take care of you, meaning I'll pay, within my ability, for food, necessary clothing—whatever is sensible. For how long, I don't know. A few days, a week, more, whatever. I don't *expect* that you'll stay and I don't expect that you'll go. I don't expect anything. I don't have a plan. I'm making this up as I go along. I'm doing it because I want to. No expectations. You don't need to feel—I'm saying you don't owe me—okay?"

She just looked at me.

"If there's something you want me to buy at the supermarket—"

"Wait—" Dolores interrupted, shaking her head. "Wait a minute."

"What?"

"I just want to be *sure*. Just because you don't have any expectations doesn't mean I don't. Now I got to ask a few questions, okay?"

I nodded.

She glanced up the stairs. "First off, who else lives in this house?"

"No one." I set the steaming cardboard cartons out on the table. There were still a few odd plates and silverware in the apartment's cupboard and I got those.

"This whole house?"

"Just me."

"You drink?" she inquired, folding her arms together. "I mean you get drunk?"

"Rarely. I relax with it, you know."

"You got drugs in this house? I won't have Maria around people who do crack."

"I would never use crack, not in a million fucking years, Dolores," I told her, remembering Roynell Wilkes, who did use it. "I tried drugs years ago but not since then. What about you? You do drugs?"

"I swear on my father's grave no."

"Good."

"You gonna keep your hands off of Maria?"

I looked at Dolores, stunned that she could even ask that. But some men would touch a child. "I'm not going to do anything—"

"Because I don't want to come home someday and find you doing something, okay, you know what I'm talking about, and then hear you say that it was just friendly, you know?"

"Yes," I began in irritation. "But—"

"Because I'll kill you if you touch her." Dolores whipped a straight hand through the air. She stared at me, her lips set tightly against each other.

"We've got to have respect going both ways here, Dolores."

"I don't like shrimps!" Maria said, pointing at one of the containers of Chinese food. "I want chicken."

Dolores spooned some food onto Maria's plate. "Maria, you eat that, it's good." She looked back at me. "She's all I got left. I figure the deal is like this: You trust me with your house and I trust you with my daughter."

"Fine."

"Number three," Dolores said. "I'm not a cleaning woman. I'll clean up after Maria and myself and everything, but I'm not making your bed or washing out your toilet or any of that."

"Of course not," I told her.

"I mean, I'm gonna go out and get myself a job soon as I get some rest. Then I'll be moving out. I'll be out of here real soon."

"There's no rush so far as—"

"*Now*," Dolores interrupted, appearing to have a complete list in her head, "the last thing. You better not be expecting *sex*." She gave a derisive laugh, almost a snort. "Because *that's* just not part of the deal. I mean, we kidded around back at the hotel, okay, but that was just kidding around, so I want to get straight on that. You might be thinking that I'm gonna pay up that way, you know? No way."

"Look," I answered, "I'd be lying if I said you weren't an attractive woman, but just remember, Dolores, I wasn't planning to invite you to come live with—"

"Well, I don't see a new wife or girlfriend here and no *sign* of one neither, so if you think I'm gonna fuck you for my room and board, then you got another thing coming, you got a lot of things coming and they're not too nice."

"I do understand—"

"'Cause *that* has only gotten me in trouble." Dolores gave a dismissive little wave with her slender brown hand. "I've had enough of *that*."

We ate the rest of dinner in a difficult silence and afterward I left them to take a walk around the neighborhood to contemplate the new situation. Outside the stoop I looked back through the ground-floor windows and saw that Dolores had already set about straightening up the apartment. She's scared and tired and strung out, I told myself, but then again, maybe you are a fool and this is an immense mistake. I'd taken them off the street and all I'd received from her was grief. Of course I could simply change my mind and kick the two of them out of the house. But I would never do that, not now. The little girl seemed happy to be here. It might be sort of interesting to have the two of them in the house; I'd never ever truly gone out of my way for my fellow human being. Not in the manner of my father, who had spent many thousands of hours quietly listening to the members of his congregation—deaths and divorce and family ruin. His son was not the type to feed the hungry, clothe the naked. And, of course, I was acting out of self-interest, a desire to fill the house with lives other than my own. Liz and I had envisioned the two unused bedrooms on the top floor as children's rooms, and now they were empty. The echo and the unfilled shadows of these rooms mocked my old intentions to be a husband and a father. No child-sized bed, no toy box or child's dresser or dolls or reading books or any of it. We'd been a few days away from buying a crib and a changing table when Liz was killed. And I'm glad we never did buy that stuff, for I would have never been able to get rid of it. As it was, I still had all of Liz's clothes and books and shoes, her papers and hairbrushes—everything. What should you do with the belongings of the dead? You should examine them, put them in a box, and give them to a church. I knew this but I hadn't done it.

As I walked through the street shadows, I passed office workers from Manhattan getting off the subways, streaming to their homes. There were couples among them, a few even holding hands. If the city could capriciously take a woman and child from me, I wondered, couldn't it quite inexplicably give them *back*, in the form of a different woman and a different child?

◆ ◆ ◆

When I returned to my house, I heard the water rushing through the copper pipes into the deep old claw-footed bathtub in the apartment bathroom. I passed through the kitchen, where Dolores had cleaned up the dinner plates. The door to the bathroom was shut and I crept close.

"My little fish!" came Dolores's voice. "Swimming!"

Maria giggled and I heard the splash of water.

"Careful. We don't want to get water on the floor."

"I *like* being wet," cried Maria.

"You *want* to be a little fish!" Dolores responded. "Now here, *mi vida*, let me put my feet under the hot water."

I crouched at the door and peered through the old brass keyhole. Dolores and Maria were sitting in the deep bathtub together, their backs toward me. I couldn't see much, just a bit of water on the floor, the white lip of the enameled bathtub, and a curve of Dolores's bare dark back.

"Is this where we live now?" Maria asked.

"I don't know," Dolores answered wearily. "The man is going to let us sleep here a little while and then Mommy is going to figure out what to do next. That's all I know, Maria."

"Mommy's figuring out what to do next," Maria repeated.

"Yes."

"Oh, don't worry, honey," Maria said, mimicking her mother.

"Here, let me soap your hair." I saw an arm reach forward. "Push up some."

"My big toes are as big as your little toes," Maria answered over the steamy rush of the tub. And they went on, with happy nonsense about why soap is slippery and the temperature of the water and cleaning under the fingernails. And big knees and small knees. It was an intimate singsong language and Dolores sounded silly and relaxed in a way I had not seen. Perhaps there was a simple reassurance in touching and being touched by her naked little daughter. I crouched lower, trying to see more, but worried I'd make the floor creak. Dolores would hear me and whip her head around and know she was being watched. And that would confirm her distrust of me. But still I huddled next to the keyhole, spying not much more than what I'd seen before, except for Maria's plump little hand dangling over the edge of the tub. Dolores leaned forward to turn off the water and when the pipes screeched and vibrated I took the opportunity to slink away.

I paced about the half-empty apartment, wondering what they might need, and speculating too on how Dolores might act when she had rested and eaten regular meals. I plugged in the refrigerator and then opened the door; the plastic shelves were rife with mold. In the apartment's kitchen, I noticed a tiny packet on the counter. One side was a piece of cloth and the other clear plastic. I knew my old tenant hadn't left it. Inside the packet was a tiny golden hand holding a cross and several very small pieces of wood, some sort of beans and seeds, a shell from a nut, pieces of stone, several beads, a small chunk of quartz. Except for the small golden hand, the contents were un-remarkable—no more interesting than the stuff that collected in the pockets of a child. But the packet had been sewn together with obvious attention, and on the paper side was a short typewritten prayer. I fumbled in my pockets for a piece of paper. In the few minutes before Dolores and Maria finished their bath I hastily copied the prayer onto a bank machine slip:

Oh potentose amuleto
Por la virtud que tu
Tienes y la que Dios
Te dió dame suerte, paz
Armonia, tranquilidad
Salud, empleo y propiedad
Para mi y para los mios.
Que salga el mal y que
Entre el bien como entro
Jesucristo a la casa santa.

Dolores emerged dressed from the bathroom holding Maria in a towel, her wet hair flattened backward. I pretended I hadn't seen the packet and busied myself with an inspection of the wooden shutters in the front parlor. Dolores casually swept the packet into her handbag and asked me if I had any clean sheets, I'd forgotten that she and Maria would need them.

"All that stuff is in the hall closet, blankets, everything," I said, trying to make them feel at home. "Now, there's no food down here so just take whatever you want from my kitchen upstairs. Eat breakfast up there tomorrow, too. I've got some cereal and juice and toast. I'll leave the door to the stairs unlocked."

"Okay. Thanks." She pulled out a folded pair of clean pajamas for Maria from her bag.

"You have stuff for her?"

"Mrs. Rosenbluth had these, they were her grandson's."

I realized that Dolores didn't have anything to sleep in. In the closest upstairs were half a dozen old nightgowns that had been Liz's, all of them reasonably chaste, but it didn't seem right to offer them.

"Thanks for dinner." Dolores fitted Maria's feet into the slippered legs of the pajamas. "It's sort of strange to say that, you know?"

"It's just as strange for me as it is for you."

"We're going to bed now. She's going to sleep with me. We're tired."

"I've got a spare TV I could bring down."

"That's okay."

I turned to go.

"Oh, can I ask you a little favor?" Dolores asked.

"Sure."

"Do you have a little glass jar?"

I didn't want to ask why. "Under the sink," I replied.

◆ ◆ ◆

I slept terribly, listening to the darkness. Somewhere in the night I heard Maria crying and Dolores comforting her. The sound bounced right up the stairwell from two floors below. Why would she cry? The sound broke my heart. Then silence and time passed. I felt the size of my bed, I rolled around in the sheets with an erection, miserable, thinking about Dolores, worrying about Waldhausen and Beales and what, if anything, I could do to convince the Chairman to approve the deal with Volkman-Sakura. When I am in bed, the acid insinuates itself into my throat more easily, and I lay there feeling it burn upward. Maybe it was the first stages of "Barrett's esophagus." I reached toward my bed table for another nizatidine pill. From the open window came the underhum of the night—cars and faraway sirens and the remote throb of the subway, making the windowpanes tinkle ever so quietly. My thoughts turned toward my argument with Morrison over using DiFrancesco to get the V-S faxes. How odd it was that Morrison always understood that I would do what he told me. He knew my age, my ambition; he knew there is a particular moment in the lives of young executives when they believe—as if it were a freshly minted idea just come to them and to them alone—that hard work (I mean grunt work, the pushing of papers and forms, the meticulous presentation of reports that will languish unseen for weeks and then be skimmed quickly by superiors, the religious calculation of the schedule of promotions and bonuses, the cunning pretension of enthusiasm for banal projects, the pursuit of scraps of praise from malcontented and even sadistic bosses) will bring them all they desire—money, yes, but even more important, the knowledge of their own essence. He'd been there. He knew I was driven.

And for that I have my mother to blame, for during my childhood her voice was forever telling me that enough was never good enough. She was loving, she thought, but was never satisfied with me. I got the grades, I did what I was supposed to do, but it was not enough. Her eyes withheld final approval, as if praise might sate me and I would then go no further, as if I might yet prove to be my father's son. She did not consciously know she was doing this of course, and I have forgiven her in the rationalized manner of an adult. My mother, these days, is up early and showered, while Harry sleeps the dreams of the well pensioned. Their house on the Gulf coast cost $920,000. She is sixty-one years old. She is thinking of things, but they do not include me. If certain unfortunate events have occurred in her son's life, it is not her affair. She worries about what will happen to Harry if she dies first. Of course, if *he* dies first she'll be fine. She is looking toward the first tee-off. This is what she cares about. For her age, she's an excellent golfer, wins senior women's tournaments in the region. She drinks her coffee in the car. The golf course clubhouse is close enough that she could walk, but her foursome of women like to be the first to tee off in the morning. The greens, softened by the night moistness, cushion the teeshots and slow the putts. You get a lower score that way, and my mother has always kept score. Yet her own private world is never revealed. She could dream each night of being ravished by the Miami Dolphins and no one would ever suspect. My mother has her sunglasses on in the car and the sunscreen lipstick greasing her mouth. Her teeth have been whittled down to stumps and then recapped; her new smile is beautiful and grotesque in its youthfulness; it aggressively repulses certain widows at the golf club from being too friendly with Harry. Her hair is expertly colored and cut in the manner of the leisurely retired. Her diamond engagement ring, with four stones each as big as a kernel of corn, is kept in the box on her dresser—it interferes with her golf grip. She holds her coffee in one hand and smoothly steers the big Mercedes with the other. What is in her head? I don't know, maybe I never knew. She has not telephoned me in over three years. It is up to me and I call every month or so. I end up talking about the equities market with Harry. He asks me about the Corporation's stock price and I remind him that federal securities law bars me from discussing it with him. For all I know, he could go off and buy a block of stock and start telling his club buddies to do the same. Once men like Harry reach a certain age, they expect to be forgiven small white-collar crimes—they've earned it, they've paid taxes for forty years. This is why Harry always asks. My mother resents it that I don't tell him. After all that he did for me, she says: the roof over my head, the tennis lessons, the years of school tuition, my first car. "You should be grateful," she scolds me. "Come visit New York, Mom," I respond. "I'll take you to a show. Some good restaurants. It'd give me a lot of pleasure." There's a pause. "I can't," she answers. "I'm terribly busy right now." Of course, she is not busy, but I do not press her. I miss my mother and I have missed her for a long time but I do not know what to do about it.

And how absurd it is that she was once married to my father, who each morning places his knotty, pained feet upon a cold, plain wooden floor, alone, the minister who no longer can minister, a stooped man so poor he buys the supermarket's generic brand of macaroni, a man who watches television with too much credulousness. As soon as I hit the big money at the Corporation, I paid off the remaining six years of payments on his small house and arranged to have three thousand dollars a month transmitted electronically from my money market account to his checking account. I would have sent him more but he didn't want it, and he gave away half of what I sent him. Did he want to live with me? I asked. No, he told me, he couldn't possibly leave his garden. And a few older members of the church still came around for solace. He was starting to have prostate trouble, he'd told me, and, I could see, was slouching toward a soft-edged senescence. He was a slender, pale wreck of a man, a soap peeling of a man. His failure had driven my success. It is unlikely that I have the parents I do, but so too was it unlikely that my wife should die by a random bullet and that in my loneliness I had invited strangers into my house. But there it is.

♦ ♦ ♦

Morning came with an insistent slapping on my shoulder. Then a tiny finger poking my arm. I opened my eyes and Maria, standing next to the bed, waited for me to see her. "Is 'Sesame Street' on?"

"Oh, good morning," I croaked.

"Good morning, Jack."

I squeezed my eyes. "What is *your* name?"

"Maria!" She pushed me onto my side. Her hair had been brushed and was pinned back with two red plastic barrettes.

"Maria who?"

"Maria Salcines."

"Do you want to watch 'Sesame Street'?" I asked.

"No!"

"I like your earrings." Tiny gold studs.

"I like, I like . . . I like your funny hair!"

She had a bit of hot cereal on her little T-shirt.

"Did you have pancakes for breakfast?"

"No," she answered playfully, holding one arm behind herself with the other and rocking on one foot.

"Did you have chocolate ice cream?"

"No!"

"Maria," Dolores's voice came up the stairs, "you get down here."

"It's all right," I called toward my open doorway.

"She's not supposed to be bothering you."

I turned to Maria. "Did you milk the cow for breakfast?"

"No, don't be *silly*." She climbed onto the bed and I helped her up.

"Why do you sleep like a big dog?" Maria asked, sitting on the bed, bouncing slightly.

"Because I'm tired."

"Why?"

"Because I go to work."

"*Maria!*" came Dolores's furious voice. "You come down now!"

Maria ignored her mother. "What do you *do* at work?"

"Make mean faces at everyone."

"No you don't. You talk on the telephone."

"That's true."

"Are you going to marry Mommy?"

I wasn't sure how to answer. "She's already married to your dad," I said.

Maria grew somber thinking about this. Her dark eyes became unfocused and she seemed to be trying to understand something. "He . . . was . . . we left because he was very *bad*," she told herself.

Her confusion and desire to explain it to herself disturbed me. I remembered my own confusion as a child when I realized my parents had split up.

"Do you think I should eat breakfast?" I asked, hoping to break the spell.

Maria's face brightened. "No! It's too hot!"

"But I'll be *tired* if I don't eat breakfast." I slid out of the covers, meeting the world in a motley costume of stained T-shirt and sweatpants. "Did you eat oatmeal for breakfast?"

"Yes!" she said. "How did you know?"

"A tiny bug told me."

"No."

"You had raisins in your oatmeal, right?"

"Yes," she said slowly.

"Well, one of them *wasn't* a raisin, it was a *bug* watching you. And when you weren't looking it flew up out of the cereal and came to me and told me what you were doing."

She searched my face for a smile. "Is that true?" Maria asked.

"Oh, it could be."

"You have a hairy stomach!" she exclaimed.

"That's because my grandfather was a hairy old bear."

"No!" she screamed in delight.

"I have to take a shower and dress now," I said. "Will you tell your mother I'll be down in a few minutes?"

"No!" She stared at me with brazen happiness. "Okay."

When I came down the stairs fifteen minutes later, Dolores was in the kitchen with Maria standing on a footstool at the sink.

Maria looked at her mother. "Mommy, there was no bug in my cereal, right?"

I smelled eggs. "No," she said. "Who told you such a funny thing?"

"Jack did."

She looked at me and smiled an adult smile. "He's kidding. He made it all up."

I flopped the newspaper open, scanned the usual proofs of man's folly in the headlines. "Yes," I said, "I made it all up."

"Sit," she said, waving a spatula.

"Did I have eggs in the refrigerator?"

"No. Maria and I went out before you woke up. They're expensive around here."

"The Korean grocers know people will pay it."

"And I borrowed twenty dollars that was in the dish," she said. "You needed food in this house. You had so little—"

"Fine."

"I got the receipt for everything," she said fiercely.

She handed the slip to me. I crumpled it and threw it in the trash.

"I haven't had eggs in months," I told her. "I've missed them."

She put a plate down in front of me. "You had four boxes of cereal. Stale. You can't just have cold cereal every day."

"Why not?" I picked up my fork.

"It's pathetic, that's why."

I saw her smile, just a bit.

"Ah, well, I'm a pathetic kind of guy, you see."

"No," Dolores said, putting a glass of orange juice in front of me. "I don't think so."

◆ ◆ ◆

An hour later, in the bookstore in the underground concourse in Rockefeller Plaza that led to the Corporation building, I bought a Spanish dictionary and book of grammar. Spanish is an easy language compared to German. The verb endings are simpler, the words closer to English. Between the early phone calls, I worked out the message I'd copied from the packet. I was at work on this when Samantha spun into my office on her long heels.

"Here I am," she announced, lifting her coffee cup.

"Well?" I asked. "Herr Waldhausen?"

"Oh, we just had a *drink*." Samantha gave a coy little flip of her hand. She looked great, as usual, in her trim business suit and perfect nails and hair tucked away. "He's not *nearly* the man he *seems* to be. Not like in the meetings. We talked and talked! He has an unhappy marriage, his wife had an affair with the man who drives their *children* to school, and he's very upset. I *listened*."

"Listened."

"Don't be silly. It was just a *drink*."

"I had to defend your reputation to Beales."

"Mmmn?" she asked, sipping her coffee.

"He had you scripted for a night at the amusement park."

"It wasn't like *that*. Otto is quite the gentleman."

Samantha's eye drifted inward then, just perceptibly.

"He say anything about the meeting?" I asked.

"He said it's their style to sit back for a few days before warming up. He told me not to worry."

"You tell this to Morrison?"

"Yes, when he called my apartment last night at eleven."

"Samantha?"

"Mmn?"

"I just want you to know that I defended your reputation. It was tough but somebody had to do it."

"I think everybody should know me well enough by *now* to *know*."

"Yes, Samantha."

"Oh, stop." She twisted her head to look at my desk. "What's that? A Spanish dictionary?"

"As a matter of fact."

"Are you studying Spanish?"

I didn't want Samantha to know that Dolores was living in my house. "Yes."

She looked at me slyly.

"Sounds secret."

"We all have our secrets, Samantha, even you."

She could see from my face that she wasn't going to find out. "Well, I suppose so!" And then she jumped up and was gone, her blond hair bouncing after her. I continued translating the words that Dolores carried with her and when done, I was reminded of my father blessing the simple meals he and I had together when I was a boy, just the two of us in his small clapboard house in upstate New York. Dolores's prayer read, more or less:

Oh potent Charm
for the truth that you
have and that of God,
I ask you to give me luck, peace,

harmony, tranquility,
health, work, property
for me and for mine.
That the evil leaves and that
the good enters as entered Jesus to the sacred house.

My father is a man of God, yet I have never believed in prayers,
though I wish I did.

◆ ◆ ◆

Late that morning, Morrison stomped down the hall, opening
office doors and jabbing his index finger toward the conference room.
"Meeting. Everybody." His eyes were wide and despite the robust
air-conditioning on the thirty-ninth floor a sheen of sweat glimmered
at his temples. I think he'd been drinking too much coffee for so many
years that it permanently changed his metabolism. People passed
along the carpeted hallway in the hush of emergency. In the conference room there was no time to jockey for the better seats. Morrison, last in, shut the door behind him and began talking: "We have
information that within a day or so, Osada Holdings Co. will take a
big position in Chukado Electronics Corp. About a three-billion-
dollar deal. Chukado bought out MEC Systems in '91 because they
were working on a rival chip. The rival chip was maybe fifteen percent
better, I'm told, and they went ahead with it. Maybe you heard of it,
the WEKS chip. It's particularly good at integrating software and
digital images. An earlier version was used for—uh, help me here,
Samantha—"

She picked up the sentence without so much as a breath of a
pause, looking around the room as she began. "It was used for com-
puter-aided animations, in which the computer could take two images
of the same object in motion—say a man throwing a ball—and fill in
all the images in between, based on an extensive CD-ROM memory
of all positions human beings are capable of, the anatomy of the
shoulder joint, and so on. A lot of that work is showing up now in
the multimedia ROM software products just in the market now, running mostly on DOS-based systems. You get the idea. The chips
saved thousands of hours of animation labor. This was in '90. The
one guy—"

"The *wacko genius*," Morrison interrupted, squinting his eyes, "there's always a genius in a story like this—"

"Right, there's this obscure Japanese guy who supposedly goes on long walks and arranges sticks and fishbones and pieces of grass by himself and then dreams up these brilliant chip ideas," Samantha reported, unimpressed by the private rituals of inspiration. "Or *something* like that. He retired after the first chip but they brought him back and now Chukado almost has his new chip ready so now Osada is going to suck up a large part, certainly a controlling interest, maybe forty-five percent." I wondered if she had ever slept with Morrison. One always wonders if people in the office are doing it, and sometimes they are. Morrison and Samantha had that ease, that tremor of intimacy in their voices when they spoke to each other. On the other hand, it was unlikely. On the third hand, there was my own history with Samantha, which I'll get around to.

"They saw that chip and got hungry real fast," Morrison added. "I mean, wham, like a fish hitting a lure. Nobody saw this coming. Three billion. That shows there's capital out there, guys. Osada already owns what, seventeen, eighteen percent of Volkman-Sakura?"

"Eighteen point six percent," Samantha answered. "With twelve percent actual voting rights. And V-S owns twenty-nine percent of Osada, from before the merger between Volkman and Sakura."

Morrison pulled a cigar out of his breast pocket, stuck it in his mouth, and used a silver lighter with his good hand to light it. "Okay," he puffed, "obviously all these Japanese guys who were all in the navy together fifty years ago still play golf or hang around in steam baths or whatever old guys do in Japan. Osada is going to be able to take the technology from Chukado, specifically this new chip, and give it straight to V-S."

"Everybody said vertical integration wasn't going to work, not after the problems Mitsubishi and Sony had," Beales noted.

"I know," Morrison said. "You're right. But a lot of those problems happened when the global economy was starting to contract. It's wasn't the *idea* that was necessarily wrong, it was the timing. The cycle is turning now, anyway."

"But wait, I still don't see how the Japanese companies have the cash for these deals," Beales went on. "Everybody in Japan is half-dead from the stock crash. The real estate market is down something like forty percent."

"The guys who were shorting the market made billions, Ed," I said. "The *smart* guys."

"Yeah, but those guys aren't the same guys who—"

"How do you know?"

Beales shot his hands up in the air, a gesture of reasonableness in the face of a madman holding a gun. Like an actor on one of the Corporation's crummy TV dramas, he shot a *meaningful* glance at Morrison, but Morrison wasn't going to help Beales out, he was going to let the two of us go at each other.

"I *don't* know for sure," Beales answered, "but I'm just raising the possibility that we really don't need to be worried by this thing."

"We don't really know who has cash over there, Ed," I said. "Remember—somebody *started* that crash, somebody who everybody was watching sold at the top and sent the signal. I bet one or two of the banks sold out their Tokyo real estate and then stopped lending. They'll buy out the bankruptcies at the bottom of the cycle. So—"

"I can't agree with—" Beales began.

"*So*, there is cash out there. And, anyway, a lot of the Japanese companies are still making big money in South Korea and Indonesia. These are companies with one-hundred-year plans. We can't assume any weakness on the part of our competitors." I addressed the rest of the group. "More generally, I would urge us to ask ourselves, what are these companies trying to achieve? How do their goals conflict with our goals? I think the answer to that is scary, frankly. I really do. They want what we want. They have their own version of it, but ultimately, they want just what we want, the markets, the technologies. And they're starting to move in on the talent. We've had a good grip on that for a while, but that could erode. And this new chip will allow faster manipulation of images—"

"They'll get the jump on the virtual-reality entertainment programming, those helmets that you can wear that will provide complete sensory range," Samantha said. "Most of the stuff out there now is pretty crude. But it's coming, about two or three years away. Jack, you know a lot about this."

"Yes," I began, "the technology is developing so quickly that—"

"Wait, we need to stay focused here," Morrison said. "It's a huge step, at least in the next six-month time frame. Here's our problem, as I see it. This information will be around the world within a day. V-S will have the technological means to get out in front within a short period, without buying a ton of our stock in a merger. I think that we need to press our deal harder. We may need to argue for *our* technology more. We need to figure out what they're thinking." Was Morrison going to mention DiFrancesco? I hoped not. It was embarrassing that I was handling it. "We need to get them to stop farting around. Get them interested. We don't want them to walk away from the table. It could happen. Deals just disappear. And the V-S people may have more confidence in their own new products than in what we can provide them. And also, if they go forward with what this chip can do, that's going to sop up a lot of their extra cash—"

There was a gentle knock on the conference room door and Helen poked her head in, her eyes searching for me.

"Yes?" Morrison said in great irritation.

"I'm sorry—" Helen began.

"What could it possibly be? Big news?" Morrison asked. "Los Angeles fell into the ocean? No, don't tell me. Pakistan nuked India? China sold Hong Kong?"

"I have a phone call for Jack," she answered apologetically.

"Helen," I said, "can't you tell him—"

"What is it, an emergency?" Morrison interrupted. "We have our own emergency *here*, blooming in our faces, like a fireball."

"I'm sorry. He *insists*," Helen protested. "I tried—"

The delay was aggravating the room. I got up and left.

"I told him you were in a meeting," Helen explained as we walked back to my office. "He was *so* rude. I told him that you were not to be disturbed but he said you were just pushing around toilet paper from one end of the table to the next. He actually said that."

I picked up the phone.

"Jack, when will I be free of these troubles that you make for me?" It was Ahmed, speaking with murderous calm. "Today a man comes to my building and he demands to know where the woman is. And I tell him I do not know what woman he means and he says many unpleasant things to me that are disrespectful in front of my men."

"Was his name Hector?"

"He did not say that he had a name," Ahmed said. "Now I figured that I would call you, my friend, even though you do not deserve that favor."

"Thanks. He's—"

"Do not interrupt, or else I will not remember everything clearly. Then—then we talked about this for a little time. I told him I did not know anything. But he would not leave the office. I said I am a very busy man and he must go. He is welcome to leave his phone number. He says many more things. Lovely things. Sanjay says to the man that he must go. The man says he knows that we know where the woman is and I tell him I do not. Sanjay tells him to get out and he gives Sanjay one very strong blow in the face. And then I understand that this is a very dangerous man and I think that he is the man who broke so much on the top floor and killed the dogs, each one a thousand dollars. I think that even though I am the stronger man that I do not wish to fight this man." Ahmed paused. "My father taught me that the strongest man knows when not to fight. And then I understood something else, Jack, I understood that this is not my problem, it is yours."

I sat down heavily in my chair. "You didn't tell him how to reach me, did you?"

"Yes, Jack, I did."

"Oh God, Ahmed—"

"I have seven children. Sanjay has three children. If the man has a gun in his pocket and all he wants is a name or a phone number, then I must give it to him. I think to myself this is a man who might have a gun. I cannot have more troubles. I cannot have *your* troubles, Jack. So I told him your first name and your work number. I said, 'Call someone named Jack at this number.' That was all. He asked me for a pen and he wrote it down."

"You did that?"

"Yes."

"Today?"

"Yes."

"Is that all?"

"I asked him if he was her husband. And he said yes. Once I gave him the number he was not so troubled. He said he wanted his wife and child back. I saw that he was no longer a problem to us. I told him that if my wife and children were gone I would look in every room in every building in New York City to find them. I said in my country a man has no honor if he abandons his family. This man shook my hand when I said that. I am telling you these things because I want you to understand that there was something in this man that is not bad. Then I gave him her things."

"What do you mean?"

"The things that were left in the apartment. Sanjay had them in a bag. Clothing, little things, some children's crayons. Some of the woman's makeup I think."

"He took them with him?"

"He held them and he smelled them."

"*Smelled* them?"

"Yes," Ahmed said, ready now to hang up. "I should expect that he will call you."

♦ ♦ ♦

The day was bad, already, but it was going to get worse and I started to swig the thick white antacid goop straight from the bottle, which is not especially good for the stomach either. I've gotten sick from *that*. Morrison, as it turned out, was wrong. The information about Chukado Electronics was worldwide within an hour, not a day, and the price of Osada foreign investment units went up 16 percent, lifting the stock price of V-S by 4 percent. A photocopy of the full story that ran on the Reuters Information Network was on our desks at one. Morrison came into my office later that afternoon as I sat there waiting with equal unease for the Chairman or Hector to call me.

"What was the interruption?" Morrison asked.

"Something private," I answered.

"I thought you didn't have a private life."

"Everyone has a private life," I said in a low voice.

Morrison looked at me like I was losing my mind, decided to skip past the topic onto more important matters. "Where is the Chairman today?"

"The islands still."

"You get that fat kid going on the faxes?"

"Yes." I was still dazed by Ahmed's phone call.

"This Chukado thing puts even more pressure on us. Lots more heat. V-S is going to have leverage on us." He meant that V-S could drop us and go after one of the Corporation's smaller, more easily digestible U.S. competitors such as Disney or Paramount, both of which were very attractive targets.

Morrison came up to my desk. "Jack, a deal is like landing a C-5 military transport, the biggest plane in the world. I've seen many land and I've seen one crash. It's the crash I remember. We used to practice our touchdown bombs with a football *inside* the fucking empty cargo hold. If you land a C-5 right, everybody gets what they want. Everybody on this floor is working their ass off to see that we make a smooth landing." Morrison's mangled hand lay on my desk, twitching. "But one thing must happen. Must, must, *must!* The Chairman of this corporation *must* agree to do what we tell him to do. I mean, Jesus, he's an old man who doesn't give a damn. He's not a player anymore, he never does any deals, never pushes the board on a decision, doesn't do any hard thinking anymore . . . he's been out of the chase for ten years. His balls are hanging low, he goes and visits his old pals in the Senate."

"He's still got some kick left," I said, thinking of our long evening together. "He can still *drink*, that's for sure."

"I don't see why it's such a big problem to move him onto our side of the table," Morrison complained. "Shit, he makes money on the deal! All those old forty-dollar stock options would have to be accommodated. But without his agreement, we don't land. We crash. We don't have wheels. You are the wheels, Jack. You got to get in there and start banging him around."

◆ ◆ ◆

Later Samantha opened my door. She was wearing white heels with blue toes. I watched her walk in.

"Where do women learn to walk like that?" I teased her.

"Like how?" She smiled.

"So that the legs sort of cross in front of one another."

"We learn it when we are fourteen practicing in the mirror after school." Samantha sat down in front of me. "We learn that and then we learn some other things."

I had a certain affection for her. Whether this was prudent or not I didn't know. "One day lollipops and dolls, the next day executives of billon-dollar German companies?"

"One thing has a way of leading to another in life, don't you agree?" She smoothed her long fingers over her dress. "Now, *look*, Jack, are you all right? I mean, all this stuff is going on."

"Stuff?"

"Some woman and her child in your office last week and Spanish dictionaries and then you get called out of a meeting—"

"Don't ask, Samantha," I told her.

"No?"

"Not if you're my friend."

She looked hurt and checked my expression for humor but there was none there. "Then I won't ask," she concluded testily.

"Look," I said in a softer voice, "Morrison is chewing on me pretty good to induce a mystical revelation within the Chairman's head," I told her. "I spent that day in Washington with him and all he did was get drunk on the train and babble strangely to me at the end of the night."

"You get a chance to tell him that Morrison is planning his forced retirement?" she asked.

"Not exactly."

"You need to get past Mrs. Marsh," she said appraisingly.

"I was afraid you'd say that." Only one road led into the Chairman's schedule and it ran past Mrs. Marsh, his heavy-hipped secretary of twenty-five years. Powerful, well-known men often are, contrary to their public image, almost pathologically dependent people. In the case of the Chairman, it was Mrs. Marsh who ran his life. No one could recall what her first name was. She directed her own two secretaries, whom she chose for their efficiency and plainness (so as not to distract the Chairman). They handled much of the Chairman's Corporation business, while she alone handled his personal affairs. Mrs. Marsh loved the Chairman with great unconditional secretarial love, never expressed, of course—a love in which his foibles and weaknesses were forgiven—and in this she was set apart from his wife and children as well as everyone else, except perhaps his dead mother. I had heard that Mrs. Marsh alone had access to the account out of which he paid for his mistresses (and probably his exertions at the club where he'd taken me) and that he had delegated all decisions as to what sums they should receive to Mrs. Marsh. It was known that a showgirl who had once seduced the Chairman thirty years prior was now living in near poverty and received a monthly stipend from the Chairman's personal foundation, in violation of the federal law governing not-for-profit organizations. Mrs. Marsh's loyalty was immovable and her quiet manner masked a ruthless code of protection of the Chairman.

"Anyway," said Samantha. "Morrison wouldn't have told you to do this unless he thought you would succeed."

"I was pissed as hell when he told me. That whole joint operating plan is mine."

"I know."

"Beales suggested this to Morrison," I ventured after seeing that the door was shut. "He wants me out of the negotiating group. I *am* out of the group."

"I think you're a little paranoid about that, Jack," Samantha disagreed. "Really. Morrison just tried to figure out what was the best way to use people. He knows you like a good fight and that you can talk off the top of your head to people. I think he figures you'll get into a discussion of the whole idea with the Chairman, start bringing him around. He has to do it that way because he himself doesn't get along with the Chairman and because the board is so tricky. He *can't* go through the board—they might smell what's going on and protect the Chairman."

"Beales—"

"Don't *worry* about everybody's motivations, Jack," she replied. "Just do what Morrison says and get the results. That's my advice. C'mon. You need to see Mrs. Marsh."

So I trailed down the long hallway to the northeast corner of the floor, where the Chairman's offices were. It was said that when the building was designed in 1974 he had chosen this corner because he could look out his windows and see his six thirty-foot-high Chinese magnolias on his penthouse garden fifteen blocks away. What was I doing back then? Following Mike Schmidt's home run statistics and contemplating growing a beard. Mrs. Marsh was in her office.

"Got a minute?" I asked.

"Yes, of course, Mr. Whitman." She was one of those women who, having grown stout, had translated her fat into authority. Her fleshy neck and thick ankles and a daily uniform of white blouse and plaid calf-length skirt all bespoke order, manners, and many years in Catholic school. Her only indulgence was a bowl of candies on her desk; she sucked on them constantly with prim fervor.

"You may know that I've been assigned to work with the Chairman on some matters, and I was wondering if I might schedule a meeting with—"

She was already shaking her head.

"He and I discussed this," she said. "You're to be available when he needs you. He hasn't instructed me to set up a meeting."

"We have to discuss a couple of things we've been at work on together."

Mrs. Marsh inspected the polish of her nails with insulting concentration. "Generally I know everything that he is working on," she said. She conferred with the lawyers and bankers for him, wrote and signed out his checks with her exact replica of his signature, and in some matters, it was rumored, possessed power-of-attorney for him. I had little doubt that had the Chairman suddenly met his demise, that she would have been called upon to be the executor of his estate.

"I need only a short appointment," I finally said.

"He tells me who his appointments will be."

"Yes, I understand that," I went on, "but I need just a little time next week. Just fifteen minutes to go over—"

"I'm afraid I'll have to ask him about it first," she said, her eyes on mine. "You see, his schedule is unclear."

"But he'll be back in the office on Monday?"

"It's not clear."

"Not back Monday? How about Tuesday?"

"He might be," she said. "But generally his schedule is a private matter. I will *note* that you would *like* an appointment and if it is appropriate—"

Her idiotic formality was a pure power play.

"I won't take this polite bullshit," I told her. "You're a gate-keeper, Mrs. Marsh, and no more. I want to know on Monday morning by ten o'clock when I can see him. Mr. Morrison has requested — no, he has directed, he has *ordered* me to talk with the Chairman about certain matters and I insist upon my right to do that."

Mrs. Marsh inhaled in surprise, but she had been around a long time, dealing with all manner of assholes and furiosos.

"I cannot tolerate such rudeness in this office — "

"I cannot tolerate such unwillingness by a *secretary* to accommodate a *vice president* of this company!" Then I quieted my voice and drew close enough to her desk that it made her uncomfortable. "You would be well advised, on your boss's behalf, Mrs. Marsh, to make sure that people have a chance to talk with him."

♦ ♦ ♦

At the end of the day, Freddie Robinson, the ancient black man who shined shoes in the building, wheeled his cart into my office. "I'm late," he said.

I sat, furious and tense, in my office chair, waiting for the phone to bring me more bad news. Robinson silently pushed a bench under my right shoe. He had been shining shoes at the Corporation for over fifty years, enduring any number of changes in management. Although he technically was not an employee of the Corporation, he had his own tiled alcove off the thirty-eighth floor men's room where he kept his supplies. He shined only the men's shoes, but repaired women's shoes, too, each day beginning on a different floor. In this way he worked through the whole headquarters in about a week, popping his head into any office with impunity, saying, "Shine?" He was a holdover from the old days and yet no one, frankly, seemed embarrassed that an aged black man stooped at his feet to buff away the grime and mud and dogshit of the streets. The older men treated Robinson with greater warmth, as if he were a pet, while the younger men, who may actually have felt guiltier by his presence, accorded him a cold aloofness. Was I the only one who felt embarrassed? No doubt my shame indicated my own patronizing attitudes. Robinson didn't appear to mind; it was the old days he pined for, and sometimes he would shake his head and say, "Back in Mr. L.'s time . . ." and by that he meant the illustrious founder of the Corporation, dead decades before.

"What do you hear around the offices?" I asked Robinson as he dabbed shine onto my shoe.

"Ahh ha." He shook his head. "You know I don't understand all the mumbo-jumbo you all speak."

"You know I know that you know."

He looked up at me and winked. "I know *you* smarter than most the rest, I know that."

It was a marvel Robinson kept going, mile after mile of carpeted hallway, into and out of the elevators all day long. He was a wiry stick of a man, dressed each day in suspenders and a white shirt. One could always see the pattern of curled white hairs on his head as he worked. Sometimes in the spring or summer he would have a small portable radio with him on his cart and a plug in one ear, listening to the Mets at Shea Stadium. A lifetime of stooping had resulted in an arthritic back and there were days we didn't see him and later we would find his back had hurt too much for him to work. And all other times I could catch the wintergreen smell of analgesic balm. He buffed and whipped his rags over my shoe with mechanical intensity, perhaps for four minutes, and then tapped the outside of the heel with two bony fingers to signal the left foot—and said, "That's it, boss," as if there was no indignity in him saying this, even to twenty-one-year-old assistants right out of college.

"So you hear about any big things happening?" I asked again.

"Well, sure. That's easy. I been here a long time, Mr. Whitman, a long time. Just gimme a minute on it."

Robinson reached into his ancient wooden cart for a rag. He seemed to have a second sense as to when not to enter an office, and no one could ever recall when he had ever entered inappropriately. He had been at the Corporation so long that he simply knew the rhythms and patterns of activity in a way that accorded him a sense of where and when to go. The other side of it, too, was that no one minded where or when he entered an office, mostly, like the janitor who emptied wastebaskets near the end of the day. Men continued to have conversations on the phone while he came around their desk, set up a footstool on which the foot was set, and went to work. They'd dig a few dollars out of their wallets, lay the money on the desk for Robinson to retrieve, and keep talking, perhaps taking notes with a pen as they listened, barely noticing that their shoes had been cleaned and Robinson was gone.

"So," I reminded him, "any big things going on?"

"Sure," he said in his throaty old voice.

"How do you know?"

" 'Cause they order up a whole mess of that caviar for the dining room. Bill, my friend who runs the kicthen, he tells me. And them guys in the parking garage rope off that section just inside the ramp for the big cars, I seen they doing *that* again. But there always one *sure* sign."

"What's that?" I asked, feeling his fingers on my foot.

"Everybody"—and here he looked left and right theatrically, as if they were all secretly listening to him—"everybody says, 'Robinson, what do you hear around the offices?' " He laughed the velvety laugh of the aged, bemused at the furious anxieties of the young. " 'What's going on, Robinson?' 'What do you hear up on thirty-nine?' 'What are they saying down on sixteen?' "

"You got me again."

"Naw. You remarried yet?"

"Well, I might have a little problem."

"What's that?" he asked with amusement.

He was the only trustworthy soul in the Corporation. "She's in my house but her husband's looking for her."

"Yessir, that *is* bad. I been there once . . ." Robinson looked up and into his past, a gentle smile playing on his face. ". . . somethin' like thirty-five years ago, I had that. She wasn't going to live with her husband no more so she came to live with me. Had a little boy, too."

"This one has a little girl."

"When they got the kids, that makes it worse," Robinson said.

"What should I do?" I asked.

"You go to church and pray he a nice, friendly fellow." He tapped my foot. "That's it, boss."

I handed him his money. The price was three dollars, but he got four for his trouble, which meant, I'd once figured, that, shining perhaps four pairs of shoes an hour five hours a day could bring him a decent living, especially considering he was an uneducated black man in his seventies.

"Good afternoon, Mr. Whitman." Robinson smiled. We liked each other. Or at least I liked him. He might have just been faking it for the money. He wheeled his cart toward the door.

"Wait. I've got one more question."

Robinson stopped to turn back at me, his face a soft leathery smile. "Hmm?"

"You shine the Chairman's shoes?"

"Yessir, twice a week."

"You doing it next week?"

"Monday morning, eight o'clock."

"That a regular time?"

"Reg'lar as rain."

"But maybe he'll be out of the office on Monday."

"No, I checked the appointment with Miz Marsh, see. Today I did that."

There, a piece of information I could use.

"You ever hear any of them talk about me, Robinson?"

"You know I don't hear nothing," he answered casually as he shuffled out of the office. "Old man like me lucky he hear the alarm clock."

EIGHT

I F YOU GOT A JOB, YOU DRIVE AWAY, proclaimed the sign at the Brooklyn car lot where Hector Salcines worked weekends. It was Sunday morning and I stood under an umbrella in a heavy spring drizzle in jeans and a T-shirt, rather pleased with my own cleverness. Calling from my office, it had taken me only about twenty minutes with the Yellow Pages and a street map of Brooklyn to find the place. I'd picked out half a dozen used-car places within a reasonable distance of the Sunset Park neighborhood Dolores had lived in and then called each, asking for Hector Salcines. Simple. The man answering the phone at the fourth place said Hector worked weekends—*something I kin hep youse with, guy?* No, I'm looking for Hector, I told him, you see he showed me a car. *Then youse come roun Sunday mornin'.* The lot was located on a triangular, otherwise useless piece of property way down on Fifth Avenue and Twenty-Fifth Street behind a twelve-foot-high chain link fence. The cars, many of them with cheap new paint jobs, were parked in tight rows with prices painted in big white numbers on the windshields, some with a short message: $300 TAKE HER TO CONEY ISLAND. $1,250 CHECK IT OUT. $1,800 SHE WANTS A NICE CAR. $3,650 JERSEY SHORE THIS SUMMER. Strings of faded red, white, and blue flags flew high above the lot and intersected at the sales office, which was nothing more than an old steel-sided trailer set up on cement blocks. I stood at the curb, coughing lightly from the acid, worrying now that I was about to do something monumentally stupid.

Three days had gone by since Dolores and Maria had moved in. Dolores continued to get up before me, making me eggs each morning. I was even a little tired of them, but said nothing for fear of discouraging her. Dolores, for her part, had been going to bed early in the evenings, taking care of Maria and doing little else, regaining her strength, I figured. Already, her face seemed less drawn by fatigue. There was greater energy in her expression and voice. I'd given her a hundred dollars to buy the things she said she needed—clothes for Maria, whatever. "Spend it," I told Dolores.

And after a moment or two of protest she did. After only a few days, the two of them were starting to take liberties, which I liked— Maria exploring the house wantonly, pulling open my underwear drawer, pawing through the kitchen cabinets, taking the scissors to old issues of the *Wall Street Journal* and slicing them into long crooked ribbons. Dolores had fixed up their bedroom a bit, put a spray of daffodils from the back garden in a vase in the dining room. Their kitchen was spotless now and the refrigerator half-full. Dolores cooked me something she called *tostones*, which was mashed-up plantains, fried and served with garlic. I didn't expect to like it, but I did. I hadn't yet asked about the jar of water, which Dolores had put in my living room on a side table near the window. And each evening on the way home I picked up something for Maria—books, watercolors, a "Sesame Street" puppet, all kinds of stuff.

But in those first days, despite the pleasant nature of these interactions, Dolores and I talked very little, and the silence between us did not get easier. I was sure she was thinking of her husband, in some way, thinking of what he was doing, or what she was going to do next, now that she was away from him. Hector was the unseen player, the man who had killed two dogs to get to Dolores and Maria. I wanted to see what kind of man he was. Call it market research, I told myself. And I could do this safely, I figured, because even though Hector knew my name, he didn't know my face or my home phone number.

That morning I'd told Dolores I was going out. And when I'd said good-bye to Maria, I found her perched on my bed watching morning cartoons on one of the cable stations telecast by Big Apple Cable. All Corporation executives in the New York region received complimentary service. It was strange enough that Maria's father installed the wiring that transmitted the very show—if not in my house then elsewhere in the city. But that was just the start of it and I'd lingered for a minute, watching Maria and marveling at the weird tangle of ironies. The cartoons appeared on a children's cable station that was 10 percent–owned by the Corporation. We'd received that portion of ownership—worth about twenty-three million dollars as I recall—simply in exchange for providing to the cable station five years of use of some of the Corporation's extensive celluloid cartoon library, much of which was created in the 1950s. I had done the deal four years ago. It was a small deal but one that had a certain elegance I was proud of. The majority owners of the children's station were pleased with the agreement, since it gave them, in addition to programming footage, the Corporation's prestige and name recognition. But the Corporation had the real advantage. In exchange for a truckload of old cartoons, we received annual profit dividends of about three million dollars, not to mention the steady appreciation of the stock, which could serve as collateral for bank financing of other Corporation projects. There was also another advantage: the cable station's repetitive broadcast of the old cartoon properties amounted to free advertising for our feature-length cartoon movies that used the same characters (each of which we rereleased every three or four years, garnering twenty or thirty million in profit each time), as well as for the licensed spin-off products—toys and clothes and stuffed animals, sleeping bags and kiddie watches, you name it. Little Maria Salcines, sitting on my bed watching television, was consuming my work.

But now I was at her father's car lot, standing under a wet gray sky. No other customers were on the lot and the place looked decidedly unprosperous. I crossed over to the office and climbed the steps. It was impossible that Hector would know that Dolores and Maria were living with me, but still I felt a quietly urgent beating of my heart, knowing that it takes more physical courage to assault a large dog than it does to attack a man. I stepped nervously to the door.

"Anybody here?"

"Come in!" came a voice.

Inside, three men watched the Yankees play Oakland on the West Coast—two heavyset older men, both Hispanic, and a younger one: Hector. I had no doubt about it. He was shorter and far more handsome than I expected, dressed in a silk tie, loosely knotted on this steamy day, with a gold chain around his neck. He hadn't shaved that morning. He glanced at me, perhaps sensing my attention, his eyes full of derision for fools. I eased inside the trailer with the bored look of a half-interested customer arranged on my face, distributing my attention to all three men, only incidentally glancing at Hector. The older man sitting behind a desk pulled his cigar out of his mouth and gave a small wet spit into a coffee can. Then he moved his red, discouraged eyes back to me. "Something I kin hep youse with, guy?" he said.

"I'm looking to see what kind of cars you might have."

"In this rain?"

I shrugged.

He seemed to be listening to my voice. "You call a couple of days ago, yesterday maybe?"

Yes, I had, looking for Hector. But I shook my head. "No," I said. "I'm just out looking."

"I'll take you out."

I wanted to be with Hector, alone.

"Tell you what," I said, "I'd like a younger guy's perspective, if you don't mind. Nothing personal."

The old guy nodded, relieved not to be wasting his time. "Sure. Hector here'll take you out."

Hector glanced up at me, then turned back toward the set. "Waitaminute, watch this—McGuire is gonna hit this motherfucker."

We all stared at the set as the tall, powerfully built slugger came to the plate with million-dollar ease. He took two balls and a strike. I noticed a clean, large bandage on the side of Hector's throat. His hair was slicked back and he gave a small grunt as he watched McGuire miss.

"Hector, why not show this man the merchandise? He come here to see a car, not you watchin' television."

"Waitaminute. I gotta see this."

The man turned to me, and smiled. "We run a very professional operation, heh. But you're gonna like our prices outside. We just ain't had too many customers today, so we're kind of runnin' slow."

I nodded. "No problem."

McGuire fouled two away. Full count. On the third strike he crushed the ball, his torso spinning with oiled grace until his bat was wrapped around the other shoulder. The Yankees centerfielder waited for the ball, unconsciously punching his fist into his glove. Hector bent forward, watching. The centerfielder backpedaled and stuck his glove up at the wall to catch the ball.

"Ah, Jesus," Hector said, leaning back. "Three fuckin' inches."

"Shit no, he didn't even *jump*," the other man argued. "He coulda jumped at least two feet. He was nowhere near a homer."

"What kind of car you looking for?" Hector said to me quickly, finished with the baseball, sizing me up as a customer.

"Something dependable," I answered, "easy to get around in — you know."

"All right," he exhaled without much enthuasiasm, "let's go see what we got." He stood, and there was that moment when we both realized how big we were in respect to each other. I was the taller, by a good four inches, but Hector's shirt was tight against his chest. He had that kind of wiry strength you see in a welterweight boxer, ropy arms, narrow waist, stronger than size would indicate, tough and quick, with a mean confidence. He stuck out his hand. "Name's Hector and I'm here to help you out, all right? You think you see something you like, let's see if we can't put something together, all right?" His voice had that quintessential Brooklyn confidence, the syllables thudding hard and tough — there's a certain brutal poetry to it. Hector fingered a gold ring that circled the pinkie on his left hand. "You work with me on the car and I'll work with you on the price."

The rain had eased and we walked down the wooden steps.

"What're you lookin' to spend?" he asked me.

"Actually maybe a couple of thousand, twenty-five hundred."

"So you're lookin' used, then. Very used. I was thinkin' maybe you wanted a new car. We got a few of them, actually, basically almost new."

"Do I look like a guy who can pop for a new car?"

He waved his hands. "Far's I can see, anybody can pop for anything. You never know. I had a guy last week, he look like a fuckin' crack addict, I mean he smelled bad, you know what I mean, *bad*, and he come in here and I asked him what he wants and he said let me have that Town Car, and before I could start talking to him about the price, he pulled out a wad of bills that was like three inches thick."

"Well, in my case, you know I can only go up to about twenty-five hundred."

"Got it, guy."

We walked over to a row of cars. With the prices on the windshield, there wasn't much to talk about. He watched me look at the cars.

"You from around here?" Hector asked. "I mean the neighborhood, or Bay Ridge, or what?" The question meant, of course, *You're a white guy and you're not Italian or working-class Irish and you don't speak like a guy who buys used cars.*

I didn't bother to look back at him. "Not too far away."

"You got a regular job?"

I nodded.

"Good credit?"

"Sure."

"I know that's personal," Hector said, "but you wouldn't believe some of the customers we got, we got to run a credit check on everybody, just to see, you know. I can tell you that right now."

"No problem."

"Some girl come in here couple months ago and bought a old Impala. She looked okay, all kinds of diamonds and shit on her hands. We took a personal check. It cleared but then we got a call." Hector laughed. "Turned out her and her old man, they broke up like three months before and she had a bunch a his old checks."

I inspected car after car.

"You going on your way to work or is it for weekends?"

"Weekends." We stared at a couple of old Chevys and Toyotas. "These are kind of small, I was looking for full size."

"We got a nice old Caddy back there. How big are you looking? You got a family and all?"

His question presented an opportunity. I looked at the ground, with what I hoped was a glum expression. "No—I'm not married anymore."

"Yeah, I hear you there."

"My wife ran out a couple of months ago," I said. "She left and she took the car and so that's why I'm here."

"What kind of car?"

"It was a '90 Taurus. I was pretty happy with it. But I got to go somewhere down the scale. I'm making payments still on that car and also to her for the kids."

Lies, my father used to preach, have no legs. But here I was, spouting them effortlessly. Hector started searching for a key among a couple of dozen he had on a chain. "My old lady left me, man, just like that, and she took my daughter so I know what you're sayin'. Wish the fuck I knew where they was at."

"You going to look for them?"

"I'm going to do *something* when I see my wife again, I'll tell you that."

I looked at him, and at the white bandage on his neck. "I don't know how you deal with it," I said. "I mean seriously, it's fucked me up, you know?"

He gave an easy laugh and it suddenly seemed that he didn't care what had happened to his wife and daughter. "Shit, there's a lotta fish in the sea, man, lot of lonely ladies out there, you know? This place you got all kinds of lonely ladies walkin' around. Lotta fish. You gotta keep like a shark that's gotta keep moving to stay alive. I just keep moving." But then his voice quieted. "But when it was good, it was *good*, you know? I mean . . ." He broke off his sentence and unlocked the Cadillac. We both got in. "This is a fine piece a car. I can tell you that right now. Heavy, with good power. The power train is still under warranty, incidentally. Tires are good, too."

"Why's the price so low?"

"The backseat is torn up."

So it was. The inside of the car was perfect except that the backseat had been slashed down to the springs and backboard. "Why didn't they just fix it up?"

"The guy *used* to own it is dead" — Hector shrugged — "so he can't do it. And nobody here wants to fix it up. Cost a lot for that upholstery job."

"What happened?"

"The way I heard it was somebody was mad at somebody so they messed it up with a box-cutter. I say just throw an old blanket over it and it'll be fine. The outside looks good and it rides nice. Want to go for a drive?"

"Why not?"

He gave me the keys and we got in. I slipped the key in the ignition.

"You don't mind, maybe you could put on your shoulder belt there, guy," Hector said. "It ain't my business but I tell everybody that. My dad, he didn't have one and he got clipped by some fucks in a mob garbage truck, thing just clipped him with one corner going the other way and he went right through the fuckin' glass, seven years ago, and the lawyer said don't try to sue them, and my moms, she still cries every day . . ."

"I'm sorry," I said, stunned by his concern for my safety.

"Ahh," Hector waved his hand, "it's just one of those . . . now, all right, this is the thing"—he pointed to the car's engine—"it's heavier and smoother. Put the power windows up and you're not going to hear a fuckin' pin."

I pulled out onto the steamy wetness of Fifth Avenue. The rain had stopped and the wind from off the bay was drying the streets and tops of cars. We cruised by the squat two-story brick row homes, past old Italian ladies sitting on newspapers out on their low stoops, tonguing their dentures, watching the street. Then I turned left onto Fourth Avenue, the crazy speedway that travels into South Brooklyn like a long needle bent twice. We rode the lights for twenty or thirty blocks, sliding past walls of graffiti: BOOSTER SHOT, ZEUS, SLICK "D" & FUNGO, XL, CHILLER Z, BUGMAN, MR. TORQUE. A truck next to a warehouse was selling wooden boxes of grapes out of the back.

"They're gonna make wine. Lotta these older wops make their own wine," Hector said, narrating the drive yet staring past the boxes of grapes, bright dark eyes focused on the far shore of his thoughts, his face relaxed and not set in expectation of conflict. He possessed a sweet innocence in that moment and I glimpsed the younger man he had been, the younger face that Dolores no doubt had loved.

And then he turned to me and back to the task of hawking a second- or third-hand Cadillac with a sliced-up rear seat. "You like it?" he barked out with friendly aggression. "Ride smooth, don't it?"

"Yeah."

We drove on and I started to wind through the Forties, where the streets were narrow and you had to be sure you didn't hit kids or guys working on their cars, usually with a big radio coming on a wire off the battery or from extension cords out of the house. Guys underneath the cars with a speed-wrench and a beer. More graffiti ribboned along the walls in colored loops and slashes: TREY-SIX, NYNEX, STRATE, JAM MY ZAM, TENSION. The ubiquitous Brooklyn block: newsstand, barber, toy store, bodega, video store. And in most of them, the Corporation was somehow making money—even in the barber shop, where the clients might even later buy some of the music they heard while getting a haircut, songs recorded by artists under the various labels of the Corporation's music division. Up on Eighth Avenue, at the light, I glanced into some of the Chinese sweatshops, where dozens of women worked under fluorescent lights at a sewing machine next to mountains of pieces of cloth. Slave labor. What is it that is so perversely fascinating about differences in class? The poor, of course, study the rich, can hardly avoid not doing so in our culture, but the rich and well off and "professional class" also study the poor, if only for comfort and morbid fascination. The Corporation's various publications pumped out endless articles on the poor and how violent they are and how their babies die at higher rates and how guns and drugs wipe them out at high rates—the whole line. Well, here I was. The people didn't look so bad. No Manhattan tension on the street. They looked more relaxed than the people I knew. "It's hard to make decent money, nowadays," I speculated.

"Man, I hear ya there—I *know* that. The guy who owns the lot is a hard-headed Guinea, doesn't pay shit," Hector answered. "All I been wanting is a few numbers, just give me a few numbers. I got four of them right once and won fifty-seven bucks. All I want is just a million off the lottery. Can tell you that right now. Get my wife back and take care of everybody, then invest the rest."

"Yeah?"

"Yeah, I'd buy me a laundry in a good neighborhood and import some Chinese," he laughed. "I'd let my moms run the place. I had my own business once, flooring, the mob fucks got me. Hate them bastards. Ahh, turn left here and we'll work our way back. Rides smooth, don't it? No, my moms, she don't know I play the numbers. I play it a lot but ain't no *gambler* on it. I had dreams of winning it, though. I *had it*, you know?"

I laughed with him, hoping to seem at ease. We passed a wall where a teenage boy was bent over at the waist, face to the bricks, while on the other side of the street, three other boys took turns throwing a rubber handball at his rear end.

"What's that?" I said.

"That?" Hector said. "That's pooty. You know pooty? He lost the handball game so now they get to try to hit him in the asshole."

We drove farther.

"See those four garage doors?" Hector pointed. "The green ones."

It was a nondescript warehouse with pull-down metal doors and nobody outside. "Looks closed."

"They got probably something like a million bucks' worth of cars in there. Mercedes, Lexus, BMW, cars from Jersey, Connecticut, Long Island . . ." He glanced at me for my reaction. "Stolen. They're gonna chop them up. Those doors are closed all day, every day, except maybe from like three A.M. to three-thirty A.M. Or sometimes they just stick them on a boat somewhere."

"Some serious money involved there," I said. "Big money."

"Yeah, I learned you don't mess with the big money."

"Oh?"

"Yeah, but that's another story."

The car nosed along another block.

"Actually, man, I missed my big money," Hector went on, in a confidential voice, still looking ahead. "I coulda had it."

"How?"

He smiled with what seemed to be real sadness. I suddenly realized, strangely, that I *liked* him. "I was in the army, man. Down there in Georgia. I joined, you know, to get the school money and to learn computers. Some guy stabbed me and I never sued. I coulda sued and all."

I hit a few red lights on purpose to stretch out the conversation, and with my prompting, and with Hector comfortably nipping at the small flask he had pulled out of his coat pocket, the story came out. In

Georgia, during the first few weeks of basic training at an army base he could no longer name, Hector and another recruit, a local, had gotten into a fight outside a whorehouse. The other man had pulled a long-handled fish knife out of the back of his pants and lunged at Hector's heart. At one of the lights, he showed me how he had crouched and swung his hand up to protect himself, and the fish knife—a poor weapon to use for a forward thrust—had skittered off the meat of Hector's thumb and caught the underside of his wrist. The sharp, serrated blade, usually used to saw through the spine sockets of thirty-pound yellowtail tuna, cut into the tendons and arteries of Hector's wrist below his right hand. The bleeding was immense, and when he woke up, the army surgeon was explaining the possibilities of microsurgery.

"I coulda sued them but I was young and foolish. It was between us two guys, not the army and me. They said I could get my hand fixed up and get out of the army if I wanted, since I'd only been there two weeks. So I left."

"How's your grip?" I asked, thinking of the manual work at his cable-installing job.

"You tell me." He shot his hand out and grabbed the thick part of my arm above the elbow and crushed it for barely a moment.

"Jesus." I was almost in pain. "Nothing wrong with *that*." I was shocked that he was touching me. It seemed proof that we were connected, that his child and wife were sleeping under my roof.

"Yeah," Hector went on, rubbing his hands now, "I was getting a check each month, not too much, you know, just a little something that I always gave to my moms, but then a paper came and the money didn't come no more."

I fiddled with the radio to see if it worked. The baseball game came on. I listened for a minute then thought of someting. "Was that game on cable back there at the lot?" I asked innocently.

"You mean the TV in the trailer?"

"Yeah."

"No, just the regular station," said Hector.

"I've been thinking about getting it. Cable. Everybody seems to have it now."

"You should, it's pretty decent."

"But you have to buy a whole lot of lines, right?"

"But they're good," Hector said. "You got Cinemax and the Disney Channel, and HBO, and the SportsChannel and CNN, which I never watch, and everything. And in Manhattan they got Channel J where all the girls do all that nasty shit." Hector laughed. "I mean, I turned that on the other day, there was this pregnant girl lying on her back with some guy pissin' on her. Then she says call this number to talk to her. All you could see was the splash on her face, you know? I mean, it's fuckin' *sick*. I install the lines during the week."

"The cable line?"

"Sure."

"Really?"

"Yeah, I stick it into the house."

"How's business?"

He shrugged. "I'm busy enough, I get a couple of jobs a day usually, but we're gonna be bought up by the Koreans."

"Wow," I said vaguely. "I didn't know that."

"The whole fucking thing." Hector spat out the window in disgust. "Koreans. We got guys in the union who know everything that's going on. They seen all the key documents, tell us what's goin' down, you know what I mean? I think it's North Koreans or something. Guys goin' buy up the whole damn fucking thing. I'd like to see them guys try to wire a fucking apartment building, crawl around like a goddamned monkey all day. People try to steal your tools and shit. It ain't right."

I murmured my agreement, my eyes on his hands. I wondered how he could have hit Dolores's pretty face, and at the thought of this my mood hardened.

"You want the car?" Hector asked.

I paused, as if to consider the question. "Probably not."

"But we drove around."

"And I'm pretty sure I don't want it."

"But it rides smooth. Engine's good."

"I don't want it."

"Why the fuck you been wastin' my time then?"

I looked at him. What a bastard I was, really. "I didn't see too many other customers on your lot."

"Yeah, because it was raining and nobody buys cars when it's fucking raining, you asshole. Why the fuck you wasting my time? Shit." Hector crossed his arms. "I shoulda seen you was just lookin' for a joy ride."

"No," I said, figuring a way to finesse my way out. "I'm looking for a car. I like the salesman, but I just don't like the car."

There was an uneasy silence.

"Really," I said.

"I missed like two fucking innings of the game, so don't give me this kinda shit." Hector looked straight out the front of the car. "I don't need the aggravation, I got pressures, the wife and all."

I pulled the car back into the lot. Then I asked, "You don't mind me mentioning it, but what happened to your throat there?"

Hector's hand touched the bandage. "Ahh, shit, I got attacked by a dog."

I handed him the car keys. "Bite your throat?"

"Yeah." We got out of the car. "But not for long. Dogs useta scare the shit outa me, but not anymore. Hate the big ones, the shepherds. Motherfuckers. Tell you the truth, if it paid well enough, I'd kill 'em for a livin'."

◆ ◆ ◆

That was all I needed to hear. Hector was angry and dangerous, and I was going to have to be careful about him. After you have seen your wife gunned down, you understand the unpredictability of violence. And it makes you tense. So that same Sunday evening, intending to unwind and think about the coming week at work, I said good night to Dolores and Maria and retreated to my roof with a glass, ice, and bottles of gin and tonic water. Drinking is very bad for my condition; as my doctor said, it loosens up that sphincter at the base of the esophagus and all manner of pain bubbles up. But fuck it, I figured, I needed to relax. The sun had fallen away at the west, and around me was the sprawling mass of Brooklyn, including Hector to the south of me, wondering where his wife and daughter were. I drank that in as heavily as I tossed back the booze I had carried up to the roof. Have I said yet that Brooklyn is a great and romantic place? Its simultaneous multiplicity catches in the brain, it is a streaming, strange place. Its history is generally unknown to the immigrants who arrive each generation, who come to the church spires and endless blocks of row homes, the places named after the dead, the names themselves Anglicized versions of the words used by the Dutch settlers who seized that green heel of land where the Hudson meets the Atlantic, where Canarsee Indians, a branch of the Coastal Algonquins, lived in the lost manner, century upon century, and where later the British drove ashore forcing George Washington to retreat into the fog of the East River upon a low wooden ferry. Where my famous ancestor stood on the shore while the wind whipped his unruly beard and hair while he sang his elegiac, celebratory song of America and buttfucked young sailors above the saloons. Where thousands of Italian boys fresh from Ellis Island learned how to sling a neat bed of mortar onto a row of bricks using a pointed trowel. Block upon block of brick buildings squatting in the lengthening metallic haze, long carpets of sunlight gliding across the streets, cars stopping and streaming like cells of blood through a great and thickened heart, the trees always dying, some of them old plane trees brought over from London that spread their wrinkled bark over the sidewalks like melted wax, while meanwhile children played nearby, still only children, watched solemnly by the old women, their bellies long fat, hips ruined. And forty feet underground sits the token clerk, setting found items behind the booth window for the public to claim: a school pass, a set of keys, a cheap engagement ring. The clerk nods at a young transit cop who superstitiously keeps a laminated picture of his sweetheart taped to the inside of his policeman's cap. I've seen that, and the two dozen black men slapping drums and shaking gourds on the Jamaican coast of Prospect Park, a pounding circle of rhythm surrounded by several hundred onlookers and a few dozen fevered dancers in the surging whirlpool of sound, with fried chicken in tinfoil sold from coolers on the side. In Brooklyn, no one apologizes for their desires. I've seen the line of people waiting outside the car with the newly hijacked cellular phone, ten bucks for ten minutes, anywhere in the world. And the hulking box of the nursing home in Fort Greene, where old Chinese women with little remaining hair blink in the sunlight, bottles rigged above their wheelchairs dripping into their arms, catheter bags filling with yellow from below. I have seen all of these things at some point, I know these things even if I do not remember them: the wheezing personal injury lawyer painting the horrors of the car accident to the jury in the civil court downtown, and the Salvadoran refugee of dubious legal status, his mind stuffed with horrors (the dismemberment of his brother, the shallow grave), silently stripping layers of lead paint from the fine Victorian wooden moldings in the house of a Brooklyn Heights decamillionaire, the refugee alone and wanting the aloneness, no radio even, content in a room of fumes; and the mugger watching his victim paw through her handbag for her keys in the apartment house foyer, watching her, waiting for the voice to tell him to pull his knife and *go;* and the retired bus driver setting up his little canasta table on his nineteenth-floor terrace facing the ocean in Bay Ridge, his union pension secure, a man who once saw Brooklyn's own Jackie Gleason getting out of a white Cadillac convertible and still talks about it, who turns on the television and then, giving a low surprised cough, drops dead, the cards slipping from his hands and fluttering off the terrace, red-white, red-white . . .

All of it, the heavy soul of Brooklyn: the priest shaving carefully before the first Sunday mass, forgiving himself for masturbating (and with such guiltless abandon); and in the diabetes ward of the hospital, a roomful of overweight black women in their sixties, lying in their beds and cackling, gossiping, waiting on the Lord, awaiting their various amputations below the knee; and the Korean shopkeeper showing the new relative how to shrug when the customer claims he's been shortchanged a dime; and the Mexican man trimming cut flowers each day outside that same shop, remembering his mother living in Mexico City above the bakery; and the advertising space saleswoman swimming laps at 5:00 A.M. in the club pool, reciting in silent fervor the twenty-minute pitch to get the Japanese car account. And the Bangladeshi man squatting against the brickwork in the sun, remembering the dung patties slapped up to dry on the wall of his family home in the hard sun of the Indian subcontinent; and the middle manager at Chase Manhattan noticing the slight bit of blood in his stool and then forgetting it again along with the day's headlines as he walks his son to second grade at St. Ann's. And a judge in the courthouse in downtown Brooklyn watching a fly taste the corner of an eight-hundred-page complaint that alleges that the mob runs the window-cleaning union in the city, thinking to himself that wisdom and personal corruption may often go together in a man; and a fellow dancing in drunken terror and joy on the roof of his Park Slope brownstone, while below him, beneath three sets of hundred-year-old joists and oak floorboards, a dark-haired woman with a fierce and beautiful face is wondering why she is living now in the house of a stranger and thinking of her husband, who, she knows, still loves her in ways he cannot understand, each day drilling the hole through which the cheap electronic entertainments will flow, wondering where his wife is, wishing that some Sunday he could sell a car or two to the deadbeats and assholes who come onto the lot, feeling that time is running against him—as it ran against all of us, he, we, us, Dolores, Maria, Hector, and me, living flecks of the heavy hard soul of Brooklyn.

♦ ♦ ♦

I woke up at about 4:00 A.M. on my roof, shivering and stiff and sick, the empty bottle and glass rolled into the gutter, and I descended the roof ladder slowly. The pressure is getting to you, I thought, you're drinking too much and acting weird. I knocked back a quarter of a bottle of Mylanta and slept a few hours, then Maria came up to my bedroom to watch "Sesame Street" while I turned myself into a man in a suit, which is how I understand myself. Later, I got up from the breakfast table to leave for work and said to Dolores, as I used to say to Liz, "I'll be home around nine o'clock."

Dolores was brushing out Maria's hair. "Okay."

"Just so that you know, that's all."

"Need anything?" she said, meaning at the store.

"No. Yes. Do you mind if we had some hot cereal one of these mornings?"

"You want some?" she asked.

"I do, actually. It's what I grew up eating."

Maria handed her mother each small plastic barrette as it was needed. I realized that she had worn the same pants the day before. Dolores would be taking Maria to the park and it occurred to me that all the kids there would be wearing bright, expensive stuff from the better stores.

"Do you have enough clothes for her?" I inquired of Dolores.

"I've got that new stuff but I have to wash out things usually."

"I'd like to get Maria some clothes," I said. "The whole set."

"She *could* use some socks and—"

"No, I mean the whole deal. Socks, shoes, little dresses and tights, whatever little girls wear. Ten dresses, ten of everything. I want you to go to Macy's in Manhattan—"

"Macy's will cost too much, Jack." Dolores frowned.

"How much?"

"That'a a lot of money for these things, especially shoes. Kid's shoes are *expensive*."

"Spend it," I told her. "Go get every damn thing she needs. And make sure you buy decent clothes, not some cut-rate crap. Go buy Maria the best stuff." I pulled out my wallet. "Here's my card."

"They won't take it." Dolores shook her head. "I'm not your wife or anything—"

"Take this one then." I handed her my American Express Gold Card. "They won't ask any questions. It's considered an insult to the customer."

She took the card and looked at it. "I can't do this."

"Why not?"

Dolores looked at me.

"I just want to take care of Maria, Dolores."

"It's a lot of money."

"It's just *money*. I have plenty of money. Maria needs clothes. I'd like for her to have them. It would give me pleasure."

"So maybe I could buy a few things?" Dolores ventured. "You know, just get some things I need—"

"For yourself? Get it. Get it all. Go on a shopping trip. Take a taxi home. I mean it. Have fun."

"The bill will be too high," she protested. "Really. It'll be too high, Jack."

That very morning, that absolute moment, I had something more than $79,400 in my money market account. But I didn't tell her this.

"Shouldn't Maria be going to some kind of school now, some sort of kindergarten?" I went on. "There are plenty of these little programs in the neighborhood."

"She could, maybe a couple of days a week, to learn the socializing and reading, you know. But that costs money, too."

"Why don't you sign her up for one?" I said. "There must be half a dozen in the neighborhood. Just find one you like and we'll get started."

Dolores stared at me and then looked away.

I ventured a hand onto her shoulder so that she would face me. She didn't move it. "You don't understand, Dolores. The money is not a problem. The bill *can't* be too high."

"Why? Why do you say that?" she said, her brow confused.

I thought then of Liz in the morgue at Columbia-Presbyterian Medical Center, her flesh gray and cold and firm. And I thought of her killer, Roynell Wilkes, the crisp hundreds stuck into his mouth. "Why, Dolores?" I said, opening the front door to go. "Because the bill was paid a long time ago."

♦ ♦ ♦

Later, in my office, I remembered Hector's words—*Dogs useta scare the shit outa me, but not anymore. If it paid well enough, I'd kill 'em for a livin'*—and requested that Helen call the division vice president of Big Apple Cable, a fifty-year-old smiler named Harry Janklow whom I'd met at the annual stockholders' meeting, a rigged carnival game if there ever was one. Janklow knew now that he would never rise any higher and when we met that first time, he'd inspected me for some ingredient that he lacked. On the phone I explained to him that I wanted the personnel file of one of his employees, Hector Salcines, sent to me. He wanted to know why, of course.

"It's a stupid reason," I complained. "We have these consultants who are testing how well we move information around, not just the important information but the other stuff. They say we're too bureaucratic and want to start chopping out departments. Morrison told them they could get any information about the company within twenty-four hours."

"He said that? That's total bullshit."

"Yes, but he said it. In our meeting last week." I knew that Janklow would have no idea of what was happening on the thirty-ninth floor other than what he read in the business pages each morning and heard through the grapevine, distorted and twentieth-hand. He was too low.

"What were some of the other things?" he asked.

"Stupid stuff. Like total recording division receipts for the Southern California market last Friday."

"It's impossible to get that sort of personnel info fast."

I heard the hesitation in Janklow's voice, his worry that agreeing to do such a strange thing violated protocol. He didn't care about Hector Salcines, of course; he just didn't want to get in trouble. So I set the hook further: "Also," I added, "it's not just you guys. It's offices throughout the whole operation. Morrison wants a report from me how fast the info is available. He thinks he can identify the weak divisions, informationally weak, I mean, and the strong ones."

"I *see*," Janklow said, happy to be informed. "What was it he wanted?"

"They picked a name at random from the master employee list, a big printout. The guy just opened it like it was a phone book and picked—let me see the name again—here it is, Hector Salcines."

"How fast do you guys need it?"

"Tomorrow morning."

"Won't be a problem. I'll have my secretary messenger it over."

"Right."

"Anything particular? Part of the file?"

"No, just the whole thing. The job application form, whatever else is on there, this Salcines guy's file."

"Consider it done."

I did. Like most people, he needed to please his bosses.

At eight o'clock I walked to the other side of the floor and there was Mrs. Marsh, watering the plant on her desk.

"I'd like a few minutes with the Chairman," I said.

"He's not available, I'm afraid," she said sweetly, as if she did not remember our conversation from the previous Friday. "He has an appointment."

I looked at her.

"C'mon."

"He's in a meeting."

I didn't want to be unpleasant this time. "I know exactly who he is in a meeting with and so I know that I can see him."

Mrs. Marsh raised an eyebrow. "I doubt that."

"He's getting his shoes shined."

Mrs. Marsh's mouth fell open into a little red oval and I took the opportunity to walk past her into the Chairman's office and there he was, reading the same bound volume by Trollope, having his shoes shined by Robinson.

"Good morning," I said. "I'd like a few minutes."

The Chairman turned his head.

"Very good!" he exclaimed, as if he had thought of the idea himself. "Let's talk. About what? Anything you like. I don't know how you got past Mrs. Marsh, she must think very highly of you."

Robinson stood up, done, and nodded.

"Thanks, Freddie."

Robinson must have remembered our conversation the previous Friday. He did not look at me and left.

"Now then," the Chairman started.

Mrs. Marsh stepped into the office in her sensible shoes and, glancing at me with candied politeness, set some papers before the Chairman. "This is the lawyer's agreement," she indicated with a sibilant whisper, "three places to sign . . . good . . . and . . . the letter to that Professor Zacks . . ."

"The historian?"

"Yes."

"We donated the books he requested?"

"Yes."

The Chairman looked up at me. "Remarkable fellow. I bought a rare book in London twenty years ago, an account of the habits of Parisian courtesans in the eighteenth century, and he tracked me down."

"This is the letter saying no to Mr. Hitt," Mrs. Marsh continued in a hush. She stood close to him in her bleached blouse, smelling of soap.

"This fellow," the Chairman explained, "has a show on public television, a lot of talk. I can't go on it. He's too smart for me."

He turned back to the letters before him. "And this is the university president?"

"Yes."

"Here?" he asked.

"Yes." He signed as instructed. She ran his life. "The car is downstairs now," she said.

"I'm on my way out, Jack, which I'd forgotten. Why don't you take a ride with me to the heliport?" He picked up his briefcase. "I want some company."

"Where're you headed?" I asked amiably.

"I'm going to give a speech at my granddaughter's college."

"What's the message?"

"Haven't read what they wrote for me yet. Globalization, the changing American economy, you know, the usual. Today's wisdom. Baked up just right."

We rode down to the garage in the elevator. The Chairman said nothing.

"You understand my problem, don't you?" I ventured. "Why I need some time to talk with you?"

He watched the red digital numerals of the floors flick downward.

"No, I'm not sure that I do."

"I've been assigned to broach a subject with you. We began something of the conversation the other night—"

"I don't remember," he said.

And maybe he didn't. He'd had a hell of a lot to drink that night and may have had even more after I left. His car was idling at the curb by the elevator and we got in, facing each other. In a minute we were inching through traffic toward the East Side.

"As you no doubt know," I began, "there are many new possibilities in markets around the world. Some of those markets are wide open and some are not. A couple of other international companies have very good complementary markets, complementary to ours, I mean—"

"We talked about this?"

"Yes."

"I don't remember."

"In fact, you were beginning to argue that—"

The Chairman's eyelids closed halfway and I wasn't sure if he was leading me on. "Didn't I tell you something about terror?" he said casually. "Something along those lines?"

The car crawled past Third Avenue and stopped at the light. We watched the women, the wind billowing and pressing their skirts. I love that little valley in women where the legs and the belly meet. The Chairman was looking at the women too. I decided to just jump in. "I need to talk to you about the proposed merger of this company with Volkman-Sakura," I said. "This is why I've been assigned to you. You know this. But I think you don't want to talk about it—"

"You know," the Chairman interrupted me, "I realized something today. I realized that uncertainty behaves very much like classical physics." He was stalling me, like a boxer clinching so close that the other man can't get in any good blows. "Uncertainty—call it risk—is moved from one entity to another. It's the basis for insurance, but it has—it has a more subtle *plasticity* to it. We may move risk from one person to another, we leverage other human beings in order that they may assume our risk . . ." His eyes traced the pedestrians on the sidewalk. "We—"

"I'm asking for an hour of your time," I insisted, "ninety minutes, tops. Sometime this week. I'll make my pitch. I'm assigned to do that."

"No," he said coldly. "You are assigned to do whatever I tell you. To talk as required. To be silent as required."

In anger and shame I turned my head toward the window. The car edged toward the East River. We arrived at the heliport and the Chairman waited until his luggage had been put on the helicopter. He found a cigarette and stuck it in his mouth as the helicopter's engines started to whine. His cool blue eyes peered into mine.

"Do you like messing around with me this way?" I blurted.

"No," he said. "It's very unpleasant. But your Mr. Morrison is messing, as you put it, around with *me*." He huddled in the lee of the open car door and lit the cigarette with a lighter. "I would prefer to say 'fucking with.' That would be the correct idiom. Mr. Morrison is *fucking* with me. That's more to the point, don't you think?"

Now I was scared. "One hour," I said. "Just one hour, you and me, no Mrs. Marsh hovering around."

"You made quite a negative impression on her."

"*One hour.*"

The Chairman looked at his cigarette and took a hard draw, his eyes squinting in the sudden release of smoke that followed, and said, "You're already scheduled. Thursday evening at six. And in the meantime, I should say that while I've figured out why *I* was sent you, you would do well, my terrorized friend, to figure out why *you* were sent to me."

♦ ♦ ♦

So there it was: inside two weeks Morrison had set me upon Volkman-Sakura, whose executives, having seen all the Broadway shows and eaten in the best restaurants, and sampled, no doubt, the finer call-girl services, and were now starting to negotiate in earnest, and the Chairman had allowed me to be set upon him by Morrison, and I had set myself upon Hector Salcines, who, oddly enough, had not as yet made use of the phone number provided him by Ahmed, and whose estranged and beautiful wife was now learning to live in my Brooklyn brownstone.

There was plenty to worry about. But the weather was good, the Mets looked like they might win a few, and most important, as the trees along my street leafed out, Dolores and Maria quickly established the first patterns of a new life and seemed to have forgotten the turmoil that had brought them to my door. I began to trip over small toys around the house and find that during the day Maria had taken certain of my belongings and put them elsewhere: I discovered my best leather shoes being worn by a teddy bear, my starched shirts taken off the dresser and laid down like playing cards on top of my bed. Dolores was also moving things around—the toaster to a different plug in the kitchen, the silverware arranged, for once, by fork, spoon, and knife. I said nothing and she took my silence as tacit approval. Day by day she seemed better, happier. The pallor of exhaustion had left her face completely. Her eye had healed and she had gained a little weight, which I could see in her breasts and hips especially and which enhanced her voluptousness. It was hard not to stare. Of course I thought constantly about sex with her, but I forced myself to remember what she had said that first evening in my house. And there was one moment when I realized that the situation remained emotionally volatile: Maria was helping put plates on the dinner table and she took four, not three, off the counter. She set them carefully at each place and said, almost to herself, "Maybe if I put a plate here, Daddy will come." She looked hopefully toward her mother, but Dolores answered flatly: "Maria, you and Mommy already talked about this." And nothing more was said. None of us looked at each other. Maria did not cry. My heart was breaking for her.

But that was just one sad moment in the midst of a great gust of activity as a new household was being created. Dolores asked me if she could do the shopping, since she didn't have much to do except take Maria to the park in the afternoon. So I gave her my account card for the local supermarket and soon the kitchen was stocked with a new variety of foods, vastly different from the unimaginative staples I usually bought. She was cooking all kinds of things now: *tostones, rojas,* pink beans, and something she called *mofongo,* a Puerto Rican dish made of a pile of fried plantains, beans, and pork, with chicken broth poured over it. The house smelled different, it smelled better. Every morning at six-thirty, Maria's little feet drummed up the stairs. "Jack, get up!" she commanded happily. And she would wait in my bedroom while I showered and got dressed in the bathroom and then I would ask her to pick out a tie for me. And, then holding her carefully, I would carry her downstairs. And now, while the radio played marimba and salsa in the kitchen, I ate chewy Jamaican spice toast with cereal or the eggs Dolores still kept cooking for me, scrambled or fried. It had been so long since Liz died that I had forgotten about the domestic routine—the sound of water running elsewhere in the house, a door being closed on another floor, the need to empty the trash more often than once a week. My electricity bill tripled, as the refrigerator was opened and shut more often, as the television played during the day, as Dolores ran the blender in the kitchen, as Maria turned on lights and forgot to turn them off. The gas bill went up—stove and hot water. I loved it. Where it was going to lead I didn't know. But I was happy now, happier than I had been in a long time.

Yet that was not all. Not nearly, as I discovered after I realized that the house was getting hot, as it always did early in May. Old Mrs. Cronister had explained that this defect was caused by the placement of the maple trees too far to the rear of the garden; the sun now climbed high enough that it warmed the back of the house much of the day. Even though the building didn't have central air-conditioning, the furnace system included an electric fan that was supposed to circulate air through the registers in the walls. The fan wasn't operating, however. One of those evenings, after I'd worked late and come home around midnight, I went down to have a look at it. I passed Dolores and Maria's apartment—the door was shut, as I'd expected. They had gone to bed and I continued down the stairs. The basement was a cool, dark space. On the street side, if you bent down in the gloom and raked your fingers across the crumbly, century-old concrete floor, you would find small chunks of coal from the era when the coal trucks used to deliver through the ground-level coal chute on the front of the house. I had never swept up all the old coal, liking the comfort of it, the history of it. I fiddled around with the fan, unable to get it going. The wiring was frayed and ancient and I tracked it across the basement ceiling toward the main line, over and around water pipes and defunct telephone wires, and while walking with my chin up and eyes on the posts and joists of the floor above me, I walked directly beneath Dolores's room, and heard her say, "Oh, come *on.*" Then nothing. There was no telephone in Dolores's room. The sound had traveled from her room through an open vent that fed into a sheet aluminum heating duct that carried her voice perfectly. I heard her speak again, just a sound, with an exasperated, insistent edge to it, almost a whimper as if she had hurt herself. Then there was silence, half the squeak of a bed spring. Then another whimper, then a low, throaty sound, a voice I'd never heard her use. "Oh come *on.*"

Dolores was masturbating. I was sure of it. It started again, the bed springs rasping ever so lightly. Who was she fantasizing about? Hector? Someone else? My neck hurt as I stared at the old wooden beams above my head. I measured my breathing, afraid she would hear me beneath her, realizing that Dolores Salcines was coming back to life.

NINE

ou want to see what I got?" DiFrancesco asked me over the phone, wheezing a little. "I'm set up and I'm starting to get some stuff."

"Is it in German?"

"Looks like it. Better bring your German dictionary."

"Messenger the faxes to me."

"No. Messengers keep very good records."

I could only retrieve the intercepted faxes in person, DiFrancesco insisted. A matter of security. So I took down his address and then a cab to Canal Street in Chinatown, down where you can buy just about anything, or a piece of it, on the street. I've seen new engine blocks for sale down there, dentist's tweezers by the box, shotgun shells without the pellets, motorboat sonar systems, plastic buttons by the thousand gross. The card read DIFRANCESCO ENTERPRISES, 568A CANAL STREET. Number 568 was a windowless metal door next to a fish store. It was locked. I saw a buzzer and pressed it a couple of times. The door opened a half inch, no more.

"Aahwhadoyawant?"

An eye moved furtively at shoulder height behind the door. I was dressed too well to be a detective and too conservatively to be a Mafia guy.

"I'm looking for this person."

I pressed the card up against the crack. The door opened a few inches and a hand came out and snatched the card. Then the door shut again and I heard the chunk of a bolt. I banged on the door. Nothing. Everything smelled of fish. I stepped back out on the street and looked up at the second- and third-story windows, one of which was sealed off with plywood, save for a small homemade stack pipe that belched a whitish smoke every few seconds. All sorts of illegal industry went on in buildings like this. The fact that I was here was absurd, this wasn't how international corporations did business. And worse, while I was here Beales was at the Plaza in the negotiating group.

"You! Mister sir!" came a voice. A Chinese woman in her fifties beckoned to me and I followed her into the storefront on the other side of the metal door, past air compressors, crates of onions, and beach chairs, and through a small office where several children played. She stopped at a stairwell and pointed up. It didn't look promising, it looked like the kind of stairwell that suckers in good business suits with wallets full of credit cards should never walk up. But then she nodded insistently, and from a fold of her dress produced the business card I'd slipped through the crack of the door moments earlier. So I climbed the stairs, my feet heavy on the old treads. At the top was a small door plastered over with Grateful Dead stickers. I knocked.

"Open!" DiFrancesco's voice.

I pushed inside. Hunched in front of one of perhaps a dozen computers, half of which were missing their cases, DiFrancesco typed furiously, dressed only in a gigantic pair of black gym shorts that said UNIVERSITY OF IOWA HAWKEYES on them. His beard was tied off with a rubber band into a ponytail. A gold rosary was beached on the immense orb of his belly. About five hundred empty Pepsi cans littered the room.

"So you blew downtown for some examples of hackitude," he wheezed, not taking his eyes from the screen.

"This is the real you, no doubt."

He laughed. "You got it."

"This is where you work?"

"My sanctum insanitorium."

"For multinational corporations the world over?"

"Mmhmm."

"What're you doing?"

"A featurectomy in order to escape from a pessimal situation." He typed furiously.

"You mean you've got some sort of problem?"

"Fucking dink maggotbox can't deal with Chinatown. Too much dirty power."

I think he meant his computer. "Why are you in Chinatown, anyway?"

"Because these Chinks, they can hide anybody anywhere," he said, pushing a button on the computer and spinning around on his chair. "Chinks are the smartest people in the world, just in case you didn't know that, except phonefreaks and crackers. Me, I'm not so smart. Except for computers, I am the stupidest person I ever met. So I got the Chinks to hide me." He fiddled with a cable. "Vicious, too, when they want to be. The gangs down here are the toughest in the world."

"I still don't get it," I said. "You do work for companies like mine, from *here?*"

"No, not technically. Well, *technically*, yes. But not on *paper*, no." DiFrancesco shrugged his mountainous shoulders. "It's all quantum bogodynamics," DiFrancesco said. "When you got that, you got just about anything."

"How are you hidden? I found you pretty easily."

"See all these beige toasters and chiclet keyboards?" He pointed at the stack of computers. "They use something like six hundred kilowatts of electricity a month. I don't pay the bill—there *is* no bill. I'm wired into the city. The Chinks can do this, though a lot of the power is dirty. Very bad for a hackintosh, too. They dug the fucking Ho Chi Minh Trail, they can do anything they fucking want with New York City."

"The Vietnamese and Vietcong built the Ho Chi Minh Trail, not the Chinese," I said.

He ignored me. "See that line there? Into the fax machine? NYNEX thinks that's a public pay phone."

"What happens when they send the guy around to get the money out?"

"They don't send him, because I can hack into their service schedule for this switching station quadrant and tell the computer it's already been serviced." He eased himself off his chair and walked over to another table. I followed him. "Aahh, don't look too carefully at the stuff on this table, or else you'll have a low regard for my character," DiFrancesco said. Of course I looked anyway, and saw a stack of pornographic video tapes, all in their glossy boxes. "Aah, I knew'd you look."

"Believe me, I really don't care," I said.

"I know it's wrong but I can't help myself. I'm a lonely guy. Lonely guys are forced to whack off all the time."

"How're we paying you, actually?" I asked.

"Certain automagical manipulations."

"Like what?"

He shrugged. "You got a huge lunchroom on something like the six floor, right?"

A couple of hundred employees ate there every day. I checked my watch. "Yes."

"And you got an execudroid dining room up on the five-hundredth floor, right?" Of course no building was that high. "So maybe they got to buy a lot of fish every week. Swordfish for the *most* executively *executive* execudroids and some kinda garbage fish, cod or scrod or something, for the rest of them, right? Maybe they buy some fish from some of my Chink friends down here. Or maybe they make it *look* like they bought the Chink fish, with requisitions and all, and so most of that money goes to me."

I couldn't imagine that Morrison would set up such a ridiculous subterfuge. "You're full of shit."

"No, you're the one in a bogosity potential field. You think what I said is out of the question? Every fucking droid corporation has some suit who sits in his office and tells the computer to pay the bills. These big old mainframes pump out checks twenty-four hours a day, a couple of hundred an hour. All you got to do is have a bill sent to the bill department with somebody's signature on it. No big deal. Nobody keeps good records in the fish business—"

"Fine," I cut in. "How about the faxes?"

He handed me a folder of faxes, all of them originating from the V-S fax machine at the hotel over the previous few days. V-S had German-language word-processing equipment in the hotel and the faxes duplicated the longer European stationery. My German was good enough so that I could read the messages rudimentarily. Most of the faxes, which seemed to have been dictated by Waldhausen, were to the V-S liaison with Deutsche Bank, the gigantic German national bank that provides financing to German corporations. This suggested that V-S had capital to draw on, but we knew that. The faxes said that following the first few days, the negotiations were proceeding "as anticipated, and we will proceed or delay as you direct."

Why would the V-S team delay? I couldn't think of a reason. If the merger deal looked bad, they could always call off the talks, but to delay merely wasted everyone's time and money, unless they had a reason to wait for information or a decision. The rest of the faxes included copies of projected market summaries, which Morrison and the others had provided the V-S people, and correspondence related to routine matters within V-S. There were, however, two intriguing items, the first, a typewritten note from Waldhausen to his wife: *Liebe Gretchen, Ich vermisse dich sehr mein Schatz. Wir arbeiten schwer und sonst gibt es nicht viel zu tun. Gib Lotte einen kuß für mich . . .* "Dear Gretchen," I translated, "Miss you very much, sweetheart. We're hard at work here, not much to do. Give Lotte a kiss for me. And please have the roofers leave a copy of the bill." And then second, a hand-written note from Waldhausen: *Cornelia, Es ist spät und sicherlich schläfst du also werde ich dich nicht mit einem Anruf wecken . . .* This one was more intriguing. "Cornelia, it is late and surely you are sleeping so I will not wake you with a call. It is possible that you will read this letter at breakfast. I am, at the moment, high above the street in New York. A grand hotel. I am lonely. I miss you, and long for our quiet afternoons. I had a dream last night that I was doing squats with the barbell, as I did in university. Doing them naked. Maybe one hundred kg. I could do that then—you have only known me as an older man. And you were beneath me with your mouth open. Every time I came down, Cornelia, your lips were open . . ." And so on. The usual stuff that men can't say to their fifty-year-old wives. The letter was to Waldhausen's mistress, no doubt.

"You got any more work for me?" DiFrancesco said. "Because if you do, give it to me, and if you don't, I got other things to do. I got this set up now, it's automatic."

"More work?"

"Sure, other fax numbers, whatever."

I thought a moment. Morrison wanted results with the Chairman. I pulled out my electronic date book and started to scroll through all the numbers at the Corporation.

"This one." I pointed it out to DiFrancesco. The Chairman's office fax number. "Hack this one and see what you get."

"Okay. Where is it?"

"It's in our building, thirty-ninth floor."

He looked at me. "You sure?"

"Yes. You need access to the PBX?"

"It's a Northern Telecom," he said.

"How do you know?"

"I noticed it in the lobby."

"You need some kind of special access phone number?"

He thought. "I can do it. I'll have to go through the—"

"No, no. I don't want the explanation."

"Okay."

"All right, what else . . ." I looked through the numbers. Samantha's home number, her number on her boat, Beales's home number, Morrison's office extension, his office fax, his home numbers in Connecticut and the vacation homes, his private fax number at home. "Can you hack a fax in a private home in Connecticut?" I asked DiFrancesco, being sure not to show him that the home in question was Morrison's.

DiFrancesco squeezed his eyes shut. "New England Telephone . . . very hard."

"If it's impossible, then—"

"No! Yes! I got a friend who specializes in New England Tel."

"Sure?"

"It'll take a while, but yes."

I gathered up the faxes to leave.

"One more problem," DiFrancesco said.

"What?"

"I'm supposed to write everything up for Shevesky. Report this shit to him."

"Don't do it."

"Just call you?"

"Yes," I said.

DiFrancesco looked at me, his eyes watching, understanding. I knew he was surpassingly intelligent. "You wish to control what information reaches your boss, Morrison?"

I nodded. "Shevesky struck me as your basic fuckwad hustler salesman."

A big smile appeared on DiFrancesco's massive face. "A maggot middleman."

"He'll do anything Morrison tells him to do, right?"

"Even if he had to bend over."

"So our deal will be that you just call me, any hour." I wrote down my home number. "If Shevesky calls you and says where is my documentation, tell him I said no summaries of the faxes are to be created. Blame it on me. He won't complain to Morrison, because he's scared of him, but if he does, I'll say I ordered no summaries. And one last thing, under no circumstances tell Shevesky these two numbers I just gave you. Okay?"

DiFrancesco smiled. "You live in a nasty world, Mr. Whitman."

I nodded. "Gets nastier every day, too."

♦ ♦ ♦

Back in my office, I was wondering how my windows got so dirty on the outside when Helen buzzed me and said a Hector Salcines was on the phone.

"Tell him I'm in a meeting."

"He called three times while you were out."

I gripped the edge of my desk. "In a meeting," I told her.

"*Okay.*"

"And, Helen," I asked, "how do you generally answer the phone?"

" 'Mr. Whitman's office.' "

"That's what I thought. How did this Hector Salcines ask for me the first time?"

"He asked for Jack."

"And Jack Whitman subsequently?"

"Yes."

"Okay, if he calls again, say that I'm not available."

"You want to avoid him?"

"I don't even want to be on the same planet with him."

Perhaps Hector Salcines had decided over the weekend to contact me. He now knew that the man who had arranged to house his wife and child was named Jack Whitman, thanks to Ahmed. And he had my work number. I could also assume that Hector knew I was at the Corporation, because if he had called Helen once while she was out, the call would have bounced out to the receptionist, who greeted callers with the Corporation's name. He did not know where I lived, of course, and thus not where Dolores and Maria were. If he was given to research, he would dial directory assistance in all five boroughs and even the suburbs and call every J. or John Whitman listed. But that wouldn't succeed; since Liz's death, I'd had an unlisted phone number. And I counted that as a lucky thing, since I didn't need any more difficulty from Hector Salcines. It was troubling enough that he knew where I worked.

◆ ◆ ◆

That night, home late after Maria had gone to bed, I found Dolores sitting on the living room rug with the photo albums of Liz and me. We used to take a lot of pictures—meals out with friends, vacations, whatever. Jack Whitman with a thirty-two-inch waist and weaker glasses. The photographs revealed that I was not going to age well, the flesh falling from my face just like my father's. I hung up my coat. "Long time ago," I said, pointing at the stack of photo albums.

"I *like* them," Dolores said quietly, turning a page. "You were so young. Both of you. She was good-looking."

"Yes."

"She was very rich?"

"No, not at all—she grew up working summers in a lobster pound."

I told Dolores how Liz had learned the restaurant business from her father, a widower with a face of ruddy disapproval who ran a string of lobster houses on the Massachusetts and Maine coasts that went belly-up not long after he died of a massive coronary while pushing a lawn mower. In retrospect, I think his doctor had told him many years before that his heart was not good and, when he was turned down for life insurance, he began to pull money out of the restaurant business, perhaps even cheating his partners, so that he could pay for Liz to go to Harvard. He was a lousy father, too authoritarian with his wife and daughter, but after his wife's death, Liz was all he ever cared about. He left her all that he still owned, which wasn't much: the proceeds from the sale of his house and a refrigerator full of beer. Her grief was tremendous and she clung to me in those months. But her father had trained her well, and soon after that Liz was hired to manage a large midtown restaurant that catered mostly to the business trade, and she loved getting there early, making sure the daily orders had arrived, that the floors had been vacuumed overnight, that the fresh bread was in, that the laundry service had delivered the napkins and tablecloths. It's notoriously difficult to prosper in the restaurant business in New York City but Liz had thrown herself into it with the same reckless confidence that had taken her up to 168th Street after dark on the evening of her death.

"I *knew* she worked hard," Dolores said. "You can sort of see it in her face." She had been sitting with the photo albums awhile, studying each of the photos, ingesting my past, my marriage to Liz. "I looked at *all* of them," she added, a little playfully.

"All of them? Oh—there were a couple . . ."

"Mm-hmm." She pulled one out of its sleeve. "This the one you're thinking about?"

I looked at the photo and froze—it was one I'd taken of Liz in her third month. As her pregnancy progressed, her breasts had swelled. She was baffled and slightly embarrassed by their new size. I celebrated this sudden gift, telling her I intended to get all the time I could sucking and fondling her breasts before the next generation took over. By this point in the conversation—we had it often in the months that she was pregnant, for I enjoyed the topic—my hands had spidered their way up around each nipple and she playfully slapped at my fingers, saying her breasts were too big and complaining her bras no longer fit. But, I answered, when would I ever again have an opportunity to appreciate such magnificent breasts? High, full, fertile, and heavy? She didn't understand, I would moan good-naturedly, she suddenly had *amazing tits.* "Like the bows of whaling ships! Like erotic sculptures in India!" I exclaimed. "Attention must be paid *now*, for someday in the far future I will be a broken-down old man with rotting nuts and a useless hose between my legs and you will be a hag with leathery fallen dugs!" "That's a *horrible* thing to say to your pregnant wife," Liz responded, pleased nonetheless. "A man," I said solemnly, "needs to bank some memories against the onslaught of time." Could I take a picture of her from the waist up—so as to remember? My wife, lusty in bed but modest in most other respects, agreed, and so one Saturday morning she knelt on the sheets with the morning light coming through the windows while I fussed with a thirty-five-millimeter camera. She was sleepy and silly and had just brushed her hair. Her breasts stood pale and firm, lifted into the light, faint deltas of veins newly visible, the aureole of each breast larger and darker since she'd become pregnant. In the picture, Liz is looking at me beneath amused brows, a smile curled on her lips, with one hand modestly lifted to her shoulder—her hand is beautiful in the sun, too—as if about to cover herself. Her wedding ring glints ever so barely in the light.

A picture of happiness. Yet I could not look at the photo without thinking of the last *actual* conversation I had with Liz, a conversation that, coincidentally, had do with breasts belonging to *another* woman. It's not a pleasant incident. It doesn't reflect well upon me. I've already set forth the basic, unhappy details of Liz's murder, but there is one last aspect of her death that still needs to be told. On the evening of her death, only a few hours before it, Liz and I talked by phone; Liz was due to visit her friend Susie at the hospital. I wasn't happy with this; as far as I was concerned, Susie was a whining tart who lived off her trust fund and for years had talked about how she wanted children and meanwhile slept indiscriminately with married men—lunchtime rendezvous in a hotel, no demands. She had helped to wreck at least two marriages. Susie's bout with breast cancer elicited only grudging sympathy from me. "You're too tired to go all the way uptown," I told Liz. "Really, why not do it on the weekend? Susie's not going anywhere."

"I want to go tonight because Susie has just had the surgery," Liz said. "You could meet me at the hospital and we'd just hop on the subway home."

"I've got this work."

"You always have work," she answered, the effort of patience audible in her voice. "You have *decades* of work ahead of you, Jack. This is a friend of ours who has *cancer*."

"I know. But this is stuff I have to get done. If it's good, there's a chance this guy Morrison will see it."

"It's very important to *me* that you go see Susie," Liz insisted. "She's miserable. She's got tubes in her and is very, very depressed. They took off both her breasts, her mother said. She doesn't have anybody except her parents. What's-his-name, the jerk she's been sleeping with, won't come to see her."

"Can't do it," I told my wife. "Okay?"

"You're really being a shit about this," Liz answered. "A prime-A, jumbo-sized shit."

"I have to do this work, Liz."

"You haven't visited Susie *once*."

"Sorry."

Liz sighed. "I'll be home around nine-thirty."

"Okay," I said, thinking her anger was spent.

"And, Jack?"

"Yes?" I answered my wife, hoping she had softened.

"Fuck you."

She hung up. That was the last thing Liz ever said to me. *Fuck you.* She'd said it before and would have said it again, a flash of anger typical of a normal marriage. We had traversed many such moments, a few needing talk and negotiation, most forgotten quickly by both of us. As I have said, we had a good marriage. But my slight, for which I had been unable to apologize, was to weigh on me, fill my mouth with bitterness and self-loathing. It wasn't just that my last words to Liz were less than affectionate, but also that had I acted with greater charity, had I only decided to go uptown and meet her, then perhaps it might all have been different. And, probably, we would have taken a cab home, because I did not like to see her struggle heavily down and up the subway steps. That the chain of causation of Liz's death had passed through my hands, so to speak, became the source of unutterable grief for me. The fact that Susie had recovered completely, been fitted for new, larger, unnaturally pert breasts, compliments of her trust officer, and then continued to chase married men, even having

the gall to smile wetly at me once or twice, confirmed the senseless-
ness of Liz's death. I'd spent many evenings sitting at home thinking *If
I had only . . .* , promising myself that if ever I somehow found a wife
again that I would be different, that never again would I make the
same selfish mistake.

I put Liz's photo back in Dolores's soft dark hand.

"What is it?" she asked.

"I was just thinking."

"About what?"

It was hard to say. I didn't talk to anyone about this anymore.
"See, this was when my wife was pregnant."

"She was pregnant?" Dolores reacted with alert attention, her
dark eyes seeking mine. "What happened to the baby?"

"Liz was pregnant when she was killed. The baby was eight
months—"

"Could they save—"

"No. It would have been a girl. A little baby girl."

"You lost a *baby*, too?" Dolores's voice trailed off and she turned
her head toward the slight breeze that moved through the open
window. I stood there, wrapped again in the grief of it. And Dolores
too seemed to suffer a confusion of emotions. Several streets over we
heard a momentary passing of sirens. I wished then that I could go to
Dolores. I wished I could beg her to let me put my head in her lap and
shut my eyes. With her cool hand on my forehead in the manner of
kindness. It had been years since a woman's hand had been on my
forehead. Dolores stared up at me, her face soft in thought. She hung
now in the balance, we both knew, between the life that was behind
her and, quite possibly, something vastly different. But then the
moment seemed to have passed. I was tired from the day and saddened
by seeing Liz's picture and so I started up the stairs.

"Your wife—" Dolores called after me. "She's happy in these
pictures. She looks like you took care of her."

"I did," I said pointedly. "I took very good care of her."

♦ ♦ ♦

Late that night, maybe 1:00 A.M., I found myself restlessly riding
the gray edge of consciousness. Outside my bedroom window came

the rush of the gloom and the rustle of the twisted old pear trees luminous with papery white blossoms, each no bigger than Maria's fingernails. Information was moving globally. You could almost feel it, invisible pulses and bytes streaming through the air, silent cells of light pulsing across continents. You can sense the global picture changing, the computer manufacturers and consumer electronics firms—AT&T, Matsushita, Xerox, IBM, Microsoft, Apple—all converging on the technologies, pushing at the Corporation. Underneath his bluster, Morrison knew this, knew that if the Corporation was to survive, the Chairman would not be the man to lead the charge. I lay in the dark tasting the residual chalkiness in my mouth from the acid medication and wondering if the next day's meeting with the Chairman would be any good.

Then I heard what had woken me, a foot on the stairs in the darkness. The old brass hinges of the door creaked. I rolled over and there was Dolores next to the bed, naked, her belly at my eyes, her heavy breasts above me, with their sad, mortal beauty. Her dark tangle of pubic hair had a forthright fullness. She bent down and held my face tight in both hands. I could tell she'd been drinking wine in the kitchen and she peered at me with great seriousness—I think she wanted to be sure it was going to be honest between us—and then pulled the covers away and got in the bed. My head was hot with sleep and my breath foul. I hesitated, but she did not. My head cleared quickly. That certain urgent energy was suddenly available. *Don't say anything to her yet.* I wondered if she felt obliged to do this. It had been a long time, and I wanted to go slowly, to have it come back to me. But Dolores pressed quickly, straddling me, pushing hard against my chest. It all came rushing back after a long lapse, the wet slipping in and out, the tension and breathing, the sweet rank odor of Dolores filling the room.

When we rolled over she grabbed her hands against my ass, forcing the rhythm. People who have just met rarely screw hard. It takes a shared desire for oblivion, a certain courage on the woman's part. And if you are a man, you never quite trust yourself not to go too hard at it, not to put a heavy hand on the woman's collarbone for greater leverage, or thrust your hips at such an angle so that under no circumstances can she shut her legs. It's what men really want to do.

All men know this in their hearts and Dolores let me, urged me, was not afraid. Her bent legs lifted high, the rough bottoms of her feet rasping the back of my legs, and I went after her with the frantic heat that ends with the heart kicking against the lungs.

And we lay there silently afterward. The sweat on my chest cooled and my limbs felt pleasantly heavy. I held Dolores and felt the rise and fall of her ribs.

"I've got a ridiculous question," she said into the darkness. "It's not romantic, you know, but I was just thinking of it."

"Sure."

"What's that *thing*—"

"That 'thing'?" I laughed. "You don't know what 'that thing' is?"

"Not *that*," she said playfully. "Let me finish what I was saying, okay?"

"Absolutely."

"What's that thing, that little place where they cut out the wall when you're coming up the stairs? I never saw that before anywhere."

"You mean where the stairs go to the right and there's a deep indentation in the wall, like a little curved shelf cut out?"

"Yes."

"That's called a 'coffin-turn,' " I said. "When these houses were built, it was back when most people still died at home in a bedroom. Nobody went to the hospital to wait around and die, like now. Then you had a body in a bed. They had to be able to get the coffin down the stairs without breaking the plaster or standing it on its end."

"You think people died in *this* house?"

"It's a hundred and ten years old. So probably."

Dolores considered this for a moment, then lifted her leg over the side of the bed. "Now I'm scared and have to go check on Maria." Her voice was anxious. "Okay?"

I watched her naked silhouette move through the dark. Her feet creaked down the stairs. Dolores had displayed a certain eagerness that had little to do with me, I believed; her passion was centered elsewhere, within herself. A few minutes later she returned to the bedroom, murmuring that Maria was still asleep. She stood above me.

"I *knew* something was wrong," she whispered with delighted surprise.

I was looking at her form above me. "What?"

"The bed—it's tilted! The head is higher." She bent down and looked at the legs. "You have something—*telephone books!*"

"Under the legs at the head of the bed."

"Why?"

"I have this problem with my stomach. It helps to keep the bed higher on one end."

"What do you mean?"

"Acid comes up into my esophagus, the hydrochloric acid in the stomach, and if it comes up through a little sphincter, a little opening, at the base of the esophagus, it burns up the mucous membrane and damages what are called the esophageal cells."

"That's why you cough all the time?" she asked. "I was going to maybe say something."

"Yes."

"Does it hurt?" she asked kindly.

"It can."

"Do you throw up?"

"Sometimes, if there's a lot of acid."

"Did you see a doctor?" she asked, climbing back into bed.

"A bunch of them."

"Does sex make it worse?" she teased.

"No."

"Good." She put her fingers over my mouth, hard, at the same time laying her other hand on my groin—optimistically, I thought—but she spat generously into her palm and patiently manipulated an erection with a frank brusquesness that had nothing to do with my arousal and everything to do with hers. She rode me hard, harder than was comfortable, with her hands resting on my shoulders, her nails rhythmically clasping into my skin. Then her right hand slipped toward her own groin and quivered against herself, two rigid fingers pressed expertly, moving with electric speed, and she came, contracting backward, her left hand leaving my shoulder for a second and then falling against my face, her palm shoved hard into the curve above my nose and her nails against my forehead. My thoughts flowed sideways back through the day and it occurred to me that Dolores knew nothing of computers and media wars and warp and woof of the capitalistic structure. She was *here*, a woman in a room fucking a man. Complete in herself. In the grayness her eyes were shut and her bottom lip bitten under the upper one in concentration. The room was large with her smell. When she tired of this position she fell to the sheets and quickly rose on her hands and knees with her rear end high so that I could insinuate myself between her cheeks from behind, slipping it in from underneath, my fingers yanking her hipbones toward me, enjoying the extra tightness of the vagina the man feels when from behind, the gross animal bruteness of it, and one of her hands crawled backward to touch herself again. She moaned and stopped to rest. Sweat dripped from the valley of her back down her ribs.

"Now," she breathed loudly in the room. "Now you're going. To like this." She rolled her head forward so that it was supporting her weight and slipped both her hands underneath herself in frank service of my pleasure, one hand cupping me from underneath, playing and stroking me, the thumb and forefinger of the other hand forming a second ring of tightness, slipping back and forth in countersyncopation to my thrusts.

"Jesus," I exclaimed.

"Do it," she answered.

And I did.

Afterward, we lay there for some minutes, listening to the wind and the cars speeding up the streets. Dolores murmured something about being with Maria when she woke up. She lifted the covers and disappeared into the darkened doorway. She did not bend down to kiss me and she did not return that night.

◆ ◆ ◆

"Why *do* you wear a tie?" Maria inquired of me the next morning while I was dressing. In the shower I'd felt that sweet ache in my groin from the night before. But already, stupidly, obsessively, I was worrying about the meeting that day with the Chairman. Morrison would be looking at me with a grimace pasted on his face, as if he were about to be forced to do something distasteful, and I sensed that he was making reassurances to the V-S people. We were moving inexorably toward the moment when some public announcement of the negotiations would have to be made, in accordance with federal securities law. If I didn't get the Chairman onto the field, Morrison would make a brutal move to the board of directors. Where that put me was anyone's guess.

"Why?" Maria repeated, pointing to my necktie.

"Because I'm going to work and it's the rule," I told her.

"Why?" Maria said, holding my electric shaver.

"Why do they have the rule? Because that way everybody *looks* ready to work. It's a silly rule, actually."

"How come you have it then?"

"Because adults like to make up rules."

"We're going to the playground today, see all the kids."

"In the park?"

I walked downstairs with Maria leading me.

"Maria, would you get the newspaper for me?"

"Yes!" She stomped down the stairs to the garden floor that led to the door under the stoop.

Dolores and I had not yet spoken to one another and I wondered how she might act after the previous night. In my experience, you look at the woman the next morning and you know instantly whether the previous night was a mistake or a gift. Dolores stood in the kitchen, making breakfast, her hair pulled back. I noticed the wine bottle in the trash. She was wearing one of my flannel gardening shirts.

"Good morning."

"Have a good appetite?" She smiled.

"Absolutely."

"Good." She spooned some hot cereal into a bowl. "There's more when you want it."

"More?"

"If you want more," she said with a certain smile, "you'll get more, you know what I'm saying?"

◆ ◆ ◆

That morning, just as I stood from my desk to go see the Chairman, Helen opened my door and handed me a colored sheet of paper. "There's a man downstairs who sent this up, the man who called yesterday." She stared at me, without sympathy. "The note is on the other side." It was a flier from a men's clothing shop a few blocks away and on the reverse, written in carefully legible block letters, were these words:

DEAR JACK WHITMAN,
I WAS TOLD BY YOUR FREIND AT THE BILDING DOWNTOWN THAT YOU KNOW WHERE MY WIFE AND BABY-GIRL IS LIVING. PLEASE ANSWER MY CALL, SIR, PLEASE. MY HOME NUMBER IS 718-555-4640 AND YOU CAN LEEVE A MESAGE ON THE MACHINE. OR YOU CAN COME DOWNSTAIRS AND MEET ME HERE, I WILL BE HERE TO 12 NOON.
SINCERELY, HECTOR SALCINES

He was down in the Corporation's lobby, pressing his claim. He'd probably taken a day off from work. But Dolores had left him. What did I owe him, what did he deserve? Not once had she mentioned going back to him, and it was she who had come to my bed. I slipped the note into my desk and decided to do nothing. I would like to believe this was a reasonable thing to do.

◆ ◆ ◆

The Chairman was at his desk, a steaming silver teapot at his elbow. "Now just talk, dammit," he said to me when I came in. "Just say what you need to say."

It was a good twenty steps from his office door to his desk. I pulled up a chair. "I've started to, a couple of times, and you dodge me," I said.

"Why, do you think?"

"Do you want a candid answer?"

"Yes," he said, not blinking his blue eyes.

"Fine." It wasn't going to be nice. "I believe you're resisting my desire to open discussions with you because you refuse to accommodate reality. Chances are you're afraid of death. That's okay—you follow in a fine tradition. You feel that the death of the Corporation as you know it, as you *built* it, metaphorically presages your own."

There it was, laid out in front of us both—the imaginary pale corpse of the Chairman, suspended in the air—a wrinkled bag of skin and bones and hair, the eyes sunken and closed, the hollowed mouth gaping upward in a leer of death. The red rims of the Chairman's eyes watered angrily.

"Get out," he said.

I didn't move from the chair, not a twitch. "Why not listen to what I have to say?"

He swirled his spoon around his teacup without answering, so I kept talking, kept running in the air: "Look, you, above all, should be able to see that the Corporation is ever changing. We cannot help but to try to manage that change. It's coming down to four or five big companies, big global companies and a couple of dozen very aggressive, very smart smaller ones. If we don't grow, we shrink."

"Very good. You have just updated me to 1978."

"In theoretical terms only. Now the technology is upon us."

"So I'm told. Everyone tells me this. Everybody in this damn company sings the technology anthem, the whole idea of synergy among products doesn't work."

"It doesn't work *yet.*" I could feel his resistance. "The Corporation and V-S can have huge markets around the globe if the whole thing is put together right. *Huge.* Think of it. We can put the squeeze on Disney and Paramount. They're expanding very quickly, and we have to front them aggressively in some of these markets. Also the regional telephone companies are coming on very strong, now that they can transmit television signals through their phone wires. With a merger with V-S, we protect ourselves. Bertelsmann, Sony, none of them will be able to link so many pieces of the machine. We do have competition from Phillips, Toshiba, and MCA. But we can beat them. It's so *clear.*"

"What's clear," the Chairman said, sipping his tea, "is that you and all the other crystal-ball wizards on this floor are suffering from another pitiful *fad.* Another windbag theology, whatever the headline writer wants to call it. I've seen a lot of theories over the years, Jack. We were all going to be riding around in jet-powered cars by the year 1980. Honestly. I'm seventy-one years old. Life . . . life has its own limitations—there are human truths that supersede all technological advances. You may be too young to see that. You can't jam together two things that were never meant for one another. Someone loses, someone gets the bum end. Believe me, I understand where you are coming from, I was like that once, I had grand schemes when I was young—"

"All the other media mergers so far have been within the same countries or between giant industrials and smaller properties," I continued. "V-S has so much of what we want. They have telephone systems in developing countries, cable systems all over Europe, a satellite system, access to the Japanese research into the new chips and the new plasma display screens—"

"New *screens*," the Chairman complained. "Why is this all I ever hear about? Who needs them? We're a movie and magazine and cable television and recording company. We do this well enough. We had an absolute net profit of eight hundred and ninety-two million dollars last year, right? We have smart people working on all the things you've mentioned, right? Why do we have to shake hands with a bunch of Germans and Japanese?" He shook his head in disgust and seemed to have reached a conclusion. His look told me he thought we were done.

"All right," I told him. "Just *listen* to what I have to say. Listen to it like you have never listened to anything in your life, because what I am going to describe is going to happen with or without you, here in the Corporation, or elsewhere, and it will happen everywhere."

The Chairman was silent. I looked straight into his pale blue eyes. Set within the folds of his dry, too-tan skin, they remained bright, not at all frightened by me, not frightened by my invocation of his death, keen to rule as much of the world as he could, to play chess with me, the young court jester appointed as a temporary amusement. Maybe that's all I was, a court jester dressed in a business suit.

"Right now, as I talk, there are probably only a thousand people in America who understand what is going to happen. In 1981 there were four million personal computers in America. By 1991, that number was eighty-five million. By the year 2001, there will be one hundred forty million. It's part of the culture. Even the working-class poor now buy computers for their children. Why shouldn't they? The price keeps dropping. At the same time, free broadcast television viewership is dying, as you know. It will be forty-five percent of its historic high in the year 2000. Now then, the personal computer, as a metaphor, as a conceit, is finished. The phase is through, like electric typewriters. The movement is to interactive, portable, specialized. It will be a few years before Congress figures out who uses what wires—the cable companies, the telephone companies, whoever. Like I said, the FCC is going to allow the regional phone companies to transmit television on fiber optic. It will take at least ten years to completely rewire the country with fiber optic. But that's just the conduit. We will have *products* that can move through any conduit—cable, fiber optic, radio, television, direct-broadcast satellite, whatever. Why the hell do you think you were in Washington a few weeks ago? To set up a fucking game of golf with a senator? No. Because this company, whether you give a damn or not, is moving into the future. That satellite is *important.* We're well positioned there. The telephone utilities are slowly being deregulated anyway, so we could start buying them if we wanted. There will be different modes and types of boxes. No one knows what the complete menu will be. Multiple avenues of transmission. It will shift. Some will do well and then be replaced by others. Some will be outflanked by industry standards, like Beta tape was by VHS—"

"You're preaching the same old religion," the Chairman said wearily. "I don't think—"

"The *point,* dammit, is that what is *possible* is going to *change.* People will catch information or entertainment in new ways and they will be able to use it in new ways. We're positioned well for all of those technologies, *domestically.* Our 1992 gross revenues from TV shows and movies is going to come out around two billion. The cash flow is consistent, our debt is basically in hand, and the analysts love us—at least this week. The time is good to do a deal. And Volkman-Sakura wants to push back Phillips in Europe and Toshiba in Japan; they have incentives. V-S is well positioned in Europe and Japan. They may get the fiber optic contract for Russia. Think about *that,*" I told him. "*Think* about the market that is opening up there. Their communications system is hopelessly out of date. They'll have to scrap the whole thing and buy a couple of hundred million miles of fiber optic wiring from Owens-Corning. They'll do it, too, once they get the economy stabilized. And what are they going to want? They're going to want what *we make*, our pop culture. And they're not just going to have VCRs, they're going to have the same magic boxes we do. The magnitude of this change is enormous. The whole world eventually interacting with massive global computer systems of entertainment. The cost-effectiveness ratios are doubling every year. Intel has a chip that is eighty percent faster than the P-Five they brought out last year and thirty percent cheaper. They announced that last week. With this kind of advance—"

"Religion . . . nothing but religion." The Chairman flipped through his papers listlessly. "We've been farting around all these years with optical discs and magazines on TV and all kinds of other Frankenstein monsters that cost hundreds of millions of dollars of R and D—"

"No, no, wait," I said. "There *have* been some huge and costly mistakes. But the right product will come along. I mean, in about eighteen months, two years, I'll be able to hang an HDTV screen on my wall, like a poster, maybe an inch thick, except it will be as big as a doorway. Then I'll slip a disk in and I'll have Madonna dancing and singing her new single in front of me. It will make MTV look like an old celluloid movie, and the sound will be better than any current CD player on the market. But you have to realize it will be better than all the multimedia stuff now on the market. Those are just very fancy video games. Once the technology is in sync with the product, you'll be able to walk up to the screen and look in Madonna's eyes and be able to see the *tiny red veins!* Then when she opens her mouth you'll be able to see back into her throat. You'll be able to talk to her and she'll talk to you! She'll call you by name and she'll take her clothes off if you ask her to. It will be better than anything we have now, better in a sense than *reality* because you can stop it and make it start or back up or in the case of Madonna, you can fiddle with a switch and watch her rotate until she's facing away from you and still singing."

The Chairman's eyes crinkled. "God, the pornographers will go wild."

"Yes, actually, that's right," I said. "You'll be able to slip a disk in and watch life-size people fuck from any angle, you'll be able to control what they do. In fact you'll be able to decide how big the woman's breasts will be, make the man's dick fifteen inches long, whatever turns you on. But what's important is this kind of technology is incredibly exciting. People are now accustomed to computers in the home. Watching television passively is boring—"

"But the American public is a stupid, nonthinking mass that gets stupider every year," the Chairman said. "We are getting stupider as a nation, as a culture. I honestly believe that." He sounded genuinely distressed. "We don't vote, we don't read books."

"Some of that is true. But these new technologies will create a kind of electronic reality that will be irresistible."

He pressed his spoon down on the wet tea bag. Ten seconds went by.

"It sounds evil."

"It's not. It's the same old appetites given new forms of satisfaction. It's an inevitable product of man's ingenuity. The pictures on the wall of the cave become inscribed on a laserdisc. But in order for the Corporation to compete, we need a global system. With V-S's Japanese microchip connections, we should be able to get integration with basic computer design and have six-month lead times over the competition. We can get on top of the market with new products. The products will follow a certain technological sequence, and each new interactive product will be downwardly compatible. Sooner or later, for example, all CDs and videodiscs will be about the size of a dime and they'll hold a thousand times the information they do now. People will be able to buy entire libraries of information or catch it out of the air. We'll have a satellite doing nothing but pulsing the five thousand most popular movies in America downward on a regular basis. The home receiver will capture and record the movies, even though different companies hold the different rights. With a few massive corporate players, the other companies will have to buckle in order to achieve access to the consumer. All the technology will be cross-indexed and cross-compatible. Let's say I want to see *Casablanca*. I call it up, I get it, the original black-and-white version. You with me so far?"

The Chairman nodded noncommittally.

"All right, now for a gag, I want to splice in one of the soliloquies from Laurence Olivier's *Hamlet*, where I please, and make Bogart speak the words perfectly—make his lips actually move and speak

Shakespeare's words in Olivier's voice. And then I can colorize the lips if I want to, or I can freeze the frame and blow it up and put tiny pictures of the president of the United States into the pupils of Bogart's eyes and then I can shrink the frame back to normal and then start the movie again, and I'm doing all of these things either by voice command or by moving a mouse attached to the computer against a menu at the margins of the screen, and then I can make, say, Daffy Duck, appear in a little floating box over Ingrid Bergman's head, and I can do all of this fluidly with no forethought or special training or superexpensive equipment, just improvising for the hell of it, and then I can make the Terminator appear, a tiny one, the size of a fly and make him shoot Daffy Duck and then the both of them disappear on screen. So Bogart and Bergman continue, except for the colorized lips, say. Then I can get the computer to scan its ROM memory for a couple of pages from the Bible, say, or the front page of that day's newspaper, and then make Ingrid Bergman speak that material in any written language, mind you, any, the idiom and inflection perfect to the ear of a native speaker—and of course I could patch in Vivaldi as a background music and then I can save the whole thing, the *exercise*, and then zap it to my friend in Hong Kong via fiber optic so he can play around with it and change it and then he can zap it back to me and I can watch it, and no one else, and *this* is what the future looks like. Can you get that?"

The Chairman looked at me a long time. He'd forgotten to light his cigarette.

"Now," I continued, "what you got off that is the basic on-line monthly fee paid to the local franchise, sort of like cable TV now, plus the rental fee for the original movie, the royalties for the use of Daffy Duck and the Terminator, calculated on the digital equivalent of a frame-by-frame usage, the fee for the software used to manipulate all these images, software which is leased to the local on-line franchises but developed centrally, the fee for first sale or on-line retrieval of the Vivaldi music, and the line fee for the transmission of the thing to the guy in Hong Kong, and a satellite user's fee on the turnaround. A fraction of money to be made at every step."

"There are political implications of this type of—"

"Yes. They're huge," I agreed. "Let's pretend you're the president of the United States and I'm one of your speechwriters. You tell me to write you a speech on, say, the economic turmoil in the U.S. You want me to do a good job, I want to do a good job. I go to my White House press office, sit at my computer. Punch up a file. There, on the screen is you, the president. Your face, in color, frozen. You're seated at the Oval Office desk, as if before the television cameras. I talk into a little microphone. 'My fellow Americans—' And just after I say it, you, the president's image, say it, in your voice, with perfect inflection, with your lips moving in perfect articulation. I work on the talk, first saying this, then deciding on some other phrase, and sooner or later I get it right. I show it to my bosses. You, the president, may or may not see it. On the tape you speak for twenty minutes. We broadcast it to the networks, what's left of them, and that's it."

"I see." The Chairman still had not lit his cigarette. His eyes were far away now. He's got it, I thought, he's finally got it. I went on, pressing whatever advantage I might have gained.

"And along the same lines, in time, when the technology is far enough along, you will be able to scan in photos of someone who doesn't live and interact with them. Scan in ten or twenty pictures of your late mother, say, maybe also a tape of her talking . . ." I froze—I would be able to do this with Liz. "That would be enough information. You could just see her again. Or anyone who was dead and who had pictures taken of them when they were alive. Imagine having a conversation with Marilyn Monroe. How great that would be, her eyes sultry and half-opened, her lips saying your name, that soft voice responding to your questions."

"They commodified her corpse, if you ask me." The Chairman shook his head. "I was there when she sang 'Happy Birthday' to President Kennedy at Madison Square Garden," he mused. "I was in the audience." His old blue eyes became unfocused. "I realized, on that very night . . . I realized that we live in a pagan society. The men around me were seeing a goddess sing to a god. The power of her image was actually dangerous, I think. Pagan idols. We worship them. And this, incidentally, is the secret of the entertainment business, Jack. Monotheism is a learned habit. Paganism is the baser instinct."

"Then you see how the technology plays into the human psyche."

"You know," the Chairman said, changing topics, "you cough a hell of a lot. But you don't seem to have a cold and you don't smoke. I noticed it when we were in Washington."

"It's my stomach," I told him. "I've got this acid problem. It's bad today, actually."

"Taking stuff? Pills?"

I nodded.

"Ulcers or reflux disease?"

He had an old man's knowledge of illness. "Reflux disease," I answered.

"Jesus," he noted to himself. "They do Nissen's plication for that."

"How do you know that?" I was astounded.

"Because they did it to me, thirty years ago."

"Is it bad?" I asked fearfully.

The Chairman didn't answer. Some other thought had come into his head and I felt a sudden odd fear. "It's a hell of a thing for a young man with a bad stomach to mock an old man's ever-nearing death." He drank off his tea. "It's—"

"It's my only advantage," I interrupted nervously, trying for a joke.

"Get out." He meant it this time, waved his hand brusquely. "Get out."

♦ ♦ ♦

I did get out, with hateful quickness. It now was of no concern to me if the Chairman lost control of the Corporation in a bloody internal fight. He was a rich old bastard who probably had a maid put on his socks every morning. When he was dead shoe leather in a box, I'd still have another forty years. Let him be publicly humiliated, did I care? I was swimming in the strong current of change. Morrison had been right that the Chairman was just an old drunk in a new suit. He was too cautious for the game, slow in the head, and I decided to report to the others that they should just go ahead and run him over. Let the board buy itself off with huge stock plays. Let Morrison send in the marines with charts and reports and all the hyper-rationalized argument. Get the PR windmills revved up. Fuck the Chairman.

I returned to my office and stood at my window watching the odd antlike activity below and thinking of my father, what he would say to me if he knew how I'd just spent my last hour. "What you're doing," he would tell me, setting a tomato seedling into the earth, "is wasting your mind and your heart. Remember that, you're wasting your heart, too." It was after 6:00 P.M., late enough on a low, clouded day that the lines of the other office buildings were indistinct against the sky, a time when Manhattan has a brooding melancholy, when men such as I stand at their office windows and wonder how it was that the boy had become the man in a suit in a lighted box above the street. I floated over to my desk to gather up some papers. Helen, who had left at five-thirty, had put something on my chair so that I would see it — with a yellow note in her handwriting stuck on it saying that this had been delivered at the end of the day. It read:

MR. WHITMAN,
I STAYED HERE THE WHOLE DAY. YOU MUST TELL ME. THEY IS MY WIFE AND BABY-GIRL.
— HECTOR SALCINES
P.S. I'M SERIOUS.

I placed this note in the same drawer with the first one, and just then the phone rang in Helen's office. I picked it up.

"Jack Whitman," I said as usual.

There was no answer, just the far buzz of a phone line, maybe traffic sounds. A pay phone.

"Who is this?" I asked.

"Where is she?"

Disguise your voice, I thought. "Think you got the wrong number, guy."

"Look, Mr. Whitman, *wait*," came Hector's voice, a sad, beaten version of the personality I'd met at the used car lot. "You gotta understand. I don't have nothin'. All I ever had was my family. Now, now I got *nothin'*. You can't understand that . . ." He hadn't recognized my voice. "Dolores and me'll work things out. We always did before. Maria misses me, I know. And I miss her, miss my little girl. You can't take that from a guy, you can't take that away from me, it ain't right. I want you to tell me how I can talk to my wife. Let me talk to my wife."

My meeting with the Chairman had left me in a brutal mood. Hector didn't scare me. I said nothing.

"You gotta let me see my wife!"

"I'm afraid I can't do that."

"Why? Why the fuck not?"

I hung up—gently, as if this mattered.

TEN

I wanted her body to forget Hector, to make its accommodations to me. Dolores came back to my bed that night and the next and all those that followed, and I was devotedly energetic in my attentions, not only because I enjoyed this newfound bounty of flesh and warmth after my long loneliness but because when you do it over and over again, a certain corporeal loyalty takes effect. An expectation of the other. The sounds and smell and weight. There were, now, the first shades of habit and familiarity in how we acted with one another. Each evening at nine o'clock Dolores would warm a bottle of milk for Maria, which comforted her, and after Maria had fallen asleep in the bed in the apartment, curled around her "Sesame Street" dolls, Dolores would climb the stairs to my bedroom.

"Maria okay?" I'd ask.

"She's all right. I got to get her off the night bottle."

"She likes it, though."

"Maybe soon," Dolores would say. "She's almost four."

Then, as I watched from the bed, she would take off her clothes and stand in front of the mirror in her bra and panties to brush out her hair. Her body was firm, abundant in the breasts and hips. But most striking was the basic strength in her shoulders and back and thighs. It occurred to me that either her mother or father had been quite physically strong. Picking up a hairbrush, Dolores would bend her head down, exposing the soft nape of her neck, and brush the dark mass from the back of her head forward. I watched the muscles of her arm and shoulder flex and relax, flex and relax as she brushed, her eyes cast downward at the floor, thinking to herself, knowing she was being watched, enjoying the exhibition. Then she would flip her hair back and brush it the other way.

Later, afterward, we would lie in bed. Eventually one of us would get up. I did not mind that Dolores saw me swigging the awful acid stuff, I did not mind that standing in my underwear I did not appear as young as I once did. You get past this as you get older. And, to my relief, Dolores seemed free of the need to appear as anything other than what she was; I knew this the moment that she padded barefoot into the bathroom one night and forgot to close the door. I heard that discreet and once-familiar feminine tinkle into the bowl, the sound muffled, then the flap of the toilet paper roll spinning, and I smiled — it set me right somehow, it was real. And we talked about birth control; she was on the pill and had refilled her prescription. Soon after that we abandoned any pretense that Dolores and Maria were living in the apartment downstairs and I moved Maria's new bed, which I'd ordered from a children's catalog, into the front bedroom.

But still there was much that was unsaid. The question of who Dolores Salcines was, *really*, dangled before me like a fascinating fruit. Strange how it is that men and women may be naked together but keep great secrets within themselves. I realized that the fact that she had left her husband didn't mean that she did not mourn the end of their marriage. And until now she had protected her history with Hector, dodging around it, telling me only a little of this, a little of that. He was a car salesman, he installed cable, he had cared very much about Maria, and so on.

I did not press Dolores, however, for I felt redeemed that the house and my life were suddenly warmer, full of life. Maria seemed to accept the fact that her mother and I now slept together, and each morning she ran into my bedroom — *our* bedroom — throwing herself onto the sheets, wriggling and giggling and hugging me with abandon, as if she had once done this every morning in her home, as if all her child's love and need for a father had found expression with me. My own daughter would have been born within a few months of Maria, and when Maria flung herself against me, I felt a certain bittersweet confusion. *So this is what I would have had if Liz hadn't been killed,* I thought to myself, reaching past the veil of fate and time to see my own self in bed with Liz asleep on one side, with our baby girl between us. *This is almost what it would have been like.* A roof, the light of early morning, the smell of sleep, warm bodies in bed. I believe that we are more like each other than we realize, across place and time and other distinctions. And so now I could understand Hector's torment; what I had here, this flesh gathered in both my arms, was once his. I felt a strange vicarious sadness for him. My pleasure came at his deprivation. My guilt, however, was not so great that I admitted to Dolores I had seen Hector at the car lot or that he had attempted to communicate with me in order to reach her. Would it have made any difference, later, if I'd told her? I don't know.

♦ ♦ ♦

The night after my meeting with the Chairman, Dolores put Maria to bed while I prepared some notes for the next day. Then she knocked on the door of my office and came in, holding an empty bottle.

"She wanted you to say good night to her. She wanted you to sing to her."

"I can sing 'Take Me Out to the Ball Game,' that's about it."

"She doesn't care what songs. Sing to her tomorrow night."

"How about 'Silent Night'?"

"Anything, Jack," Dolores said. "She's so crazy about you."

I turned toward her. There was something new in her voice. Dolores let her fingers trail over the papers on my desk. Tonight wasn't going to be about sex, I saw. I suggested we go up to my roof. The air was cooler and it was a clear night. We climbed up with a bottle of wine and some bread and cheese and fruit. I poured out the glasses and we sat there in the dark.

"Did you expect it?" Dolores asked me suddenly.

"It?"

"You and me," she said.

"No," I answered. "It's the craziest thing I heard of, you and me. I hoped it might happen but I didn't assume it."

"*I* knew," she laughed. "I kind of knew all along."

"You knew I wanted to?"

"Well, *of course*, but I mean I knew we'd do it. You have to realize I was so sick and tired. I thought about it the first night, though. Something about a clean bed made me want to." She rolled over. "And you had so much money."

I felt a jolt of irritation. "So much that—"

"No, no. You don't understand, Jack. I never fucked a man who was so rich, so I had to do it just because of *that*. I got nothing but me, right? And you got so much and I wanted to see what it was like to do it. And also 'cause I felt sorry for you losing your wife like you did."

I laughed. "You felt sorry for me and you liked my money. Great."

A soft hand flew playfully out of the darkness and slapped me.

"I want you to have better reasons than that," I said.

"You know," Dolores said, "I'm not looking for love, exactly."

"No?"

"I'm looking for a life. Life after Hector."

It seemed Dolores was ready to talk. This was the first time she'd brought up the topic of her husband. "Why is he so jealous?" I asked.

"Because he loves me, why do you think?"

"Well, a lot of men wouldn't be as crazy as him."

"A lot of men haven't had to deal with *me*." She laughed, finishing her wine. "He knows what I'll do. He knows I'll do it. My *tías*—that means aunts, they never liked him. I didn't tell you I had two aunts? My father's older sisters. They were *santera*—"

"That's sort of a mix of Catholicism and voodoo?"

"*Santería*—it's the Catholic saints with other names, the old African names," Dolores explained. "And my aunts would go to the *babalawo*, the santeria priest, and they went to the botanica every day, maybe to get a little *incienso*, a little bit of anis, some *sal de mar*, *mostasa*, *ajonjol*, *linaja*, that kind of stuff, herbs and things, I never could keep them all straight—"

"Wait," I interrupted. "Now you have to tell me about the jar of water."

"Oh, that's nothing," Dolores protested, giggling too easily.

"I don't believe you."

"It's nothing."

"You had it in that crappy hotel room and you had it in the apartment in Ahmed's building and now downstairs. It's not like I haven't seen it, Dolores."

"Nothing."

"What?"

She sighed. "You put it out to collect evil spirits."

"You believe that?"

"Well, *no*, but . . . it makes me feel better," Dolores said. "It's good luck. Too many bad things have happened to me."

Of course I had to ask. "What?"

"Just things."

She was quiet, a dark shadow. I heard her breathing. *You have no idea who she is*, I thought. "Nothing bad's going to happen," I finally said.

A minute passed, the two of us silent in our own thoughts.

"Anyway," Dolores went on, "like I was saying, my *tías* didn't like Hector. He was too dark. They said I could find a man with lighter skin. They wanted me to have children who were lighter. That's what you're supposed to do in the D.R. You get a darker child, that's *un paso atrás*, like, a step backwards. And they didn't like him because he couldn't speak good Spanish. He just knows a little bit, can't really speak it. Kitchen Spanish, you know."

"He's Puerto Rican?"

"Yes."

"But born here?"

"Yes."

"Well, I can understand that his Spanish wasn't that good."

"I know, but my *tías* couldn't. They said he was too hot, Hector is too hot. Hot is good, but too hot, no good. The nuns in Catholic school always said *santería* was no good, that it was stupid, that you got to be ignorant if you believe in it. But most of them didn't have all these aunts always cooking up some crazy things and looking at their little books and everything. Hector never understood it. Puerto Ricans think Dominicans are all *jíbaros*. Country people. His family never liked me, they think people from the D.R. are no good. Always . . . there's this word for it, *chinchorreando*, gossiping, like bedbugs, all crazy and running around. If you're Puerto Rican you think you're American, and you think Dominicans are just trash, like they just got here. Hector once tried to pull that shit on me and I told him, 'You tell me how many cousins you got on welfare and *then* you joke about my papi.' If he had ever met my papi he would know. He knew he better not make jokes. My father was a strong man, his calves looked like they had softballs in them or something. He worked in the piano factory. Hector never could pull that shit on me. But there's another reason, too. See, like I said, I'm a little bit lighter than him, just a little bit. He likes that. I know he always wanted a white woman and he was glad I was lighter than him."

"To me you're very dark."

"Because you spent your whole life with white girls!" Dolores laughed. "I saw that picture of your wife and you know what I thought? I said to myself *that* was Hector's dream woman, right there, he never had a white woman with the blue eyes and all. I think actually he wanted one with real blond hair too, California-girl hair. He told me before we got married that it was something he wanted and never had, I mean, he had some light-skinned girls who were sort of Puerto Rican–Italian, right? You get a lot of that down in Bay Ridge. But no blondes, you know, real blondes. I told him that if he ever looked at some girl that got *real* blond hair I was going to make him regret it. He wanted to ask me some things but I think he didn't want to know the answers. He was always afraid I wanted black guys. Maybe I did. I used to say give me Lawrence Taylor, *please*."

"The guy who plays linebacker for the Giants?"

"Oh, *please*." She laughed, tipping her head back, the city lights bright on the curved surfaces of her eyes. "Me and my girlfriends used to talk about how big he was and everything. Just to, like, be *under* him. Like maybe he would just *kill* you. But anyway, I never told Hector all the things like that because he was just going to get pissed. You see, Hector is a romantic. You are, too. You're kind of romantic about me and Maria 'cause we're different, right?" Dolores looked at me to be sure I was listening. "But I don't have some big problem with this stuff, okay? My papi told me, he said Dominicans, they been free something like five hundred years, mixing everybody around. I don't have some kind of problem with this."

"Right."

"I mean I been with white guys, whatever. It's inside is what counts."

"Yes." Dolores didn't want to talk any more about our racial difference. But she was clearly in the mood to talk. "So, are your aunts still alive?" I said.

"No. The second one died about three years ago. She was in a nursing home . . . it was sad, she came here with my papi after my mother died."

We sat in silence.

"It's late," Dolores said. "You want to go to bed now?"

Her voice was husky and full of want and I realized that just mentioning her mother and father and dead aunts, about whom I knew nothing, had made Dolores feel vulnerable and sad. Her people were gone.

"Hey," I said softly. "Dolores."

"Yes?"

"Tell me."

"What?" she said, almost in tears.

"Tell me who you are. Everything."

She put her head down. "Jack, if I do that then I don't know what it means, you know? I don't know why I'm telling it to you. There's so much . . ."

I took her lovely smooth face in my hand and turned it toward me and the light from the city caught the wetness of her eyes and she stared into my face, lost in the sudden compressed awareness of the unpredictability of life. I sensed that she had suffered a great loss, and I tried to convey tenderly that there was nothing she could not tell me, that I would listen to her for however long it took, and that I desired above all for her to release herself to me. "Tell me, Dolores," I said again.

◆ ◆ ◆

We sat there on the roof, facing the night, and Dolores began to speak. She was born, she said, in 1965 in Santo Domingo. That year the government was overthrown, the schools were closed, and U.S. troops came ashore. That was all that had ever been told her by her two aunts, the sisters of her father, all years older than he. Her mother was a large woman with great breasts and a mouth men liked. Yet sensible, too. A robust daughter of a fisherman, Dolores's mother, Paloma Martinez, had carried Dolores seemingly without effort. A midwife delivered her, so Dolores learned, a woman who had come hastily from another delivery and who hadn't had time to scrub her hands properly. Midwives typically sweep their fingers back and forth within the vaginal opening of a woman about to deliver, in order to stretch the flesh and allow the baby through without the woman tearing. But she ended up making a small cut anyway, for Dolores was a big newborn, with a large head like her father's, and as soon as the flesh was opened, a route of infection was created. Dolores's mother was sick with septic infection within four days of the delivery and her milk never came in. The aunts consulted the local *babalawo*, who advised that Dolores be nursed by her mother's sister, who had a year-old son. Dolores's mother died of septicemia when Dolores was two weeks old. Her father was heartbroken and vowed to raise his daughter in a country that had a future, where healthy twenty-year-old women did not die because God was looking elsewhere. Where there were doctors, not old women who did not read newspapers and forget to wash their hands. Santo Domingo was hot and wretched and reminded him of his wife, whom he had seen waste away from the robustness of pregnancy to a spectral, shrunken presence attended by her sisters, who chanted prayers and burned incense in her room as she slipped toward death. The only thing he would miss would be his amateur baseball team, for which he played catcher. He was by trade a jeweler, a man who wore a crisp white shirt each day and read the newspapers. His friends told him not to go. But his two older sisters urged him to make the trip. He would support them and they would care for Dolores. One sister had never married and the other had lost a husband and never had children. Yet when he came north in 1965, taking a bus from Miami with his infant daughter and two sisters to New York, it was soon clear that he was going to be unable to work as a jeweler. For the first time in his life, Roberto Martinez understood that he was *a black man*, at least in the eyes of America. The jeweler's trade was still dominated by Jews; to set up his own shop he needed at least a couple of thousand dollars, which was out of the question. Every dollar—the old, thin dollars of the poor—was counted and folded, recounted and saved for necessities. The local banks at that time were run by the Irish who had settled Sunset Park around the turn of the century, and few were willing to lend to the population that was driving the Irish out, even from St. Michael's Roman Catholic Church on Fourth Avenue, an immense, magnificent structure, built with the dollars of Irish widows and the pennies of Irish cops, and *now*—so went the reaction to Dolores's father's request for a business loan—*now the fuggin spicks, from P.R. or whatever goddamned country, were arriving by the fuggin planeload.* Dolores's father knew he had to look for a job, any job, and he was lucky to have a strong back, built as he was with great stocky width through the shoulders. For a time he worked at the immense Brooklyn Army Terminal at Fifty-ninth Street and Second Avenue, where the army was shipping munitions and tanks to Europe during the Cold War fortification of West Germany. The job paid reasonably well, but he had three other mouths to feed. He saved every dime, Dolores said, becoming a man so frugal that he would set a can of beans over the pilot light of the gas stove each morning. Heating slowly, the beans would be ready by evening.

Then a friend told him that the Steinway & Sons piano factory up in Long Island City liked to hire men who had built boats, because they understood the mysteries of wood. Grains and knots. Glues and bracing. All the two of them needed to do, the friend said, was show up and claim to have built boats in the harbor of Santo Domingo. Who would know they hadn't? The men drove to the factory and Maria's father was hired as soon as the manager saw the width of his back. The other man was dismissed. It was a long commute for Dolores's father but steady work that paid enough. In 1966 America had more children than ever, and schools and families were buying pianos. For the first few months there, Roberto Martinez worked in the rim-bending operation, a low dark cavelike room, with a crew of other powerfully built young men who, standing in tandem, bent and set the long layered and glued sections of hardrock maple onto a press. When the wood was set and dried it became the case of the piano and moved through the immense factory, gradually being finished. When she was older, her father walked with Dolores through the factory after hours, showing her every step of the manufacture of a piano, shuffling through sawdust and wood scraps. Each piano had thirteen thousand parts, he said. As a jeweler, he understood fine work, and thought that he could do it. When he mentioned his former trade, one of the managers—a Ukrainian immigrant himself and enlightened then as to assigning jobs by talent rather than race—found Roberto

Martinez a new job sitting at a bench in the "action department," assembling the delicate trip hammers made of wood and green felt that struck the piano's strings within the instrument.

It was also possible that Roberto Martinez was promoted simply because of his quiet, selfless dignity. Dolores remembered that he slept each night in the kitchen on a sagging cot behind a screen. The aunts needed to be close to the bathroom at night and the only other room where one could sleep was Dolores's. Next to her father's bed was a small dresser table he had found discarded behind an apartment building and its one small drawer became the only private space Roberto Martinez had. But Dolores knew what was in it: his set of jeweler's tools, his own father's watch, which did not work, a modest box inlaid with mother-of-pearl that held a few pieces of his wife's jewelry, and a manila envelope with his diploma from high school, his jeweler's certificate, and the yellowed wedding notice in a Dominican newspaper. He kept a piece of muslin over these items. On the top of the table was a cross and a framed black-and-white photo of his wife.

Roberto Martinez's grief over his wife was a pure and holy thing, but he slipped away some evenings and occasionally brought a girl-friend home for dinner. He had a life that was private from his daughter and sisters, and whether he had ever wanted to marry again was something Dolores never knew. Her aunts were a formidable pair and they bluntly inspected whomever their younger brother brought home. A wife would mean a larger apartment and the diminishment of their authority. Eventually Roberto Martinez ceased bringing his occasional girlfriends home. He seemed content to sit at night and ask Dolores to bring the newspaper or the department store catalog to him. They would page through it, looking at the jewelry ads. He would point to a photo of a diamond ring and say, "Now, here, *mi corazón*, is a diamond solitaire. See the way the light goes up and down these edges? When you finish school," he told her, "I will make you a ring." This she remembered vividly.

When Roberto Martinez was no longer interested in looking at jewelry catalogs Dolores understood he was losing his sight. He went to a succession of Brooklyn eye doctors. After a year in which he made increasingly more mistakes at the workbench, he was transferred to the Steinway delivery crew as a foreman, for which eyesight was less important than judgment, patience, and on occasion a strong back, which he still possessed. He oversaw the loading of the pianos into the black Mercedes vans and the unloading into schools, music stores, and private homes. The company salesmen had a habit of saying that if an assembled piano would fit within a room, any room, then the company could get the piano *into* it. Any room. That made selling pianos easier and delivering them more difficult. It was during the summer of 1972, Dolores told me, when her father was a week short of his fortieth birthday and when she was seven that the Juilliard School took delivery of fifteen new nine-foot concert grand pianos with ebony finish. They were delivered two to a truck, and a train of eight Steinway vans rolled into Manhattan's West Side. The temperature had reached past the nineties that day, touching one hundred, and, so Dolores was to learn from her aunts, her father stood for hours out on the hot pavement, giving directions to the drivers and movers, co-ordinating the arrival of freight elevators, and listening, no doubt, to the heaving and creaking of the mammoth instruments, each of which cost twenty-three thousand dollars, as they were delicately lifted onto the wooden dollies. With customary dedication, he took it quite seriously.

And so there was a certain sad glory in Roberto Martinez's last day, for he completed the delivery of a third of a million dollars' worth of pianos, his biggest delivery ever. He took the subway home instead of returning with the empty trucks to Long Island City for his car, and the subway that evening was notoriously hot. Dolores remembered the blank, drained look on her father's face as he came in the front door of the apartment in Sunset Park and moved unsteadily into the kitchen for some water. She was only seven, but old enough to see that he was not himself—there were deep rings of sweat under his neck and armpits, and instead of getting to the refrigerator, her father sat heavily down on one of the kitchen chairs, bought from the local furniture store on lay-away, and said to her in a quiet, confused voice, his last words, "*Dolores, mi corazón, donde está tu mami?*" Where is your mother? And at that his heart ruptured and he collapsed to the linoleum.

◆ ◆ ◆

"After Papi died," Dolores explained to me, "we didn't have any money and we had to move. We lived on *Tía* Lucinda's welfare and her dead husband's pension from the D.R. army." It was, indisputably, a poor living—in a peeling apartment that faced Brooklyn's Eighth Avenue in which the windows rattled at night and the roaches ran up through the floorboards from the bodega restaurant downstairs. But her aunt Lucinda was kind, if a little slow, and Dolores had a bit more freedom than other girls. Her father's meager fourteen-thousand-dollar insurance policy was to be spent on the cost of parochial school.

In a few years, Dolores said, she was a dark-haired little girl in a St. Anthony's uniform, the white blouse and green tie and the plaid skirt and matching green knee socks. Her aunts considered returning to Santo Domingo but that would mean Dolores would not be an American. They had become increasingly dependent on *santería* for their version of reality and sometimes Dolores came home after school to see that the apartment was full of burning candles, her aunts chanting quiet prayers in Spanish before an altar. They went to mass nearly every day, and, in retrospect, she saw they were simply two uneducated Dominican women in their fifties who had expected that their robust younger brother would take care of them until their deaths; now they were terrified by the fluid complexity of American culture. They knew they were losing Dolores to this new place. Eleven, twelve, thirteen, she was getting older, looking more like a young woman. There was a strength in her expression, almost a ferocity, and this they knew had come from Dolores's mother. Dolores finished the ninth grade. They did not like the way she dressed, or what was shown on television, or the way the boys acted. They especially did not like the young man who called her every evening. She was only fourteen, tall for her age, but that did not mean she was ready for Micky O'Shea, a hulking Irish boy who worked in a garage down on Fourth Avenue.

"They hated him," Dolores said. "He was so dirty, they said he had grease in his *teeth*. I didn't really *like* him, but it was exciting, you know, when you are so young, and he wasn't really from the neighborhood, and he spent a lot of money on me real fast, like we saw movies in Manhattan and he brought me these little bracelets, and then one night he said let's walk across the Brooklyn Bridge, and it was very late, I guess I remember *that*, and it was very romantic and I was tired and then he sort of threw me down, like, and the next thing I know I'm looking up at all those cables and wires and stuff and he's raping me, with all these cars and trucks going by underneath. Humming, right? I'm like a *virgin* and he's doing it hard, my head is going bang bang bang on those boards where you walk, and all the time, his armpit is in my face, just shoved into his armpit, and I'm thinking my aunts are going to kill me, they are going to tell everybody, scream and run around and everything . . . so it happened, he kept *explaining* and I remember he threw my underwear off the bridge because it was torn up and then took me home and let me off in front of my building, and he was going to say, like, don't tell anybody, but I already knew I wasn't going to do that. I knew I was okay . . ." Dolores looked into the distance. The far skyscrapers of Manhattan and night air were somehow conducive to remembrance. "I was fourteen years old and I was going to be okay. I don't know. I didn't have anybody anymore, no brothers or sisters, no parents, right? So I got pretty wild after that, I starting hanging out, you know, everybody kind of knew me, I did some things with some boys, but I kept doing my homework and everything, I remember that, but then it started to change. My aunts started getting sick. And we didn't have any money. The guy that ran the bodega said he couldn't keep giving me credit 'cause my *tías* hadn't paid him anything on it in like two months. Somebody from the church, a young priest, came and talked to us. The whole thing was just, you know, falling apart."

At eighteen, now understanding the economics of necessity, Dolores found a job at a unisex hair salon at Forty-third Street and Seventh Avenue in Brooklyn; she liked to cut hair but didn't have the money to go to beauty school in Manhattan and so she asked Carmella Quintano, the owner of the salon, if she could do the wash and pick up a few customers when it got busy. Carmella, a heavyset woman who enjoyed her movie magazines from Puerto Rico more than she did cutting hair, would get a larger cut than she did from her licensed beauticians. Carmella needed male customers if the place was going to make any money, and realized that an attractive eighteen-year-old like

Dolores could be useful. So Dolores was hired to wash hair, and she sat on a stool in the back of the salon until a customer came in; then she would have the customer sit back in a special sliding chair next to the sink, and she would first rinse, then lather, then rinse the hair, careful always to get the soap out and not get the faces of the clients wet—especially the women, who didn't like to have their makeup smudged. The salon was a busy, noisy place with Spanish-language soap operas on the television and people talking loudly over the sound of the blow dryers. She was often alone in the back corner, such that she was almost forgotten by the other hairdressers much of the time, who were more interested in the next drag on their cigarette or with chatting up the customers for a better tip than with talking to young Dolores. But she had some money coming in—with tips she was able to make seventy-five or a hundred dollars a week. Sometimes the older women, those who plucked their eyebrows too thinly, Puerto Rican and Cuban women whose sense of fashion was frozen in the fifties and who plastered too much rouge and makeup over their eyes, complained that she had pulled their hair or left soap in. The older men who were vain enough to have their hair styled told her she reminded them of their daughters or granddaughters and apologized that they didn't have much hair left. Sometimes they dared to look up at her as she leaned close to rinse their hair and she saw their sentimental lust for her. They tipped her directly, for her beauty. They were the same age as her father would have been if he had lived and she would whisper a Hail Mary under her breath for them when their eyes were closed, the mask of exhaustion most evident.

It was one afternoon, Dolores went on, that she was sitting reading one of Carmella's movie magazines when she realized a customer was waiting; he was young and a bit short, but his body was muscular in a slender way. He was Puerto Rican. "Please sit yourself here," she said in Spanish.

He slid into the chair and tipped his head back. His eyes were clear and dark and she realized while looking at him that she had not turned on the water.

"Today I got some big things goin' on," he began in English, as if they had already been talking and without seeming to care whether she wanted to listen, "so I'm getting an important haircut."

"Yes?" Dolores said.

"It's got to be good. I'm going to get a job, in Manhattan, so do a good job."

"I always do," Dolores sang back at him.

"I *coulda* gone to a fucking barber shop but they don't know how to cut it right. Those guys're too old, you know?"

"Do you have the job or do you *think* you have it?"

"I have it," he said, looking up at her coolly, stretching his muscular neck. "I *have* it."

She wet his hair then, feeling its thickness, and she bent a little closer to him than usual. She washed his head slowly, massaging the scalp, and he shut his eyes but kept talking.

"This job is excellent. I'm going to make eleven, maybe twelve dollars an hour, get my car fixed up, and save that money for something, then maybe I'm going to go into business for myself—" And Dolores thought to herself that for someone so young—he looked twenty at the most—he was awfully confident. Her eye fixed on a tiny gold crucifix among the dark hairs of his chest below his open shirt collar. So many people in the neighborhood did not have any real confidence, especially the men, and as she began to rinse his hair the first time, she suddenly felt his hand brush her calf. She was standing between the wall and the wash chair and so none of the other people in the shop could see and besides, she wasn't the type to scream, but then the hand crept under her skirt and up her leg with warmth and firmness, all the while as the young man kept talking. ". . . so I'm gonna hire a lot of people and get my businesses going, you know, make me some really big money—" The hand expertly stroked her thigh. She wasn't scared but excited, and she leaned forward so that her skirt billowed slightly and hid the arm beneath it, and with this, her subtle permission, the hand continued upward until it found the elastic border of her underpants and with serpentine ease slipped up beneath the fabric, stroking there with a middle finger. The young man's closed eyes opened then and he stopped talking. They looked at one another. His finger twitched and a shiver went through her. Then, fast as it had come, his hand went down.

She swung her fist hard at his face. But he grabbed it. She swung her other fist and it caught him flush in the mouth. He didn't flinch, and a squint of amusement ran through his eyes.

"I have been watching you for almost three days, Dolores Martinez." Then he pulled her toward him slowly, pulled her close, and whispered in an older, more serious voice, the voice of Catholic mass given in rehearsed formal Spanish, his tongue moving between his teeth. "I knew you worked here, I asked your name. Forgive me if I have offended you. It is because I desire you above all women."

Dolores's romance with Hector Salcines moved very quickly after that, for she was drawn, she said, to his confidence in himself. He assured her that with him her life would be better. After all, she told herself, she was an orphan, and there was nobody to take care of her. Her aunts were useless and the elder, Tía Maria, was living on a respirator in a Catholic charity nursing home, too sick to stand, with a suppurating bedsore as big around as a saucer on her rear end, licking her mouth constantly as a side effect from the medication. How Dolores hated to visit there, all the half-dead people slumped over in their wheelchairs. On one visit her aunt was asleep with a paper straw stuck in her mouth like an elongated cigarette, the pint carton of milk spilled in her lap . . . And so he, this boy, was *life. La vida*. After what had happened with Micky on the Brooklyn Bridge, she had slept with eight or nine boys, in the hurried and fumbling way of teenagers, and so it was not that she offered her virginity to Hector Salcines, it was something much more important — she offered him herself, her future to him, and soon they were fucking in his small apartment every night, Hector vigorous in the way of twenty-year-olds, fucking repeatedly, telling her how best to give him blowjobs by putting a firm hand behind her head, forcing her all the way down, all of it making her feel suddenly older with the understanding that of course *this* was forbidden by the church because it was *muy fuerte*, so strong. She did not care that her aunts saw her with Hector; they held no sway over her, they were old already, their bodies dropped and ruined. Soon they would be dead, she knew, and soon they were.

"Me and Hector used to just lay on the bed telling everything to each other," Dolores said, her voice thick with remembrance. "He said he wished he could meet my papi. He never really got loved by his own dad much. His father and mother, they were scared, you know?

They came here from San Juan in like the fifties before Hector was born and just worked. That's all Hector did since he was fourteen. He just worked. He believed everything everybody said that if you work you can be rich. He always said he was going to get rich and retire his dad and moms. But his dad died when his car got hit by a garbage truck and his moms lives somewhere in Queens, she had to move, I guess. He used to go see her on Sundays with Maria. Not so much in the last couple of years . . . she was going back to San Juan and staying there a lot, I guess. Hector always loved his moms."

Hector, Dolores went on, had grown up in an apartment building in Queens, within the tangle of highways near John F. Kennedy International Airport. His father ran the crew of men who cut the hundreds of acres of grass surrounding the runways. The grass had to be cut more or less continuously during the summer months, kept low in case emergency vehicles needed to race across it and to discourage the flocks of sea gulls who would use it to nest. They repainted runway markings during the winter. And there were always innumerable cracks and patches in the runways that needed repair. Hector worked one of the gang mowers one summer, wearing protective earphones against the low roar of the jets. He and the other boys would have push-up contests on their breaks. There was nothing in Hector's boyhood that Dolores remembered to me that suggested obvious damage. He was a bright, good Puerto Rican kid with a handsome face who loved the Yankees and thought maybe he'd go into the army. Dolores remembered Hector's father as a kindly, worn-out man whose health had failed after being sprayed by jet-fuel. Hector's mother had never learned English very well and her only passion was for raising turtles and listening to Puerto Rican mambo crooners. Hector's parents were quiet people who wanted no trouble, Dolores said, and I was given to understand that Hector had been wounded by their inconsequentiality. His father's dreams had reached only as far as the small tile patio in the cramped yard in the back of the house.

But there is nothing that gives a young man hope like catching a smart, good-looking woman. The world has revealed one possibility and thus more might follow. By the time Dolores and Hector had married in 1985, he had a plan, she said. There was a real estate boom on. The market value of everything was rising—the huge brownstones in Park Slope and Brooklyn Heights, where the young whites with money lived, four-story homes that ran half a million easy; the squat three-story brick row homes the Italians lived in; the twelve-family apartment buildings like the one he and Dolores lived in. The banks were *giving away* credit cards. There was money everywhere, snaking through the neighborhoods. Speculators were all over Brooklyn, buying and reselling buildings even in marginal neighborhoods like Sunset Park. The eight-family units were up to 230, 240. Hector had been watching this. He wanted to make some real money. He didn't have enough to buy a property, to become a player. But he saw that every time a building turned over, the new owners put some money into it. You could see it by the stuff that ended up in the dumpsters outside the buildings, most of which needed work. New owners needed floors sanded, new roofs, new windows, tools, paints, all the materials for renovation. Hector had worked in a flooring store while in high school. He knew the products; he had installed ceramic tile, linoleum, glue-down wood floors, peel-away, all kinds. This, he told Dolores, was his idea: He'd rent a store that fronted Fifth Avenue between Forty-eighth and Forty-ninth Streets in Sunset Park. Three thousand usable square feet on the first floor and five hundred in the basement, enough to store inventory. New 220 wiring that could power display lights. There was a subway stop three blocks away and plenty of walk-by business. And as for the traffic pattern, the avenue was choked with cars, practically a goddamned parking lot on Saturday afternoons. The place had an off-street loading dock in the back, perfect for receiving deliveries during business hours without disrupting the customers. The owner was a nice old Jewish guy who simply wanted to ride the rent for a couple of years before selling out and retiring, and he was willing to give a young guy a break. The old guy wanted two thousand a month, which was just below market price, plus three months' security. Hector would need to hire two guys to sell to customers and do the installations, and a girl to run the register. With utilities, insurance, and payroll, his monthly costs would be five grand a month. Add to that the fifteen thousand he would need for start-up inventory. To make a go of it for six months would require forty-five, fifty thousand cash to start up. Hector had nine thousand of his own money saved. He was only twenty-four, without any kind of track record with repaying loans, no education, no collateral. Even with credit so easy, the banks wouldn't touch him.

But with Dolores worried about how they would repay the money, Hector pleaded his case to a Chinese businessman who figured his sums with an abacus. Why a Chinese man would even consider lending outside his own people was a mystery—perhaps he figures, said Hector, that he's gonna buy the business cheaply if I fuck it up. But I never saw a Chinese flooring store, responded Dolores. It didn't seem to stand to reason but the businessman loaned Hector the thirty thousand, which left him six thousand short, and he worried constantly to Dolores that the store space would be rented out to someone else at any time. He didn't want to go into it without the proper amount of money. Most small businesses failed because they were undercapitalized, Hector told her. The landlord couldn't lower the rent, the old Chinese businessman wouldn't cough up any more cash, and besides, Hector didn't want to borrow another dime if he could help it; he was paying the Chinese businessman 21 percent interest—blood money.

So he called his friend Alberto, who had been arrested sixteen times since high school, and they worked out something, *a little deal between you and me and who will know anythin' about it?* Hector agreed to mule coke to make the last six thousand, Dolores said. The coke was moving from Philly to New York, five hundred per trip. After the first round-trip Hector realized that the undercover cops had to catch a few people every day, a quota, and that they were tired and lazy and content only to catch the stupidest people. So Hector figured he would play it safe and make the trip via Pittsburgh. New York to Pittsburgh to Philly back to Pittsburgh and back to New York. It took a lot longer but the odds of getting caught were much lower. He did it twelve times. You simply tied the waterproof bundle of coke with fishing line to the deodorant holder wired to the underside of the toilet bowl in the bus toilet. Then you jam a lot of toilet paper in the bowl. Then you take a shit. Nobody looked very closely. He took a differently scheduled trip each time. Get out at the Port Authority terminal, meet the guy a block north of the station. Twelve round-trips . . . six thousand, the last six thousand.

And when he opened the store, Dolores explained to me proudly, Hector began to make money. He worked fifteen hours seven days a week, killing himself, doing everything he could, the inventory by himself, washing the outside windows, wiping down the samples so that they would gleam, stacking boxes of silicone sealer and floor wax, buckets of tile adhesive, squares of self-stick linoleum. Whoever said Puerto Ricans were lazy had never seen Hector work. He would collapse at home at the kitchen table, worriedly figuring the day's gross against the expenses. And when he had made the break-even amount and seen that there was more cash left over, he'd begin excitedly: "Dolores, everybody and their mother came to my store today. The goddamn *world* came to my store today. My daddy use to say that Brooklyn was dead. All the wops and paddies moving to Staten Island, out the Long Island Expressway. So what? *Let* them fucking leave, I got five guys from Bangladesh come in today, they got the contract on nineteen bathrooms in a office building somewhere and they want to buy low as possible. I gave them a good price. Why not? I move the product, make a little profit, and they'll be back. They bought two thousand square feet. And some old Russian guy came in, with his son to translate. You shoulda *seen* him droolin' over some of the urethane-gloss tile. The son translated and said the father never saw that kind of shit in Russia. And a couple of women from Haiti. Some fat bitches, all they did was look at this sample, look at that sample. One of their kids pissed the floor. We're going to make some money, Dolores. I know it. It's going to work, I can feel it. It's the location. There's Frankel's up the block across the avenue. People come knowing they can get hardware there and pick out flooring here. And not have to park again. Some of them Koreans came in looking for a remnant that was twenty-two by twenty-six. That's too big to be a remnant. They didn't care about a pattern. I sold them three pieces of Congoleum Valuflor 03691 that didn't match. Everybody comes in, you got a apartment, you gotta get new linoleum for the kitchen, 'cause your mother is going to see the kitchen and scream about how dirty it is. Even if you're just renting. I was on the phone and this yuppie bitch come up and buys a sheet of Armstrong Solarian Supreme, most expensive stuff I got, four-fifteen per yard, light blue geometric pattern for her bathroom. She drove out here all the way from the Heights because she was looking for a special pattern. She asks me how much is next-day installation and I say a hundred bucks, 'cause my crew is backed up. Make it sound like we're real busy. I'm thinking, like, no way she's going to go for that, but I said it to see. It's going to take Manny and Luiz maybe forty minutes tops to bang that piece of shit in there, maybe take an hour total what with the travel. And I'm paying them eight an hour under the table, Dolores, I'm gonna clear maybe eighty bucks on the installation alone. The lady she says put it on the Visa and goes off to look for some bathroom tile. It's workin', Dolores, it's workin'."

And on he went, spinning out scenarios of profit. The store lost money at first, and despite Hector's optimism, for several months it seemed it wouldn't work, that the enterprise would fail, but then, like wind slowly filling a sail, the whole operation began to move. People were charging the limit on their cards and the banks didn't care. Even in the struggling lower-class neighborhoods of Brooklyn, money was moving around like nobody could remember. Some of the best-looking neighborhood girls were making one hundred bucks a night in the good Manhattan bars just putting beers down in front of white guys in ties. If you could type you could get a night job on Wall Street inputting data into a computer — a lot of the older women who didn't have kids to worry about were getting twenty, twenty-five thousand a year doing that, money they never dreamed of. Hector made an early payment of a thousand dollars to the Chinese businessman. There were minor hassles of course, like late deliveries of inventory and the guys who worked for Spinelli's Carting Service, the mob trash hauler. The guys on the huge green Spinelli truck now wanted eight dollars a load, cash. Something about what's on the books and what's off the books. It came out to twenty-four dollars a week. One thousand, two hundred, and forty-eight dollars a year. Off the top. You paid or you paid, the saying went. He hated them; they reminded him of the mob fucks who had driven their truck right into his father's car. Bump, his father is dead and the fucking garbage truck isn't damaged. They knew there was nothing you could do. The cops didn't give a shit about it. Eight dollars a load. Hector looked into it and found that was the price everyone else was paying — the fish market up the street, the laundry, the hardware store. Everybody paid eight dollars a load and when you figured the thousands of loads a day, you could see how the mob guys had so much money. He decided to pay it, without saying anything. Then the Spinelli guys tried to jack it up to twelve dollars a load on account of the hard sixteen-foot cardboard tubes that the linoleum came rolled on. The cardboard in the tubes was three-quarters of an inch thick and didn't compress easily in the truck, so the Spinelli guys said. That wasted space, made the truck fill up faster, cost them money. Hector responded that he'd see that the tubes were cut lengthwise. He could do it with a handheld power jigsaw with a reciprocating blade. The Spinelli guys said no, it was gonna have to be twelve dollars a load, cut tubes or not. Hector told them to forget it. Cancel his carting contract.

The trash started to pile up and after two weeks the big trucks from the flooring manufacturers couldn't make their deliveries easily in the back because of the trash, so Hector jammed the trunk and backseat of his car with sawed-up tubes and hauled the stuff out on the Interboro Parkway one night and dumped it in a rest area near the highway and turned around and came back and did it twice more. It was wrong but what choice did he have? The loading dock was clear now and he would figure out what to do later. But the carting company sent two guys back in a car who asked if Hector would reconsider his contract. Still twelve dollars a load? Yes, they said. He wouldn't pay it, he said. The mobsters, two older men with recently cut hair, nodded their heads. Maybe they were tough guys, maybe they weren't. You could never be sure who you were dealing with. One of the men put a toothpick in his mouth contemplatively, Hector remembered aloud to Dolores, and said well, we can't lose your business, and asked Hector to put out his hand so they could shake on some kind of a deal. When he did, the bigger man grabbed it tight. The other one pulled out a power box stapler from his coat and there was a sudden *dok, dok, dok*, and Hector was left on the sidewalk, clutching the meat of his thumb.

"Fuck you!" he screamed after them.

Hector called other carting outfits. They asked his location and when he told them, they declined the contract, saying the store was out of their territory. Clearly the mob had carved up every street of Brooklyn and given each piece to specific carting companies. It was, as

Hector told Dolores, the fucking principle of the thing. Eight dollars he could understand. It was a little grease to keep everything running smoothly. But a 50 percent hike was unfair, especially since he'd promised to cut the tubes lengthwise. He *worked* for that money. When he thought about the risks he had taken muling the coke, just to have the money taken by a bunch of mob fucks.

A week later the men in the car came back and said they'd heard that Hector had complained to some of his neighboring businessmen, which was true. They didn't like that, they said. Bad for their reputation. He offered them ten dollars a load. He'd cut the tubes lengthwise, and then into short sections and tie up the bundles. A piece of cake for the guys on the truck to pick up. He'd even have *his* guys put the stuff on the truck. What more could they ask for? The men smiled coldly and said the price was twelve dollars a load. Hector said he wouldn't pay it. They looked at each other and knew that the problem wasn't about money. They left.

That week was a good one at the store, with clear profit of two thousand dollars, and Hector came home to dinner late and announced to Dolores that he'd just bought a new Chrysler LeBaron, a businessman's car. You get some respect, he told Dolores, and the monthly payments aren't so bad. And now I think we can look for a new apartment, too, *chica*. They were thinking about having a child, Dolores told me, and wanted a place with more space. Hector was tired of saving every cent, tired of living in a three-story walk-up. "We got to live a little," he told Dolores proudly. "I'm going to start buying some things, you know, some clothes and all. We only got one life and we got to live it." They found a place with three bedrooms, right across from the actual park in Sunset Park, the first floor of a house. The landlord liked them immediately—they were a clean, good-looking couple and the husband had a job. It would be quieter than the apartment building, where you could alwa s hear people arguing and fucking and using the bathroom above your head and where there was always a mountain of bags of garbage in the doorway at the street. And the baby, when he or she came, said Dolores, would have a nice large bedroom. They'd set up a new television, they'd paint the kitchen over, they'd have a little changing table in the baby's room, they'd put money aside for the baby's education from the very start—

all kinds of financial vehicles were now available, Hector explained solemnly, maybe put a little money into the stock market, since everybody was getting rich now doing that. Maybe put wall-to-wall carpeting down in the bedroom.

That night, sleeping in their old apartment, they were awakened by a phone call at about 4:00 A.M. Somebody had pulled a tractor-trailer up to the back of the store. Did Hector usually take deliveries so late? asked the caller, the man who ran the laundry two doors up. The unmarked truck was idling in the cold weather, rear doors open, the trailer flush up against the back wall of the store, so tight you couldn't slip a Sunday newspaper through the crack between the truck and the store. There was a guy sitting in the cab of the truck drinking coffee, looking relaxed.

By the time Hector had run the ten blocks from their apartment, the truck was gone. They had burned open the store's loading bay doors with acetylene torches. The light was on and every piece of inventory was gone. In fact the salesroom looked rather neat, swept out. They had taken the cash register. They had gone into the basement through the steel gauge lock, taken the inventory there as well as taken the three cartons of toilet paper he stored down there. All they left were the baited rattraps. He figured it must have taken five or six guys only an hour working hard, especially if they had a mini forklift inside the truck. He'd offered ten dollars a load, instead of twelve, and so at three loads a week he was just six dollars off per week. Times fifty-two weeks. A lousy three hundred and twelve dollars a year — that was what his pride was worth. Insurance covered some of the inventory but it would take weeks for the police and insurance inspectors' reports to be processed. In the meantime he had no inventory. Nothing could be sold. There was no way for him to make any money. He'd lost his own savings and he still owed Mr. Chu fifteen or twenty thousand after the insurance refund, depending on whether he could get some of the rent deposit back. By the time Dolores got to the store Hector was weeping with anger and frustration and had broken his right hand on one of the walls. "That was my one fucking shot, Dolores," he told her. "That was *it*." They couldn't move into the new apartment, they couldn't do anything now.

"And after that," Dolores said, gazing upward toward the stars, "we were like, not the same. Hector had to give the old Chinese guy the new car and he took over the rent on the store and kept it going. Same name, everything. It's still there. I mean we kept trying and everything and Hector paid back the money, but it was like, it was like when you hit a *dog*, you know, you hit him really hard and that dog is never going to be the same, it's always going to be afraid. And it kind of made Hector mean, too. Life was going to start being harder now. We needed money bad. He got a job cleaning apartments in Manhattan. They made him wear a uniform with his name on the pocket. Sewn on the pocket. He hated that. They see that and they know you're nobody. He used to say that. I'm nobody, Dolores. He used to tell me about the apartments, how much money the people had. One lady had thirty-seven rooms. He said he counted. It took them a week to clean the place. They had to put little pieces of tape on the rug so they put the furniture back in the right place. Antiques and stuff. The lady locked her bathrooms on purpose so they had to go down to the basement. He hated that job and he quit and he did some other little jobs and then he got that cable job. At least he got to work in Brooklyn and be around regular people. We still loved each other. I used to hold him at night and tell him it was okay, that I loved him and it was okay, it wasn't his fault, how was he going to know they were going to do that, right? I used to tell him that every morning so he wouldn't be depressed. 'I love you Hector, it wasn't your fault.' I told him that every day."

Dolores turned her dark eyes toward me in silent recognition of her husband's pain. Only later would I understand that although all that she had described to me that night was heartfelt and true, she had also been very selective in what she had said, cleverly excising certain facts that begged for explanation and which, had I known of them, might have caused me to alter my behavior. But for the moment I was consumed with the vision of Hector and his torments; I could not help but admire him, and thus feel a great shiver of guilt. Although Dolores certainly might suppose that Hector was looking for her, she didn't know of her husband's brief letters of appeal to me. Dolores did not know what I was doing. And neither, really, did I.

ELEVEN

A nxiety, like sound, can suddenly get a lot louder. Early the next morning I got a call while still in bed.

"This Mr. Whitman, Mr. John Whitman?"

I told him yes.

"This is Jimmie Fitzpatrick, assistant building services supervisor down here at work? I got your number from security, here, sir. Hope you don't mind me calling this early. I'm calling — it's a pretty strange thing, sir — somebody spray-painted your name in front of the building last night, Mr. Whitman. I got my crew working on it already — "

"My name?" I said sleepily, eyeing the clock radio. It was two minutes past six.

"With a message, actually."

"What was it?"

Dolores stirred next to me.

"I got that written down so I could read it to you."

"Yes?" I could tell that he was stalling; there was a problem.

"It read like this, see," the man continued, "big capital letters: TELL ME WHERE MY WIFE AND BABY-GIRL IS, JACK WHITMAN. Tall letters, with a big spray-painted arrow going right up to the south doors."

"Jesus."

"I thought I'd let you know, in case somebody asked, see."

"Thanks."

"I got the mess covered up with brown paper and sawhorses out there so that everybody goes around it, but we only found out about maybe half an hour ago and so I know there was some people who saw it and saw your name. I don't know who-all of course," he said. "It's still early and nobody else is gonna see it."

"Thanks," I stuttered, feeling sick.

"I kind of think he used some kind of pressurized paint sprayer, not just a little aerosol can, seeing as how the paint went on pretty heavy and is deep in the stone," the man went on, apparently worried he might be accused of not moving quickly enough to clean up an embarrassing graffiti about one of the Corporation's high executives. "You're talking about letters maybe five feet high, with the lines maybe a foot wide," he went on. "I got my crew working on it. But I got to tell you, Mr. Whitman, that it's going to be a couple of hours before my men get it cleaned up."

"Why?"

"If he had just spray-painted on that regular cement out there next to the street, we could paint gray over it," came the voice, matter-of-fact, certain of the physical world, if nothing else. "That woulda been easy. But it's them polished Italian marble slabs that he hit with the paint. You can't just paint over it, it'd look terrible. Won't match all the swirls of white and black and everything. See, that stone comes from the quarry in Italy and it's all polished up nice. But you got thousands and thousands of shoes goin' over it every day and the smoothness gets worn down, like. It's got these little seams and crannies and cracks that the red paint went deep into, so you got to get some high-concentration methylene chloride that heats the paint chemically and makes it expand. Then you can dig it out with a steel brush. I got my men pouring it on the marble."

I got out of bed then and into the shower, where I let the water pound my head.

■ ■ ■

When I arrived at the Corporation plaza I walked around to the south side. There the men from the maintenance crew were, four of them, on hands and knees in their neat uniforms—blue pants and matching cotton sports shirt, with the Corporation logo on the breast. They'd set up work lights to see the stone better. I stepped closer.

"Is it working?" I asked one of the men casually.

"Yeah," he said, not looking up, as the chemical bubbled in the cracks of the marble. "But it's never going to look right again."

I was early—perhaps no one important had seen the graffiti. Inside the building, the same tired man pushed the floor polisher over the expanse of floor. Upstairs on thirty-nine I walked past every office on the floor to see who was in. It was only seven-fifteen. A few secretaries from the financial offices were making coffee—they'd just arrived, too late to have seen the message, I knew. But when I passed Samantha's office, there she was, her hair in a ponytail, her back erect, red fingernails clacking lightly on the keys in front of her screen.

"Jack?" she called while keeping her eyes on the screen. "That you?"

"Morning."

I stopped in her doorway, trying to reconstruct her subway ride from the East Side and figure what direction she walked from the station. The corridors under Rockefeller Center led everywhere. Samantha looked at me, her blond hair perfect, her clothes bright and perfect, her legs long and perfect, her left eye not perfect, and a thought passed across her face before she remembered to trigger her smile. "What?" she said in her high voice. "Oh, good morning, just good morning."

I needed to get her started on another topic. "What's happening with Herr Waldhausen and company?"

"We're close. I mean, I *think* we're close. We're talking about little stuff. Those guys from Salomon and Chase are working on it now. We're going to have to make some sort of announcement in a week or so, about being in negotiations at least, is my guess."

"And then we'll get a couple of dozen shareholder's suits." We had already discussed how to handle shareholders who were angered that a great American institution such as the Corporation had merged internationally.

"Oh, we'll get everything!" she said dismissively, fingering the bracelet of gold and ivory that encircled her wrist. "But it is going to work. How're things with the Chairman?"

"He hasn't budged. I've given him the whole argument, too. Nobody should expect that I'm going to be successful, because so far, *nothing*, got that? Morrison had better be prepared to muscle with the board of directors. It could come down to that, Samantha. You can't make any kind of announcement without the Chairman of the damn Corporation going along with it."

She stared at me. "You notice that mess outside the building this morning?"

I stiffened. "Where?"

"On the south side?"

I shrugged. "I use the other side."

"Of course," Samantha said.

"Any more dates with Herr Waldhausen?"

"Last night we went out for dinner, as a matter of fact." Samantha arched her eyebrows. She had the inside line on the deal now, I could see; everything went through her or close by. She was smart, too, she knew not to lord this over me.

"Morrison must be proud of you."

"All he wants is the deal. He says just keep Waldhausen talking."

"Is he?"

"Well, he keeps asking me about things." She hit the save key on her keyboard and turned around. "He wants to know everyone's responsibilities. He even asked about you."

"Me?"

"He wanted to know where you were after the first day."

This surprised me. "You told him?"

"I told him you were doing some work for the Chairman. He asked me how it was that Morrison expected to do this deal without the Chairman's approval."

"And you said—"

"I said we *thought* we could bring him around to see it our way."

"Oh, come on, he's got to see that Morrison wants to force the Chairman out of the airplane. How did Waldhausen react?"

"He smiled." Samantha frowned. "I guess I expected him to push the question—you'd think he would, but, on the other hand, if he doesn't push the issue, doesn't challenge us, then that signals to us that we have his support. I mean, he's a smart guy, he knows about the Chairman—"

"Maybe Waldhausen and his people see the Chairman as an impediment, too, and they know that by dealing only with us, Morrison and everybody, that strengthens our position for us if a fight with the board develops."

"Or maybe he's just hoping we resolve it internally so he doesn't have to deal with it."

"Or maybe he's got a fucked-up perception of the situation on the thirty-ninth floor."

"How could that be?" Samantha said.

"Morrison told *us* that he had spelled out the truth of the situation to Waldhausen beforehand, but maybe in fact he misrepresented it, or himself. Made it seem like he was the main guy. That could be done very subtly."

"Waldhausen isn't going to fall for that."

"No?"

"No, I mean we've talked *a lot*, about a lot of things . . . how he perceives American culture, what kids in Germany are like now, his wife," Samantha noted, examining her nails. "Ulna, Ulna this, Ulna that."

The wife's name on the fax was different—Gretchen, as I remembered. "That was her name?"

"Yes, about how she neglects him and won't take care of the house, the whole thing."

"Is he the sort of man who has a mistress?"

"I asked him and he said no, he was too heartbroken over his wife. We talked about a lot of things. He said he was shocked at the homeless problem here. He told me he was in Central Park and saw a man cooking a dead pigeon. What else . . . he's impressed with Morrison, thinks that he's just coming into his prime as an executive . . . that sort of thing, we just talked."

It was one of the few times I knew something that Samantha did not and I intended to say nothing and thus maintain the advantage. Assuming the fax to his mistress was real, Waldhausen was lying to Samantha, creating fictional scenarios in order to induce her trust. His letter to his wife, with a different name, seemed genuine. As for the mistress, his lie was expectable—why should he tell Samantha about that? He was working Samantha somehow, and she didn't know it. Why? I couldn't think of a reason, I could only just stare dumbly, marveling at how pleased Samantha was with herself. I knew what had come next. "Then you seduced him of course."

Samantha tilted her blond head and opened her big beautiful mouth. "Of course!"

"Lucky guy," I said.

She crossed her legs. "Other guys have been lucky, no?"

"Ah, Samantha . . ."

"Yes?" she teased. "What is it?"

I sat in her other office chair. "It's still a little weird for me, even after all this time."

"You're just sentimental," she said with seriousness. "You're a sentimental guy, Jack. You have the requisite mean streak in you, but ultimately the other is stronger." She stared at me, one eye turned in. "I'm sure of this."

"Perhaps."

She shook her head. "No, definitely."

The light was coming up in the windows behind her.

"I saw the graffiti outside the building," she said.

I let out a breath. "I thought you might have."

"Is it about that woman and little girl I saw up here a couple of weeks ago?"

"Yes."

"She was very . . . very striking."

"She was in bad shape when you saw her."

"Yes, but she has a rather remarkable face. Such a *strong* expression. I think that a man could see that face once and not forget it."

I nodded. "That's exactly what happened, Samantha. I can't really explain it."

"And the little girl, too? That's part of it?"

I nodded. "And the little girl, too."

Samantha shook her head and looked down. "I was always sorry about what happened to Liz, Jack. You get old enough and all you want is for people to have decent, safe lives." She looked back up at me. "I always felt terrible about what happened . . . you know that."

We were quiet a moment. "I can't have anybody knowing about this graffiti, Samantha. Not Morrison, not now."

"Yes." She looked at me, her expression soft. "He'd be really pissed. I found the letters this morning, Jack. About five-thirty when I came in."

"So *you* called Fitzpatrick, the building services guy?"

"I told him to get it cleaned up immediately."

"Jesus, thanks."

We sat there in her office, a man and a woman, each in suits.

"Hey, Jack, it's *me*, right?"

I gave her a smile. And we heard noises down the hall, ending the moment.

"Okay." I rose to leave Samantha's office.

"Okay."

I walked to my office, feeling relieved. It had been years since our brief affair. Reagan had still been in the saddle. Neither Samantha nor I confused what had happened for anything other than the satisfaction of mutual curiosity. It was early in my time at the Corporation and Samantha and I were both cutting through the junior-exec levels. My marriage to Liz was fine, too—truly. We were happy. I strayed for no good reason except that the chance was available to me. Samantha and I had been to L.A. on a business trip together, we had talked in the hotel bar. I knew instantly that it would happen. It was a matter of a drink after work a few nights later while Liz worked late, and a cab to Samantha's apartment, which at the time was still a drab two-bedroom affair on the West Side that she shared with a roommate, a brilliant young Japanese pianist whose bedroom was entirely filled by a Steinway concert grand. The woman slept under the piano each night, as if protected by a massive, three-legged animal with a shiny black coat. (How odd it is that, conceivably, Dolores's father had worked on that piano.) I think Samantha and I slept together to get it out of the way, in a brotherly-sisterly manner, and to ensure a certain loyalty from each other. Just one night. "We did this now and it was fun but you're going to stay with Liz and I'm going to keep looking," Samantha informed me in bed. While she showered I perused her apartment and found a list taped to the refrigerator in the kitchen, entitled "Weekly Goals." The goals that week: 1) LEARN D-BASE SOFTWARE. 2) STOP BITING FINGERNAILS FOREVER. Samantha was just twenty-seven, sweeter and more succulent then—her skin *impossibly* soft, still just a girl's skin—and in retrospect I think she was just starting to understand and experiment with the possible intersections between work and sex. Women *do* do this, no matter that they rightly decry the practice when a man imposes himself upon a female of lesser position in the office. It would be later that Samantha started to look *harder*, more polished; it was later, when she began to make the big money, that the months would go by and man after man after man was summoned to her apartment to try to fuck away her loneliness.

I have never been capable of bitterness toward women I have slept with—the relationship may have ended in flames, but I remember each woman—or girl, as the case may be—with a certain wistfulness at the perishability of intimacy, at the younger, more innocent version of the both of us. Even my functional congress with Miss Najibullah, the paid courtesan at the Chairman's club, would eventually be painted over with cheap nostalgia. I think this is a character flaw in myself and I think that Samantha saw it and knew that she could sleep with me and thereby inoculate herself against the possibility that we might be vicious competitors at some future moment at the Corporation. But I didn't realize this at the time. I remember coming home the night after we'd done it—a matter of a fifteen-block walk at the time—and taking a shower. Liz returned home late and undressed next to the bed, still smelling of the restaurant, the smoke and spilled beer and squeezed lemon rinds and half-eaten swordfish fillets, and as she flung her clothes to the floor in exhaustion before falling into bed I thought that life had a certain weird richness to it that I could lie down twice in one night with two different women. What I'd done was wrong, for I'd promised Liz I would never do it and there was no reason to break her trust, but it was utterly delicious. I *knew* that I would never get caught and I never did, unless of course you take into account the fact that Liz was killed before I gathered the courage to confess to her, which I always meant to do, considered it each day, in fact. When you are denied the chance to confess, you are also denied the chance to be forgiven. In that respect I *was* caught, caught terribly.

◆ ◆ ◆

I spent the morning worrying that everyone in the building knew that Jack Whitman, a vice president on the thirty-ninth floor, had been the subject of a graffiti attack. I chewed antacids. It didn't get any better when Beales stopped by my office. His big, handsome frame filled the doorway. "Let's eat lunch today," he said. "To talk."

"Talk?" I wondered if he had heard about the graffiti.

His face was set. "You and I *need* to talk."

Perhaps he was right. We agreed on one o'clock at an expensive Indian place draped in great bolts of maroon fabrics such that you felt you were caught in chambers of a giant heart. I got there first and was shown a seat in the back, which was more private. Keeping my eyes on the tablecloth, I listened to the two men at the table next to me.

"When they call, don't say, 'I decline to comment,' " said the first.

"They love that—it can be construed as guilt."

"Yes. Exactly. So instead, what you say is, 'I can't help you with your story.' That's very good. It can't be quoted and yet it is not a formal refusal to comment and it validates the reporter's role. Says you understand he's got a job to do. It's very subtle, but it works."

" 'I can't help you with your story . . .' " the other man mused.

"Yes, that's what you say when they call."

On my other side sat a heavyset man dressed in the pseudo-relaxed literary manner, his hair pulled back in a ponytail. I supposed that he was a magazine or book editor. He was talking to the famous South American poet who made his reputation singing the torments of the Brazilian slums (and who now, I'd read, spent most of his time in San Francisco, Paris, and New York). While the waiters obediently scraped crumbs from the table into brass trays, the two men delighted in berating the administration's vicious indifference to the lowest classes. In but a few minutes, they had analyzed America's foreign policy toward Latin America, the current direction of the United States Supreme Court, the cultural wretchedness of the suburbs, and the succulencies of the salad vegetables now in vogue. It occurred to me that Dolores had probably never eaten in a place like this.

Beales came in, shouldering rudely past the Indian busboys, enjoying his greater size. He was in a hurry and he would be in a hurry until he got to his grave. He saw me, but then he noticed someone from CBS whom he knew and paused to chat, standing to be seen standing. Despite all his tennis, he was thickening around the middle. Years back, when we were trying as hard as possible to be friends, he used to insist that after work we slip into this little place on Broadway between Fifty-second and Fifty-third. It was a topless bar, with a stage. You went down a narrow, grimy flight of stairs. An immense black man in a suit and tie showed you to a chair next to the stage and asked what you wanted to drink. The colored lights swirled, the mirror balls spun. Meanwhile the girls dancing onstage already had their g-string in your face, the little garters with tiny cloth roses, the leather, whatever. Some were bored or faking, but a few looked like they meant it. They were very good, this being midtown Manhattan. The drinks cost too much, the complementary buffet loaded with the worst cheesy slop. But we were married guys and it was a cheap thrill. There was a very firm Texan girl, who looked no older than eighteen, her hair a silky curtain that played around her body, which was slender as a snake's. When she spun hard around the brass pole, you could hear the screws groan in the wood. She did nothing for me and so I wondered with detachment if she knew, *really*, what she was doing with her mouth as she danced. But Beales, whose wife was a heavy-hipped blonde who had birthed three babies, each over nine pounds, was fascinated by this young girl, her compact smoothness. She looked *tight*. He must have put a dozen bills in her garter that first time. After he was made a vice president, he started going to the club by himself and coming back to the office late after lunch. Then, without telling his wife, he bought a tiny studio apartment a block south of Central Park—ten feet by eighteen feet, no bigger than a large rug—eighty thousand bucks, a sum low enough that his wife wouldn't notice a change in the family's living standard from the outgo of monthly mortgage payments. It would have been a great investment but Beales didn't rent it out. He took the bar dancer there maybe twice a week at lunchtime, and occasionally before getting on the commuter train home to kids and dinner. The evil pleasure of a quick pop. This kind of thing is common; the pressure pushes men into new, harder versions of themselves.

Beales came to the table.

"Okay," he said after we'd ordered, "why do I want to talk? Because all of us, you, me, everybody, are knocking our balls together trying to come up with a deal with V-S and Waldhausen, and we're actually getting pretty close—"

"How close?"

"Basically it's down to management questions. All the marketing stuff is worked out. But that's not what I want to talk about, Jack." He paused to see if I was ready to switch topics. "I think you and I should just call some kind of truce. When we fight in front of Morrison, it doesn't help either one of us. I know you and I are not exactly in love with one another, but you're acting really pissed—"

"Yeah," I jumped in. "I am acting pissed, because you got Morrison to cut me out of the negotiating team and start farting around with the Chairman."

Beales's eyebrows arched. "I didn't do that."

"The fuck you didn't."

He opened his hands in the air. "Morrison must have dreamed it up."

"No, I don't think he did," I replied. "I really don't think that. He had me working on the merger plan from the very first moment. He had me in there as one of the guys that knew everything. It's actually stupid for him to have done this."

Beales sat back in his chair. "I agree."

"You agree?"

"Yes, I agree, it was stupid. I didn't understand it at the time."

"And you didn't say anything?"

Beales shook his head. "No."

"You saw it as to your advantage, of course."

"True."

He was forty, too old to take chances. He had worked hard for almost fifteen years, finding and laboring in the dense seams of power in the Corporation, just as we all had. He was older mentally than he should be. He loved the nonreality of air-conditioning, knew he was safe in air-conditioning, one of those men who wanted the future locked up and put in a Merrill Lynch Cash Management Account. His shins were rubbed smooth of hair by the elastic in his expensive socks that his wife bought him three times a year from Saks. He hated that, because it made him know he was going to die.

"So," I went on, "you might as well have been the one to suggest it to Morrison."

He didn't say anything. Our soup came.

"You realize that I know *none* of the V-S guys?" I continued. "That Samantha has been busy with Waldhausen and you and Morrison and the bankers and everyone have had a *fucking party* together using my work? You realize that, don't you?" My voice was getting louder and people at the other tables glanced over.

"Yes," Beales finally said, smoothing his yellow tie.

"And I suppose you guys are going to work it through the board, leaving the Chairman on some side road holding a suitcase, or dinking around in his rose garden in the Hamptons. And that was the idea all along."

"Look, Jack, do I mind that Morrison's got you on a fishing expedition? No. I'll be honest about that. But you've got to believe I didn't put the idea in his head." He was moving his big tanned hands around in emphasis. "Somebody else, and who, I don't know. Maybe the consultants, I don't know. And I'm saying why don't you and I just avoid hammering each other right now? It's not worth it for either one of us."

He was protecting himself. "You're full of shit," I told him.

Beales shrugged, sipped his soup, and then put the spoon down. "You know what?" he said.

"What?"

"I thought I could just reason this out with you but I can't." Beales looked around the restaurant, stood up, and fished into his pocket for a couple of bills. He flipped them dismissively onto the table. "I'd rather get a turkey sandwich at a deli."

I watched him go. The restaurant was full of men like Beales, hunched over talking business, getting today's angle, the buzz, the advantage. Men in their late thirties or early forties who now carried a wife and several kids, the house. Strapped in for the long ride, boys. And at this level to stop moving was to die. Those not promoted carried a certain malignancy that sooner or later assured their professional death. You have to be promoted or be given a new project every year or two or else everybody knows you've run aground, turned to stone—I'd already seen men and women who were *finished* at forty-three, forty-five. They got that look, that worry playing across their faces. Meanwhile legions of other smart people crowded to take your place, pushing from behind like you did, from underneath, clawing at your feet. Once you're above a certain level, nobody will ever feel sorry for you if you falter, they will trample your corpse into the sand as they run past. If you were a Beales with a wife and three kids, the tuition payments would be murder, the mortgage was five thousand a month, and he was probably looking around for a decent beach place on Long Island, somewhere to dump the family for a month in the summer (renting was a pain, no mortgage deduction on the income tax), and if you had a place on the beach, you needed a boat to show you weren't cheap, and that was another seventy-five grand, easy. I knew Beales; he understood that all he had to do with the V-S deal was hang around the picnic blanket and that would prove he had the real corporate stuff, that he hadn't *needed* the eighties, not like the others had—the deadbeats and smilers all lifted by the big tide. He knew his time was now. The big money wasn't too far away. Everybody was out to get theirs. Beales was going to get his. And I, greedy Jack Whitman, was going to get mine.

♦ ♦ ♦

But what you get is often different than what you want. When I returned, Helen told me I was due to go listen to the systems consultants that afternoon. Even at the high levels, one is forced to waste time now and then.

"I can't go," I told her. "These things kill me."

"You're scheduled," she said.

"Everyone else go back to the Plaza?" I asked.

"I think so, yes."

"So I could skip this meeting and no one would know."

"*God* would know."

"He already knows everything, Helen. What has happened, what will happen. He knows my sins, too, and they depress him. He thought I had a shot at the big cloudy show—you know, angels and harp music and conversations with Mother Teresa. But now it's out of the question."

"Get out of here," Helen said in mock sternness. "You're late."

I elevatored down three floors to a maze of offices where the carpeting is older and the corners of the hallways are smudged and damaged by the mail carts that go around each day. A merger agreement with V-S would mean linked computer systems. I found the meeting room. The door was closed—I was late. The conference room was too dark for me to see who else was there and I slid in just as the presentation began. In the front, facing the group, stood the information systems consultant, a young black guy in a stiff suit, one of the new high priests of accounting technology who had been brought in to discuss the logistical problems of hooking up the Corporation's computers with those of a theoretical corporation the size and complexity of V-S. The consultant blinked almost constantly, as if to accommodate the speed of thought within his own head: ". . . and before I get to the prepared diagrams that demonstrate the particular macro network that you may wish to consider, I thought I'd quickly run through—" Useless information, which the consultant could always just pass out in ring-binders if he wanted. But his outfit was probably getting about sixteen hundred dollars per billed "team hour" and so they'd give us the whole show. ". . . in order to integrate a far-flung decentralized network typically composed of DOS PC's, OS/2's and Digital VAX minis and maybe a Hitachi AS/EX-80 mainframe in Germany and convert to GAAP standards for use over here and to get all the baud rates to match, my friends, we would propose a KAP accounting system designed by Roma Grupo S.p.A. in Italy that runs on the IBM S/370 architecture, because it performs in eight languages and will incorporate Swedish umlauts or double-byte Japanese Kanji characters or even those incredibly long German nouns."

The consultant gave a soundless little laugh and then smiled patiently, a holy man waiting for his message to reach the pews.

"Can it handle South American figures?" I asked dutifully from my chair in the dark. "You've got to figure those as a possibility. Brazil's inflation is something like five hundred percent a year."

"*Yes,*" the consultant responded, no doubt pleased by a further complication. "A point *considerably* well taken. You've got to have accounting packages that will deflate and revalue those crazy Argentinian and Brazilian hyperinflation numbers. That means very large currency blocks in the software so that numbers in the hundreds of billions in the local currency can be processed. But how would such a system be configured? Well, friends, we must remember that two marginally compatible systems are being networked here, so the Roma Grupo KAP would sit on top of those two. Let's call the two systems A and B. Both are stand alone systems and of comparable current technology, maybe system B is a bit bigger, but A is thirty percent faster. The data can travel from B to A or from A to B. The question, essentially, is one of *control*. Who controls the information? Is system A a stop for the division financial data on the way to . . ."

And so on, interminably, an invisible freight train of information. The consultant's blinking became worse with the effort—he was brilliant in his ability to project the complexity of an enormous computer system within his own imagination—one of those people who could have been happy in another age carving endless, unbroken meanders on endless palace doors for the endless glory of the Medicis. Then came the computer-generated graphs and charts and diagrams with catchy graphics and pull-down menus on a large-screen TV and he stood in the darkened room of the silhouetted heads. The colored high-resolution screen flickered from one image to the next, switching into deeper levels of detail, and it all seemed like a kind of sickness that people would spend their time on these things.

In the darkness I began to fall asleep. Perhaps I actually dozed off, for when the hand came down on my shoulder from behind I jumped. I sensed a presence next to me, a smoker's breath, a drift of after-shave cologne. Then came the words whispered close to my ear: "You have an exasperating habit of saying interesting things, my friend, and so this old man would like to have one more discussion with you." The hand remained firm. "Two days from now. But this time you have to come up with something better, something *new*." The hand patted my shoulder twice. "I'll do my best to stay alive until then."

Then, as the consultant droned on, before I had quite understood what had happened, the figure moved silently through the flickering gloom and slipped out the door. The Chairman.

He was in the game.

♦ ♦ ♦

At home that night, I turned on the news while Dolores cooked dinner for the three of us. First Peter Jennings—the subtly sardonic tilt to his head. Then I channel-hopped to Rather on CBS—a cigar-store Indian with a moving mouth. I'd once seen him walking outside Black Rock, the CBS headquarters, looking lost, wearing thick glasses that made his eyes into huge liquid oysters. When you see him on TV, you don't realize how stout the man is.

Maria came and jumped in my lap, taking the remote unit.

"I'm going to change the channel," she said.

"Maria, this is the news, and I—"

She flicked. A car skidded across a dusty horizon in slow motion, all poetry and color and money. I wanted to drive it, even though I had a car already, kept in a nearby garage, rarely used. Maria flicked again. A beer commercial, everybody twenty-three years old, having the best time of their lives. I wanted to be there with them. The advertisers know me so well. In America, if no one knows you, at least the advertisers do.

"I want to watch Bambi," Maria said.

"You can't," I explained. "You have to put in the tape and the VCR is hooked up to the TV downstairs."

"Why?"

"Why is the VCR downstairs?"

"Yes."

"Because I just have one and I had to put it with one TV or the other."

"Oh." She looked at the screen. "I want to watch it here!" she shrieked, testing me.

Maria saw no reason why she could not control what she saw and where. If what she wanted to watch could be played on the side of a soap bubble or on the surface of the milk in her cup, she'd be momentarily enthralled and then accept it as reality. She was young enough to have that happen. The magic of technology did not intimidate her, not yet, at least.

"Maria, let me ask you something, okay?"

"No!"

"Just one question."

"All right." She wriggled impatiently.

"Why do you like looking at Bambi shows and TV and things?"

"'Cause it's fun."

"Suppose the TV was on a computer?" I asked Maria.

"Could you still get Bambi?"

"Sure."

"It might be fun."

"Supposing you could watch it and tell Bambi what to do?"

"I like it. Let me do it!" She grabbed the remote control and flicked it through the channels. Then she called up the small alternative channel box in the screen and looked at the other shows with that too. When I was a kid, all we had that was unusual was cartoons on the local UHF channel—no cable, no VCR, no big-screen TV. Yet here was Maria, not quite four years old, and the new technology was part of her understanding of reality.

"How did you learn to do that?" I asked.

She bounced in my lap. "I don't know! It's fun."

I knew then, suddenly, what I would do with the Chairman. That night, while Dolores was giving Maria a bath, I called our NewMedia subgroup head in L.A. and asked him if he could send their latest prototype to New York. He panicked. It wasn't ready for formal presentation yet, he said. There were bugs that had to be worked out and the whole project was nine people in seven rooms and they were all working on separate pieces of software.

"It's informal," I told him.

"You looking for next month, or what?"

"Day after tomorrow. Get the software, the box it runs on, and the technician on the plane tomorrow."

"That's an impossible request."

"No it's not," I said. "Get your people on a jet. I don't care how you get here as long as you're here tomorrow to set up."

"Impossible. Really. And it's an outrageous request."

"It's merely a pain in the ass."

"No, it's *impossible.*"

I said nothing and let his words linger in the space between us, the faraway buzzing and popping and murmurings of the dead, the hum of continental space—just a few seconds.

"Who's the audience?" he finally asked. "A bunch of analysts or something? Wall Street guys?"

"Just one person."

"One?"

I said the Chairman's name.

"Come on."

"It will be me, him, and a technician that you would send to hook it up and make sure it runs. But primarily him."

He was considering.

"It's all icon and menu-driven, and has the best new voice-synthesis stuff, right?" I asked.

"Yes, all that's very good now."

"Voice synth usually takes a couple of hours to adjust to the individual?"

"No, no. We're down to fifteen minutes, tops."

"And the image and motion encyclopedia we were talking about a few months ago?"

"We've scanned in . . . let me remember the figure—we've got a guy who's been doing it—it's about four hundred million, something like four or five hundred million discrete frames. Stock footage, all kinds of stuff."

"Jesus."

"Yeah." He laughed. "It's pretty good. We're pretty fucking proud of that."

"The whole bucket of bolts actually hangs together and works, right?"

"It's not production standardized, but—"

"But it works, we have *one* copy that actually works?"

"Yes. But don't I have to clear this with what's-his-name, vice president for—"

"Forget that," I told him. "It's on my head. Really. That's not going to be a problem. We're playing at a whole different level."

The line was silent.

"You'll get it here? Floor thirty-nine. Expense everything through this office. Not a division expense. Pad the expense, too, if you could use it in your budget."

"You're talking maybe a hundred and fifty thousand easily, to fly the stuff in. Commercial carriers won't take what they call level-nine technology without special flight insurance. There's excessive vibration insurance, there's accidental mishandling insurance—I mean, it's really a pain. We've run into this with trade shows. It had to be loaded and unloaded specially on originating flights, not connecting flights. And there's special packing and overtime for the technicians . . ."

"No problem. I'll sign off on everything."

"Who should I ask for?"

"Me. Ask only for me."

♦ ♦ ♦

An hour later Maria was asleep and I was at my desk with papers strewn around my chair. Dolores came into my office. "I was looking for an extra pillow upstairs in the closet," she said. "You have all of your wife's clothes."

I hadn't been able to throw them out. The walk-in closet on the top floor of the house was full of dresses, blouses, skirts, pants, a few maternity clothes. Even all the socks and underwear and bras were packed away up there. I'd meant to give it all away to a local church, but sometimes late at night when I was unable to sleep, I'd drift upstairs and stand in the closet, perhaps succeeding at catching some faint, fleeting smell of Liz. It was sick and stupid and yet I hadn't been able to get rid of the clothes.

"You want to try them on?" I said.

Dolores stared at me. "I'm not your dead wife."

"Of course not," I said. "I know that."

"I don't even know if they'd fit me."

"Then don't bother," I told her.

But ten minutes later Dolores came in wearing one of Liz's old business suits. The fit was pretty good; whereas Liz had been a little taller, Dolores's wide shoulders and heavier chest filled out the blouse. She was in her stocking feet.

"The shoes didn't fit," she said at the bottom of the staircase. "How do I look?"

I couldn't tell her, of course, that Liz had worn that very suit on the day she came home from the ob/gyn office to tell me she was pregnant. "You look great," I said finally. "You could go to work tomorrow in it."

"Of course it's not really *me*." Dolores smiled. "And I'm not her."

"Very different," I said, "in most respects."

"How?" Dolores teased.

"She's dead and gone. You're alive and kicking."

Dolores took off the suit.

"You're here," I said.

"But you *remember* her."

"Yes, of course."

"How well?" She stepped into the clothes she'd had on previously.

"Everything."

"Everything?"

"Yes, honestly."

"She as good in bed as me?"

"I thought only men were hung up on that."

"You going to answer my question?"

This was only half in fun. Dolores could not reach into the grave and bring Liz before her in order to make a woman's private comparison. So she humbled herself by asking. In a certain respect, it was similar to my wanting to find out who Hector was, except that I had the advantage that he was alive. "You really want to know, don't you?"

"Yes." She nodded. "Tell me."

All those teenage summers Liz had packed lobsters by day, she had run wild on the beach by night. Cars and beer and a couple of boys each summer. She'd known a few things.

"It's a tie," I said. "You're just as good. Different but just as good."

Dolores seemed satisfied by this answer, as if it elevated Liz to her level. My answer meant, in her understanding of things, that I had been married to a real woman, not some uptight princess who was photogenic and had nice clothes. She pulled open my file cabinet.

"You mind?" she asked.

"Just don't misplace stuff." All my financial records were in order in the file cabinet in my study, the usual stuff: bank statements, canceled checks, mortgage agreements, insurance papers, health records, a record of home improvements, Liz's death certificate and autopsy report. Dolores idly picked up a sales spreadsheet for one of the divisions with break-outs of monthly sales figures.

"You like being a businessman?" she asked.

"Not these days."

"Mmmn." She pulled another paper out of a file and then looked at me accusingly. "Hey, wait a minute."

"What?"

"This house cost five hundred and nineteen thousand dollars?"

"Yes."

"That's *a lot*."

"Not in New York City."

"You paid all that?"

"Well, I've got a mortgage for a lot of it."

"Yeah, but—"

"You're right, it's a lot."

She spied another piece of paper and yanked it up to her eyes. "You have something like seventeen thousand dollars in your checking account?"

"Yes."

"Your *checking* account!" Her voice held a shrill edge. "How much do you make? Like a hundred thousand dollars or something?"

"What are you saying to me, Dolores?"

"How much!"

"More than that."

"How much?"

Her father was a man who heated beans on the pilot light of the stove to save a few pennies.

"It's not important," I said softly.

"Tell me, so I *know*, all right?"

"It's not your business, Dolores."

This made her furious. "Oh, and it wasn't your business when I told you just about every last thing about myself, about how some guy raped me on the Brooklyn Bridge and everything?" She sank down onto the chair, the fingers of her right hand pulled together in a point that supported her forehead. Her shoulders shook, just a little. She looked up at me then, her eyes mad and wet. "You don't understand how hard some people got to work just to make a couple of hundred *bucks*," she said. "I mean, Hector, my husband, some of the things he *did* to make money . . ."

"Yes," I agreed.

"What do you mean *yes?*" she snapped. "You don't *know* anything, you're just some rich—white—asshole like some people are always talking about. I never really understood it, like, how unfair it was."

We didn't speak for a few minutes.

"I'm going out," Dolores announced.

"C'mon. It's ten-thirty."

But she was already heading down the stairs.

"Will you listen if Maria wakes up?" she called back.

"Sure, but—"

"I'm going to be a while."

I followed her down the stairs. "When will you get back?"

"Maybe two hours."

"I can't ask where you're going?" I said in exasperation.

"No."

She closed the door on the way out, and I worried immediately that she was going to go see Hector, that she would call him for some sort of rendezvous. But how? As of that morning, Hector didn't know where she was. I couldn't leave the house to follow her; if anything happened to Maria while I was gone I would never forgive myself, nor would Dolores. I looked out the front door. She was halfway down the block. It was long past dark, when the streets of Brooklyn change, new populations creeping out from the shadows. I stood at my door worrying. Across the street a tall, slender homeless man foraged through the cans.

I stepped outside. "Hey," I called.

He lifted his head and looked around. "Yeah, who?"

"Come here, I want to talk a minute."

He saw me and slowly pushed his shopping cart across the street. When he drew close to my gate I walked down the stone steps. "You want to make some money?"

"I'm makin' money this minute, soon as I find me my next can."

In the lights I saw that his face was cave-cheeked with ruin.

"No," I said, "I mean some real money, say a hundred bucks."

He squinted at me in contemplation. "Sound dangerous. I don't do that kind of work."

"No," I said, "this is easy."

"Why you payin' so much?"

"Because I'm stupid. See that woman?" I pointed down the street. "She just—*there*—she just turned the corner."

"I seen her."

"I want you to follow her and find out where she goes."

"That could be anywhere."

"I think she's going to stay on foot. No car. Just walking."

"She in trouble?"

"No, not necessarily. But it's private business."

"Private enough t'get me shot?"

"You follow her, and I'll give you fifty bucks now and fifty when you come back."

"That could be all night, my man."

"No, she told me she'll be back in three hours or less. And if she's not, then you come back in three hours."

"Got the fifty?"

I opened my wallet and handed the bills to him. "What are you going to do with your cart?"

"Take it with me."

"You're going to push it along? Why not leave it here, in the bushes here."

"'Cause some guy like me come along an' snatch it, that's why."

"If you say so."

"Don't worry about me. I'll be back."

"Come back before she does, just see where she goes."

"You got it." And off he went, with new purpose in his stride, pushing the shopping cart back out onto the street, its contents rattling and flapping. I went back inside, wondering if I'd just thrown away fifty bucks.

♦ ♦ ♦

But I hadn't. Almost two hours later I heard a discreet knocking on the door. I opened the inner door and looked through the glass. It was the same man and I slipped outside.

"So?"

"That is a *strange* woman," he muttered with wild excitement, and I could see he'd been drinking. "I go just like you tellin' me, an' that woman can walk, she can't even slow down for thirty blocks, an' then she goes into this lounge up out there on Sixth Avenue an' maybe Twenty-fourth Street, right?" His face was shiny. "An' so I think that's the deal. She's gonna slip into one of these places an' meet some dude an' that was what you wanted me to find out on her. I'm thinkin' that you was pretty slick to put the spyin' eye on her like that, I was congratulatin' you an' *me*, 'cause I got some money out of it there, you know, an' I slipped into a liquor store an' bought me a pint an' I figured I'd come back here, get my other fifty, but then I see she's comin' out an' I expect some sugar daddy be somewhere 'round, somewhere *good*, right, I mean, I been watching her butt go back an' forth for forty-five minute, but there ain't no dude, just another woman, some woman what got some kinda big ole ass like a Sunday turkey, an' they talk an' I can't hear nothing, I'm on the other side of the street—*cool*, you know."

I leaned back against the doorjamb, worried now. "All right," I said. "Then what?"

"Then she starts walking again an' it ain't back here. No sir. An' I'm like, shit, this ain't over yet. She got some kind of bag in her hand now, not too big, a shopping bag. So then we start off again but this time she's going down to Fifth Avenue an' Twenty-third Street, in there, an' I'm thinkin' so she's goin' to meet the dude at his house, maybe she just *called* him from the lounge. It's gonna be some dude with some money or crack or somethin' because she's a good-lookin' woman, right?" He cackled. "I mean that's why the fuck anybody cares where the fuck she at, right?"

"Where'd she go next?" I asked tersely, not interested in his analysis, but whether Dolores was safe.

"We go to that cem'tery right there on Twenty-second Street, you know, that Greenwood Cem'tery where they got so many people buried?"

I knew it—rolling acres of tombstones, shadowed by many old trees, surrounded by a high spiked iron fence.

"—an' I'm thinkin' I ain't goin' in *there*, it's dark an' them places is full of guys with guns an' shit, some serious shit goes down in that cem'tery sometimes, you know, because they got all those freshly dug graves an' shit an' I heard tell some dudes talkin' 'bout how you can put someone in there an' then never find 'em once the grass grows over it an' nobody want to go *lookin'* for a body in somebody else's grave 'cause you gotta get a court order an' shit, so I'm thinking damn if she ain't goin' to go messin' around in *there*. I mean it's got a chain out on the main gate but there's gotta be a hundret ways to get in where the fence be broke, an' so she goes in one of those! Like it's the fuckin' *supermarket*. An' fuck! I'm thinkin' this is one motherfuckin' brave bitch, she be goin' messin' around in a cem'tery full of murderers an' ghosts an' shit an' so now I can't take it no more, I'm gettin' *worried* an' shit, thinkin' I'ma lose her, so I ditch the cart in the bushes an' start following her, quiet."

His face was bright with excitement and he drew a deep breath. "She know *just* where she goin'. She got it figured, right? We ain't in the section for the rich graves with all them statues an' tiny houses made out of marble, it's the *poor* section where the graves is small an' then we go to where the graves is *flat* an' about the size of a piece of paper, an' you know that's where it can't get no poorer than that. You be poorer than that, you *dead*, right? Course you dead *anyway*, heh! An' then I see some guys way off, one of them got a lighter on, doing crack or some such shit, killin' somebody or somethin', an' I'm thinkin' so she goin' to see them an' they're goin' catch me an' kill my ass. But your woman just go real slow like an' then find the thing she's lookin' for an' it's one of them *tiny* poor people's graves, an' she stops there an' kneels down an' I'm maybe thirty feet away, quiet you know, an' she lights these little candles an' starts chanting an' something, like a moan. Sort of like she's sad an' sorta like she's gettin' fucked. An' then these other guys, they see something is goin' on an' they's laughin' an' I can tell they been drinkin' some, the way they was laughin' an' so I take my hit off 'm my bottle, you know, an' then they start comin' over like they gonna fuck somebody *up* an' then your woman there says, 'Don't mess with me, I'm praying.' Somethin' like that. Like you *better* be able to say it right the first time or else there ain't *goin'* be no other time. They goin' laugh an' stick you quick. She said it good, but these niggers think that's real funny. That's the funniest thing they *ever* heard an' so they come closer with their flashlights an' shit an' then they get close enough see she's a woman an' you *know* they thinkin' about rapin' her. I mean, *I* been thinkin' about it for a hour. But then she pulls somethin' out of the bag she's got an' it be *alive!* It's a bird or a chicken or *somethin'* an' that stops them an' they see she's got a little knife an' she screams somethin' in Spanish an' then cuts that bird's head off an' throws the body up an' it starts runnin' like, without its motherfuckin' *head.* An' I'm fucked up! I'm drinkin' now, boy, an' these fuckin' homeboys see *that* an' they fucked up bad by *that* an' they get the fuck out of there, go run- nin' off, go kiss they momma's tit, an' I hear a couple of gunshots like they think they're shootin' at the chicken or somethin', an' then mister I just got the *fuck* out of there myself an' I don't know if she saw me or what all, I just want my fifty dollars so's I can get me some rest."

I stared at him in disbelief.

"That's it, my man."

"Is she coming back?" I asked anxiously.

"Back any minute. Now, that fifty."

I gave it to him. He'd earned it, too. "You'll get some food with that?" I asked hopefully. He drew a greasy, blackened piece of twine from within his clothing. On the end of it was a small bag and he quickly secreted the money in the bag and the bag back in his clothes.

"Food?" he answered. "I'm goin' to get me some *steak*, boy."

♦ ♦ ♦

Dolores came back not long after that, turning the key in the front door lock. She walked in and without looking at me dropped onto the couch, her dark hair wild and damp, her skin flushed, eyes sullen. I sat in a chair across from her clutching the arms, not ready to talk to her just yet, unnerved by how different she looked, wild and *tough*, clearly the daughter of a sturdy Dominican woman. She was brazenly disheveled, as if she had just been with a lover, though I knew differently. And in that moment, the antique mantel clock ticking politely, Dolores raised her dark eyes to mine.

"What're you looking at?" she spat.

"I know where you went," I told her.

Her lips became a bitter half smile. "I doubt it."

"The cemetery."

Dolores's dark eyes burned at me. "You left Maria?"

"No, I didn't leave her." I kept my voice as even and reasonable as possible. "I had a homeless guy follow you. He told me the whole thing, about the chicken, the whole thing."

"You had no fucking right to do that."

"He told me you visited a grave."

Dolores stared at me, then let her eyes drift past me.

"My father," she finally said in a low voice.

"Oh."

"Okay?" she asked irritably, cutting her eyes back at me.

"Did you *need* to go at night?"

"I wanted to."

"You could have been hurt. I don't want you running around at night like that. You've got Maria here, and—"

"And what?"

"And I don't want anything to happen to you."

She contemplated this. Her face didn't soften. "I could have gone out *dancing*," she said scornfully. "That's what I *should* have done."

"I'd be jealous," I said.

"You and Hector." There was nothing but disgust on her face. I realized then that unlike many women, she didn't fear men, not at all. Perhaps this was what I found so exciting.

"He's pretty jealous?" I said.

"He knows what I'll do," Dolores told me, running her fingers through her hair. "I did some things, you know. He didn't know about them, but he knew about them, if you know what I mean."

"For instance?"

"You don't want to know," she said again, her voice laced with meanness. "It's not like the *ladies* at your office, it's not like your *wife*."

I said nothing.

"You want the worst?"

"Sure."

She checked my expression to see if I was serious. "I guess if we're going to be hanging out together, you should know some stuff. But you're not going to like it."

I was tired and strung out from work and fearful about what awaited me the next day: I had to plan the arrival of the NewMedia project, check with DiFrancesco, figure out the meaning of the Chairman's presence at the computer system meeting. And I still hadn't told Dolores that Hector was looking for her. Things were getting ahead of me. But I understood that Dolores was ready to cut new ground with me, and I felt a headlong intoxication at the mystery of her. "Tell me, Dolores," I said. "I can take it."

"We better go up on the roof with some of that wine," Dolores said, "if you really want to hear it."

♦ ♦ ♦

"I did some things I shouldn't have done. I don't regret doing them, you know? But still I shouldn't have done it. This was when Hector and me were not getting along so well. I used to think Hector was the strong one." The wind was whipping Dolores's hair. "I used to think I was lucky I got him. He was so strong and macho and confident, you know. But I got it wrong. I was too young to see it. That was his best, right? When Hector was twenty-four, he was the best he was ever going to be." She smiled. "He used to fuck me so much, it was like breathing. We even did it three weeks before the baby came, even though the doctor, he said no. But later we had some little problems."

"What?"

"Just . . . money and everything. He was having trouble keeping a job and was unhappy a lot of the time. He was messing around with some girls who hung out at this bar nearby. I don't think he was really doing anything. But I was pissed, you know, and he wasn't paying much attention to me. I was just kind of *unsatisfied* with everything."

She had been shopping in the corner bodega, Dolores said, when she noticed a couple of fire engines outside an apartment house down the street and walked toward the scene, looking for smoke or flames. When she got near, it was apparent that there was no real emergency, just a bunch of Irish firemen standing around in their fire pants and big rubber boots turned down at the knee so you could read their names written on the inside while the fire chief checked everything out. One of the firemen was disconnecting a hose from a hydrant and she asked him what had happened.

"Ahh, nothing much," he responded, not looking up. "They got some old guy smoking in bed. Just a smolder. Didn't do nothing."

The fireman had taken off the heavy yellow rubber coat and was working in his blue T-shirt with NYFD in white letters across his back and Dolores watched the large muscles in his arms. And a funny jolt of desire ran through her: she realized that she wanted him to do something to her. He pulled the hose off the hydrant.

"Just a little fire, huh?" she said.

The fireman stood up. He was pure Brooklyn Irish, big all over, someday a man with a gut but now a twenty-seven- or twenty-eight-year-old with thick short hair and eyes blue as a mailbox. He looked at her. "Yeah. What's your name?"

"Dolores."

"Well, Dolores, you want to fuck?"

She looked at him in shock.

"That's the real question here, ain't it? I can't talk now but that's the question, far as I can see. You're a hell of a good-lookin' woman. I drive by this corner when I get off my shift, at ten o'clock, so if you wanna meet me here then, let's go."

There it was. As simple as that. The fireman went back to work. He was clearly an asshole, Dolores thought, but there was something about him, perhaps a little like Hector used to be, and she wanted sex so badly. And the fireman was white. And he couldn't have AIDS because everybody knew they didn't let gays be firemen. And so that night she arranged for her girlfriend to watch the baby, and to tell Hector she was out if he came home before she did. She didn't really give a damn what he thought. And she stood on the right corner at ten o'clock and after a few minutes a Trans Am pulled up and flashed its lights. She got in and they didn't say much. He drove her to his home, a split-level on Staten Island, and they had some drinks in his living room and then he came over to her and turned out the lights. She worried he might hit her but he didn't. His name was Patrick, and he gave her a hard kiss and they started taking off their clothes. . . .

Dolores's voice filled the dark air above us, seemingly existing of its own accord, a voice of anger and frustration and appetite, and I wondered what it was that had driven Dolores to betray her husband so casually. I still did not understand why her marriage to Hector had disintegrated so quickly but before I could ask about that, Dolores continued. "We did the usual stuff, you know, but then he wanted to put it in my ass. Hector never did that, he said it was bad luck. And I thought that was going to hurt, and it did hurt a little, but he was careful. And then he reached for this little drawer next to the bed and pulled out . . . one of those long rubber penises, a dildo, you know, and he had me on my hands and knees with him going in and out of my ass and then he asked me if I wanted the other thing. And I didn't know. I was afraid it was going to hurt . . . I didn't say yes and I didn't say no. He said he knew what he was doing and that it wouldn't hurt. If it hurt we would stop. So he reached around, you know, and he did it, both at the same time, the dildo in front, and I have to admit it was something . . . it was something I'd never felt before, both at once like that. I just sort of shut my eyes and I was biting my lip. It was . . . so strange, it hurt but it was *good*. And it was so strange that a Catholic girl like me was doing this, and I was married and a mother. I sort of hated myself and I sort of didn't. And later when he drove me home he asked me if I liked it and I said I guess so and he wanted to know if I'd do it with him and his two friends if I looked at them and said they were okay. And I was thinking, did I get hurt tonight? No. I felt a little weird. But I felt kind of *happy* too, like I discovered something that I wasn't supposed to do and it wasn't so bad . . . I wasn't hurt or beat up, right? And so I told the guy okay I'll consider it. And so maybe a week later I got out of the house again without Hector knowing and this guy Patrick picked me up and we drove to his house again. And his two friends were there, Irish guys like him, but they were cops. And married, too. And I looked at them and thought they didn't look so bad. I mean they were clean, not fat and disgusting. And they lowered the shades and we started to drink and one of the guys started to do some coke but I said no thanks . . . and they had some music on, the guy who plays the saxophone, you know, Kenny G., and Patrick asked me to strip and I did. Then the other guys did too and I told them if they were rough with me then forget it, I didn't care if there were three of them. Not to mention their guns on the table. So everybody took off their clothes and we did it, you can imagine, and the guys switched around a lot and I remember somewhere in there I laughed and they asked why and I said because we're all Catholics, that's why, and they laughed, too. Ha, ha, we're all Catholics. Then they went at it pretty good and they called me a spick and . . . it got, you know, it got a little rough. But I remember that even though it was bad, I was bad, I liked all those men being on me. I kind of expected they would be mean but they weren't mean. They didn't *hurt* me. They said some things, you know, but that was really for the others and it was exciting for them and we all sort of knew it was going to be the only time. I mean, I know it was degrading, like when I was on my back and they were above me and doing—you can imagine, but there was something about *that* I sort of liked, to be honest, I know it's not what women're supposed to want. I was sore all over, they fucked me pretty good, my ass and my mouth hurt, everything. And two of them did it again while the third guy watched, because he couldn't get it up again, he was thinking of his wife and all the guys laughed at that, you know? It was sort of sad. And afterward I took a shower and had some more drinks. I thought I was going to cry but I didn't. The two guys who were cops had to go on duty and Patrick drove me home. He said when would I see him again, and I said I thought that was it, you know. That we had done it and nobody got hurt and that was it. I didn't want to start something. That I loved my husband. He got a little mad but said he understood. So I thought that was just the end of it, but I was stupid about that. There were these rumors that went around the neighbor- hood, like how I had sex with six firemen, or like every week I did it with four policemen and everything . . . I guess one of the guys had done some talking—at the fire station all they do is sit around and talk and wash the fire engines. One of them spoke a little Spanish, maybe he talked. Hector knows everything about me, that's why he's so jealous. It was the wrong thing to do because I had a baby and because of Hector. But if I wasn't married? Was it wrong? I don't know. I didn't get pregnant, I didn't get diseases, so I'm not unhappy about it, you know? Of course when Hector heard about it he wanted to beat me. But he was afraid the cops would come mess him up. He wanted to know if it was true, the rumors. I told him I'd never tell. He knows though. He knows me, he knows."

Dolores's words faded out over the roof. It occurred to me that she had a certain courage.

"I told you about what happened to his store and everything, right?" Dolores continued. Around us, the wind moved through the trees. "That changed him. Things change you . . . you never know when something can happen . . ." Dolores looked out over the roofs. "He's not like he was, I mean he's still got a temper and he still can kind of get crazy about something, you know, but also Hector is like, sad now. I used to worry if he was going to jump off a bridge or something. I used to tell him, 'I can't take this.' He used to say that guys like him were fucked from birth to death. Just like his moms and pops and *their* mothers and fathers before them. I can hear him sayin' it. See, Hector always wanted to be rich. That's why I'm glad he doesn't know where me and Maria are now. I got to go get a divorce lawyer or something."

"Do you still love him?"

Dolores paused. The red lights on the top of the World Trade Center blinked.

"Course I still love him. But that's not what we're talking about."

Dolores seemed finished and we sat quietly up on the roof, the wind pushing at us and bringing that odd consciousness one feels when slipping past old boundaries. As a man, I understood Hector's anxieties about Dolores. One may glimpse the expression on the woman's face while in the midst of it and know with certainty that she is far, far away from you. I understood now that when Dolores and I had sex she was fucked by and did fuck all her previous men at the same time, like a corridor in the mind that one has traveled many times, even perhaps including the man who'd raped her when she was so young and thrown her panties off the pedestrian deck of the Brooklyn Bridge. Her mind held all of her past. There was no possessing her. As a younger man, I would have been jealous, have despaired over this, been tormented by it, tried to suppress it. But flesh moves on. I think Dolores knew the same thing was true of me, too. She knew of Liz and could have guessed about the others. It's in the nature of what happens between men and women. So when Dolores and I fell into the darkness, as we did later that night, we did fuck and were fucked by our past lovers as well: Liz, Hector, Samantha, the fireman, the girls of my youth, the boys before Hector. The room and the bed and the sweat were hovering shadows of time and death; I think we both knew enough of life, saw the essential tragedy of it, that we hastened toward the momentary refuge of pleasure. In some couples, the closeness comes afterward, in the embrace that follows the spasm. For us, it was in the spasm itself, my forehead flat and wet upon hers, her tongue thrust into my mouth, sucking it as if to pull it from my head, which would leave a sweet pain later. Spent, we fell away from each other, fell back into ourselves, sweaty, done.

◆ ◆ ◆

The next morning, when I arrived at work, my body heavy from sex and lack of sleep, I checked Helen's in-box and found an intercorporate envelope on her desk. It was the report I had asked Janklow at Big Apple Cable to send me, many days late, so much so that I'd forgotten about it. I untied the string binding the flap and slipped the contents out. There was an obsequious cover letter from him, apologizing about the delay, with a concurrent copy going to the Chairman — he would never see it, I knew — dutifully reprising our conversation in order to document his compliance. Ah, the small posturings our jobs force upon us. The file itself looked disappointingly thin. I sat with it at my desk, knowing quite clearly that I was trespassing upon Hector's rights as an employee and as a private individual.

There was no order to the slim sheaf of documents. The first was a backward-running log of comments by Hector's supervisors, recorded at three-month intervals; clearly this was perfunctory, for the entries were terse and repetitive: "Works good. OTR good. [This I took to mean On-Time Record.] Attitude good." "Works good. Can calculate dB loss. Splicing is good, trained to do roof dish, understands channel splitter and amplifier good. OTR good, attitude good." "Works good with other men. Trained coaxial cable panel. Cut hand 5/12 — one day out. OTR good, attitude okay." And so on. Hector, for all of his anger and suffering, was a model employee. In three and a half years, he had missed only four days of work. I continued to flip through the pages, realizing that it was leading nowhere; sheet after sheet indicated Hector's unswerving dependability to the Corporation, and if I had somehow expected to come upon a useful psychological profile of Hector Salcines, then I was mistaken. After all, he was but one employee, a small man. The Corporation reached into the lives of thousands of men and women like him. Like most executives

in large corporations—those with over twenty-five thousand employees, say—I did not know anyone who worked in the lower bowels
of the corporate body. While we generally liked to believe ourselves to
be compassionate toward these lower workers, the fact that we didn't
actually *know* any of them meant that when it came time to cut back on
dental benefits or the Corporation's retirement plans or to spin off
divisions or close certain operations, it was emotionally painless. It
would be wrong to say no one cared, but it would be correct to say that
it was expected of you that you would not care too much.

And as I turned over each page of the file, I couldn't help but
contemplate the thin connection between the Chairman and Hector.
Both men knew about each other, if only in the abstract, and it would
be safe to say that each was a small part of the other's consciousness;
each bore a relation to the other. You could lay the highest of odds
that they would never speak to each other—and yet those odds would
be almost as low that Hector and I should ever converse. We had
already done so, several times, but as far as Hector was concerned I
was more or less indistinguishable from the Chairman; we were the
same version of man, only at different moments along the arc of
power. Hector could hate me in the way that men without power may
rightfully despise those who own them. For Hector, I was the
Corporation incarnate; as it had fucked him over with lousy pay and
soul-killing labor, it also was stealing his family.

Meanwhile, as the file indicated, he dutifully and dependably kept
putting in his time installing the cables, wiring the city's homes with
conduits of mass culture, and how tiresome it must be, drilling holes
through window frames and using the oversized power staple gun to
secure the thick cable as it wound around floor molding and door-
frames to whatever room it was where people watched television. The
men wore light blue uniforms with red pinstripes on the shirt and a
name patch over the breast pocket. They drove around in a Ford
Econoline 150 with a ladder chained to the roof rack. A lot of the work
was done outside, and in the cold and rain and heat. Hector dealt each
day with the domestic realities of the company's customers—kids,
dogs, playrooms, housewives, invalids—and thus must have possessed
a great well of information against which to compare his own life. And
some days, Dolores had told me, it was hardly worth the trouble

because he was paid a fixed amount by the job, not by the hour, and doubtlessly he encountered difficult backyards, where the main cable was unreachable through the customer's yard, and other times the customer missed the appointment or decided he didn't want a wall drilled through. And Hector simply drew a line across his carbon-form appointment slip, called the office and got the next appointment, and went there. This is why he was forced to moonlight at the car lot, trying to foist rebuilt wrecks and wheezing clunkers onto the un-suspecting. From what I understood, his nearly fruitless effort would have been worth it if he had Dolores and Maria to return to each day. A man, I knew, would endure all manner of discouragement if he believes that doing so has a purpose. But for Hector Salcines, there was none of this satisfaction. Dolores and Maria were gone. His despair could only build.

Then, paging to the back of the file, I came upon Hector's original application for employment, which he had filled out by hand in the same choppy capital letters that had appeared on his notes to me. The form listed him as married. The paper was stamped HIRED in red letters and stapled to it was a copy of his employee information sheet. It looked regular enough, listing his current home address, Dolores's full name and birth date (3/20/65), and other expectable details—except that Hector had listed himself as the father of two children, not one. For a few seconds I was confused. *Two?* But there it was: Hector Roberto Salcines, age three; Maria Paloma Salcines, age five months. *Three and a half years prior, Maria was a little sister.* Was Dolores the mother of both children? I wondered, then thinking *yes*—each child's middle name had been the first name of Dolores's parents.

I closed the file and sat back, feeling numb, a headache finding its way into my thoughts as outside I heard Morrison charging down the hall. *There was another child in this mess*, a fact that Dolores had skillfully neglected to tell me. Hector's insistence upon reclaiming Dolores's heart changed then for me; there was a secret I didn't know, something driving Hector, and I felt humiliated and stupid, caught in the great foul wreck of things. Life was never as it seemed. Dolores had lied. Oh, had she lied.

TWELVE

orrison had it now. He had the deal with Volkman-Sakura firmly
in hand, or rather, clutched in his seven fingers; it was sweetly his,
and fuck anybody who might be foolish enough to try to take it
away from him. I saw this in his face that next morning when I stopped
into his office to remind him about the faxes DiFrancesco had intercepted and about my meeting the following day with the Chairman.
But, sitting magisterially in a dark blue suit — almost a navy uniform
like the one he had once worn — Morrison watched me with abstracted
tolerance, as if I were an ant climbing a piece of string. I knew he was
thinking about the piece in the morning's *Wall Street Journal* that
speculated that the Corporation was considering an international joint
venture on an unprecedented scale. The piece named V-S and several
other international conglomerates as possible suitors, including the
strange new Malaysian group that was slyly buying up
all kinds of properties and was rumored to have ten billion in cash.
The article went on to suggest that such a match would be problem-
atic at best, given differences in corporate cultures, FCC limitations on international ownership of American media, and so
on. What the Corporation really needed, argued the reporter, was
a simple cash infusion, such as a new stock offering, which would
only anger the current stockholders, who would see their holdings
watered down, or a straight cash infusion from an outside investor.
Like a lot of business journalism, it was only half-right. But the fact
that it was in the paper meant that Morrison had instructed one
of the Corporation's PR flacks to float a message into the jour-
nalistic ether.

"I think we should find it *worrisome*," I began, "that Waldhausen's
fax to his mistress conflicts with what he told Samantha . . ." I told him
about the Chairman's presence at the computer meeting. "I can only

conclude . . ." I told him that I had called the NewMedia Group people and that they were flying in the Corporation's new entertainment technology along with a technician so that I could show it to the Chairman. "It seems to me that the expenditure, which will run about a hundred thousand dollars, is worth the chance that . . ."

Morrison wasn't listening. I stopped talking. He didn't notice. So I sat there. There seemed little doubt that I was out of the picture. No one in the negotiating group had wanted to talk to me for days, and this indicated that the negotiations were moving briskly. The secretaries on the floor, who knew enough to know that they weren't supposed to know anything, were nervous. Except around me. I was the waterboy now and they knew it. I stood up and left.

In the meantime the information about Dolores's son ate at me and, except for the moments when I had to speak to any of the others, I stood at my office window and pondered her purposeful silence. She had told me she had been raped as a girl, she had told me the contents of the drawer next to her father's bed, she had admitted her pleasure at being screwed by three men at the same time. Why hadn't or why *couldn't* she tell me she had a son? I rechecked the file, worried that I had missed something obvious that might indicate that the boy was not her own. But he'd been born after Dolores and Hector had been married, which of course didn't necessarily prove she was the mother, but he had her father's name. And there was no previous record of marriage on the employment form. Was the boy living with Hector? Or some relative, Hector's mother perhaps? I calculated that Hector, Jr., would now be six years old. Was he asking for his mother? Was he asking his father why the family was apart? These were the questions I had inquired of my own father. *Dad, how come . . .* As a small boy I had stood before my father and asked him why he and my mother no longer lived together. I remember thinking that I would promise to be good if the two of them got back together. My father had looked down at the floor in shame and sad knowledge that I would always be pierced by the dream of family. Hector, no doubt, desired to put the Salcines family back together before that same dream died. I couldn't fault him for that, not at all, and I wished that my own father had shown Hector's determination when my mother had left.

I was not ready, however, to ask Dolores about her son. The question rose in my mouth that evening as she played with Maria, as she folded fresh laundry, as she brushed her hair for bed, tilting her head to one side so that the hair fell straight down in a dark curtain. I wondered how often she thought of her son and the strength it took not to mention him.

♦ ♦ ♦

The next day was the day I was to meet with the Chairman again. And this time Maria was coming with me. Under a high blue sky we held hands on the way to the subway as it crossed the Manhattan Bridge above a barge churning down the East River. Dolores, who was going to meet us for lunch at my office, had dressed in a new pink dress and put her hair in pink barrettes. Except for the fact that Maria didn't look a bit like me, we might well have been father and daughter out on a visit to the Museum of Natural History.

When we arrived at the Corporation building, I told Frankie the guard that Dolores would be coming up later. Then, in my office, I found Charles Kales, the technician from the NewMedia group, a tall, gentle man with an acne-pitted face. He had the equipment set up when we arrived, a couple of suitcase-sized computers, and one the size of a large trunk, which he had configured with cables and power lines, one color monitor for Maria, and a standard keyboard and small monitor off to the side for him.

"You'll help us?" I asked Kales. "If we get stuck?"

"Sure. But that's not going to happen. She'll get it in about a minute. I have three daughters—I know."

I took Maria by the hand and we went down to the Chairman's office. He sat at his desk, dressed in a marvelous blue suit with a paisley tie, drinking tea and reading the old book by Trollope. I hoped I looked that good when I was his age.

"Here we are."

The Chairman looked up and saw Maria.

"*Well,*" he said, rising, "I knew you would try anything, Mr. Whitman, but I never expected *this.*" He bent down to shake Maria's hand and introduced himself.

"Hello, young lady."

"I'm here with Jack!" Maria said, holding my hand and swinging on it.

"She's the daughter of a friend," I explained.

The Chairman looked down and smiled. "She seems to have a lot of affection for you," he said, as if he knew more about me than he would declare right now.

We walked back to my office. Kales had pulled a chair up to the screen and put Maria in it. I turned to the Chairman.

"I've been racking my brains how to get you to see that this deal needs to go through. I've given you the rational, quantifiable arguments. You knew them anyway. I think Morrison expected me to do this and then to give up. So that would seem to be all that I could do."

The Chairman settled into a chair, attentive at the novelty of my presentation. "You have been wrong about your position with me in every instance," the Chairman said. "But that is all I will say."

"Well, at any rate, there's something I want to — *give* is the closest word I can think of, and this is how I'm going to do it. You've listened to every damn thing I've said and you've argued with me over some of it, but you *have* listened. So I'm going to give it another shot."

"I hope you won't be digging my grave for me again."

"No. But it came to me that what you might *like* to have is what you can't have, really, which is the future. We all want that. What a thing it would be if you could experience the future, before it comes. And perhaps this way I could be persuasive." I turned toward Maria, who was quietly not understanding. "What we have here is an average-to-bright girl aged three years and eleven months. As far as you're concerned she was born yesterday. But the chances are that she will live to the year 2074."

"That's something to think about." The Chairman stood behind Maria, his hands folded behind his back. "I hope we've solved the national debt by then."

"Maria is not overly familiar with the uses of the computer, no more or less than most children her age, which means that she has seen it used on television and that kind of thing. She's not some young Mozart of programming or anything, okay? Just a regular kid. Right, Maria?"

She tugged on my hand. "Can we play the game now?"

"It'll be just one more minute, honey." I turned back to the Chairman. "At Maria's age, there is sufficient eye-hand coordination to ride a tricycle. She can say her ABC's by heart easily and can count up to a certain number, maybe thirty. In the future, one of the widely used developmental thresholds of children will be when they are able to use a computer of a certain standardized complexity or simplicity, whatever that standard is, I don't know. It's immaterial here. But this will be true of all the classes. Of course, the upper-middle class and the wealthy already have computers available for their children. These kids will be the next generation of the information elite."

"So what are we going to see?" the Chairman asked. "There are all kinds of computer toys and programs and disks and encyclopedias and stuff available now for kids. My youngest grandchildren have all sorts of stuff."

"Yes, but nothing on the market is more advanced than what you're about to see. And what you are about to see is designed for children, even though there are comparable adult possibilities. I have Maria here to make the point that if a kid almost four can grasp the essential plasticity of this technology, then—"

"Then we have a whole new generation of users, of consumers." The Chairman nodded, intent on speeding me up. "I think I can figure out the commercial possibilities, Mr. Whitman, assuming there are any. Bill Gates and I have discussed this, incidentally."

"Now, we've got here the best new voice synthesis software, the animation, high-resolution screen. Great sound, just about everything that's coming along now." I nodded at Kales and he typed a couple of commands into the computer.

"Speak your name into that little microphone there," Kales said to Maria, pointing to the front of the computer.

"My name is Maria Salcines," she said in a sweet, eager voice.

"Good. Okay, again."

"My name is Maria Salcines."

Kales peered into his screen, hit a few keys.

"How old are you?" said the computer in a feminine voice.

"I am three years old and my birthday is June tenth," Maria said.

"Good." The technician nodded to me. "We're ready. It will recognize her voice and no one else's in the room. No mouse commands, no keyboards, just talking to the machine. I've been working on this for seven years."

"How does that work?" the Chairman asked.

"Well, basically, the computer electronically chops her words into slices of time that are ten milliseconds long. Then it analyzes the frequencies of each slice and matches it against a data base of normal speech sounds. This technology will be everywhere in five years, incidentally. It's going to change the way we do a lot of things." He hit a key and Maria's screen went dark. A few numbers flitted on and off, program-loading information regarding memory and various disk drives. Then a cartoon village appeared, England in the 1600s, home of my ancestors almost four hundred years ago. A little boy in knickers and a cap walked along the lane, stopped, and waved at Maria.

"Hello," the boy said.

"Hi!" Maria answered spontaneously.

"What's your name?"

"Maria Salcines."

"Where do you live, Maria?"

"I live in Brooklyn," she said happily, ready to play.

"Brooklyn, New York?"

"Yes."

"Never been there."

"Oh."

"Do you want to know my name?"

"Yes."

"It's Christopher." He pulled a hammer from his back pocket. "I want to build something." He pulled out a toolbox that rattled with tools. "I need your help."

"Why?" said Maria.

"Because I need you to tell me what to build."

She looked at me. "Anything," I said to Maria. "Tell him whatever you want to build."

"A boat!"

"Okay," Christopher said. "A boat it is. A boat you shall have."

On the screen the boy walked down to the harbor, his little shoes clip-clopping on the cobblestones, taking several right and left turns and down narrow lanes. He passed a cobbler in his shop, the walls piled high with old-fashioned shoes. The cobbler, an old fat man, looked out of the screen and said, "Hi, Maria."

"Hi." She turned to me. "I like it."

"Do you like my shoes?" the cobbler said.

"Yes."

"Touch the ones you like most."

Maria leaned forward and touched an old pair of boots on the screen. A whiskery mouse with a red cap on popped out of the shoe and scampered away. Then the boots themselves popped up in the air and leapt onto the cobblestone street, where they danced a moment in a frenzy of loud bolero music, and flew back into the cobbler's shelves.

"C'mon, Maria," Christopher said.

The boy arrived at the village harbor. There was a sailing boat lurching against the ropes.

"Maria, do you like this boat?" Christopher asked.

"No!"

"Why?"

"I want a new boat. A big boat."

"What kind?"

"A ocean boat."

Christopher gave a little shrug. "No problem, Maria."

The creaky old galleon grew in length and height while its mast shriveled and smokestacks and decks grew. The wooden boards of the hull strained and popped off, landing on the deck in a bundle of neat lumber.

"The program is making a transition between images, while a subprogram is deciding how to integrate the old image into the scene, deciding what to do with the lumber, for example," Kales said. "We've got all kinds of different possibilities in this program, so many that there's almost an infinite number of story lines to take. I've never seen what this is doing now, for example."

Christopher had taken his toolbox and used the old lumber from the galleon and quickly hammered together a neat gangplank that led to the lowest deck of the ocean liner.

"Do you like it, Maria?"

"Yes."

"Let's look at a plan of this boat."

He magically withdrew a large scroll of paper from his pocket and examined it and then turned it around. It was an engineer's diagram of the ship, from three perspectives, and it grew larger so that the whole screen was filled with it, each part labeled precisely. Maria leaned forward and impulsively touched the engine room. Instantly the screen filled with bright footage of an ocean liner engine room, where men in nautical uniform stood in front of dials and gauges, working. The giant turbines throbbed noisily.

"That's real," the Chairman said.

Maria touched the screen again and we went back to the ship's diagram. She touched the ship's galley and instantly the screen showed a long gleaming row of stainless steel counters, where men in high white hats pushed an immense kettle of soup across the shiny floor. On the far wall were rows of spoons. Someone walked by with a pushcart of desserts. The soup splashed and then the cartoon Christopher stuck his head out and said, "Maria, let's get going, okay?"

"Okay."

Now we were back to the dock, with Christopher wiping his face with a handkerchief.

"I want some dogs on the boat!" Maria said impulsively.

The screen froze for a moment, the computer humming beneath the table, then the screen filled with a selection of color photographs of about twenty different breeds of dogs.

"That was not a smooth transition," Kales interrupted. "Christopher should have *introduced* the dogs. It was a bit abrupt."

Meanwhile Maria had picked two dogs to come onto her boat, a small poodle and a spaniel. These two appeared in cartoon form on the gangplank of the boat, smiling as dogs do, wagging their tails. A crew of sailors and a captain appeared at the top of the gangplank and welcomed them aboard. The captain looked at his watch.

"We depart in two minutes," he said in a deep and kindly voice.

"I want Mickey Mouse, too," Maria said.

Christopher turned. "You want Mickey Mouse? Hmmm."

"The program is stalling now." Kales said. "It's seeing if it recognizes what Mickey Mouse is and then if it can match the word to an image. I don't know if we'll have that, since that's a Disney trademark. It depends on what's been scanned—"

"Hello, boys and girls," said Mickey Mouse, poking his head through one of the ship's portholes with a popping sound. "I was here all the time."

"Good!" Maria said.

"They must have run a little sound in when they scanned it," Kales concluded to himself.

"One minute before we sail!" the Captain said.

The Chairman leaned forward to Maria. "Honey, ask the little boy if Tom Brokaw can be on the boat."

"Who is *that*?" Maria asked.

"It's a man on television, a nice man who is a friend of mine. Tom Brokaw."

"Tom Brokaw!" Maria yelled at the screen.

"Let's go find him," Christopher said, jumping up on the deck, searching behind some suitcases.

"Is the program stalling?" the Chairman said to the technician.

"No," came the answer from Kales, "it's loading a special imaging system which takes stock footage and digitalizes the pixels in order to video-animate, which means—"

"Hello, everybody," came the deep, reassuring voice, and then Tom Brokaw appeared, a living moving image of him. "Maria, I understand we're going to go on a trip."

"Why is his hair blowing?" the Chairman asked. "His hair is blowing but nothing else in the picture is."

Kales grimaced at the screen, thinking. "That means that when the footage was scanned in, that he was probably outside, doing a live feed from Russia or China or somewhere and the wind was blowing. The program is recapitulating that moving hair, since it understands it to be part of the image. The fact that nothing else in the picture is blowing is because it's not programmed in. Also, he could be a little taller. There are certain subtleties we haven't worked out yet. Complexities solved means complexities created."

"From what little I understand," I began, "the memory requirements must be absolutely—"

"Yes," he interrupted proudly. "Broadcast-quality video runs at thirty frames a second and each frame requires as much as two megabytes of memory. That's a lot. It's been one of the hurdles. But we're using the new experimental DRAM chips, here."

"DRAM?"

"Dynamic random access memory. These are two-hundred-and-fifty-six-megabit chips—*huge*. IBM and Toshiba are working on a two-hundred-and-fifty-six-megabit DRAM, but that won't come into commercial production until 1997 or 1998. Except for U.S. military research, we're way out front here."

Meanwhile Maria had gotten the boat moving, with the dogs and Mickey Mouse and Tom Brokaw on deck. She and the Chairman sat together working the program and I nodded at Kales and we moved away.

"You did a great job with this," I told him.

"I worked on it most of the night, just getting some of the little bugs out. I had to get a modem-feed from the West Coast for a little more programming they were working on."

"How far are we from mass production?"

"Three years, minimum. But it will be three years better."

"Cost?"

"*Today* this would cost, maybe . . . seven or eight million dollars, at least."

"What about when you get it down?"

"I bet we can get it down to ten, fifteen thousand dollars in five years," Kales figured. "Then the chip prices will fall and it'll be more reasonable."

"What's the secret to all this?"

"Ultimately?" he asked. "The chips. They've become the greatest works of human ingenuity. I mean that in all seriousness."

I looked over at the Chairman and Maria. Tom Brokaw was painting the great white hull of the boat with a big paintbrush and as he moved the brush, da Vinci's Mona Lisa appeared on the curved surface, taking into account the variations of rivets and portholes. Then he painted another picture, this time of himself, reading the news, which I recognized as about a week old. "That's pure footage," Kales said. "Four months ago it was technologically impossible to run that out of a disk-based retrieval system. Needed too much memory.

Now we're doing it. You can get these kinds of special effects in movies, but each image is planned — scripted. Here, the technology is responding spontaneously — there's no subtle menu driving here, certain effects can't even be repeated, probably . . . you can't just loop back to where you were . . . I mean, we're *really* out front here."

On the screen, Mickey pulled the rope scaffolding up and lowered himself down. Together he and Brokaw painted over the televised Brokaw and the Mona Lisa with moving footage of themselves painting themselves painting themselves.

"That's the replicator program."

"Amazing," the Chairman murmured. "Our media company becoming a computer company."

Then Christopher dumped a can of white paint down the hull and they started over, on Maria's instructions from the Chairman. The New York City subway map began to appear.

Maria sent the program through one image after the next, talking to the screen, touching it when necessary, and I saw that the Chairman had looked away from the screen and instead was watching her, enchanted.

"You get the point now, right?" I interrupted. "How if we could get into, say, the Japanese and German markets via some of Volkman-Sakura's existing marketing arrangements, not to mention — "

"Yes, yes, of course." The Chairman waved me off.

"I mean, it's conceivable that what we're seeing here could be an on-line service, either through cable or the telephone lines. You just turn it on like a TV, start playing or researching. A ten-year-old doing a school report could download an image to a printer, integrate that into standard word-processing or page design software. That's the marriage of the *product* with the distribution system. Like I said before, maybe the distribution is by a hard line or even satellite. We don't know, but — "

"Every moderately wealthy household in the world will want this," the Chairman interrupted. "Paris, Hong Kong, Rio, everywhere — "

"And with our film stars, our books, our music videos — "

"Yes, *yes*," the Chairman said. His tired eyes had turned from mine and concentrated now on the young face before him.

♦ ♦ ♦

Later, when Maria and the Chairman had just about exhausted themselves trying out the prototype program, Dolores knocked on my door. There she was, in heels and a great blue-and-white dress, her hair piled high on her head, just a strand curling down in front of each ear, with Liz's pearl earrings on. Her makeup was different, too, more subdued, and I noticed she held a new handbag like the ones many of the women in the office owned.

Dolores twirled flirtatiously on one heel. "I'm looking for a man in a suit."

"You look terrific."

"Yes?" She was pleased.

"*Well,*" the Chairman exclaimed, the cigarette in his mouth going up and down as he glided over, all ease and grace, "now I know why Jack has so much trouble concentrating on his work." He held out his hand to Dolores, and introduced himself, as did she. Like all old men who wanted to possess young women, the Chairman acted as if I were not there, as if Dolores were my woman only as a result of his beneficence; he flirted with her as compensation due him. "Are you the mother of this very clever child?"

"She's mine, all right."

"This is Dolores Salcines, Maria's mother."

"I am truly pleased to meet you. She's a sweetheart." The ashes of the Chairman's cigarette broke off and fell onto the carpet.

"I'm glad she behaved, that's all." Dolores laughed nervously.

The Chairman glanced at my shoes, thinking to himself suddenly, and for the life of me, I could swear that he'd just thought of something *unusually* clever. "Jack, I want you and Dolores to come out to my place, this weekend. Sunday. It'll be informal. I do hope you can come, Dolores. How's your game of tennis?"

"Uh—sorry, I never played it."

"Then you can swim and enjoy the sun."

"Can I bring Maria?"

"Of course," the Chairman beamed. "We'll have scads of children there." He turned and eyed me directly, the tone of his voice just different enough that he made it clear that he wanted me there, just cold enough not to indicate how he had been affected by what he had seen. "Mrs. Marsh will provide you with the directions, Jack. And thank you for this interesting demonstration." He smiled at Dolores and then bowed to shake Maria's hand. "Good-bye, Maria. I have very much enjoyed my time with you. And, if you'll excuse me, now I must go."

♦ ♦ ♦

That afternoon Morrison waved me into his office. "We're moving quickly," he said. "They've come around. Samantha and Waldhausen have really led this deal. We've got a lot of agreements roughed out now. We make a preliminary announcement in less than a week is my bet," Morrison said. "I'm going to start calling board members, loosen them up on the idea."

I told him about my meeting that morning with the Chairman. Morrison played with the wooden duck on his desk. "Maybe he actually will go along with the merger idea," I said.

Morrison returned his eyes to me, and could not help but smile. "He's an old man, Jack, he's over seventy, his time is over."

"So you assumed all along he wouldn't change his mind, right? You decided to waste my time on that basis?"

"These aren't questions you should worry about," Morrison replied. "We've got other stuff to think about. We're going to have a lot of activity around here soon. I brought Waldhausen over yesterday to show him around. We've been talking about carving out a suite of offices for them in the building, maybe a floor or two below."

"Sounds good."

"But I need you to do something for me."

"What?"

"Get rid of Robinson."

"Get rid of him?"

"Fire him. Get him out of here."

"Nobody seems to mind—"

"I mind. I mind a lot. Waldhausen was telling me at lunch yesterday how bad race relations have gotten in Germany lately, and how he was afraid they were going to become like this country. And then we're in my office yesterday and in comes Robinson. He's got the baseball game in one ear and he asked me if I wanted a shine. Mrs. Comber missed him, she was in the ladies' room."

"What did Waldhausen say?"

Morrison reacted angrily. "He didn't have to *say* anything. Saying nothing was saying everything. Just get him out of here, for good. It's racist just to have him around, it's fucking embarrassing, like we're running a plantation."

"The guy needs the job—"

"Don't push me on this, Jack. It's a small thing. Robinson is just some old guy. You're gonna fire a lot of people in your time. Believe me, I've done it. This is just one lousy old black guy who shines shoes."

But this was not what I was hired to do and I told him so. We had two whole floors of personnel people downstairs sitting around on their asses, filling out forms and doing not much else. They had nice women with clean fingernails who *specialized* in firing employees. I told Morrison that, too.

"Yes, and because he's been around thirty years and everybody loves him and will want to have a retirement party or something, it'll be a month before they do it," he said. "I don't want to have memos written, I just want the guy *out* today so I don't have to worry about it when Waldhausen and the other V-S guys come around in the next few days and weeks."

"Let me work out something," I offered. "Get him to take a little vacation so he isn't around."

"No. Just get him out."

"What about a pension or something?"

Morrison turned toward the window and contemplated the haze of apartment buildings to the north of Central Park. "If he begs for money, give him something . . . I don't know, something like—"

The phone trilled. Morrison picked it up and I watched him talk without thinking, hear without listening. He was keeping his thoughts to himself and he was *appearing* to keep his thoughts to himself. I'd noticed him having breakfast in his office the last few days, before heading over to the Plaza for the negotiations, sipping orange juice, pouring cream from a small silver pitcher. He was drinking more coffee. The new stance was internal as much as external. He was telling himself that soon would come his finest hour, that he had lived fifty-three years and endured innumerable abuses and detours and idiot cocktail parties and plowed through roomfuls of paper in order that he might find himself poised on the moment of greatness. The vanity had a long root. It went back to that original military cockiness, maybe further. He had lost a bit of weight, perhaps ten pounds, which in corporate executives, as it is for politicians, is a sign of ambition for higher office. Morrison felt that he had been anointed by fate, that the gods only give to those who give to themselves, and he did not intend to screw up this opportunity. He did not intend to be standing in his rose garden twenty-five years hence, retired and forgotten and wearing a floppy hat to keep the sun off his face and realize what his wrong move had been. He would, he felt, play chess with all of them at once — the Chairman, the board, the V-S guys, and all those whom he commanded — like a grand master who plays a dozen matches at once in one room, looking at a particular chess board for a moment, angling defensively, setting up a coming attack, or even suddenly making the perfect brilliant coup de grace, and then moving onto the next match. A situation in which the greatness was not in one game but in the ability to play a dozen or more games simultaneously and win. To be good at this, one must keep one's own counsel. There is one side and all else is the enemy, including one's advisers, because although they might mean well, they are capable of error. Even I, his trusted lieutenant, was his enemy, or at best, a piece on his chessboard, tactically disposable in the right moment. He had measured my words and offered little response. There was a plain coldness in his face, and in the hallway recently his laughter sounded purposefully fraudulent, laced with some extra tone of irony, as if he was laughing at those who would try to make him laugh.

"Hang on a second," Morrison said into the phone. Then he turned toward me. "Out by the end of today."

He returned to his call. I'd have to get rid of Robinson and I hated Morrison for that. But he didn't care. He had come, now, into a season of ruthlessness.

◆ ◆ ◆

In upstate New York, my father was chopping at the earth with his hoe, thinking of the slender green tomato seedlings he would set into the earth as soon as the nights were dependably warm, perhaps thinking about his son in Manhattan, yet not knowing that same son was about to fire an elderly black man. I had Helen call building services to find out where Robinson was and he came through my door about thirty minutes later, pushing his sad little cart.

"Listen, Mr. Robinson, I have to discuss something."

"What's that? My Mets? My Doc Gooden?" he said with a smile.

"No. It's not that." Better to get to the hard part, I figured. "Listen, you're going to have to leave us."

"What? I'm okay. I'm good." He thumped his chest with a fist. "Don't you worry about Freddie Robinson. He's all right."

"No, it's not that," I said. "You can't work here anymore, Freddie. You're going into the wrong offices at the wrong time."

He stood there.

"What'd I do?"

"You're going into the wrong offices when you shouldn't, Freddie. That's all."

"You know I'm honest."

"Nobody said you weren't, Freddie."

"What they *sayin'* about me, then? Last time I talk to you, you ask me what they sayin' about you and now here I am asking what they sayin' about me. Everybody likes Freddie Robinson. Everybody here smiles at me and I smile back. I like people, Mr. Whitman. I've been in this building since it was *built* and now you're going tell me I can't work here no more?"

The fingernail of a corporate dictator, cut with idle detachment, falls to the floor, killing a man. Robinson's fate was Morrison's whim, nothing else.

"I want you to give Helen your address and we'll get you a check, help you out."

"I don't need no check, I need to see my people every day," Robinson said, with greater agitation. "Some people in this building and me go way back. These people my family, Mr. Whitman. It came from up top, didn't it? I don't have no grandchildren, Mr. Whitman, my own son got killed twenty years ago. I'm a old man. I'm sixty-eight years old. Gotta do something. Can't go shine down Penn Station. That's all them Brazilian kids. Take me years to get in there. I can't go shine outside Port Authority. Not Grand Central neither. Weather'll kill this old man, summer and winter. I can't do it."

I stared at him, admiring his courage and eloquence, and considered going back to Morrison. But that would aggravate him and be useless. It would demonstrate that I would question his directives. He had once been a good manager, not reactionary, soliciting advice from all. But conciliators do not become kings. Robinson stood in front of me, with his sad beaten little cart. He deserved better than an ignoble end to his work, and I knew that Liz, for one, would have been shocked that I had gone along with Morrison's irrationality. But life, and business, is a sequence of transactions. Morrison was trading Robinson's livelihood for his own peace of mind. I was trading a percentage of my conscience for Morrison's approval and Morrison would be back on the floor within half an hour, expecting that Robinson would be gone. It was that simple, that ugly.

"I'm sorry," I said. "The decision's been made. That's it."

I thought he would leave then. But Robinson frowned in bitterness. "You think I don't know what all is goin' on around here?" he said combatively.

"What do you mean?"

"I been around the block. I see what's happening."

"What?" I asked.

"Don't you be fresh like that. If you goin' to fire me outa here then I got to say my fill. You know better'n me what all's goin' on. You part of them." He looked genuinely aggrieved. "I thought you was a nice fellow. I thought you was going to help out my Chairman."

This shocked me. "What?"

"I told the Chairman you a fine young man. I told him how they killed your wife some years back."

"He asked?"

"Sure he asked! He asked all kinds of things about you! How you think *he* know what's going on around here?"

I drew a breath. Some kind of higher game was being played. I basically didn't know what the fuck was going on.

"Now you still gotta go fire me outa here?"

"Yes," I told him.

Robinson checked my expression for a flickering of reprieve. "You sure about that?"

"Sure."

He turned and set his hand against the handles of the cart, pushing it out of the room, the small bottles of shoe polish clinking softly as he went. His silence confirmed what a bastard I was.

♦ ♦ ♦

Janklow, the vice president at Big Apple Cable, called that afternoon.

"You get the file?" he asked. "Looks okay?"

"Looks fine."

"Thought it would get to you faster."

"It's fine."

"That's it?" Janklow asked hopefully. "I mean, if there's anything else you guys are looking for . . ."

Schmoozing me, looking for the open door, a special assignment, a handle to grab hold of. It occurred to me I could probably have Hector fired, just by saying the word. But that would mean he'd have more time on his hands, would feel greater desperation. And he would suspect, naturally, that I had ordered it. And then I would have unfairly fired two men in one day and my soul would be worth about as much as a scrap of old tire littering the West Side Highway. I wondered if I could maybe make Hector's life a little easier, take the sting out of losing Dolores and Maria.

"How many positions are at the next pay grade?" I asked Janklow.

"Maybe four dozen. Field supervisors."

"They work hard?"

"They supervise," he grunted. "Supposedly. They train the new installers and make sure the work orders are carried out quickly. That kind of stuff. Pretty simple."

"Could this guy Hector Salcines do this job?"

"I never met the guy. But field supervisors aren't exactly brain surgeons. It's just guys who have run cable for more years than the other guys and got tired."

"Longer hours?" Maybe a promotion would distract him, too, keep him busy.

"Maybe longer hours but easier, too. More paperwork in the office, checking the accounts by computer and stuff."

"I want you to promote this Hector Salcines to the next level, to supervisor."

"Oh?"

"Yes. Don't tell him why, just promote him."

"And may I ask why such a strong imperative is coming from the thirty-ninth floor all the way out here about some guy who makes maybe eleven bucks an hour?"

I didn't say anything. This is an effective technique in conflict.

"Just promote him? Just like that?"

"Yes."

I had another call coming.

"Just do it," I said, sounding like Morrison, switching lines. The new call was from DiFrancesco.

"Got some more stuff," he wheezed. "You want to come get it?"

"I don't have time. What is it?"

"Looks like more of the same. It's coming *in* to that second number you gave me."

"Which number?"

He read off the digits. It was the Chairman's fax, in Mrs. Marsh's office.

"I don't understand," I said.

"I don't either."

"Fax them to me here."

"I don't fax things, it leaves an audit trail."

"C'mon. I don't have time for your paranoia."

"No faxes."

Everything irritated me. "We're paying you to provide the service!"

"No trail."

"Fix it up to that fake New York Telephone line you told me about. Couldn't you do something like that?"

There was an appraising silence. "Won't work."

"Then go the fuck around the corner to a copy shop and fax it from there, you fat, lazy bastard! This is what we are paying you for!"

Five minutes later the sheets came spilling out of the machine in Helen's office. I plucked them from the machine as they scrolled out and looked them over.

I called DiFrancesco back. "You said these came from that other number I gave you?"

"Absolutely."

"You didn't screw it up somehow?"

"No chance."

"But some of these are substantially the same—they *are* the same English documents that went out from the Plaza Hotel a couple of days ago."

"It looks that way."

I examined the other documents coming and going from the Chairman's fax machine, all mundane stuff: a real estate deal involving one of his children, a letter from an old friend.

"I think you screwed it up," I told DiFrancesco. "All the other stuff makes sense."

"Wrong."

"But this is *exactly* what was sent from the Plaza to Germany. It's the stuff that was provided by our people to their people in meetings. There's no reason why it would be sent back the other way—"

"There is a reason, you just don't know what it is," DiFrancesco answered in anger. "Because I *never* make mistakes."

♦ ♦ ♦

At six, I took the elevator to the lobby. Frankie the guard stopped me. "There's a guy been askin' for you. He didn't have an appointment so we didn't send him up. He's over on the other side of the lobby—*there*—he's not lookin' now—"

Hector. Standing in jeans and baseball jacket, watching the wrong bank of elevators, the one that only went up to the twenty-fifth floor.

"You don't want to talk to him you could go right now," Frankie said. "*Right* now."

So I did, slipping into the river of workers headed for the subway, walking quickly, weaving unnecessarily to make it harder to follow. After a hundred yards, just to be sure, I looked back.

Hector was there thirty yards back and I suppose he'd seen me turn around because he was looking away from me, cap pulled low. I turned quickly and accelerated my pace. I could go above ground and try to catch a cab, but the traffic crawled at this time of day. I passed through the turnstile and proceeded quickly to the downstairs track. The D train was on one side and the F train on the other, both Brooklyn bound. Hector was behind me and would be down the stairs in an instant. The D train's doors chimed and I jumped on, hoping that the train would leave the platform before Hector could get on. It started to move. Was I safe? Hector arrived at the spot where I'd boarded, looking through the train window to find me. He ran along-side the train, dodging other commuters. He saw me.

And then I swept down the track. Safe now. I resolved to deal with Hector straight-on tomorrow, call him on the job perhaps. Jesus, I'd had the guy promoted today.

We stopped at, then left, the Forty-second Street stop. Hector's only chance was the F train back in the Forty-seventh Street station under Rockefeller Center but it hadn't caught up. But my D train slowed after it pulled out of the Forty-second Street stop. The train crawled twenty yards, then picked up speed. It was on the busier track with Q and B trains in front of it. And then the F train, which ran local farther downtown, roared past us one track over, the riders illumin-ated in the dark tunnel. I didn't see Hector, but I was sure he was on that train. It had probably left only seconds after my own train. Then the D train picked up speed again. We pulled into the Thirty-fourth Street station. The F was there, waiting for the transfer. Hector was on the platform, with one foot in the doorway of the F. He didn't see me. He was looking at the wrong car, unsure whether he should switch onto the D, which now had lurched to a stop. The warning bell for both trains chimed and they both closed their doors at the same time. Hector was still in the F train, peering through the door win-dow. He looked at my car, he looked at *me*.

Both trains began to move. Both stopped at the West Fourth Street station, I knew, but, presumably, the D train would make it first, since the F was a local and stopped at Twenty-third Street and Fourteenth Street. Assuming the D arrived at West Fourth Street before the F, I was safe. I would have two options: I could stay on the train or get out, fly up the stairs before the F rolled into the station, and then be lost to Hector completely. He would get into the West Fourth Street station and not know whether I was on the D train, which would have just departed, red lights disappearing down the track, or had gone upstairs. He would know that he had one more shot at me on the D train, which stopped at the Broadway-Lafayette stop. Or, he would think, he could run upstairs and see if I was there. But by then I would be gone.

But that didn't happen. Just south of Twenty-third Street my train slowed in the rush-hour congestion. The other riders shook their heads in disgust. The F train drew abreast of the D and both trains came into West Fourth Street at the same time. And there was Hector looking for me through his train window. My breathing tightened and I looked around wondering what to do next. His train pulled ahead by half a car and I took the opportunity to walk to the back of my car and open the door to the next car back. But it was crowded. There was not time to shimmy through all the commuters for a couple of cars and emerge on the platform farther down. Too many people, tired and aggravated. It was harder to move now. I'd made a mistake.

My train pulled to a stop. Across the platform, the F train was discharging passengers. Hector would be looking for me in the car I'd just left. And now I could not leave my own car easily. Not *in time*. I couldn't get out now. The doors on the D closed and the train began to move toward the Broadway-Lafayette stop. Was Hector on my train or not? If yes, then I had to get off at Broadway-Lafayette, because from there the D went over the decrepit old Manhattan Bridge, where it always stopped because of flag conditions, and that would give Hector ample time to search backward through the two or three cars to find the one he knew I had to be in.

The D train was moving now, drawing even again with the F train. Was Hector still on that, or on my D? I glanced toward the next car up, which I'd just left. Hector was there.

I pushed rudely through a few people, crouching a little in case

Hector looked through the window at the end of his car. It was a good thing he was on the short side. I saw a guy in a black raincoat.

"Sir," I breathed quickly. "Sell me your raincoat."

"What?"

"How much?"

He looked at me like I was a nut.

"Christ, I dunno."

"I'll sell you my *hat*, man," said another man. It was a red baseball cap with an oil company logo on it. "Twenty bucks."

"Let's do it."

I gave him the money.

"How about a hundred for the coat?" said the other man.

I bought that too, swaddling myself in the coat and pulling the hat down low on my head. I kept pushing toward the back of the car, putting more people between me and Hector. The train swept into the Broadway-Lafayette station, last stop in Manhattan. The F train also came into the station. In my disguise I stood with my face against the door window. Out of the corner of my eye I saw Hector enter the far end of my car. Hector had not seen me, or if he had seen me, he didn't realize it. My door opened. The F train's doors were open, too. I left the D and stood in the middle of the platform. I could go up the stairs and get a cab—but traffic at the intersection of Broadway and Houston upstairs would be very slow. Murder to get out of there. Then a wave of transfers from the number 6, the Lexington Avenue local, came down the stairs. It would be hundreds of people. I couldn't fight my way upstairs against the wall of flesh, so I ran down the platform, away from Hector, and stepped onto the last car of the F just as the doors shut.

The F train didn't go exactly where I wanted it, but it deviated at this point from the D train, which was good, since I believed Hector was still on it. The F stopped at the far end of Park Slope, at Ninth street and Seventh Avenue, and fifteen minutes later, not seeing any sign of Hector, that is where I got off. Safe.

As I walked I took off the hat and looked at it. The crown was stained with sweat. The hat smelled, too. I chucked it in the trash. A few minutes later, six blocks north on Seventh Avenue, I walked into

my laundry. Grace, a sweet Filipina woman who knew all her customers' laundry numbers by heart, greeted me.

"That's not your coat," she said.

"You're right."

"Whose is it?"

"That's a long story." I pulled the coat off. "Is it worth dry-
cleaning?"

"This?"

I hadn't really looked at it carefully.

"I would just throw this away. Give it to the homeless."

"I paid a hundred dollars for this coat."

"You pay ninety-five too much." She smiled forgivingly. "I have
your shirts." She pulled down a paper package from the shelf. I turned
around to glance behind me.

Hector was standing across the street, inside a pastry shop. He was
not looking for me, he was looking *at* me, waiting for me to lead him
toward Dolores and Maria. He didn't know they were living with me,
but perhaps he had guessed. We were only two blocks from my house.

"Grace," I said. "Do you have a back door?"

She quietly led me into the back room. I slipped past half a dozen
young Filipina women folding towering mountains of laundry on
wooden tables, and emerged in a backyard. Grace pointed toward a
low fence that ran along the facing backyard and I clambered over it
and trespassed my way out of this yard and then another to find a
driveway to the street on the other side. An old woman rapped on her
window two stories up when she saw me—some guy in a business
suit frantically hopping her fence—but then I was out on the street.
It had taken only a minute and then I was close to my house.
I went in quickly and pushed the huge wooden door shut and
locked it.

♦ ♦ ♦

When I got in Dolores was holding the phone.

"There's someone at the laundry who wants to talk with you," she
said. "I don't understand it."

"Mr. Whitman?"

"Yes."

"This is Grace at the laundry."

"Grace, what can I do for you?"

"I have something serious to tell you. There was a man here pretending he lose his ticket, but I have never seen him before. He lied and said he came when I wasn't here. I asked him what was his number and he said he didn't remember."

"But you know everybody's number by sight."

"Yes. Then he ask if he can see the book, where we write down the dry cleaning. My boss was there and so I said yes, but please hurry up, I have to look up somebody's ticket."

"Like when I always lose mine."

"Yes, I look it up. He says he not have ticket so can he look at book to get the number."

"What?"

"He wanted to see the book so he could see your name, I think."

To get the address, I realized, which was always written in, in case dry cleaning was lost and the customer needed to be located.

"I took the book from him and told him it was wrong book. I gave him laundry book, which not have your dry clean number. He checked the book for some more time. Then he say do you know Jack Whitman's number. I say no, how am I supposed to remember two thousand three hundred customers' numbers on their ticket?"

"That how many customers you got?"

"Yes."

"Grace, thank you very much."

"Yes. I say something that maybe you don't like."

"Go ahead."

"It is none of my business but I know that you have different clothes in your laundry now."

"You mean women's clothes. And a little girl's?"

"Yes, but I know you are not the father. And I remember this when I see your ticket number when he is looking for where you live."

"Grace," I said. "You are far too smart to be working in a laundry."

"Yes," she laughed. "I know."

◆ ◆ ◆

That night, late, the ringing phone carved a channel in my head. I got it before Dolores woke.

"Speak."

"Dolores, please."

Hector. There was that pause while we both realized who was on the other end.

"Think you got the wrong number, guy."

"This Jack Whitman?"

"Who is calling?"

"Well, you should fucking remember me because I fucking remember *you*." I heard music in the background and a television set. Hector was probably at a bar. "I'm going to find out where you live, asshole. I got real close today, didn't I? Gimme a couple more days, I'm going to figure it out, go down to City Hall, look in the records, whatever."

"How'd you get this number?"

"That guy Ahmed, down at the building. I went back this evening. He was there."

I said nothing.

"I want my wife and daughter back, you got that?"

He waited for an answer.

"You *tell* Dolores she had better just come on back here or else a lot of shit is gonna happen, man."

There were certain things I could have said to him: that I would go to the police, that I could hire a private detective or even a couple of goons; that his wife no longer wanted to be with him — any of it, but each of these reactions would only have angered him even more. And Dolores was asleep next to me. I did not want there to be a psychological bond between Hector and us — that of the pursuing and the pursued; I wanted instead for him to be unsure of whether he had reached me. I hung up.

He could always call back, waking Dolores or Maria, so I disconnected the phone next to the bed and crept downstairs and disconnected that extension too. Of course, we would have to plug the phone in the next day.

Then I had an idea. I dialed DiFrancesco. A message came on: "If you understand quantum bogodynamics, then your message will make it past the bogon filter, otherwise you will crash this unit. Speak now."

"This is Jack Whitman. Pick up the phone."

He did. I asked him how long it usually took New York Telephone to change an unlisted number.

"Maybe a week."

"Can *you* do it?"

"Sure. Cake. Icing on cake."

I gave him my number and asked him to change it.

"Now?"

"Yes."

"You just woke me up."

DiFrancesco afloat in bed: a horror. "How much?"

"How much do I want for it?"

"Yes."

"I'll do it tomorrow morning for a hundred bucks."

"Do it tonight and it'll be worth a thousand dollars to you. Bill my company."

"Call me in the morning and I'll have your new number for you."

I fell back into bed. Forty minutes later the phone issued half a ring. I picked it up. The line was dead, and I figured that DiFrancesco was at work. Hector may well have been at work too, but for the moment I was ahead of him.

◆ ◆ ◆

I am a heavy sleeper but later that same night, I woke to a peculiar smell, this time stronger than ever before, a sweet burning in my nostrils that immediately made me worry that the house was on fire—my greatest fear, since a house with so much wood in it would burn quickly. Dolores was not in the bed. As soon as I was out from under the sheets I could tell that the smell was *purposeful*. But where was Dolores? I listened. No sound came. I stood frozen in the middle of my bedroom wondering what to do next—and then I saw a weird flickering of light on the plaster walls above the stairs from the parlor and was seized with a great dread. I eased down the stairs in my underwear and socks, keeping much of my weight on the banister, down toward the source of the weird light.

My living room was covered with tiny flickering candles, at least a hundred of them, and the light seemed to exist in a room of swaying shadows, a room without walls or ceiling or floor. In the middle of the room, Dolores. She was kneeling before the fireplace mantel, her hands pressed together in prayer, her lips quickly whispering in Spanish. Softly, then louder and faster, her voice breaking higher on some words and then falling into a hushed fast patter. Singing almost, a hurried singing. In front of her was a small realistic statue of Christ in his agony, such as are sold in the many botanicas in the Latino parts of Brooklyn. She must have hidden it in a closet. Christ with his eyes rolled upward at his wreath of thorns, his hands and feet impaled. Candles burning all around the figure threw twisted shapes up the walls, a hundred dead men writhing. Dolores spoke directly to the figure. I could not understand her prayers but recognized a few words: *Oh, Dios mio! Quien eres Tu . . . Dios omnipotente, justica suprema . . . mi angel de la guarda . . . Jesus . . . en las aflicciones de la vida . . .* As she prayed she lit a match to little piles of powder set out on the plates from my kitchen. Had I let a madwoman in my house? No, my father would have counseled, only someone with faith in God. *Dios mio, tu que eres grande, tu que eres el todo, deja caer, sobre mi, pequeño, sobre mi que no existo . . .*

I watched for a few minutes, thinking Dolores was about to be done. But then she consulted a small orange book and began another prayer. I didn't dare disturb her. The chanting began again, Dolores's voice rising and falling, nearly breaking into tears, sometimes going fast, other times slow and then halting, upon which moment she would consult her book again, reading aloud. I stood frozen on the stairs for what seemed an eternity as she chanted, my legs stiffening, my heels aching. It was after three o'clock, but Dolores seemed only to be in the middle passage of her ritual, far from whatever final shore of exhausted redemption she sought. My eyes were heavy in the spinning, hallucinogenic light of the room and I felt a sudden vertigo, as if I might pitch headfirst down the stairs. I'm a white man. I fear mysticism, I fear everything about it, I fear the voodoo stuff that went on in Prospect Park, the headless chickens and goats. I did not know how to talk to Dolores about it, and I knew that I must not break her reverie. This was from another part of her I did not yet know, far from the tidy Presbyterian church services my mother took me to, the pews hard, the sermons delivered with reserved erudition. There were no blood and feathers and tiny bags of dirt in anything about me. I could not understand the world this way. No chanting or magic or incense. So I retreated quietly up the stairs and eased back beneath the sheets, which were now cold.

♦ ♦ ♦

I woke early that next morning, a warm, overcast Saturday, Dolores dead to the world next to me. She slept with her mouth open, her lips pressed against the pillow, her hair a dark tangle over her eyes. She emitted that faint warm odor of a sleeping body. I bent close to her head, and thought I smelled a pale whiff of the incense from the night before. But I couldn't be sure. I wondered if I'd dreamed the whole thing and as I shot through my regular routine—shave, shower, dress—I figured that remnants of Dolores's ceremony would be littering my living room when I went downstairs. But the room was as ever, not a paper disturbed. Perhaps, I thought, perhaps you really did dream the whole damn thing. The house had been aired out, no ashes in the kitchen garbage can, no candle drippings. Nothing.

♦ ♦ ♦

That afternoon, while I was in the garden showing Maria how to prune the winter die-back in the roses, Dolores called out the window.

"There's a guy who says you have to come to his office immediately," she said.

I looked up, tired of being chased by the telephone.

"Who?"

"He won't say his name. He sort of wheezes, though."

It was DiFrancesco. "I got all kinds of stuff coming in, now. You want to see it?"

I told Dolores that I would be gone for an hour or two.

"Where are you going?" she asked.

"I'm going to meet a guy who we're paying a lot of money to break federal telecommuncations law."

"To break the law?"

"He's got a way to steal information from fax machines. That has to be illegal."

Dolores contemplated this. But she remained silent.

♦ ♦ ♦

I took the subway to Canal Street and walked to DiFrancesco's office, past dead fish, roasted pigs, and little old Chinese ladies doing their day's shopping. DiFrancesco met me at the door, drippings of honey and jam and peanut butter streaking his naked chest, his hair greasy and wild. I looked closely at his face; it was pale, a great, smooth melon.

"Jesus, you shaved off your beard."

DiFrancesco shrugged. "I started to smell it," he admitted. "I couldn't get it clean."

"Well, the weather's getting hot—"

"But I still have it," he interrupted.

"You still *have* it?"

He pointed. I looked around and noticed something hairy in a Tupperware container; it looked like a small animal had been stuffed in it. "You're a weird guy, anybody ever tell you that?"

"Sure."

I stepped carefully past the junk on the floor over to his computers and he handed me a couple of papers. On the top was a fax in German from the V-S Bonn headquarters to Waldhausen's group in the Plaza. I glanced at it quickly—translating enough in my head to see that it had to do with the structure of management of the merged corporations. The second was a fax to the Chairman's office machine regarding the purchase of the estate in the Bahamas. The cost: thirty-five million dollars. Sounded like a nice place. Hope they have off-street parking. Next was a fax from the Plaza to Bonn regarding the purchase of a new Polish music label. Someone from the V-S group must have been involved in those negotiations. The next fax was from the Chairman's fax machine, to Bonn. It was addressed to a

W. Fricker. This puzzled me. Fricker, the guy who had preceded me as the Chairman's assistant, was supposedly incapacitated by mysterious headaches and on indefinite sick leave. But here, next, was a memo from the Chairman, typed out by Mrs. Marsh: "We missed you by phone and assume this will await you when you return. We need a fax sent from Bonn to Plaza asking for the proposed executive structure under the new, joint-operating plan," the memo instructed. "The top ten or fifteen positions on Corporation side. This you will fax back to me immediately."

I flipped back through the faxes to the first one that DiFrancesco had given me.

"These all were sent today?"

He nodded.

"You gave these to me in order or out of order?" I asked.

"I don't know. Bunch of papers is what I had there."

I looked at the faxes in frustration.

"You mean pagination or sequence of receipt?" he said.

But I was ahead of him. From the small hour printout at the top of the pages I could see that the Chairman's fax had been sent from New York to Bonn that morning at 11:02 A.M. and the fax from Bonn to the Plaza, which carried out his instructions, had been sent about 1:00 P.M. New York time—early evening in Bonn. This second fax, in German, instructed Waldhausen to ask Morrison for his best guess of the executive structure in the new, merged company. I knew that in this theoretical structure Morrison would elevate himself over the Chairman and place his own people—Beales, Samantha, at least a half dozen others—in key positions. In effect, the Chairman was asking that Volkman-Sakura be provided documentation that Morrison intended to force the Chairman out, as well as a list of Corporation executives loyal to Morrison. A list of traitors provided by the traitors themselves to the Chairman. You had to hand it to him.

It was Saturday, so the Corporation switchboard was closed. I needed to find Morrison, let him know what was going on. I called information in Westchester and got his home number. While the phone rang I looked out the window. An old Chinese man was taking tomatoes out of a huge packing box and putting them into small two-pound bags.

Morrison's wife picked up the phone and I asked for him.

"I'm afraid he isn't here," his wife said easily.

"Is he at the pool or somewhere I can reach him?"

"Why no," she said. "He's in Manhattan."

"Will he be back home soon?"

"Well, no."

"At the office?"

"No . . . I don't think so."

"Do you know?"

She paused. Yes, of course she knew. Wives of executives making four million dollars a year always know where their husbands are.

"He's in Manhattan, I can say that."

"This is important," I said politely. "This is Jack Whitman, we've met a couple of times."

"Yes, Jack."

"He's at the Plaza Hotel?"

"I really can't tell you. He said no one was supposed to know. I'm sorry."

They were meeting at the Plaza and I didn't even know about it. Bad, very bad. They were definitely cutting me out. But I still had to play it straight—the Chairman certainly wasn't my champion and so I needed Morrison. Perhaps he would see to it that I would receive an interesting position in the merged corporations. I had to protect him—it was important that the request from Bonn *not* be answered. I watched the old man select tomatoes and dialed the executive suite at the Plaza where the group was meeting. I reached Beales.

"Ed, I need to talk to Morrison," I said.

"We're really busy here."

"Let me talk to him."

"He's in the next room with Waldhausen," Beales answered with purposeful lassitude. "I don't think it's a good time to interrupt him."

"Samantha, then."

"She's not here yet."

"Let me talk to Morrison."

"If it's important you can talk to me."

I supposed I had to.

"Listen," I said. "You guys are working out the structure of the new executive group today, right?"

"Well," Beales said vaguely, "we're working on things, various aspects of the deal, you know."

"Don't fuck around with me, Ed. I know Bonn has faxed you a request for a management structure."

"We're going to send it to them in a few minutes, as a matter of fact."

"Don't."

"What do you mean?"

"Don't fax it to them. It's going directly to the Chairman, via Germany."

"What?"

"I'm getting something here," DiFrancesco said, looking at his screen. "Incoming fax to the Plaza machine."

"Hang on," I told Beales. I set down the phone and went over to the screen. "This fax is coming into the V-S machine at the Plaza?"

"Yes, here . . ." DiFrancesco said. "It's coming . . ."

I looked at the screen. It was unreadable.

"Wait a minute," DiFrancesco protested. "I can fix this."

"Jack," Beales said in my ear when I picked up the phone. "What do you want? I got to go back to the other room."

"You guys got a fax machine there?" I asked him.

"Do we?"

"I mean one that's different from the V-S machine."

"No, why?"

I wasn't sure. I was confused and trying to keep everything straight.

"Hey, hey," DiFrancesco said, "I got this readable now."

I glanced at the document on the screen. A request to Waldhausen's people for an immediate answer to the previous fax. Why the hurry? It occurred to me that someone somewhere was trying to time a sequence of events.

"I'm going to have to hang up," Beales said.

"*Wait,*" I told him. "Who has the fax with all the new management structure on it?"

"They got a couple of secretaries here," Beales said in exaspera-tion. "One of them, I suppose."

"Can you alter a fax as it goes through your machine?" I asked DiFrancesco across the room.

"That's a fascinating question—"

"Yes or no. Could you do it now?" I insisted.

"No. I mean it *probably* could be done, but I'm going to have to think about it."

"Ed," I returned to the phone. "Don't have that fax sent."

"Why, for Christ sakes?"

"Because—"

"Hold on." Beales covered the phone. Then he came back. "They tell me they just got another request by fax for the document, Jack. I can see the girl, the secretary, across the room—we worked all this out here, we agreed on it and it's been typed up. In fact I just looked it over—"

"Don't fax it!"

"You're just pissed because your name won't be on it," he blurted. So. They were cutting me out completely.

"Okay," I said calmly. "Listen to me. I'm being straight with you. Get your name off the document—"

"What?"

"Get everyone's name off that—"

"You're out of your mind. How'd you find out about this stuff?"

"Let me talk to Samantha," I said.

"I told you she's not here yet. Why do you want to talk to her?"

Below me, the old man was putting bad tomatoes under good ones, hiding them. That was the secret, I realized. I could fuck over Beales nicely. "Listen to me, Ed. Get your name off that management structure and make sure that Samantha's is on it. I'll say it again, Ed. You're going to wish you did what I'm telling you. Get your name off the document, and make sure Samantha—your colleague whom you so much admire—make sure her name is on it, okay?"

"You're out of your fucking head," Beales whispered harshly into the phone at me. "You're out of the loop, pal. We got it all figured out on this end. Hey"—he called across the room—"give me that, yes—

that one, I need to make an adjustment, very fast . . . here, yes, thank you, just . . . just this page, I need a pen, get me a pen . . ." His voice returned to the phone directly. "We don't need you anymore, Jack. I've been listening to your arguing and bullshit for too many years. I can say this because it's all wrapped up here, Morrison has signed off on it, I guess he was going to tell you on Monday, but—"

"Fuck you, Ed." I hung up.

DiFrancesco looked at me.

"He wouldn't do what you told him to do?"

"No."

"Is that bad?"

I glanced out the window. The old man spat on his hand and polished up one of the top tomatoes in a bag. Shiny and nice, with the rotten ones underneath. My life was one stupid game after another. "You should be getting something on your machine very soon," I said finally.

"I . . . uh, yes, it's dialing in now . . . looks like an outgoing fax from the Plaza Hotel machine to . . . that same number in Bonn," DiFrancesco said, staring at his screen. "Cover sheet says six pages . . . I'm getting it."

A minute later he had the document captured on his screen. I scrolled through it, not bothering to translate the German. I knew what I was looking for. On the fourth page I found a schematic diagram of the new management structure, all boxes and lines of power and new titles. The whole group from the Corporation at the Plaza was on there, with one position or another. About a dozen. Yet one name had been hastily scratched out. Just a thick black line through the neat little box. I scanned all the other names—there was Morrison as "Co-chairman," with V-S's chairman, there was Ed Beales as "Executive Vice President for International Market Planning and Development," the position that by rights would be mine. My name wasn't there, and neither was Samantha's—*hers*, I realized, was the one that had been hastily scratched out. As I'd hoped, Beales had assumed that I was lying to him. If I'd been telling him to remove his name from the document, then, in his logic, his name should remain on the document. And telling him to keep Samantha's name on the document had elicited the opposite action—he had quickly blacked it out, assuming that doing so would confer to him some advantage over her.

"You get what you want there?" DiFrancesco asked.

"I might have," I told him. "Don't know yet."

A few minutes later, that same fourth page was sent from Bonn to the fax machine in the Chairman's office, with a cover note by Fricker. As I expected. It was sent to the attention of Mrs. Marsh, and, no doubt, it was that very moment curling out of the machine into her soft, plump hand.

THIRTEEN

er lips looked great. She leaned in close to the mirror and puckered them and rolled the shiny tube of lipstick just so, along the border of each lip. Then she ran her pink tongue across her teeth, touched up her eye makeup, lifted the lashes one last time with the black tip of the mascara applicator. Her face was coy in the mirror, pouting, flirting. She knew she looked terrific. Her hair, washed and rinsed with conditioner and brushed to a high luster, was pulled up above her neck with some sort of mother-of-pearl clasp she'd picked up in the Village, and she had a new pair of hundred-dollar sunglasses perched sportily on top. It was a summery, fun look. From the bed, I watched the preparations step by step. The nails on her fingers and toes were a cherry red, her legs were shaved and creamed, her underarms smooth and spritzed with antiperspirant, and her new sundress, a flowery, three-hundred-dollar cotton print charged on my American Express card at Bloomingdale's, was cut low and made to be worn without a bra for the few women who could pull it off, and just high enough on the back of the thighs that one knew instantly that *the bitch be game*, as they say in Brooklyn, that here was a woman who was ready for a good time, that here was Dolores preparing for our trip to the Chairman's place.

"Do I look *cheap?*" Dolores spun in front of the mirror suddenly worried.

"You look pretty expensive, actually."

Dolores didn't like the joke. "Jack . . ."

"You look fine," I assured her. "It's a weekend thing. People are supposed to be dressed casually. You look sexy and casual and great."

"Good. That's *just* what I want." Dolores turned back to the mirror. "I got a new bathing suit and one for Maria."

"Can I see yours?"

"It's a surprise."

"Is it a bikini or one-piece?" I asked, packing some towels and a swimsuit for myself.

"Oh, you'll have to wait," she teased.

"Sounds sort of scandalous."

"Might be, you never know."

I nodded. "Good."

"Will it be warm enough to swim?"

"It's supposed to be pretty warm today, but the pool will be heated if necessary."

"He must have a lot of money."

I laughed.

"Does he?" Dolores asked earnestly. "I mean, a *heated* pool is a *lot* of money."

"We'll get out there and you can tell me if you think he's rich," I said. "You can give me your opinion on it."

Maria, washed and brushed too, was outfitted in a cute little red sundress and sandals. She and Dolores went on getting ready and I wandered downstairs. There had been no new information since the previous afternoon when I had been at DiFrancesco's office, and as of that morning DiFrancesco hadn't intercepted any more faxes. I assumed that Morrison, Samantha, and the others had continued their negotiations with Waldhausen and the other V-S people at the Plaza Hotel. I was tempted to call Morrison at home or Samantha but didn't see the use. Morrison's wife would have told him I'd called, even if Beales hadn't. And Morrison knew I was going out to the Chairman's Long Island home, but in his scheme for the management of the new merged Corporation, it didn't matter where I was. If anything that Morrison considered important was to happen out there, he would have primed me, told me to report back to him. But he clearly didn't care what I was doing now. I was extraneous, I was old news.

So, in a mood of discouragement, I accompanied Dolores and Maria out to Long Island on the Long Island Railroad, picking up the train at Atlantic Avenue in Brooklyn, and after a two-and-a-half-hour trip, we were met at the Southampton station by an elderly man in a tweed coat standing in a slant of sun on the platform. "Out for the day to see us?" he smiled, by way of introduction, taking the bag of swimsuits and towels Dolores had brought. "My name is Mr. Warren." He led us to a boxy new station wagon with LITTLE MARSH FARM painted discreetly on the driver's door. We followed the Montauk Highway east for a few minutes toward Bridgehampton, so forcibly neat, and then down a winding road. Each side was lined with impenetrable hedges twelve feet high, with an occasional flicker of a gabled roofline or an elaborate brick chimney rising from behind. This was serious money, not Jack Whitman run-down-brownstone money. Dolores and Maria lolled in the backseat of the station wagon, the sun flickering across their faces, the wind pushing their hair back and toying with the hem of Maria's sundress. I suddenly realized I was happy. So fuck Morrison, I thought, life has its compensations.

Then I turned back to Mr. Warren. "Is there a special gathering out here today?"

"No, not especially. There's usually people for tennis and swimming here on the weekends." He was slowing down and checked his rearview mirror. "Friends, you know."

Dolores pressed her face into the open window. "I smell the ocean."

Mr. Warren smiled. "Yes, we're very close to the water now."

We proceeded up an unmarked private road, and continued for five minutes past marshes and fields of wild rose and through a stand of virgin oaks and poplars, each a good two hundred feet high, and then through a rolling field of grass, where pruned, hundred-year-old copper beeches gracefully lined either side of the road. The station wagon dipped and rose and several Japanese luxury sedans flew past us going the opposite direction, with a friendly wave from Mr. Warren out the window. As the road leveled out we saw the brick chimneys first, and then beneath them rose the shingled Georgian mansion about the size of the New York Public Library. Behind it was the hundred-mile haze of the Atlantic.

"Oh my God," Dolores whispered.

◆ ◆ ◆

The Chairman was not available to greet us, said Mr. Warren amiably, but he had asked to see that we were comfortable. We were led around the house and directed to a large pool, where perhaps a dozen young children and adults played—no one I recognized as Corporation people, which was a relief. The grounds were extensive, and across an expanse of lawn sat a sleek black helicopter. Farther off came the sounds of tennis balls being hit on several courts and I could just make out a few older men in tennis togs, their sagging chests distorting their whites. But they remained at a distance. Inside the pool house was a table of finger sandwiches, salad, fruits, juices, beer, and so on. Dolores and Maria disappeared with their suits into the women's cabana. They emerged a few minutes later, Maria first in her cute pink suit with a frilly skirt, and then Dolores. She had chosen a striped bikini that lifted her breasts up nicely, and as she led Maria over to the pool, I watched the other guests adjust to Dolores's sexuality. She and Maria were the only dark-skinned people at the pool, but no one seemed particularly interested in this fact; they looked rich and that was enough. Maria quickly made friends with another little girl and the two of them splashed happily in the shallow end. Dolores swam tentatively and it occurred to me that she'd never had much chance to swim, growing up in Sunset Park, Brooklyn. The three of us played in the water for a while. I noticed the helicopter leaving and arriving. At one point in the next hour I saw Mr. Warren at the house, shielding his eyes from the sun with his hand as he looked toward the pool, perhaps looking for me. Then he disappeared. Dolores and Maria and their new friends drifted away from the pool to play a game of croquet. I swam a few nervous laps, wondering if I would see the Chairman at all that afternoon.

Time passed under the sun. Most of the children seemed to have run off down the hill and, left alone, I found one of those absurd pool chairs made out of Styrofoam and aluminum that floats even as you sit in it. Fortified by a cold beer that fit in the arm of the chair, I fell into a stuporous half slumber, rocked by the light lapping of the pool, the sun searing pleasurably through my closed eyelids. It had been years since I had enjoyed such an afternoon, and almost two decades since I had enjoyed a summer of such afternoons. What is it about the pleasure of burning beneath the sun? My mother and Harry McCaw had joined the tennis club and the summer I was fifteen I'd spent a lot of time there, working on my serve, aware somehow that it was my last summer of freedom, cultivating a precancerous tan and pursuing the legendary Betsy Jones, the daughter of the club's owner, only fifteen and already notorious for her sassiness, drinking, and remarkable two-handed backhand . . . those were vanished, memorable weeks. It was rumored then that Betsy was dating a University of Pennsylvania sophomore (which turned out to be true, since she eventually married and divorced him), but I was sleek and energetic and at ease in my tight little tank swimsuit, which I tied with a little string halfway between my navel and crotch, and after a summer of insipid teenaged flirtation, we did the great deed late one night at the club in a five-foot-deep wooden closet, atop hundreds of folded linen tablecloths. She knew what she was doing, and I didn't, and the actual act probably lasted less than three feverish minutes, with no ultimate satisfaction for Betsy Jones, but afterward I believed myself to be transported to a new level of manhood, as if, say, I had just been drafted into professional football. I remember saying good night to her sometime after 2:00 A.M. and then streaking on my bicycle in crazed jubilance through the dark streets toward home, my sockless toes gripping the clammy insides of my tennis shoes as I pedaled with my hands off the bike's handles, raising my fists over my head in a mad celebration of victory. I remembered this more than the actual act of sex. I never saw Betsy again. She was shipped off to a new boarding school and we lost touch.

A shadow moved above me in the sun. I heard my name. Mr. Warren appeared at the side of the pool, looking hot in his tweed jacket. He was holding a towel.

"If you have a minute, Mr. Whitman?"

I knew by his polite expression that I was being summoned, that the afternoon had a purpose after all.

"Do I have time to get dressed?"

"I'm afraid not, Mr. Whitman."

"I'd really like to just go back to the pool house and throw a shirt on, at least."

"I'm sorry. He would like you this very moment."

I climbed out of the pool, irritated with this silliness, my swimsuit dripping, and looked around for Dolores and Maria.

"They're with the other children." Mr. Warren handed me a

towel, implying that there was no time to find Dolores and tell her I'd left the pool. For a butler, the guy was tough. I followed him in my tender bare feet along a path of bricks set in a herringbone pattern that wound under ornamental cherry trees toward the main house.

"I'm still wet," I said, pointing to the parquet floor as we stepped from the bright sun through a sliding glass door.

"That's all right, Jack," came a voice from inside the room. "We know you're a slippery fish." The Chairman. My eyes adjusted to a dark, air-conditioned room of paneling and Oriental rugs as Mr. Warren stayed outside and pulled shut the glass door behind me. He was seated in an easy chair and swept his hand toward four older men, all showered and dressed in casual clothes. "Gentlemen, I'd like you to meet Jack Whitman, one of our most promising young people."

The far-off older men who'd been playing tennis, now showered and seated in padded armchairs. They nodded hello dutifully, sipping their drinks. They looked familiar. They *were* familiar. I tried to arrange the towel casually around my neck and look as if I knew just what was going on. Water ran in quick droplets down my legs, puddling at my feet. I was virtually naked, my thinning hair frizzled up by the sun and water, white stomach popping out over my waistband. There is something disconcerting about standing in wet trunks inside a house, in front of five older men, available for their inspection, representing my generation, and not a prime specimen, not at all. I was no longer the young man who had given Betsy Jones a pop in the tablecloth closet. I looked like a guy dragged out of a swimming pool and forced to stand and deliver. You had to hand it to the Chairman; he knew how to terrify a man. I had a wet jockstrap on and it chafed and bound my testicles. My knees began to shake and I felt the slime of perspiration in the heat of my armpits.

"Jack, let me introduce you," began the Chairman with a casual wave of his arm. "This is Peter Velkner—"

I nodded. Yes, I recognized everyone now. Velkner had been a board member of the Corporation since 1986. Founding chairman, now retired, of Velkner Aerospace in California. A technology genius. Key computer inventions back in the 1960s. Understood manufacturing processes. Completely uninterested in the New York social scene.

Spoke Japanese fluently. Raised hybrid coniferous trees as a hobby. I nodded hello but did not shake hands.

"Ralph Ueberoth—"

Board member of the Corporation since 1990. Current vice chairman of New York Trust National Bank. By training an economist. Had been one of the governors of the U.S. Federal Reserve Bank in the first Reagan administration. From what I knew of him, a doubter by nature, a lemon-sucker.

"Harry Doerman—"

Of course. Board member of the Corporation since 1979. Current chairman of Global Airlines; former vice chairman of Merck, the drug manufacturer; former vice president of IBM. A happy guy, a deal maker. Could sell anything to anybody, sunglasses to corpses, anything.

"And Earl Watson."

Board member of the Corporation since 1983. Founder of the Watson Corp., which ran a chain of sixty-eight newspapers nationwide. Very smart about American culture, a patron of the arts. Somewhere I'd read that as boys he and the Chairman had taken violin lessons together sixty years back, during the Depression. These were the senior members of the board, the inner sanctum.

"Jack, as you probably know, the board has a number of committees. One of them, as you know, is called the governance and nominating committee, which has a standing subcommittee for miscellaneous purposes. You may not know about this"—the Chairman conducted himself as if he and I were mere acquaintances, his tone ever so subtly patronizing—"but the subcommittee is empowered under one of our bylaws, one of our *obscure* bylaws, to bypass other members of the board and convene itself as it sees fit and wherever it deems sufficient. This is the only subcommittee that can meet officially and not notify all the other board members. I tell you that"—and here he paused to look straight into my eyes—"to be sure you realize that despite the agreeably *informal* appearance of our meeting, that this is a formal meeting." At these words, Mrs. Marsh appeared, in her frumpy dress and stockings, carrying a notebook and pen. But her hair looked blasted from behind—I realized that she had just come in on the helicopter and no doubt she had yesterday's faxes to the Chairman from Germany with her. She sat down in the back of the room. ". . . with complete recorded minutes of the meeting, binding power of vote, and so on."

The Chairman let his blue eyes settle on mine to be sure I understood. He looked alert, jazzed up. "Now, to get to the matter at hand. Jack has been making the case to me for a merger with Volkman-Sakura. As everyone here knows, with perhaps the exception of Jack, over the last six months I have had informal discussions with their representatives. We've been quiet about this, *very quiet.* I've decided, based in part upon Jack's excellent arguments, that a straight stock-for-stock swap, plus a V-S capitalization plan, makes excellent sense. Jack here has all the details, all the rationale."

He turned to me and I shivered with recognition at his cleverness, his mastery of me, of Morrison, of all of them. "I would like you to make the case for the deal to the committee, Jack, if you would."

"I am pleased to do that"—I smiled in terror—"but perhaps there are others in the executive group who should also have the opportunity to—"

"We appreciate your loyalty to Mr. Morrison and the others," Watson, one of the committee members, interrupted, "but we wish to hear *you.*"

"Yes," the Chairman answered, "you need not worry about Morrison and the others. Their roles are clearly understood by this committee . . ."

Their roles are clearly understood by this committee. I stood in the midst of a countercoup. The Chairman was presenting the joint venture plan as *his own idea* to the board.

"What we would like from you, Jack, is, first, the overall argument for the plan. You've talked to me about the penetration and addition of new markets, the ability to pass through various cultural curtains through V-S's own distribution system, and so on. Then I would like you to specify the financial maneuvers that would actually effect the venture, starting with the shell holding corporation, the valuation of their stock against ours, any bridge loan requirements, what our Eurodollar situation is like now, and then, if you have any breath left"—he gave a soft, staged little laugh—"then lay out for us the effect on each division, which operations would have to be spun off and sold, what the conflicts with federal regulations are, the market for these superfluous operations, and who, possibly, would buy them — "

And so on. In short, to summarize all the work of all the others, the useful stuff, the important figures and strategies, certain words and concepts worth millions of dollars. He knew from the satellite meetings in Washington that I had a very good memory, was a quick study. The committee members didn't care who had come up with the numbers and valuations and reports; once out of my mouth, the information was theirs, forever. Mrs. Marsh sat poised to take it all down in shorthand, her half-frame glasses on the bridge of her nose. As he finished I quietly cleared my throat—I'd be talking for an hour, perhaps more . . .

There are moments when we betray other people. Morrison had manipulated me into a position where I could do that to him, even while propounding his vision of the Corporation. He had purposefully taken me out of the negotiating group—what did I owe him now? If I did not cooperate with the Chairman, then I signaled my allegiance to Morrison, and hence advertised his betrayal of the Chairman. Either way I turned, Morrison was screwed, as far as I could see. He couldn't protect me now. And I was expendable to the Chairman as soon as I talked. My only chance was to do a good job. I was on my own, singing for the angels.

The Chairman asked solicitously, "I think you have a lot to tell us, Jack. Perhaps you would like to sit?"

More than anything, I wanted to shoot my hand into my trunks and unbind my balls from the clammy jockstrap.

"No," I answered quietly, to him and then to the four men sitting in front of me, "I'll stand."

◆ ◆ ◆

It went somewhat better than I expected. I got into it, paced around a bit as I talked, answered the questions and objections that were raised by each man. We backtracked a few times; they weren't familiar with some of the latest market information. The Chairman stood to the back, listening. He picked up a tiny Chinese jade horse from a side table and inspected it absentmindedly, nodding to himself from time to time as he heard certain of my points and responses. I ceased hearing my own voice nervously and just talked to the people in the room. They were smart; they could see that the presentation depended on analysis, not a bunch of gee-whiz charts and slide shows. And then, they had asked their last questions.

Outside, the shadows of the trees had fallen like giant fingers across the pool. Were we done? The Chairman gave a sharp little nod to me and said, "Thanks, Jack—you've given us a great deal to think about. Or maybe I should say now we're going to think about a great *deal.*" He gave a quick concluding wink and the meeting was over. Someone put a drink in my hand and each of the committee members came up and shook my hand in that dry-skinned, casual way of older men, getting close and just sort of slipping a cool, not-too-tight palm in there, as if a bill is being passed between the two of you. I belonged to them now, they had me.

◆ ◆ ◆

The Chairman quietly told me he'd see me in the office the next day, and that was the cue that screamed I was to disappear. Mr. Warren miraculously appeared again and guided me down a hallway toward another door. The warmth had returned to his manner. I passed a formal dining room where a magnificent table was set for five, warm silver bowls resting on buffet carts. Mr. Warren led me to a comfortable den, where Dolores and Maria were sitting on a sofa, dressed now, watching television. I could see that they'd had a nice day; they'd been taken care of, fed, entertained. After I changed into my clothes, Mr. Warren escorted us across the lawn to the helicopter. Dolores took my hand and squeezed it. We stepped up into the cabin, which was large enough to seat six people.

"Thank you for coming to see us this day," Mr. Warren said. Then he pointed to a cabinet behind us. "There should be a rather nice warm dinner behind you, there, with just enough time to eat."

He shut the cabin door and within a minute the helicopter lifted up.

"Where are we going?" Dolores asked over the loud vibration of the helicopter.

"Probably the heliport on the East Side," I told her. "It'll be forty-five minutes, is my guess."

"I'm scared," Maria said.

"Don't be, sweetie."

She settled down and pressed her nose to the curved window and watched the Long Island shoreline on our left as we flew west back toward Manhattan, into the last minutes of the sun. I was exhausted by the afternoon; the careful orchestration of events, with Jack Whitman as unwitting pawn, scared me. What would happen when I arrived in the office the next day? Did I belong to Morrison or to the Chairman? Where was the advantage? I closed my eyes. And then I felt warm lips on my forehead and opened my eyes. Dolores sat before me, dark eyes fixed on me. I saw that the afternoon had profoundly changed her understanding of me; she gazed at me intently, with new hunger.

♦ ♦ ♦

We landed on a huge yellow X at the heliport. A car awaited us and not seventy-five minutes after taking off we were at my front door.

"Are you tired, Jack?" Dolores asked as we stepped inside.

I flipped on the hall light. "Stressed out. I should have brought some of my acid medication along with me."

"You didn't know what they wanted from you."

"I should have guessed, Dolores, I really should have."

She was unpacking the swimsuits and towels. "Well, I had a very, very nice day."

I managed a smile. "Good."

"They made you talk that whole time?"

"Yeah."

"Why don't you put Maria to bed? Maybe it will calm you down."

So I did, impressed with Dolores's little piece of wisdom. Maria and I went upstairs hand in hand to her new room, which I'd started to fix up with a toy box and a little bed and a table for the coloring books. Maria was tired from the sun and water and I helped her into her pajamas.

"Read me *The Cat in the Hat*," she said.

"You're very sleepy, sweetie."

"*Read* it to me."

"Get up in my lap, then."

I read the first few pages in a low voice about how the little girl and little boy were inside on a rainy day with nothing fun to do when the Cat in the Hat appears. Maria's eyes became glassy. Her lids closed slowly and she went limp in my arms, her head upon my left breast, so close that my exhalation made her dark curls tremble. Her lips were fat and slackened, eyeballs gently moving beneath her lids. I might never know her—our lives might fly apart or she might nurse me on my deathbed—but in those seconds I loved her. What I held in my arms was as perfect a thing as could be made by nature, a child still years from the great neuroses and miseries of adulthood, the creeping hatreds and fears. Maria stirred, her lips smacking quietly. One arm found my hand and gathered it in. Did Hector suspect that another man held his child with fatherly desire?

After I put Maria into her bed and covered her, I checked the answering machine in my office. Two messages: "Uh, hello, this is Mike DiFrancesco . . . I got a little bit of a problem with NYNEX, when I was changing your unlisted number, I messed it up: the number is now 555-4043 but it's listed, not unlisted. The address is still unlisted and I can't figure that out, except maybe the NYNEX file got duplicated somehow in the system, and you're considered a new listing. They've been changing their protocols, so I hope this doesn't create some kind of *problem*—"

I fast-forwarded to the second message: "Dolores, listen I *know* you're there, I know you're listening . . ." Hector's voice, rattling out of the little box. I turned the volume down until the message was barely audible. ". . . I got this phone number from the phone company just now, some kinda *new* number, Whitman's been fucking around with the number or something. Listen, if you're there, you gotta be, I been figuring some things out here, 'bout where you are now, and I think I got it and so maybe we'll be talkin' real soon, Dolores, and that's good because I just want you to know that I got promoted. A new job, lotta more work. They just said, 'You, you're promoted.' I been fuckin' sweating up there more than three years and they finally give me a break. Now I'm one of the field bosses—field supervisors. I know you always wanted me to make more money, Dolores. They got me starting training tomorrow. All kinds of procedures and rules and shit. There's paperwork, and stuff on a computer, too. I told them I was gonna do a good job. It's more money, Dolores, I got more money for us and you can come back. Bring Maria back. I got fifty-two hundred more bucks coming in now, real money. Think I'll still, you know, put in those shifts at the car lot, for extra, right? I gotta work longer but—"

I cut off the tape, then erased it. My moves were going wrong, backfiring. Hector didn't care how many hours he worked, as long as Dolores and Maria came back to him.

"Jack?" Dolores came up the stairs with a blanket and a bottle of wine and two glasses. "Was there a message?"

"Nothing important."

"You're coughing, baby," she said.

"It's just . . . the acid."

She took my hand and we climbed up to the roof. I drank silently and worried about what would happen the next day at the office. Something was going on. The Chairman had given me no clue after I'd talked and Morrison hadn't called to see what had happened. And I'd chosen not to call him—if such a thing could be called a choice. Dolores approached me in the darkness.

"You're coughing *a lot*, Jack."

"It's just stress and caffeine and everything."

"What happened out there today, can I ask about that? Because I know it wasn't just a lot of fun. I never saw anybody so nervous."

"It's almost impossible to explain, Dolores. It's very complicated. I don't know what the hell's going on at work. I'm getting pushed around. I could lose my job tomorrow, I think that's a possibility."

"They made you talk so long," she said sympathetically.

"Don't worry about it, you have enough to worry about." There was something accidentally harsh in my voice when I said this, a certain tone of reserve that suggested judgment of Dolores. She looked up in hurt surprise and I believe she saw in my face that I knew I could tell her to leave at any time. "I'm sorry," I told her. "I shouldn't have snapped. There's a lot to make me tense now."

"I can help that."

"How?"

"Oh, some way." She smiled and I thought to myself, *Fuck you, Hector, this woman is mine.*

"There're some ways and there's one way," I answered.

"One way, then."

"If you're willing, Dolores, if you're willing."

I slipped off my shoes and pants and underwear and she began then, the one perfect cure for the acid and the tension, and the backs of my knees shook as I lapsed into the bizarre fugue state where it was only my penis that was alive and the rest of me that by contrast was dead while I felt that certain perfect tranquillity, the night wind against my thighs. To have a woman kneeling between my legs, sucking, only then do I not worry about the past or the future. When you are screwing, you worry about the future, you worry about what the woman is going to get out of it, will she be satisfied. But not with the other . . . maybe one of her hands goes underneath the testicles, which is very good. Sweet smoke fills my head, my lips quiver strangely, my penis feels grotesquely, wonderfully thick and heavy—the pleasure seems to actually enlarge it further than its usual tumescence, and I forget the Corporation, I forget the dead and dying, I forget that I myself am merely a putrefying bag of worm-meat set to life by a jolt of electricity. A body electric. I forget my hemorrhoids, my taxes, the fat creeping around my torso, my mother and father. There is only the hard pipe that goes from me to her, her to me, her lips sliding back and forth, her tongue sending pleasure back to me, and I am able to flatter and fool myself that she genuinely enjoys this, that she is sexually aroused by this. She sucks and fondles and soon I am in the great good place in my brain, such that in the penultimate seconds, my knees lifted high, muscles shivering, the last moment, when certainty overtakes expectation, my face changes swiftly from a straining grimace to a younger, eased version of myself, one's theoretical, unstressed face, at peace for a few seconds. I have never seen this face on myself, but I have felt it.

FOURTEEN

. . . These management changes are indeed abrupt, but their effect will be to clarify leadership in this company. We have an excellent, seasoned team now in place, and despite the inevitable coming characterizations in the business media of the Corporation as an enterprise in mortal turmoil, nothing could be further from the truth, as we have many exciting developments awaiting us, some of which may be announced soon. In short, the Corporation is on firm footing, with record gross income in each of the last three years, a rapidly improving balance sheet, and steady profits. When the economy inevitably improves, our profits will brighten even more quickly. I personally will appreciate your continued good faith and industry.

The Chairman's memorandum lay centered on every desk the very next morning, over his signature and the typed names of the board of directors, specifying who on the thirty-ninth floor had "resigned to pursue other interests": Morrison, of course, Beales, and about ten other of Morrison's pilot fish. Only minutes earlier, I'd walked out of the bright light of the morning into the Corporation's lobby and seen an odd look flung onto the face of Frankie the guard. He'd *noted* my arrival. People pick up on things. Information is instantaneous. Regimes are never more than an idea. When the elevator opened to the floor, I'd found the hallways empty, the secretaries sitting in quiet anxiousness at their desks, some whispering into the phone. Now, with the announcement before me, I went on reading. The bankers had been replaced, fired, cut out, bought off—the professional equivalent of being shot in the back of the head and dumped in the East River. The bean counters in internal accounting, gray men with worn soles and tired faces who had never done a deal, had been spared. A couple of Morrison protégés in lesser division positions had been sent packing. Bodies floating down the river, one by one, faceup, facedown. The Chairman had burned Morrison and his people out of the Corporation. Some of the firings were gratuitous—good people, smart people. Fricker, the Chairman's assistant who everybody assumed had left because of his headaches, had been elevated to senior vice president for international relations, a new position. A new fellow from Disney would be joining us. I read through the announcement carefully a second time. Samantha was not on the list of dead. I'd saved her.

Helen stood in my doorway. "So, you saw."

"Yes."

"Mrs. Marsh says you should go over to the Chairman's office in about an hour."

"What happened to Beales?" I inquired.

"He cleaned out his office at six-thirty, they told me."

"Morrison?" I asked.

"All I know is that the Chairman had three compensation lawyers and some secretaries working all day here yesterday printing out severance agreements."

"Yesterday, a Sunday?" The Chairman was way ahead of me, of everybody.

"Three lawyers," Helen said. "All day long. He was on the phone all day with them here."

"He couldn't have been on the phone the whole time," I said, "because I was in a meeting with him for a couple of hours in the afternoon."

She shrugged. "I heard they started working at five o'clock in the morning, so maybe they were done by then."

"I see."

Helen stood there.

"What is it?" I asked.

"It didn't have to be like that. Mr. Morrison worked here something like twenty years—"

"Twenty-five," I corrected. "He came to the Corporation right after his last tour in Vietnam."

"Elaine Comber was extremely upset when she came in this morning and saw the announcement. *Extremely* upset."

Morrison's secretary.

"It was going to be him or the Chairman," I said.

"Well, I don't think it was fair," Helen went on. "I know no one's asking *me*, but I think it's pretty lousy."

"Then you don't understand the mistakes Morrison made."

"What?"

"Morrison thought the Chairman could no longer exercise power. He thought the Chairman wasn't watching, that he was an old man who he could just blow past."

"So you've changed your allegiance?"

"Jesus, it's a matter of survival, Helen. Morrison was cutting me out of the picture. That's what I kept talking about. He was streamlining his management team. He had to if he was going to merge his group with the Volkman-Sakura people. He knew Beales and I could never work together, that things were only getting worse."

Helen shifted her weight to another foot. I was telling it to myself as much as to her. "He carefully got all my best work out of me and then chose to keep Beales in the group. I *wasn't* crazy to think the wind had shifted. He assigned me to the Chairman because it was a way of doing three things—loosening the Chairman up on the merger question—weakening him, placating Beales, and then, when the Chairman was forced out by the board, I would be disposed of along with him, since I would then be associated with him. It was a very smart management move but it didn't work."

"I still don't think it's *fair*," Helen protested. "Mr. Morrison worked so long here . . ."

"Well, what do you think he got for his *suffering?*" I said, irritated now. "Fifty million?"

"Nobody was allowed to say."

Helen heard something and looked toward the hallway behind her. Samantha was at the door in a blue suit with white blouse, holding her thin leather briefcase. I wondered if she understood all that happened over the last few days.

"Good morning!" she said brightly to both of us. "Helen, I need a minute here with Jack."

Helen left dutifully and Samantha shut the door. She walked toward me across the room.

"When do women learn to walk like that?" I said.

Samantha ignored the joke and came around my desk, stopping next to me. I could smell her perfume but never could tell the cheap stuff from the expensive. Samantha bent down and put a soft hand on my left cheek and pressed her lips against my right cheek sweetly. A caring, lingering kiss. She looked at me, her blue eyes wet.

"Thank you, Jack," she whispered. "Thank you."

♦ ♦ ♦

An hour later, after I had brushed my hair and straightened my tie in the men's bathroom, I stood in Mrs. Marsh's office, waiting to find out what was to happen to me.

"He'll be just a minute or two," Mrs. Marsh said, her plump cheeks lifting into a flawless smile of politeness. "May I get you a cup of coffee, tea?"

"I'm fine, thanks." Now we were old friends.

And then I went in. The Chairman stood up from his desk, his fingertips resting lightly on the wood. He'd picked up a little sun over the weekend.

"A new epoch," I said.

His old lined face smiled—slowly, generously. And with that smile, I knew I was all right. I was a player, in for the new haul. He was the father, I was one of the sons. He took my hand and shook it, holding both hands.

"Yes, a new epoch," he repeated. "And with a new epoch comes new people. Please, sit." He nodded toward a chair. "Good. Now then, we need to talk. We'll be talking quite a bit, you and I, as well as with the others. First you and I will talk. We need to start from scratch. I'll try to explain the basis for our working relationship, as I see it." The Chairman looked at me and gave a little chuckle. "I figured you out on Sunday, Jack, I finally figured you out. I'd been trying, incidentally. I'd been thinking about it, based on our time together. You and I took the train up from Washington and went to my little retreat and we had a couple of arguments, and I still couldn't figure you out. But I figured it out yesterday, Jack. I pride myself on being able to figure people out, I've been doing it for a long time. I'm interested in personality, in character. They say character is destiny. I generally agree with that."

"So what did you discover?"

"I was talking on the phone, Jack, in my study out in the house on Long Island. I have in my study a brass telescope that was once . . . that belonged to a Nantucket sea captain, one of my ancestors. It's about two and a half feet long, and it's mounted on a swivel base so you don't have to hold it. Very steady. I was talking to someone on the phone — one of the lawyers working here that day, actually — and I had in front of me a list of people here. Some were in the left-hand column and some were in the right-hand column. I was crossing out, moving people back and forth." The Chairman waited for a moment, to let the brutality of this statement pass. "And some were in neither column, Jack. I was writing down the names of people that I and the board were going to fire and the names of people we should keep." He looked at me with a certain cold clarity. "I couldn't decide about you. Your name was not on either list. I am being utterly honest about this. Things were moving very quickly at that point. We — the board members and I — had been meeting since the night before. We were all drunk on coffee, if you know what I mean. It had occurred to me that you should address the board, that you should inject your enthusiasm, and frankly, I had invited you out to my place for that very possibility, just in case, you see, in case I felt like having you talk to them. You were going to be a card I could play if necessary." The Chairman checked my expression to see whether this offended me. "I knew it wouldn't matter if you were prepared or not. You would be all right, I had that faith in you. But I didn't know whether you belonged to Morrison or you belonged to me. You understand what I mean by that?"

I nodded easily. The Chairman's face had a certain kindness in it now, a certain wisdom.

"I didn't know what resentments you might have. They could be substantial. It was clear to me from the start that Morrison was trying to get you out of his group. But he knew that you would be loyal to him, even if he was using you. He's a smart fellow—I should know, I brought him along. I could see that first day that you didn't want to be with me, Jack. You had been listening to Morrison too long, you had a certain idea of me. That's all right. That perception of me has persisted the last five years or so. Fine. I've been used to that perception. It has been useful. People tend to work harder if they think that there's a chance that the leadership will change. They're jockeying for position. I know this makes for greater anxiety in the office. But it is *useful.* Morrison has been busy making a name for himself for ten years with this very thing in mind. And you too. You wouldn't have been working so hard this last year on a joint merger plan if you didn't think it might personally benefit you. So I was perceived as being out of touch, not around. Fine. I was in touch with the key guys on the board on a weekly basis. So, now then, where was I? I'm sitting there at the window wondering if you, this very bright thirty-five-year-old vice president who has been hollering at me the last couple of weeks, are with me or not. I had the telescope and I watched you come down the hill around the house to the pool. I didn't even know you were going to be there, I just happened to look through the telescope. You had that very attractive woman friend of yours with you. And her little girl. I watched the three of you. I wondered why you were with her—she's really not your type, at least on the face of it. Not the typical wife of an executive—that's not a judgment, incidentally, just an observation. Of course, she's attractive. But that's not so unusual. I just watched the three of you, wondering what was going on. You were on the edge of the pool, you had your hand on the little girl's head. I think that you were putting some sort of sun lotion on her forehead. Maybe the sun was hot enough to burn. I'm a father, I remember doing this with my own daughter perhaps forty years ago, when I was about your age. I found this touching, Jack. This is not your little girl but here you are, caring for her like a father. I could see that you felt that way about her. Then I remembered what you told me about your father and mother, and the terrible thing that had happened to your wife."

The Chairman shook his old head in sadness at what I had suffered. And in this was more redemption than anything my father had ever said to me.

"And then it clicked for me. It all made sense. You're *wounded*. You want to be part of something, Jack. That is who you are—you want to be part of a family, a body of people, a corporation, whatever. You have been made lonely by circumstance and you want to be part of something. You need people, Jack, more than most. You want somebody to love, people to love. I believe you want this more than you want power, Jack. You have this need, not a weakness, exactly, but a need. You will innovate as necessary. My guess is that this is why you have this woman and child in your life, somehow they give this to you, perhaps they comfort you. I very much hope that things work out for you with her. That she has a child by another man makes it more complicated, I suspect."

"Yes."

"And I would bet that each of you has something of a past."

I thought, of course, of Dolores's son, wondering when she and I would talk about him. I realized that we needed to deal with the question. "You have any advice on that?"

"Yes." The Chairman nodded. "As a matter of fact I do. Be honest. Clean it up. Get it over with. Then things can move forward. You need a family, Jack. One at home and one at work. This is why you went along with Morrison's scheming. You are clearly a brilliant young man when it comes to planning and detail, one of the more brilliant I have come across in the last twenty years, but I would expect Morrison to have found people like that. Yes. But that isn't why I want you to stay on this team, Jack. I want you to stay on this team because I want people working with me who want people. I saw you with the little girl and the woman and I knew that so long as I made you feel that you were part of something here, that you had a family here too, that you would be loyal to me and would work on the Corporation's behalf. And that is why you are here in my office today."

I sat motionless, feeling very young.

"Now then, yesterday went nicely," the Chairman said, rising from his desk to adjust the window blind behind him. "And today is going to be a mess. I have already made statements to the *Times* and the *Journal* and CBS News. And that fellow from CNN. It's going to look like there was a struggle for power and the old lion won. And that's what it was. The reporters will figure it out. I'm not so sure I care. But the corporate relations people are running around trying to make this look as good as possible and they tell me we've got to get the good news out fast. I agree with that, the board agrees with that. It might be better to wait a few weeks, but there are other considerations. The stock price, for one. So tomorrow, we'll announce the V-S deal. One story will obliterate the other. The focus becomes on the future. The firings are seen less as a bloodletting than as a reorientation, a re-creation of a new company. So we'll announce the merger negotiations almost exactly as Morrison and his people worked it out. It's a very fine agreement, and the people at Volkman-Sakura are pleased. When Mr. Morrison initiated communications with Mr. Waldhausen several months ago, Mr. Waldhausen called me. I was surprised but I was not shocked at Mr. Morrison's boldness. Apparently he thought he could sway the board at the right time. Waldhausen and I devised an idea to let it go forward. He understood my position. I've been meeting with the board privately since then. This is how it played out." The door opened. "Oh—you know Wally Fricker."

Fricker came in from the next office and we shook hands. He was making about ten times the salary he had been making the last time I'd seen him and it showed in his face.

"You've been in Germany the whole time?" I asked.

He nodded.

"Jack, tomorrow morning we'll have the formal vote with the whole board," the Chairman went on. "Just protocol. I've talked to all the key people, as you saw yesterday. Then an hour later, the public announcement of the deal."

"What do you want me to do?"

"I want you to get everything you said yesterday out in Bridgehampton down to twenty minutes. It went well but it was way, way too long. Just so the full board can have the whole thing laid out for them. You should go home and think about this, actually. Go home, take off your shoes, and come up with the best twenty minutes you can think of. Time it with a watch, the whole thing." The Chairman pushed several pieces of paper into a pile. I was about to leave when he called after me. "Also, please do one more thing for me, today before you go home, please get that Freddie Robinson fellow back here. Mrs.

Marsh will have his number." He looked at me. "Some absolute *idiot* fired him."

◆ ◆ ◆

"Look!" Maria hollered to me when I came home early that day, having reinstated Robinson before leaving the office. "I'm on tiptoes!" She pranced about the living room on her toes, a little pixie in curls and a new dress and shoes.

"You're home early," Dolores said, coming out of the kitchen. They had just returned from Maria's new playgroup.

"Good things are happening," I told her.

"But you're home."

"It's the first afternoon I've had off in months, actually."

"Let's go do something."

"I want to have some fun!" Maria demanded.

The Chairman's words had put me in an optimistic mood. "We could go for a drive."

"Where?"

"Brooklyn Heights? Sit out on the promenade and watch the boats?"

"Maria and I were there last week," Dolores said.

"Well, anywhere, a drive for the hell of it, before the rush hour traffic gets bad. Maybe an hour."

"*I* want to go for a drive!" Maria said.

We walked to the garage and got into my rarely used Ford, with Maria in the back with a bunch of her coloring books. I had no idea where I wanted to go. It would be better to stay off the cratered Brooklyn-Queens Expressway at this time of day. I kept an eye out for kids running into the street after school and nosed the car along Seventh Avenue, past yuppie mothers wheeling babies in Aprica strollers, then cut down to Fourth Avenue and turned left toward the south of Brooklyn.

"Where're we going?" Dolores asked. "We're going to Sunset Park?"

"We could if you want. I wasn't planning it."

"I want to go!" Maria said.

She shrugged. "It's not so great a neighborhood."

"But maybe you could show me some of the places you told me about." I took her hand.

"Sure," Dolores said. "But I don't want to stop and talk to anybody."

We headed south for thirty blocks and then we were in her old neighborhood and I looked carefully at the cramped row homes and hulking apartment houses. I remembered the address from Hector's personnel file; perhaps Dolores's son was there this very minute. I pictured him as a sturdy, plump six-year-old, with Dolores's eyes and face. Then I remembered that Hector would still be at work, which meant, I guessed, that the boy was at a friend's house or in the park or still at school. If Dolores and Hector eventually divorced, it seemed likely that she would get custody of her son, given the fact that judges don't like to break up siblings. And that might mean the boy would come to live with me. In fact, if Dolores and I were together, then my affluence would be a factor the judge might consider when considering Dolores's ability to care for the boy. This had never occurred to me before.

"This is the place I used to buy vegetables," Dolores said, pointing out the window, "and that, that's where we used to buy candles and incense. This coming up is our old street."

"I'll turn down it."

"Okay, but I don't want to stop. Maria, don't wave to anybody."

I made a sharp turn and, reading the street numbers, slowed down in front of a crummy walk-up, five stories high, with cracked stonework in the front, and cheap window guards bought in a hardware store in some of the windows, and laundry hung out on the little balconies. I braked to a stop.

"And this," I said, a little too abruptly, "is where you used to live?"

I looked at her expectantly.

"How did you know about this?" Dolores demanded. "How did you know about this place?" she repeated, a strain of urgency in her voice.

"That's not the question, Dolores."

"What *is* the question?" she replied defiantly, and her defensiveness angered me.

"The *question*, dammit, is why you didn't tell me you have a son."

She stared at me in shock, and then slumped down in her seat, her eyes filling with tears. She turned her head away from me. I worried that she might grab Maria and jump out of the car, so I eased it down the street, back into traffic for a minute, and then back onto Fourth Avenue, back the way we had come. "Dolores, the company I work for is very, very large," I finally said. "It has divisions, many divisions. Companies that it owns."

"So?" she said from behind her hand.

"So you already know we own Big Apple Cable, where Hector works during the week. You see, in effect, he and I work for the same gigantic company, except that we are in very different places in it."

"I got *that*."

"I'm high enough up that I can get information about all the various parts of the corporation. Including Big Apple."

She said nothing.

"Not too long ago, I requested that I be sent your husband's employee file."

She looked at me, cheeks wet, her face frozen. And then she came at me with her fists.

"That's totally wrong!"

I caught her with my right arm, held her. "Yes. Yes, it was wrong. I shouldn't have done it but I did. In that file was the usual stuff but also in it was the information that you and Hector have a son, Dolores. I know about your son, Dolores. I can tell you the day he was born."

Sometime, in another life, I will learn about the physiology of the veins in the head, and then I will understand how it was that three of them pulsed suddenly in Dolores's forehead at that moment, even as her lips quivered and she stared at me with great wet angry eyes. But I was angry too.

"Your son, Dolores, *your son*," I pressed. "Where is he?"

♦ ♦ ♦

Dolores was silent on the way back, curled away from me in the car seat, staring dully out the window. When we returned to Park Slope, I pulled the car over and suggested we sit out in the garden, where Maria could play by herself in a new sandbox I'd bought her. Dolores nodded her head tearfully and we marched back to the yard, where Dolores found her wallet in a bag, and slipped out a small color photgraph. She contemplated it. Then without bothering to meet my eyes, she handed it to me.

It was a picture of the three of them, Dolores, Hector, and little Hector, taken when the boy was about two, I guessed. And that would be four and a half years prior. The intervening time had aged her noticeably. In the photo, Dolores seemed to be almost a different person, with that sort of bright healthy juiciness only young women possess. Her eyes were happy and her smile more animated than I'd ever seen it. And Hector himself seemed more robust, more confident than when I'd seen him, his dark hair shiny as glass, one hand on his wife's shoulder as she sat in the photographer's studio chair, the other casual by his side. And in Dolores's lap was little Hector, a small dark-eyed prince of a boy, obviously cleaned and scrubbed down to his nails for the photo session, looking stiff in his collar shirt and cute little fake tie, and staring into the camera with the unknowing, open-eyed wonder of a child, his little lips fat and red. I remembered Maria's age and did a little rough figuring. "Were you pregnant when this was taken?"

Dolores looked startled for a moment, then said, sadly, "Yes." Like about three months."

I handed the photo back to Dolores and she slipped it back into her wallet. "I want you to understand two things. It was an accident, but it wasn't an accident. I mean, it happened because of Hector and me. It—" She looked at me. "I want to explain it to you so that you will see why it is so hard for Hector, for *us*. We're caught by it, you know? We can't forget it."

◆ ◆ ◆

There is something self-evidently false about focusing on particular instants of a life, as opposed to the confluence of patterns that causes events to transpire, but one must find a beginning somewhere when talking about the past. So, too, with Dolores. She recalled for me the moment she knew she was pregnant with little Hector, a tickling twinge in her breasts not long after her period was late. She returned home from the doctor's office—a cheap clinic full of Indian doctors with thick accents who couldn't get work elsewhere, she said dismissively—with a sense of dread, because her own mother had died as a result of childbirth and because she didn't know if Hector would be happy about the news, or if he would believe or admit the child was his. "We weren't even married," Dolores said, "and he hadn't said anything. He did get me a little ring but that didn't mean anything. So I got home and waited for him to come off work. And he got home and was tired and I took a breath and said I got to tell you something and then I just said it all at once and—this was so surprising, he was very happy and started to kiss my stomach. He said he loved the baby and we would get married real fast. So we did, which I already told you about, and we had a big wedding, like I said already—did I say how much it cost? I think it was something like five thousand dollars and I really didn't want to spend it, but Hector, he said he was going to make us rich, he was going to go into business and not to worry. He always wanted to be rich, throw money out the window to people. So he spent all of his savings and some of the money he got from the army for his hand—oh, he was in the army for about two weeks and got stabbed in the hand and so they used to send him money for it. And I think he borrowed the rest. He looked good in his tux. Everybody looked good."

After the wedding, which was attended by the melancholy pair of aging aunts, both with swollen ankles and propped up and strapped in wheelchairs, neither of whom trusted Hector's glib boasts, the young couple shot by limousine to Atlantic City. "It had this little wall that went up between the driver and the people in the seats, and the driver told us he would be shutting it and that he would open it again when we got to Atlantic City."

"So you screwed in the seat of the limo as it was driving."

"Of course!" She smiled.

Then came the months of pregnancy and birth, which was difficult, Dolores said, not only because the Indian doctor whom she didn't trust used forceps but because it was her first labor and the little boy's head was swollen and conical from the pressure to get through her pelvis. He turned yellow with jaundice, as is common with newborns, and was kept under special lights at the hospital for four days while his liver began to work on its own. The baby had to have a tiny blindfold fitted snugly over his eyes, or else the intense lights could damage them. "The nurses were not any good. They had too many babies to look after, so I stayed up, like, three days in a row to be sure that the blindfold didn't fall off. Hector had to work the whole time. Of course the baby, he pulled the blindfold off all the time, he hated being on his back under the lights, but I just sat there and pulled it back on."

Eventually the baby was well enough to go home, said Dolores, and the three of them settled into the life of young parents—the life I'd missed by three bullets. Dolores read as much as she could about being a good mother, for she didn't trust her aunts, and, besides, she wanted to raise her son as an American, not half and half as she had been raised, Dominican Spanish at home, New York street Spanish outside, too little English, her half-literate aunts burning scents in her room at night sometimes and mixing smelly potions on the stove and pouring them into glass jars, praying in Spanish for their dead father, who had been buried in the sandy soil of Santo Domingo thirty years prior. No, none of that for her, thank you. Her child was born in December of 1985, and Dolores's aunts and father, living the first thirty years of their lives in Santo Domingo, had been born, in a sense, in the previous century. So she took Dr. Benjamin Spock's famous book out of the Sunset Park branch of the Brooklyn Public Library, and plowed through it, all five hundred–odd pages of it, with a dictionary next to her to use when necessary. Their little boy was slender, more like his father, with skinny shoulders and chest. His lashes were long and the corners of his eyes were perpetually wet. As her firstborn, she indulged him, letting him sleep with her in bed with her in the mornings after Hector had gone to work. On good days she pushed him in a stroller up to Sunset Park to meet with the other young women with children, sitting on benches and talking about all the important matters of life: children, husbands, mothers, money. The park was perfectly situated upon one of the highest hills of Brooklyn and afforded a magnificent, distant view of the blue-gray skyline of Manhattan and the white world of power and influence wholly impregnable to the aspirations of a *mujer* such as Dolores

Salcines. But no matter. Hector was bringing in just enough money, and having a son filled her. Her boy—*her boy!*—grew, he took his first chubby bowlegged steps, he cooed, he began to speak. He kicked off his shoes and threw his food on the floor and didn't want to go to bed. He suffered from diaper rash and ear infections and sudden fevers and strange blotches on his skin that came and went. He told his dad to "be the funny horse!" and rode around on his back. He learned to count to ten and to sing "The Farmer in the Dell" and ride a tricycle. Dolores wished that her father had lived long enough to see his grandson. If she could have anything, it would be that.

And then she was pregnant *again,* happily so—though it was no surprise, because after little Hector's birth, sex with Hector had gotten better. Somehow having had a baby had been the final loss of corporeal innocence; the blood and the pain and frank animalness of it had changed her. She became aroused more quickly and came so easily now, without trying. She'd heard other young mothers talk about this. And now that she was pregnant again, this time she knew enough to get her rest and take her vitamins. It was a good pregnancy, even chasing after her little boy. Hector was tense, worrying about the money. They argued sometimes. When she was almost due, he said he would find a better job, maybe check out the company that was doing all the cable-TV installations in the neighborhood. He knew one of the guys who did the wire work. The company, Hector had been told, would probably be hiring sometime in the next six months. But Dolores was not thinking about these things; she was feeling her body reach its ultimate weight, her breath short, her ankles swollen. The baby was going to be big. Her water broke on a Sunday and the delivery was quick and uneventful. Hector coached her as best he could during the labor, and when the baby was out and clearly a healthy girl, he cut the umbilicus with the surgical scissors the nurse handed him. Now we have a son and a daughter, he said to Dolores, his eyes bright.

"We were always so happy then," Dolores remembered. "Hector, he believed in everything, he believed he could make a better life for us, you know? And I told you what happened to his flooring store before Maria was born, the way they stole everything? I mean, we were happy, we were very happy about our kids, but . . . I don't know.

Things started to happen. Hector finally got the cable job after Maria was born, but it wasn't so great and so he had to start selling cars. He wasn't around enough. I used to get angry and sometime he would just go out at night. He was trying to make enough money. Maybe he was getting tired of it, you know? Things started to happen . . . it's hard to explain. We kind of fought. But things happened you would never expect. This isn't about my son yet. First I have to tell you about what happened on the train."

They were on the R train headed south toward Sunset Park one Saturday afternoon in July, Dolores explained, and Hector had a copy of the *Daily News* pulled up to his nose. They'd seen a movie, picked up some groceries. Little Hector and Maria were with a baby-sitter. Dolores watched her husband page through the sports section. He was a smart man but a slow reader and this sometimes irritated her. She read everything quickly, and always held great pride in this ability. Hector was also illiterate in Spanish. But she knew he loved to read about the Yankees, he was always talking about how ballplayers worked only a couple of hours a day for *millions*. She waited for him to glance up and see her. The subway pulled into the Union Street station. Something was different outside the windows of the train and immediately the riders picked up on it, as they do; then it was clear—there was yelling outside the train. Perhaps a gang—that was always the danger—and who knew where they were on the platform? Hector put his paper down and his eyes met Dolores's. The train stopped and the doors opened, without the conductor's usual announcement. They could leave the train or stay. They heard more shouts. And then suddenly cops started running into the car, ten, maybe fifteen, huge men in blue, their chests thickened by bulletproof vests, the black leather belts heavy with nightsticks and flashlights, bullets and citation pads, and of course guns—working their way down the car, looking at everyone in it, skipping past Dolores and the other women and the few white guys, concentrating on anybody who was black or Hispanic and young—Hector, no doubt, felt the sudden, chill fear of the innocent. When the cops came to him—they seemed to believe they had *spotted* him—one of them said, "He's got a red shirt. Let's see how tall he is."

"Get up," a young cop with a thick neck ordered. "Who are you? Got some ID?"

Hector produced his wallet, which was thin, almost no money in it. Dolores felt the condemning looks of the other passengers.

"What stop you get on at?" another cop said. The radio on his hip squawked.

"We got on at DeKalb Avenue."

"Bullshit," the cop said. "You're lying."

"It's true," Dolores protested. "He's my husband."

"I'm not lying, man." Hector wrapped his fingers around the pole that standing subway riders hang on to. Next to the cop he was smaller, powerless. "We were downtown, shopping."

They barely glanced at Dolores.

"Get off the train." The young cop put his hand on Hector's arm. "Get off the train and answer some questions."

"I didn't *do* anything! Ask my wife. Ask these people," Hector said louder, sweeping his arm toward all the passengers. "Ask them, ask any of them, I got on at DeKalb."

"It's true, officer," Dolores pleaded.

"That right? Anybody see this man get on there?"

The other riders stared balefully, stupefied idiots. No one answered. They could see the cops were agitated.

"Hey, man," Hector protested, "I been on this train for twenty minutes. I ain't getting off the fuckin'—"

The nightstick hit Hector's fingers. The police grabbed him by both arms and pulled him out, knocking over the bag of groceries between his feet. On the platform, they pulled him up against a tiled wall. Dolores quickly carried the grocery bag out to the platform. The men surrounded Hector except for one, who faced her, barring her from getting closer.

"Spread your feet wider than your shoulders, bend at the waist, hands on the wall, head down."

"I didn't do—"

"Head down!" The cops searched him, one of them shoving a nightstick deeply into his ass. Then the stick went around his neck. "Where's the fucking gun? You threw it away, you asshole, you thought you could waste a cop and then just get on the subway, right? Where's the gun?"

"I didn't do nothin'!" he screamed. The sound echoed down the platform, and other riders watched impassively through the scratched windows of the train. "Nothin'!"

"He didn't do anything," Dolores cried. "He's my husband—"

"You know what happens to cop killers, asshole," one of the policemen said, his voice thick with menace and his breath hot against his ear. "Where's the gun!"

Hector screamed. "I didn't do it! You got the wrong guy!"

The nightstick came up between his legs.

Hector gave a sickening cough of pain. They were hitting him. Dolores could see that one of the men had a hand to Hector's neck.

"Come on, asshole, give it up—"

"The slip!" she cried. "You stupid men! The slip! Look at the slip!"

The policemen were stunned for a moment.

"The slip from the store. It's in his front pocket."

"Hold it, Tommy," one of the older cops said. "Check his pocket." They pulled out a few dollars and change and the crumpled receipt that showed on it the amount of the purchase, the time, and the address of the grocery.

"What stop did you say?"

"DeKalb."

"The store is up there around the corner, Sergeant," one of the men said, checking the street number on the receipt.

"All right, give me the amount," the cop questioned Hector. "What was it?"

"Like eight dollars, man," he hollered, his lips an inch from the wall. "I got milk and bananas and bread—"

"Show me that bag of groceries, lady."

They pawed through the bag, ripping it, checking the contents.

"We bought some beans, soup cans—"

"All right, shut up," the cop said. "This paper says the time was one-fourteen. When was Dougherty shot?"

One of them radioed. The answer was about one-fifteen. It was impossible to buy groceries and blocks away simultaneously kill a cop aboveground in Brooklyn. "Let him go," the older policeman said, and then shoved him away, hard enough so that Hector couldn't see the face of the man who had been holding him. Dolores rushed to hold him, putting her arms around his ribs. His shirt was damp with sweat and she felt the quick rise and fall of his chest. The pack of policemen continued down the platform, walking quickly, listening to the radio, their footfalls heavy, determined, already unmindful of Hector, as if he had never existed.

"When we got home he got angry about things," Dolores continued, "about how everything worked, you know, the system, the cops and everything. Everything was so frustrating. The money was tight, you know, and he didn't want to think about it. And the new baby made the apartment smaller and needed things. And Hector was getting tired of working and getting nothing. My father was like that at the piano factory, you know. I understand that. He had these dreams that weren't coming true, right? He and these other guys would go to all the bars, sometimes."

That same evening was hot, Dolores said, with the neighborhood parents standing around on the sidewalks, the younger women in spandex tops, the older ones in loose cotton dresses, the men in T-shirts or shirtless, if they weren't too fat. She held Maria, who had just turned one, in her arms while little Hector played with the other children. Somebody put a boom box on the top of his car and ran it off the battery while he washed the wheels. Dolores and Hector's street was relatively quiet; the drug traffic was a couple of blocks in one direction and the stores in another. Hector stood down near the corner, sucking down a bottle in a paper bag, shooting the shit with his hombres. She could hear him telling the story again about the cops, showing where they held his head down. About how the cops are always killing men and then saying that they died accidentally. Or provoked their own deaths. He was nervy and loud, wanting revenge, drinking too much this early in the evening. Yet Hector had to drink, Dolores realized; it was the only way to let the incident with the cops slip away. She hoped Hector would drink enough to relax, not so much that he would get wild. The men laughed and punched each other. They looked okay. Hector was going to be okay. Dolores turned her attention to her son. One of the guys on the street had a long-handled fifty-pound wrench and had opened a hydrant—the police didn't care, as long as you closed it up later. Little Hector, just three and a half, and the other children splashed in and out of the spray that arced into the middle of the street, their damp feet slapping the asphalt and their voices crying in excitement, running in and out of the water while their fathers and mothers kept an eye on them. A summer evening in a poor neighborhood. Dolores talked with Ruita, one of her friends, and kept Maria bouncing on her knee. The men, still drinking and boxing and weaving a little for fun, tapping each other with light punches, were onto a new topic now, complained loudly about what assholes their bosses were and how they made them work too hard, and that became which women they would like to fuck, which movie or television stars looked particularly hot, maybe that girl on "The Cosby Show," Lisa Bonet, Mickey Rourke did it to her in that movie and the scene, it was so hot they had to cut it out, *just give it to her hard, man,* and they all smiled sagely at the many ways of fucking women—*you know, man, like they want it,* and the talk went on like this, with the fathers among them casting an occasional, domesticated glance up the street to see if their wives were watching their children. And Hector, no doubt, enjoyed the talk, the way it set him apart from his family—even though he loved his wife and kids—and the way his head felt light from the second big bottle of beer. With the future uncertain, with not enough money, the pleasure of a summer evening was redemptive. Dolores finally went inside to put the children to sleep and called several times for Hector to come inside. But he yelled up to the apartment window that he was going to go out with the boys.

"And this pissed me off, because it's hot as hell and *of course* I'm doing all the work with the baby just like always and Hector is just going to fuck around. I mean, I understood that he had to get it out of his system, what happened with the cops and all, but I was like, is this my life? Is this the rest of my life? Maybe I was thinking about that all along. I can't remember every little thing. It was three years ago almost. We had this little apartment up on the third floor. It looked out over the courtyard. I was tired of that too, you had to walk up every time and there was always a lotta noise from the street that came in the window, kids smoking and messing around."

Maria was a heavy sleeper now that she was eating solid foods, and she dropped off quickly. The crib was in the living room because there was no other place for it. Maria would sleep through the night easily and be soaked in the morning.

But little Hector was another matter. A poor sleeper, nervous and angry at his new sibling. Dolores sat in his small room, next to theirs, and sang to him. Finally he dropped off. It was not until much later that Hector came home, smelling of beer. She was tired of sitting in their sweltering apartment. The air conditioner didn't work, she'd opened all the windows. Hector rolled a little as he walked, and she was angry at him, hated him for his freedom, which depended upon her labor with the baby, his domination of her. And she wondered if he'd cheated on her that night. He seemed mysteriously pleased with himself and she knew about the *puta* trash that hung out at the bar on Forty-eighth Street. With the music playing all the time. Some of the girls, the crackheads, would troll through the bar, cadging drinks and looking for men who wanted sex. They were not quite whores, not exactly. Some even had regular jobs. She knew how men could be flattered. She asked him where he'd been.

"Out with Louie and Petito."

"What'd you do?"

"Just talk and shit, Dolores."

She didn't believe it. Both men were single and would lie to cover Hector's story. Both men were no good, as far as she could see.

"You go to that bar down on Forty-eighth Street?"

"Maybe."

"What'd you do there?"

"Well, first I took all our money out of the bank and I bought everybody fifty drinks each, Dolores, and then I fucked each one of the waitresses until they, like, started to have, like, some kind of *religious* experience, Dolores, and then—"

So she and Hector got into it from there, Hector alternating between righteousness and conceit inspired by his wife's jealousy. Teasing her. Little Hector woke up and cried. He was old enough to get out of bed and run around the apartment in his blue cotton pajamas. But now yelling scared him.

"Get back to bed," Hector told him.

"Don't yell at him."

"I want some juicee," the boy asked.

"Let's get in bed," Dolores said.

"I need some juicee."

"Get back to bed!" Hector roared. And the boy crawled back, snuffling. Dolores shut his door.

"Maybe I did," Hector said when she accused him again. "Maybe I need something I don't get here."

She didn't know if this was a taunt or a confession. She knew how frustrated he was, trying to make money, and she knew that a few beers at the bar generally relaxed him and that he may have only considered fucking one of the bar *putas*, that accounting for his guilty behavior. Or maybe he really did do that. She was hot and angry. There was only one way to tell, she knew.

"Yes or no, did you do it?"

Hector said no.

"Then prove it. Prove it now."

"I don't need to prove it, bitch. I can walk out that door and prove it to somebody who wants it."

"Prove it."

Staring with hateful lust at each other, they stripped. She was testing him. If he was quickly erect, anxious to get in, with quickening, tight breath, she would know he hadn't just had sex. If he was slower to get an erection or labored in his effort to ejaculate, she would know. And it wouldn't be the beer. Hector never had any trouble with beer. She would *know*. She was his wife, she had been fucked by him a thousand times. He couldn't fool her.

So, still angry, they fell into bed, tearing at each other, pushing, making it a little rough, then actually rough, with her hitting him as hard as she could, and him holding her down after she made his nose leak blood. *Dimelo mami, dimelo*, he said, give it to me. *Más, más, oh fuck me más* . . . They didn't care what kind of noise they made, screaming, cursing, and then when it was clear to Dolores that he hadn't been with another woman, her anger metamorphosed to a purer lust, for she had won him from the bar *putas*, with their crotch tricks (she'd heard some of them could pick up coins off a table edge with their cunts, that they yanked up their bikini bottoms and bent over to show the little puckered mouth of their assholes pursing and winking, teasingly even slipped the first inch of beer bottles up into themselves) and she was who he wanted and he was hard as stone in her fingers and mouth and insides, irrefutable proof of his fidelity, and she did not care that he was still angry with her, fucking her with backbreaking vengeance, making a lamp go over, making little Hector scream from his bed, and the upstairs neighbors pound the ceiling above her. A fragment from the Bible in English: "O Lord God, You have begun to show Your servant Your greatness and Your mighty hand . . ." It was not so much lust for her husband but for how he made her feel. *Who cares what they think, little Hector'll fall sleep soon, fuck the people upstairs, I'm gonna forget everything . . .* The minutes passed and she rocked in Hector's anger, knowing that he was not fucking her but at the world *through* her, at the motherfuckers who had the money and at people who had rendered him so inconsequential. At the asshole racist cops. So be it, *dimelo*, that was where the power was in Hector. She loved that power, yes, she did, truly. Her head and neck hung off the bed, her arms limp over her head, Hector pounding her, pounding her, muttering viciously at her, the bones of his pelvis hitting her, the end of his penis jamming in hard, making a little pain, the fine gold chain of her crucifix fallen across her lips, her tongue tasting the small links, her mind a blurring hallucination of church spires and the heavy sweet face of her father and a faceless black man she had seen on the subway months ago, a man with shoulders the size of Georgia cantaloupes, and the lifting of the gulls from the garbage near the *supermercado*, pounding her, pounding her, the gray gulls that flew into the city from the ocean, from the Narrows, near where all the old-timer Italians lived, lifting at once, a thousand of them, wheeling across a brooding low sky, over and under the elevated F train, higher, the dark shapes of the ferries plowing through the river, and far across the water New Jersey, a wedge of salmon sky to the west, and the old dreams of the millions of new Americans, the sadness of it, the Chinese women working themselves to the bone along Eighth Avenue in Brooklyn's garment sweatshops, occasionally having their fingers skewered by the thick stitching needle of the industrial sewing machines, and the young men like Hector pounding their youth into the hard cement streets, and the old Hasid in the park throwing the ball briskly to his son and the four dead black boys in front of the nightclub, yards of sidewalk slick with blood, she'd seen that once, and the lost, cataclysmic pain of the birth of her son, his birth had been much harder, and the smooth face of the priest when he saw her once on the street, his eyebrow lifted in recognition of her, and *oh, más, más, más*, in the small hot apartment in the vast choked Brooklyn night, she wrested pleasure and oblivion . . .

And then there was the silence, their hearts heaving in the sweaty pallor of exhaustion, her insides stewed, stinging, juiced, her lips mashed by Hector's face, her skin charred from his beard. Then came the pounding on the door, voices insistent with emergency. Her son. *Her son?* She leapt from the damp sheets and rushed naked to his small room next to theirs. He was not there. How could that be? And she heard the voices on the street below, coming through the window. And she knew before looking that little Hector had been so terrorized by his parents' brutal lust that he had sought escape onto the ledge of chipped brownstone by his window, where, while she always kept a watchful eye, he often played in the sun. But how far was three stories? Now Hector yanked on some underwear and was out the apartment door, flying down the stairs. She peered over the ledge to see the teenagers circled around the small figure of her son—she recognized the blue of his pajamas—and then she saw her husband push through them and fall to the ground; gathering the limp form into his arms, Hector peered upward, and by the streetlight she could see the wet torment in his face. *Dios mio. Dios mio.*

♦ ♦ ♦

Dolores pressed her fingers hard against her forehead, as if her face was made of soft clay that she could remodel into one less furrowed by grief. Then, through the bars of her fingers, she looked at Maria playing quietly in the sandbox on the other side of the yard and called, "*Mi'ja*, go get my purse."

The child obediently ran inside the house and a moment later came out, holding the purse with both hands.

"I want you to play by yourself one more minute, sweetheart," Dolores said firmly, taking the purse.

"Why is Mommy crying?"

"Because I'm sad about something."

"Why?" answered Maria with a small pout, running her finger along the cast-iron ivy vine of Dolores's chair.

"Because sometimes things are very sad."

"Why?" came the plaintive voice, wanting to know of the adult things being discussed.

"Jack and I have to talk about something now, *mi'ja*."

"Why?"

"Please, Maria."

The child wandered obediently toward the flowers, and when it was clear that her daughter's attention was diverted, Dolores drew from the purse a thick sheaf of odd-sized papers held together by several rubber bands. "She doesn't remember her brother. She was only a year old," Dolores noted sadly. She pulled off the bands and quietly paged through the papers until she drew out what looked like a worn pamphlet. She opened it and considered its contents, then quietly handed it to me. "I don't know why I kept this, but I did."

The pamphlet, printed under the name of James McGaffey & Son, Inc., Funeral Directors, of Fifth Avenue, Brooklyn, was a general price list for the services to the dead. The prices "include the local transfer of remains to the funeral home, staff services, securing of necessary authorizations, basic local transportation to the crematory or cemetery . . ." I looked up at Dolores, then back at the pamphlet, skimming the words in sickened recognition at the costly procedures of attending to the dead. I had studied much the same document when choosing Liz's burial arrangements: "If you want to arrange a direct cremation, you may use an unfinished wooden box or an alternative container. Alternative containers can be made of heavy material, pressed wood or composition materials, or may be pouches of canvas or other materials." And there followed the many prices for the various services, and a few of these had small check marks next to them in pencil, no doubt made by Dolores: "Embalming (including use of the preparation room): $450.00" and "Embalming of autopsied remains: $490.00"; "Topical disinfection: $375.00"; "Dressing and Casketing: $90.00" and "Cosmetology: $45.00"; "Surgical restoration: $52.00"; and "Crucifix: $75.00."

I handed the pamphlet back.

"We buried him in Greenwood Cemetery," Dolores whispered.

"I used to think it was nice, with all those big maple trees, but then you see on Twenty-fifth Street that's where all the stripped cars get left. And people just dump their garbage there, you know, old washing machines and broken televisions and stuff. Mattresses and stuff. I don't want that for my little Hector. If I could do *anything* I would take him to the little place where my father is buried in the Dominican Republic, a very tiny church in the town where my father was born, it's the most beautiful graveyard I ever saw, where they got flowers growing on the fence and you can smell the sea. I wanted him to be safe, next to my father, not jammed in with a fucking million other people."

"So," I ventured carefully, "that night you went out to the cemetery it was your son's grave you were visiting, not your father's?"

Dolores looked at me and I forgave her deception. She nodded. "Yes, Jack."

We sat there in the late light of the day and heard the scrape of a fork on china and laughter tinkling across the space of the other yards. An early summer dinner party perhaps, several houses down, the polite and witty chatter that had echoed along the back walls of these Victorian brownstones for more than a hundred years. The voices rose and fell. They were discussing national politics, the latest movies, the delicacies of a certain new restaurant on the West Side. Maria was kneeling at the edge of the garden, watching a bee crawl into the pink, scalloped trumpet of a petunia. The sun burned low on the brick walls and through the season's first purple morning glory blossoms along the fence. Dolores folded the papers back into her purse. She leaned forward and I saw great exhaustion in her eyes. She took my hand with a strong grip.

"You see why I couldn't tell you everything real fast, Jack? It would have been too much. Honestly, I just couldn't tell you because it's so sad for me, it was the thing that made it bad between us forever and it wasn't even Hector's fault . . . and after little Hector got killed Hector was so protective, he used to yell at me to be careful with Maria, when she was in the stroller, when we were crossing the street, every little thing. He was so upset about what happened to Hector that he got so, you know, unreasonable. We used to go to St.

Michael's on Fifth Avenue, that's where everybody who goes to mass in the neighborhood goes. Hector always said it looked like the plaster ceiling was going to come down but I liked it, it was very big. But I think he confessed to Father Baptiste how our son died, and he must have said something that changed Hector. I asked him what did Father Baptiste say but he never told me. I'm *sure* he told the priest. It didn't bother me, because it's between Hector and God. He needed to tell it."

She nodded to herself and watched Maria lifting a scoop of sand into the air. "After that, Hector was so serious when we went to confession. He polished his shoes. And he would stay in the booth a long time and people began to look at me, like, what is your husband doing in there, what did he *do* so he's gotta be in the booth so long? I knew he was telling the priest, I knew he said everything, about how he had sex so loud that it scared our little boy. And I think Father Baptiste said something to Hector about protecting Maria, maybe that God would not forgive him the death of two children at his own hand. That because of little Hector, we must be *vigilant*. Me, I didn't say anything about it to Father Baptiste when I went inside, for months, even after Maria was born. I was too afraid about what he would say, you know, that he would open the door and yell to everyone that I was a sex maniac and had killed my son. And I just knew that Father Baptiste was waiting for me, every Sunday I said all my little sins and he told me how many rosaries and then asked me if that was all, if there was anything *else* I wished to confess and I almost said it but Maria was making a little bit of noise and was hungry so I said no. I guess that's just an excuse.

"But Hector was so serious and used to tell me to watch out for drug dealers because they were all over the neighborhood, these guys who were very tough, and watch out for *everybody*. Some guys had got beat up real bad around the corner, one of them got a screwdriver in the liver somebody said, and people's cars were getting stolen and all the usual stuff. The lady next door got broken into and they stole her VCR and television. Hector went to the hardware store and bought one of those peep holes and drilled a hole in our front door and put it in. And he said that little Hector's death was a test and he had failed it and that sooner or later another test would come. He never said what the test would be but he said that when it came he was going to be ready. He said God watched us all and I guess I agree with that, because that's what we're always taught, but I wondered what happened to the old happy Hector, like where was he? Now everything was so serious. If I did anything, like I forgot to look at the light before it changed, he got so angry with me, squeezing my arm hard and pulling me back and saying that he didn't want Maria killed just like her brother just because . . . and he always meant it was my fault, you know. And he wanted to have another baby, another son."

"That's understandable," I said. "I'd want to do that."

Dolores smiled sadly. "We did it all the time, every night just about, and I didn't get pregnant. I don't know why. Maybe I was too worried. And we did it at the right time of the month and all.

"And — he used to fuck me with a sort of — he was *quiet* now, sometimes he'd *pray* before . . . before, he used to make a lot of noise and sweat and swear and tell me I was a good lay and stick his tongue in my ear but now it was just, like, climb on and do it and wait to get pregnant. I couldn't even tell if he *liked* it. I mean he was, you know, he had no trouble getting an erection but he always . . . I think he still loved me but — but he didn't care so much about getting rich but now he hated people who were rich because they stole from the poor. He had these ideas from the Bible . . . he still went to work and everything, Hector never missed work putting in the cable everywhere and selling cars. He could still mess around and make people laugh, you know out on the street with his old friends and everybody, but inside he was different.

"And I started doing some things . . . I liked this guy, Sal, who was the super's son, younger, you know, maybe twenty-one or -two and he used to come around after lunch when Maria was down for her nap. We started messing around a little bit, and then it got sort of regular. I made him use rubbers because I was trying to get pregnant with Hector. I couldn't, like, have a diaphragm lying around. I always took a shower and told Sal to leave right away. Maybe just once a week. I felt so bad about it but I just, I had to feel like — all of me was still there. Sal didn't tell anybody, he was very smart because he'd seen

Hector, he knew Hector was so jealous. I didn't even like Sal so much. He was just sweet and sort of young . . . I had to actually, like, teach him some things in bed. He reminded me of when Hector was younger, he didn't even have much hair on his chest or stomach. He was very glad, you know, like a boy. He made me feel good. But I knew it was wrong. I told Ruita what I was doing and she told me I had to get out of the marriage . . . she said she'd give me the money to get out if that was what I wanted to do. She said everybody in the building was talking about Hector, like they expected him to do something weird like jump off a roof or something. She said sooner or later something would go wrong and Hector would find out about Sal and then he would kill me or Sal or the baby or somebody. He hated his job with the cable. But there wasn't any other work. And I felt bad I was taking his money and sleeping with Sal."

Dolores inspected her hands, as if her guilt were stained on them. "But I was trying. Hector said he wanted to go to St. Patrick's in Manhattan and pray for little Hector and I said okay and I left the baby with Ruita and we did it, the place is so so big and you have all the tourists there and I thought that maybe Hector would feel better and it seemed like he did, he seemed like himself a little bit more, but after that, he was just depressed. He got older, I used to look at him when he didn't know it and I could see his eyes were older. You know, sadder. And he started to drink more, he didn't just drink on Sunday when all the guys watched football. One night he came home real late and smelled real bad and I asked him where he'd been and he told me he went up to the top of the Empire State Building and just stood up there. And I knew he'd been drinking up there and that scared me bad. I knew he was thinking about killing himself. I just sort of knew. Up there real high with the lights of the city and I remember how windy it gets and it means he was thinking . . . he never came out and said it . . .

"One night I was by myself for once, and I passed by a restaurant window, a coffee shop really, and I saw this woman sitting there in the booth, by herself. She was about my age, maybe twenty-eight, and she was smoking a cigarette and seemed, like, at peace. Like after mass, when you just sit there by yourself. Like she just knew who she was and what she was doing and wasn't in a rush. And it wasn't like she was rich, like she had a lot of money, right? She just was herself, all herself and I stared at her. I stopped at the window and it was like I was looking at what I wanted to be.

"And so I decided that night I would tell Hector I was leaving. I would tell him it wasn't his fault but I had to go. We were done. I loved him so much but we were done. I figured I could borrow a couple of thousand from Ruita. She understood, like I said. I knew I had to go somewhere Hector couldn't find me. I didn't want him to find me, I wanted it to be so that he could maybe forget, and feel better after enough time went by. It couldn't be in Sunset Park. And even though Brooklyn is cheaper than Manhattan I was afraid he would find me in Brooklyn. And I never went to Queens really. I just got that feeling. I figured I'd just find a job doing something. I mean, even though the economy is bad, I could do something and make it. I didn't need anything as long as I had everything for Maria. All I wanted was for her to have a chance for a better life. I didn't want her to have Hector for a father. She loved him but she didn't know anything. Something was dead in him, you know? He had no pride. My father had pride, even though he was a working man. He wore a clean shirt every day, he had no debts, he lived clean. I wanted Maria to have a father like that. Hector was . . . his spirit was, like, *dying.* He was getting so strange, so angry and ridiculous. Did I say that he went to mass on Sundays twice?

"So I was going to tell him that night. But I didn't. He came home and had worked all day and was tired and ate dinner and fell asleep. Then I realized that if I told him we'd just have a big fight. And he would try to stop me, so I didn't tell him. He went to work the next day, just like usual and I packed two big suitcases and took Maria in the stroller to the subway, the B train. I didn't even leave him a note. Maybe I didn't believe I was going to do it. But then I *was* doing it, it was happening, we were actually leaving and I had all my papers with me, everything important like Maria's birth certificate, I got that in my purse, too, and I had the money from Ruita, she gave it to me, like I said she would, and as soon as I got on the train I felt better, like I was moving again, like I was going to make it, the old me coming back. I knew Maria was going to miss her daddy but that she would get over it. She was still young enough. I had some good clothes and some makeup and I could look good if I needed to. I knew men would look at me. But I wasn't looking for a man, I just wanted to find a room somewhere where Hector couldn't find me and start getting a job, you know. When I got into Manhattan, some of the businessmen, like you, looked at me. One man asked me could he buy me a drink. Some older guy, in his fifties.

"I went to that hotel where you found me. I had maybe three thousand dollars and I just wanted to hide for a few days. I guess I was upset about it but I had nobody to talk to. And Maria asked me when were we going home and that—that was hard because I had to tell her that we were living away from Daddy now. I didn't call Hector at first. I knew he was going crazy and I didn't even call Ruita. I just took Maria for walks and read the newspaper and lived for a few days. And maybe about the third night I came back and my door was open and somebody had gone through the room. I had put the money in the pages of this magazine where nobody would see it but they found that. They took almost all my money and I had maybe two hundred dollars left in my pocketbook and—see, this made me think it was a woman— they took a lot of my clothes, all my good clothes and they took Maria's clothes too. I was sick. I was so upset. To take a little girl's clothes. I was so worried because I couldn't go back to Hector, not now. I had to go up to a Hundred Twenty-fifth Street in Harlem to buy some more clothes for us and I think I spent something like forty dollars. I was running out of money. Food is so expensive. I called Ruita, maybe to see if she could give me a few hundred more but Lucy her sister answered and said Hector was looking for me, that he was going crazy and asking everybody if they knew where I was. Then I knew I couldn't go back. And that night I went to the clothing store to see if I could get some shoes for Maria. I was saving a pair that little Hector used to have because I knew her feet were getting bigger and his shoes weren't worn out, babies don't wear out shoes, they outgrow them, but those shoes got stolen too. And I knew Maria's toes were rubbing inside, it was too tight, and I went to a couple of stores up there looking to buy a secondhand pair, maybe four or five dollars because the new ones, even the cheap ones, cost at least twenty dollars.

It was late and I couldn't find the right shoes and I got back on the number two train at Ninety-sixth Street and that was when you stood up and talked to me.

"I didn't know what to do. I looked at you and I guessed I figured I would take a chance. You were my chance and I would take it. I knew you liked the way I looked because you were so nervous. I was in this old coat and got maybe sixty or seventy dollars and you were in that very good suit and tie—I knew it was real silk—and came from this whole different world, you know, I could see that right away, and had a lot of money, and you were so nervous. I mean, Jack, I never thought I was going to end up living in your house or that we would go to bed together or *anything* like that! I couldn't think so far ahead. All I knew is that you stood up and gave me your card and that was something. I had *something*, I had this little card, you know? You remember I looked at you after the doors shut? I was sort of scared, I kind of knew something might happen. And that night I decided to come see you."

"What about your eye?" I interrupted.

"My eye?"

"Remember? You had a terrible black eye that you said Hector gave—"

"Oh right. Yeah. No, he didn't give it to me."

"I thought he did it."

"Yeah, I know."

"He didn't hit you?"

"I didn't even see him that night."

This amazed me. "Then how?"

Dolores looked down. "I started thinking that night about how maybe I would go see you and then I thought maybe some other businessmen might, like, you know, be interested. And when Maria was asleep I went downstairs at the hotel and I thought maybe I would just go out. There's all these little restaurants and all those people who go to the theater . . ."

"You were looking to pick up some rich guy maybe? I'd given you the idea?"

"Basically. I don't know. I didn't have any money. I didn't know what to do. I went in one or two places but they looked at my clothes and they told me to leave. So I started walking around, you know, just thinking about everything, I think I was like on Eighth Avenue, maybe Forty-fourth Street, Forty-fifth, I didn't know the neighborhood, really, and I saw some limousines and I started walking in that direction thinking maybe there was some other restaurant and then all of a sudden this big woman comes running across the street, she's got this tight little skirt, but she is big, and she comes right up to me and punches me right in the eye and starts screaming at me to get the fuck out of her 'point.' And I don't what she means, my eye hurts so much—"

"A hooker."

"Right, she was screaming at me and she pulled out this little knife and I started to run. I was so stupid to go walking there and I figured it out, that was the whole neighborhood, but I didn't know that, I never was there before, right? So I ran back to the hotel and went upstairs and I thought, oh shit, look at my eye, it was so stupid to do what I did. I didn't want to wake up Maria and I kept ice on it. I didn't know what to do. I kept looking at your little card. I put it on the table and I looked at it and I looked at it. I said to myself, 'Take the chance.' So I did. I guess I did the right thing . . . I want to live. This is the only life I got, Jack. I'm still young enough, right? A lot has happened but I'm still young enough. I can still have more children. You're a good man, you're steady and clean and I really believe you love Maria. You've known her only a little while but I believe you love her. I was watching you. I think maybe we could try it . . . if you can take me, Jack, I'll give you everything I got. I mean, I'll be good for you, I'll be good to you. And you'll have Maria. Both of us."

Dolores looked up at me with great fragile hope in her face and I thought to myself, *God has given you a gift, so don't be an asshole, don't be an idiot.* I pulled Dolores tightly in my arms.

"You got it," I whispered to her, squeezing my eyes shut and feeling a certain long-lost relief, a return to myself, a return to hope for the future. I was caught up in it, for, you see, I came from a broken family—I cannot remember ever having been in the same room with both my mother and father, and as the Chairman had told me earlier that same day, I have always wanted a whole family. I have always wanted that with terrifying longing, like I wanted breath.

When I opened my eyes, there was Maria looking at us, holding her plastic pail and shovel, not knowing what to do. I knelt down and scooped her up and held the both of them tightly in my arms, kissing Dolores and Maria back and forth, one and then the other, pressing my lips against them with reverence for their existence in the universe, and in this quiet dance, all the promises that can be made between human beings were made . . .

◆ ◆ ◆

The great German philosopher Schopenhauer wrote the following, which I read as a college student and have remembered ever since: *In early youth, as we contemplate our coming life, we are like children in a theater before the curtain is raised, sitting there in high spirits and eagerly waiting for the play to begin. It is a blessing that we do not know what is really going to happen.* These words make me think of Maria. Someday she will realize that she did not imagine the torments of adulthood. But I would add to Schopenhauer's statement. I would say that even as *adults*, studying the world, working the odds as well as we can, acting with the best part of hope and charity, we yet do not know what torments await us. We do not *know*. I was happily spinning beneath the sky with a beautiful woman and child, unmindful that I was in good health, unmindful that I was making $395,000 a year. Enough money, as I have said, to make my father wince. But I did not know what torments awaited me and, more to the point—to insert the rigid steel needle of truth into the soft marrow of happiness—*I did not know how I would torment others.* It is our crimes against others that burn most perfectly in our souls year after year. In one moment a young girl is scooped from the ground by a thirty-five-year-old man who has grown to love her as the daughter he was denied. Years from now, when Maria, grown up, is explaining her life to some young fellow, she will recall me aloud. I hope that he loves Maria with what little sense as young men may have. And while Maria tells about what later followed that moment of hope, as she recalls *what happened*—as she half remembers it, having been there when it occurred and having had it explained to her through the years or having imagined it, she will remember the wealthy man named Jack Whitman, whose house she lived in with her mother. Maria, eighteen years old or twenty or twenty-four, will have thought about *what happened* many thousands of times. Perhaps she will understand it in a way no one else could. But as she tells her story to the young man, bowing her head, then lifting her lovely dark eyes to his, her voice, now that of a young woman, will be calm. The time of tears will have long since passed. If she loves the young man and wants him to know her heart, then she will need to explain the strange set of circumstances—she will need to explain *me*, however briefly. She will recall me from the dim vault of memory in order that she may find love, and when she does this, when the apparition of memory she calls Jack Whitman appears, it will be with a certain unsolvable torment.

FIFTEEN

D awn on the day I was to get rich. A clear May morning that promised heat and leafy shade. I woke early and lay next to Dolores in the sheets with my arms behind my head letting the time pass in slow luxury. Each minute carried me inexorably toward the 9:00 A.M. meeting with the board of directors, which would be followed by the 10:00 A.M. press conference, in which the plan with Volkman-Sakura would be announced. I'd be seated next to the Chairman, close enough to follow the second hand on his watch. Beales would be sitting at his kitchen table, a man with nothing to do that day. Ha. I slipped the sheet from Dolores's shoulders to examine the clean curve of vertebrae that ran from the fine hairs in the nape of her neck between her shoulder blades down to the ripe cleft of her rear. She stirred. . . . *and now I've asked Jack Whitman—some of you have met him already—to lay out the specifics here. Jack?* I dragged my fingers across Dolores's creamy dark skin and then insinuated myself into her dreams while whispering the numbers and arguments into the air above the bed. *Perhaps the best place to begin is with a declaration, gentlemen, and that declaration would be that we are at a juncture where we either make our fate for ourselves or have it made for us by our competitors. It is time for a bold stroke. We live now in an era when gigantic segments of the world's populations are newly able to demand and pay for the products we create. At the same moment, important new technologies are expanding what it is that we call entertainment . . .* I pushed into Dolores. I'd talk for the specified twenty minutes, being sure to keep my hand movements slow and forceful and let my eyes linger on each face, the new generation explaining the future to the old. And I'd end with a brisk yet obedient nod toward the Chairman. *Thanks, Jack, that gets us going in the right direction. Now then, we may indeed see that the opportunities, especially in Eastern Europe and Russia, are impressive . . .* Dolores woke sufficiently to understand what I was doing. We said nothing, not a breath, and this continued the perfection of it. I would sit back down next to the Chairman with a sober expression that masked my elation. How different it was all going to be. *Jack*, the Chairman would say to me in a couple of weeks, *the board's compensation committee has decided that your new role with us merits a different approach to your salary* . . . And now, because greed is convertible to lust, a few fine, hardworking minutes followed, my breath hot in Dolores's ear, each exhalation florid with pornographies, the first sweet sweat of the day coming as we worked under a bright rug of sunlight, with Jack Whitman, senior vice president for corporate planning and development, fucking and thrusting his way into the certain future of a seven-figure salary and stock options in the Series D 12% Convertible Exchangeable Preferred, Dolores's dark hair fallen over her eyes and cheek, the corner of the white pillowcase caught tightly in her teeth. She, like I, was dreaming of something, but I do not know what.

♦ ♦ ♦

Afterward we heard Maria talking to her dolls in the next room, telling them in a sweet fluting voice that it was time for them to wake up and have breakfast. "Do you want eggs? Do you want cereal? Do you want bananas?" The latch of the bedroom door clicked and Maria came in, wearing only her tiny pink nightshirt and underwear. She carried five or six stuffed animals and dropped them onto the bedcovers.

"Oh, good morning!"

"Hi, sweetie," I said.

"Hi, sweetie to you!" she answered.

"Thank you."

"I'm cooking breakfast," Maria announced.

"Good," Dolores said. "Then I don't have to do it."

"No, I'm shaving!" Maria padded into the bathroom and came back to the bed with my electric battery-charged razor. "I'm shaving Jack," she said, holding the black instrument in front of me, her dark eyes wide awake. "I'm going to do it "

I presented one whiskery cheek. "Okay, but move the razor slowly."

Maria switched on the razor and held it with two tiny hands and then dragged it across my skin.

"It works!"

Dolores pulled on a robe and cinched it around her waist before heading toward the bathroom. "Maria, put some clothes on when you're done shaving Jack." She looked at me. "You're getting pretty good service this morning."

"I'm appreciative," I responded as the razor whined close to my ear. "I appreciate everything."

"Mmmn," Dolores responded, raising her chin.

Later, after breakfast, we sat out in the garden. I'd showered and dressed for work in my best, dark, summer-weight suit, lingering before the mirror, looking into my eyes to see if I was different yet. *Gentlemen, perhaps the best place to begin is with the declaration that we are at a juncture where we either make our fate for ourselves or have it made for us* . . . It was just after 8:00 A.M. The subway took thirty-five minutes minimum, and with rush hour congestion it could take ten more. *Gentlemen, we either* . . . The trip from the lobby to my office took two minutes. The first meeting was at nine. So I had a few minutes before I had to leave. . . . *make our fate* . . .

And maybe if I'd left then, things would have been different. The jets approaching LaGuardia roared overhead every forty seconds or so while I squatted down and showed Maria how to plant cucumbers, thumbing a hole in the ground, dropping in the slender white seeds and patting down the earth. Dolores sat in one of my faded beach chairs, mending a small cotton shirt of Maria's, the sun lighting her dark hair. She looked up at me. "What're you so excited about?" she asked.

"You."

"Come on."

"I am," I told her. "I'm excited about you because I think you're pretty great, in all respects, not just the *usual* ones, if you know what I mean, which you do—and I'm excited about Maria, who doesn't want me to give her kisses *ever—*"

"Never, ever, ever!" Maria cried happily as she smacked her hand on the dirt.

"—and I'm excited because we're planting cucumbers here and

they're going to *grow* all summer and we're going to watch them as they stick out their little orange flowers and Maria is going to water them every night with the hose, and that's fun, you know, and I'm excited because I have an incredibly important meeting in exactly . . . fifty-six minutes. I've got to leave now."

"All you do is go to these *meetings* all the time," Dolores complained in good humor as she looked at her sewing. "When are you going to get rich?"

I helped Maria dig in the warm earth. "Maybe soon."

Dolores lifted her eyes. I brushed some dirt from the knees of my pants and we looked at one another.

"Really?" she asked.

"There's a chance, a good chance."

"Worms!" Maria shrieked. "Look!"

A long wet night crawler contracted and wriggled in the dirt. "The ground is full of them, honey."

"Why?"

"They make everything that is rotting and dead into good earth," I said, thinking of my father. He loved worms — they did God's work.

"Okay," I told them as I glanced at my watch. "I've got to go. See you tonight. Good-bye, Maria."

"Bye!" she called.

During those minutes, we had not heard Hector break the beveled panel of glass in the outer parlor door in the front of the house, for it could not have been a terribly loud noise, especially since he probably wrapped his hand in his shirt before he broke the glass with his fist. The glass, more than one hundred years old, shattered like a thin sheet of ice, and Hector reached inside and unlocked the door. The two closed inner doors, which also concealed the sound of the breaking glass, had been left unlocked by me when I went to the front door for the newspapers. Later it was apparent that Hector had moved stealthily about the house. I think he heard us in the garden through the open windows on the parlor floor and decided to take his advantage and hurried up the stairs, looking into the bedrooms. He bounded up the next flight of stairs too, where my office was. There was a lot to see in all of those rooms, much that revealed the new life of his wife and daughter, and he could have been in the house as long as ten or fifteen minutes; I think now that what he saw influenced his mood and worked in some strange way against his rage. Depressed him, made him frantic. I had just given Dolores a quick, domestic peck on the cheek when Hector appeared at the door to the garden, panting and sweating in a heavy black coat. He was unshaven and excitable and plunged out into the sunlight of the garden.

"Finally!" he breathed loudly, taking in the sight of Maria and me. "I finally found you."

Dolores rose to her feet and held out her hand for Maria.

Hector took a couple of steps forward and looked at his wife and daughter, examined them. "This is pretty fuckin' good, Dolores, you and Maria in new clothes. I can tell you that right now. Pretty new clothes. Shoes and everything—what's that?" He pointed at the bracelet on Dolores's wrist. "I knew you was *good,* but I didn't know you was *this* good." Then he waved his hand behind him. "You know what I'm talkin' about, Dolores? I said I knew you was *good* but not like *this.* House full of computers and toys and antiques and shit." Hector's voice became bitterly sarcastic. "Not even *you* knew you was that good."

Dolores's face remained calm but she glanced at the pockets of her husband's coat, watching his hands.

"So it looks like a happy little scene here, everybody all dressed up so *nice.* Hey—" he said to me, "going to buy a car now? You're pretty slick, Whitman. Checkin' me out like that. Yeah, I figured that out. Then trying to keep my wife and kid from talking to me." He looked back at his wife. "Dolores, you know I been tryin' to talk to you for *weeks?* Did this guy tell you that? About the messages I been leavin' on some machine, long messages? Did he tell you he came to the car lot to check me out? We rode around in a car together. Did he tell you that?" Hector drilled the question at her, jabbing and cutting the air with his hands. "Did he tell you how I been trying to find you, how I been sending him letters and callin' and everything?"

Dolores looked at me with confusion. "No," she said quietly.

"I was tryin' to do that 'cause I still love you, Dolores, and I know you still love me. We're still together, baby, I can feel it. Just that your problem is you never understood love. You never really got it, you know?" he tapped his head. "You don't appreciate loyalty. I get kicked

around by about a dozen cops and so then what do you do? Couple a
months later you go out and *fuck* some of them, probably same cops
beat me up. I mean, a man's wife goes and fucks a bunch of cops and
firemen after she sees him get beat up. Is that fucked up or what? I'm
talking about loyalty. And you left the window open and the baby fell
out and got killed. And—"

He saw Dolores look quickly toward me.

"Oh, she didn't tell you *that* part, I guess," Hector spat bitterly.
"That *one little thing* that made all the difference, right? Okay? How
she left the window open because she had too much to drink even
though she knew it was dangerous? Did she talk about how the social
work lady from Family Services come around asking what happened?
How there coulda been a hearing down at Family Services? How I
forgave her for it? I forgave her everything. She killed my son and I
forgave her for that!"

His voice slid into a great angry lament and Dolores seemed
alarmed by this change—she recognized something in it. "I loved you
that time I first seen you, Dolores," Hector went on. "Jesus Christ, I
told you that. I made my promises, you know? Them vows in front of
your aunts? Spent all my money on the honeymoon? We had it good
in them times, we had everything we wanted. I always been loyal to
you, Dolores, never fucked around. Maybe I *pretended* I was messin'
with some them girls at the bar down on Forty-eighth Street, make
you a little pissed off, but I never did nothin'. I'm tellin' you I never
stuck my fuckin' cock in no other woman because I loved you. I fucked
a lot of girls before I married you, Dolores, and I liked doin' it and
then I stopped because I loved you like you never understood. A guy
don't always want to admit that, Dolores. Nothin', Dolores, I never
did nothin' because I'm tellin' myself that this ain't nearly good as
what I got back home. You was the fuckin' best. I told some the guys
that, too." He waited for Dolores's acknowledgment. It didn't come.
"And I kept bustin' my hump, right? I'm a proud man, Dolores, I got
my pride but I rather have you. I worked my *ass* off for you and the
kids and then I come home one day and you're gone and then you
move in with some guy, some fuckin' rich *white guy* who probably
can't fuck no good—"

"He does just fine, Hector, so you can shut up." Dolores stared hatefully at him, her lips pressed together. The two of them seemed to have forgotten my presence.

I realized that there was more to come, and I worriedly checked my watch. There was no way now that I could make it exactly on time to the board meeting; already I was running five minutes late. But I couldn't leave with Hector in my backyard. He might hurt Dolores or Maria, he might burn the place down, he might take them away from me. "Hey," I said to him, "let's just get a few things straight here — "

"You!" Hector hollered. "You ain't part of this, you ain't not even here, you got that? I'm not even gonna *bother* myself with you in this deal." He turned toward Dolores, his eyes softer. "Dolores, please, baby, I been tryin' to find you for weeks, you know that? I'm sorry I hadda kill a couple of dogs. It wasn't their fault. It's just that I ain't got nothin', Dolores. I don't have myself no more, you know? I been workin' so long and I ain't got *nothin'*. Nobody is buying cars at the lot. All we got out there is a lot of shit that is no good, stuff that's eight, ten years old. But that's okay because I got this promotion. I said that on the tape, too. You hear that? They made me a supervisor, Dolores, I get something like fifty-two hundred bucks more comin' in. Good money. Got a whole training manual and everything. So I figured maybe we could take a little vacation, maybe go down to the beach, Dolores. Maria loves the ocean, remember that time we went out to Coney Island? Atlantic City or something, just stay in one of them motels that ain't so expensive." Hector looked at his wife, hoping she would say something. He wanted desperately to disgorge his grief and I could imagine him sitting in confession, minute after minute as Dolores had said, talking too loudly to the priest.

"Alls I want is just you and the kid," Hector hurried on. "If I got that I'm okay. This is what I been wantin' to say and all. My heart is okay long as you and Maria come home. Let's go to the beach. Today's my day off, set up some beach chairs maybe . . ." He watched her for some sign that this might appeal to her, but Dolores's expression was unchanged, and this seemed to unnerve him. "I never begged you for nothin', I never begged nobody, I never even begged the Chink for money, I never begged for a job. Never. But I'm beggin' you, Dolores, I'm in bad shape, *chica*, you're still my hair parlor girl, *tú sabes?* Still my little *mami*. All them good times up in Sunset Park?

All them nights outside on the grass? Come on, Dolores, you useta say *besame, besame.* You can't walk away from all them times, I been out to little Hector's grave, Dolores, and I seen you been there sometime not too long ago. I seen some old flowers and stuff and I know we still got all that. We still got little Hector, Dolores. Only I know 'bout him inside you and only you know 'bout him inside me. I even stayed around the cemetery lookin' for you a couple of times. And I'm going to mass, Dolores, I'm prayin' for you and me and Maria, 'cause I'll find some way for her to go to college, Dolores, I'll do it if I gotta fuckin' cut my legs off, she can do what we never got, we have to work for that. I got a whole plan, see. Every little thing figured. Keep goin' offa this promotion, keep goin' higher. I ain't been drinkin', Dolores, I'm savin' every dollar, eating cheese macaroni—" He stopped talking. Something had occurred to him. He squatted down and opened his arms. "Maria, *dame un beso.*"

The child broke from her mother's arms and walked solemnly toward her father, head down. As she moved, Hector seemed reassured, even peaceable. "See that?" he demanded of us. "She's gonna give me a kiss."

But Maria saw something in her father's face that made her stop a few feet short. She turned and ran not to her mother but to me, since I was closer, hiding her face against my legs and wrapping her arms around me. I instinctively dropped my hands onto her head, cradling the dark mass of curls, and picked her up, holding her to my chest. Of course I loved this child, and my familiar actions betrayed that. When I looked up, Hector was staring in shock. His daughter had chosen me, not him, and his face drained of anger: the enormity of what Maria had done stunned him. He'd prepared himself for Dolores's sexual infidelity, but not for Maria's fearful embrace of another man.

The four of us stood there silently, the bees meandering in the sunlight, Hector with his mouth open, unblinking. I wish now that I could have known what passed through his mind—perhaps he wondered how his life had come to a point where he had again been dispossessed of a child, how it was that his life was moving toward the margins of loneliness and despair. The shock on his face gave way to a strange, ashen resolve and he turned toward Dolores.

"Come back now, Dolores," he pleaded softly. "I can't take this no more. I'm tellin' you, Dolores, I'm goin' to kill myself. Yes or no."

"Hector—"

"Yes," Hector whispered hoarsely, "or no, Dolores. That's it. That's what it's gonna be. I'm askin' you."

Before answering, Dolores glanced at me with torment; I saw that she dreamed of the life I had shown her. As much as she still loved Hector, a new life with me seemed a genuine possibility. My money seemed like a possibility. The *ease* of money, in contrast to Hector's noble yet futile attempt to climb out of the working class. Dolores knew that money would help Maria. And too, there was the dream of Dolores's father in her, and she wanted it to continue.

"Hey, Dolores," Hector pleaded, trying to break the spell, "I'm tellin' you . . ."

She continued to look at me until her expression changed, relaxed. She'd understood something. Decided something. Two days prior she'd been a guest with me at a Long Island mansion that was worth a good fifteen or twenty million; Hector's motel in Atlantic City no longer cut it—it was a joke, in fact, a sad, little joke. We're all like this; our appetites get richer. There I stood in my good dark suit. Three-hundred-dollar shoes, the small gold cuff links, the silk tie, the combed hair. Barely an hour had passed since I had ridden myself up into her, since the money had ridden up inside her. And perhaps she even held a certain sentiment for me, not great love perhaps, but something close to affection.

"I can't, Hector." Dolores looked back at him, her voice firm now. "You and me . . . it's all done, Hector, I can't be with you."

"That your answer?"

"Yeah." She looked at him, not blinking.

"*I'm the father of your two kids!*"

"Don't start on me like this," Dolores said. "You and me been over all this."

"Okay," I began. "I think—"

"Dolores, I ain't fuckin' around here, you know?" Hector cried, a thin edge of desperation in his voice. "I'm sayin' it plain as I can, that I got to have you and Maria back, so help me, I'm . . . I'm—"

"No," she answered angrily. "I said no. That was my answer."

"I'm no good for you now, that's it?"

Dolores stood straight before her husband. "Everything changed, Hector. Things happened. They always do."

"You gonna stay with this bastard?"

"Yeah," Dolores answered bitterly, "I just might, Hector."

"He gonna take care of you the way I do?"

"Maybe better, Hector."

"Well—" Hector stood there staring at us. It wasn't going the way he had envisioned. Maria was frozen in my arms. Maybe thirty seconds passed.

"Dolores, I have this meeting I have to go to," I announced with purposeful irritation, glancing at my watch, hoping to bluff things into some kind of settlement. It bothered me that Maria was witnessing such ugliness, too. "I'm really late. In fact I'm in trouble, too. So let's decide what the *fuck* is going to happen here."

The two of them stared at each other, all of it passing back and forth between them, I knew. But I couldn't be here, I had to go. I felt that first tick of acid in my throat—the pain didn't want to be forgotten. If I left that instant, I'd arrive in time to be considered quite awkwardly late. Everyone would look up at me. Fine. I'd carry it off. The table was big enough that you could skate on it. The wastebaskets in the corners would be empty. The carpeting would have fresh vacuum cleaner tracks. Samantha's makeup would be perfect. She would smell good, too. But five minutes more and I would be late enough that the Chairman would ask Mrs. Marsh if I'd called. He'd know how long he could wait and then he would blink once and decide that someone else would present the overview to the board. "Hector, dammit, you're not wanted here," I said now with urgency, "can't you *see* that? Can't you see that it's over? It's done. Things *end*, and other things begin. Your baby son died. I'm sorry about that. Things went bad. Your wife left you. She decided to do that. It's done. Dolores and Maria aren't—"

Hector's expression made me stop. He looked at each one of us, his dark eyes glassy with solemn comprehension, and then nodded silently. Something had passed out of him and in the warmth of the sun on the bricks he seemed to slouch into his heavy black coat.

Maybe I could leave now. Still holding Maria, I took two steps closer toward him in such a way as to direct him back into the house and toward the front door. He didn't move.

"You going?" I said.

"Yeah," he said in that same hoarse voice. "I'm *going* all right."

"Okay, then."

"You think you love my wife and daughter?" Hector demanded suddenly, stopping in front of me.

"Yes," I snapped back, holding Maria tight to me.

"You think you can take care of them?"

I was silent, worried now about his malevolence.

"You think you three going to stay together?" Hector persisted, his dark eyes burning the question at me.

"Hector, you stop this shit," Dolores said.

"You think you got my wife, my baby girl, that it?" Hector went on. "They're yours now, big man, that the idea?"

He wanted me to say it.

"Yes," I answered calmly.

"Fuck you. You don't have shit."

"Get out of here," I said.

"Fuck you," Hector spat at me. "You hear that? Fuck you. You don't have shit. You hear me?"

I watched him, feeling the heat of the day rising. They were standing around outside the large mahogany doors on the fortieth floor waiting for the subtle nod to begin. The Chairman would be the only one carrying no paper.

"One last time, Dolores," Hector cried loudly. "Yes or no."

"No, Hector," she said coldly. "Why do I gotta say it a million times? No."

I was about to again insist to Hector that he must leave but before I did he thrust his hand into his coat and pulled out a heavy old revolver. With no hesitation he jammed the steel barrel deep into his mouth; his lips were tight, as if he were sucking hard on a straw. He performed a brisk half turn toward Dolores — to face her directly one last time, to force her to see what she had done to him — and then the single shot came, the sound of it kicking the air, making us jump, and a fine spray of blood and tissue speckled my glasses and face. Hector fell to the brickwork at my feet, the blood from the back of his head bright red in the sunlight. I wiped my lenses instinctively. The shot was off to one side and Hector gurgled with a wild, choked expression in his eyes as he faced the sky. Screaming for her mother, Maria kicked and struggled out from my arms. Dolores and Maria fell to the ground next to Hector while I stood above them, knowing I must go and call the ambulance, yet unable to move, watching Hector's young, vital body fight against the certain tide of death. His fingers clutched and released rigidly. Blood came from his ears and out of his mouth.

"Daddy, Daddy, Daddy, Daddy!" screamed Maria. The sound tore through me and echoed down the brick walls of the houses on either side of us. Then there was a telling silence. Maria and Dolores knelt beside Hector, praying and crying, and with his wife and daughter returned to him, he arched his back one last time and moaned strangely, as if he still had a shred of consciousness and now, this moment, wanted his life returned to him.

♦ ♦ ♦

The ambulance arrived in just under four minutes from Methodist Hospital six blocks away and at first the EMT's worked hard on Hector, slipping off his heavy black coat and yanking his shirt open so that they could get to his chest as he lay there on the bricks of my yard, flat and rigid on his back, gold chain and crucifix fallen to the side of his neck. Their radios crackled as they tore open large white absorbent pads, jammed a syringe of adrenaline in Hector's neck, and put inflatable shock trousers on him to force the blood from his legs back into his heart. But the color was gone from his face. His eyes peered fixedly into the morning haze above us, and his waxen lips hung open, as if about to comment. Dolores stood over him in her bloodstained dress, her hands on Maria's shoulders in the same protective way she stood the first time she stepped off the subway and turned toward me on the day we met. In their shock, neither cried. Several policeman arrived and one fastidiously pulled on white latex gloves, removed the gun from Hector's hand, and emptied the rest of the brass-jacketed shells out of the chamber, enough to have killed all of us. Another cop stood off to the side, rocking back and forth on his heels, his face impassive as he wrote down the basic facts. From time to time he looked up at Dolores and Maria. They were only yards away from me, on the other side of Hector's body, but it seemed a strange, far distance.

They lifted Hector onto a gurney, leaving the black coat on the ground, and moved him into the house toward the ambulance. Dolores and Maria followed his body. I put out my arms.

"Don't touch me," Dolores said with fierce coldness, pulling Maria tight to her. She climbed straight into the ambulance, holding her daughter, and I knew it was done.

◆ ◆ ◆

The ambulance pulled away and I stood on my front stoop, alone and shaken. The appointed hour for the meeting with the board was upon me. If I left immediately, I could still arrive in time for the few minutes of chat at the end of the meeting, repeating the excuse for my lateness during the small talk on the way to the 10:00 A.M. press conference. I sat on the iron bench in my garden and gazed with dull fascination at the trampled pattern of blood upon the bricks. It seemed an insubstantial amount, given that a man had died there. Hector's black coat lay across the bricks like a fallen shadow. I dared not touch it. My shoulders and legs ached with an ancient fatigue. Time passed—how much exactly, I didn't know, but the blood had started to darken, a badge of time. The dust of Brooklyn caught in the blood's surface and dulled it. The telephone rang once, then stopped after four or five rings and then rang again. It trilled out the window, a small, useless sound. They were calling me now, to be sure I was on my way. Mrs. Marsh, standing on low heels in her office with the phone in her ear, sucking primly on a candy. Ants gathered at the edges of the blood, tasting its possibilities. And then five or eight minutes went by and the phone rang again, hard, fifteen or twenty angry, insistent rings, and still I could not rise. My father is a man of God, and I am not. His sad old eyes stare at his garden. He contemplates his weeds. He says the Lord's Prayer to himself with each meal. My mother reads the stock pages with a brandy and a cigarette. I wandered back into the house and stared at the many toys still spread across the living room rug, the tiny socks thrown on the floor, the sugary cereal in the bottom of the cereal bowl. Someone had tracked blood into the house, just a smear or two, probably one of the ambulance workers, possibly me. Next to the phone Dolores had left a hairbrush. A black sedan from the Corporation's car service pulled up outside and honked. The driver got out and rang the doorbell. I waited for him to leave. They would understand that I was not coming. Adjustments would be made. Others had the different pieces of information in their heads and could spray it out into the universe. The phone rang one last time, a few desultory rings, and then it was silent for good.

♦ ♦ ♦

I did not intend to go to the meeting, I did not intend to do anything but sit by myself until the roaring in my head stopped, but sometime in those minutes, I stumbled to my feet and without knowing what I was doing, went out the front door toward the subway. It was not that I wanted to be at the meeting, but that I was alone and the only people I knew were at work. The sight of Hector on his back played before my eyes as I rode the train, and I felt strangely thirsty. People seemed to be looking at me but I ignored them.

Forty minutes later I passed into the Corporation's lobby. It was as ever but looked different; I felt the weight of the many stories above pressing down upon the high vaulted space. I'd missed the board meeting and God knew what that meant but I could still make the press conference in the Corporation's auditorium. There was a special sign in the elevator welcoming the press and directing them to the twenty-second floor, which, when the elevator doors opened, was crowded with business, entertainment, and media reporters. The corporate relations people had set up a phone room for the wire service journalists to get the story out as soon as it broke and there were three dozen in there from Reuters, Associated Press, the British, German, and Japanese financial papers, all of them, calling it in to their editors or modeming a few paragraphs from their computers. That meant the major announcement had just been made.

I went through the doors at the back, past the corporate relations people handing out press packets. Inside the auditorium, the Chairman and various members of the board were at the front of the room up on a stage. The Chairman stood at the microphone explaining the merger deal. The room was packed. Maybe two hundred people. A dozen television cameras in the back of the room. One of the corporate relations people stopped me as I got halfway down the aisle.

"We're in the midst of the announcement, Mr. Whitman," she said with a smile. "We missed you earlier."

"Yes."

". . . advantageous to our position as a world-class corporation—" came the Chairman's practiced public voice, full of pep and optimism and humor.

"Is there anything I can do for you, Mr. Whitman?"

There was only one thing I could say, to anybody. "I just saw a man kill himself."

She blinked. "I don't understand."

"I saw a man shoot himself in the head, not even an hour ago."

She frowned, then put her pretty hands in the air before me. "Stay here please, Mr. Whitman."

Standing behind the Chairman were Fricker and Waldhausen and all the others, including Samantha. She looked great in a bright red suit, her hair done for the occasion, and held some papers in her hands. Perhaps she had spoken to the board instead of me.

"Excuse me." A photographer edged by me in the aisle, lifting his camera above his head.

"A guy just killed himself in my backyard," I told him. "He worked for this company, as a matter of fact."

"What?" he said, irritated. "Who are you?"

"I work here. I—I'm supposed to be here, doing this."

I looked up. Samantha had been quietly summoned to the edge of the stage by the corporate relations woman. Samantha spotted me but our eyes did not meet. Then she gave her instructions and the young woman bent close, nodded, and headed my way.

"What did you say, some guy killed himself?" a reporter next to me asked, flipping over a page of his notebook.

"I just saw it."

The corporate relations woman returned to me.

"Ms. Pipes says you're going to have to move to the back," she told me with icy pleasantness. "I'm afraid that—you have . . . is it *blood* on your suit?" she said in surprise and disgust. "Sort of *sprayed?*"

It wasn't so much. "I was planning on getting up on the stage," I told her. "I can do it so that—"

"Oh, you can't, I'm afraid, we've *started.*"

"Who is he?" said the reporter. "The name's Whitman, is that what you said?"

"We're not giving interviews now," the corporate relations person jumped in. "This is not—"

". . . and are confident that the formation of the world's foremost communications company will presage an era of increased . . ."

The Chairman was watching me now as a multimedia presentation flickered on the large screen behind him. He frowned. A couple of reporters turned around. They'd heard me.

"Who are you?" one asked me.

". . . we are extremely pleased by the intersection of these new markets . . ."

"Jack Whitman. Vice president for corporate development and planning," I answered dutifully.

"What's the problem?" he asked loudly. "Are you supposed to be up there?"

"Well—"

"You seem to have blood on your suit, you know that? Something happen somewhere?" His eyes brightened with an idea. "Something happen in the building?"

"Yes . . ." I began. "A very strange thing just happened to me—"

He was paying attention now.

"It happened in the building, you say, where?"

"No, no, not here . . ." I looked toward the front of the room. Samantha was standing next to the Chairman, her bad eye focused inward as she whispered in his ear, directing his gaze in my direction. He frowned and then he nodded and leaned back toward the microphone.

"Excuse me!" The room boomed with sound. "We have some unauthorized . . . yes, *you*, sir, halfway back, right there. Please let us continue with the program. I apologize to the media for the interruption." The Chairman stared right at me, as if we were strangers on a bus. "Thank you," he said conclusively.

"Please move to the back," the corporate relations person urged me.

Perhaps I resisted. Just a little, with my arms. That would be understandable. I don't remember doing that, really. But I might have. I do remember that I wanted only to say that I was content just to listen. But Samantha was still watching and she saw that I had not moved. She took one graceful, long-legged step toward the microphone and the room froze for just a moment as we looked at one another. The members of the board were watching impatiently. Waldhausen was watching. She was going to say my name. The room started to murmur with irritation. I think everyone sensed that we knew each other. Maybe it was only five seconds. It felt longer.

"You, sir," Samantha said in a cold voice to the room. "Will you please leave these proceedings?" She lifted her pretty pink hand and summoned the forces. "May we have some people from corporate relations escort the gentleman from the room, please?" Samantha appeared to be looking at me or just over my head. Or perhaps her skewed eyes confused me. I didn't seem to know her. She certainly didn't know me. She gave a reassuring smile to the audience. Then the corporate relations people appeared and cordoned me toward the door. Instantly the presentation resumed.

"Who is he?" asked a reporter getting out of his seat to follow us.

"Nobody," the corporate relations woman said graciously, as if accepting sugar in her tea. "No pictures."

"What's that blood on him?" came another voice after me.

But I was out of the room. Falling. Gone.

◆ ◆ ◆

They took me into some secretary's office I'd never seen before and politely hovered about me. "I think we should put him in a cab or something," I heard a woman say. "Where do you live, Mr. Whitman?"

She bent close to me and I could only stare into the strange pretty face, one of the faces of the Corporation. She was pretty in a gum commercial sort of way, which is how the Corporation likes its corporate relations people.

"Where do you live?" another one repeated helpfully. They seemed so civil, so professional.

Another one whisked into the room.

"Ms. Pipes said that we have to get him out of the building right away. I told her he was totally disoriented. She asked me if it looked like a lot of blood on him."

"What did you say?"

"Well, look at him."

"She say what to do?"

"She said the press conference should be almost done, so we may have to use the service elevator. Mary, will you call building services and get them to send it up here?"

"May we see your wallet, Mr. Whitman?"

They found my address and sent me home. A young man with a boy's neck inside his crisp collar was instructed to see me out of the lobby all the way to the curb.

"Make sure he gets in the cab," he was told.

♦ ♦ ♦

In the taxi I lay back on the seat watching the buildings go by. The driver looked up at his mirror. "Don't get sick in my car," he said.

The faces of the building flew past above me and I heard Samantha's voice again, *you, sir,* summoning the guards. I was now the man who had disrupted the most important press conference in the Corporation's history, a man in a bloody suit. Samantha had ordered my removal. With ease. I realized without purposefully thinking of it that it could only have been Samantha who had suggested to Morrison that I be assigned to the Chairman in the first place. Who else could it have been? That was where the coldness in her voice from the podium had come from, the brutal dispatch. She'd believed that Morrison's gambit would work. By getting me assigned to the Chairman, she shuffled me aside and set herself up to benefit from Morrison's ascendance. Now Morrison was gone, and she was not. Samantha was very good, she was a survivor, she was playing the game at a higher level. I doubt she hated me; in my shock I understood that only someone who had nothing would want everything.

◆ ◆ ◆

Back at the house I climbed out of the cab and looked up the steps at my house. I opened the door and listened. Then I saw Dolores standing at the window with her daughter.

"Maria," Dolores directed in a calm voice, "I want you to go upstairs for a minute."

The child ran past me and climbed a few steps, then looked back. I could see the terror in her face and I wanted to hold her and protect her.

"Go on, you heard me."

Maria climbed the stairs solemnly, her knees lifting her little skirt. Dolores turned to me. "We're leaving now."

"Back to the hospital?"

"He's dead. I said good-bye to him back there."

Her expression was distant.

"Then where?" I asked.

"Away."

I couldn't think. "Your old apartment?"

She didn't want to answer, pressing her lips together tight. "I don't know," she said finally. "No, not there. Anyplace but that."

"Why not just stay here a bit, and figure out—"

"We can't stay here."

"But you and I, we're—"

Maria was coming down the stairs and Dolores looked up at her.

"I want you to stay, Dolores. You and Maria. I don't have anybody else, that's the thing. We can work all this out, we could—"

"Was it true what Hector said?"

"About what?"

"About how he kept trying to talk to me? He said he was trying to call—"

"Yes."

This seemed to be infinitely sad for Dolores. "You should have just let me talk to him. I could have talked to him. It would have been different."

"I didn't think he'd — "

"No, of course not!" Dolores cried out. "How could you? You didn't know him!"

"But I was only — "

"He got all angry, thinking about everything. You can't just do that to Hector, he gets frustrated."

"Jesus, Dolores, I'm sorry. But he came here with a gun in his pocket, he — "

"He did a stupid thing!" Dolores exclaimed bitterly. "And he was stupid to love me so much!"

We stood in silence while Maria fingered some of the toys on the coffee table. She understood something of what her mother was saying. No one had turned on any lights in the living room. I could see by Dolores's distracted expression that she was playing it all back to herself, the decision to leave Hector, the decision to move in with me.

"Come on, Maria," Dolores finally said.

"Can I call you a cab?"

"No, I don't need a *cab*." She pulled on a coat over her bloodied dress.

"You don't know where you're going?"

"No."

"It would be better for Maria to stay here. Keep things stable."

"No."

She had nothing. "Let me give you some money or something. Just so — "

"I don't want anything. Come on, Maria."

Dolores gathered up a few toys and clothes for Maria, just enough that could be carried, and then handed me her copy of the house key. She pushed open the front door and motioned for Maria to follow.

"Dolores, don't go. Please. I want you here, I want you to stay."

She turned back toward me and I realized that if she had left Hector, then of course she could leave me. Her dark eyes brimmed for a moment as she played it all back to herself. Her lips were swollen. Then she blinked the tears away and her face hardened again. She gathered Maria's hand and the two of them walked down the worn steps of my stoop. Maria insisted on closing the black iron gate in front of my house and Dolores indulged her this.

"I don't want to leave," Maria cried out, dragging her shoes.

"Let's go, Maria," Dolores whispered sternly to her daughter, not looking at me.

"Bye, Jack," the child called to me sadly. They turned up the street in the direction of the subway, the old brownstones rising high and mute to either side. Maria looked up at her mother once or twice, but Dolores walked resolutely forward. The breeze moved the new green tree leaves over their heads. I wanted to believe that only good things would come to them.

SIXTEEN

I am solitary. In my wanderings about the city these days, I've developed an odd habit. Perhaps that's expectable, for I am now a man of park benches and windows in cheap luncheonettes. A man who lingers on the sidewalk, striking up conversations with the street vendors. Sometimes I stand in bookstores for hours, flipping through volume after volume. Other times I go sit in the public library in midtown Manhattan and read the magazines. Yes, perhaps it is only expectable. My new odd habit is this: when I get dressed each morning in my apartment, I slip a small three-by-five notecard into my breast pocket. It's the same card each day, softened around the edges and corners by now, and it sticks up about a half inch above the pocket. On the card is taped a smudged rectangle of newsprint, a short paragraph from the first lengthy story on the Corporation's merger that appeared in the *Wall Street Journal*. The piece was absolutely complete, laying out the merger rationales for Volkman-Sakura and the Corporation and how the financial analysts liked the deal. The article recounted the Chairman's long tenure, the "sudden ouster" of Morrison, Samantha's "new prominence," Waldhausen's increasing power at Volkman-Saukura, and so on. The expectable, the usual. The one short paragraph that I clipped out appeared toward the end of the story, far enough down that it could be cut out by an editor if space required. The paragraph read: "The announcement was briefly interrupted when an executive of the company, John Whitman, caused a disturbance. Whitman, a vice president for corporate planning and development, had apparently been a witness to a suicide in his home an hour prior to the announcement and had arrived at the press conference in a disoriented state, said a company official. 'It was just one of those weird events no one can predict,' said Jessica McGillis, a company spokeswoman. 'It has no relevance to our very important and most exciting news.' "

♦ ♦ ♦

It was on the morning after Dolores and Maria left, the morning the piece appeared in the paper, that Helen phoned.

"I'm here," I said. "Still here."

"They sort of asked me if I'd call you," Helen began.

"It's that bad, huh?"

"I don't understand," Helen protested.

Helen was being kind. I stared out my window into the garden. Hector's black coat still lay on the bricks. I didn't dare touch it yet. "I mean," I said, "that after what happened yesterday, no one *wants* to call me."

"I think everyone should understand that you were—that something had happened . . . everyone seemed quite pleased overall by the announcement."

"You're being very kind, Helen. I suggest that you ask as soon as possible to be assigned to someone else. That would be the advisable thing, Helen."

"Jack—"

"Helen," I broke in. "I wonder if perhaps you could box up everything in my office that is somewhat personal and just send it to me here."

"What's—"

"Just box it up. Please do it."

"But, Jack," came her voice, betraying her exasperation now, "you were supposed to make a presentation for the Chairman to the board and everyone is basically *shocked*, to be honest about it, and—"

"Did the Chairman ask after me?"

"Well, no, I don't believe that he did, he's been working with Samantha mostly, she ended up being the one who—"

I replaced the phone on the hook.

That same day the police sent over two detectives from Brooklyn's Seventy-eighth Precinct to talk to me, a young hound of a guy named Westerbeck along with an older man with graying hair who watched me with detached professional scrutiny. They rang the door-bell and we sat down politely in my living room.

"We're just trying to get some answers to wrap this up," Wester-beck explained. "It's sort of an unusual case, 'cause usually the guy'll kill the wife and the kid first or maybe kill the other guy. He usually kills somebody else and then sometimes he kills himself. That's usual-ly the way it goes, we got one the other day like that where the guy killed all his children first. Four of 'em, boom-boom-boom."

I said nothing.

"So what kind of guy was this Hector?" the detective asked.

I couldn't think of an answer. "Beaten," I finally said.

"Guys beat him up?"

"No. I mean things kept beating him down."

"Did you know he had a gun yesterday?"

"I guess I worried about it but I wasn't sure."

"So you didn't try to talk him out of it."

"It was too fast."

The detective nodded noncommittally. "His wife told one of our guys that he was upset because he wanted her and the little girl to come back."

"Yes. That's true."

"She said you sort of tricked this guy, made it so he couldn't talk to her."

I glanced at the older detective's patient eyes. He waited.

"Yes," I said. "That's also true."

"You took this woman and her little girl in and you were going to live happily ever after, that it?" the younger detective asked.

"I didn't have exact expectations."

The detective looked around the room, at the chandelier, the furniture. "It was an act of charity? You're a charitable guy?"

"I had my reasons for helping her. Dolores and Maria had no place to live."

"So you liked her?" he said. "The way she looked?"

"Yes."

"You were popping her?"

The older detective's expression was unchanged.

"Yes," I answered.

"And it was just chance that the husband and you worked for the same company?"

"Yes."

He took notice of the toys all over the rug, which I still had not picked up. The older detective simply watched. He seemed to understand that the fact that Jack Whitman had committed no crime did not mean that he was free of guilt.

"You worked it out so that he couldn't talk to her and then he broke in and—"

"Yes."

"You two guys, you and this Hector guy sort of had something going, a little angry jealous thing, right? You thought you were smarter than him, you thought you could sort of manage him out of the picture?"

"Yes."

"He loved her."

"Yes."

"She still loved him?"

"Yes."

"Do you know where this Dolores Salcines woman and her daughter are now?"

"No."

"She just left?"

"Yes."

"You're telling us you have absolutely no idea where she is."

"No. And if you find out, please tell her I'd like to talk with her."

"You ever own a gun?" the detective continued.

"No."

"Never owned a handgun?"

"No."

"We gotta find out where this Dolores Salcines woman is just so we could see how her version of things matches up."

"I don't know where she is."

My answers seemed shavings of the truth, which, gathered into a pile, resembled nothing of the whole matter. The detective shifted in the seat. "See, Mr. Whitman, it's unusual where the guy doesn't kill the other guy. The usual thing is for somebody else to get it. You two guys didn't fight or anything, roll around with that gun?"

"No."

"You get a hand on that gun?"

"I was a couple of feet away."

"This woman couldn't be at a relative's house or something, some friend's place?"

"She could be, but as far as I know all her relatives from the Dominican Republic are dead. The people in her old neighborhood would know who her friends are."

"We checked that out."

We sat there. The clock moved. The two men had a certain patience. People had been sitting in this room for over a century.

"You know their baby boy got killed about three years ago," the older detective said softly. "You know that?"

"Yes."

"Is that related in any way you can think of?"

"Directly? No."

"Indirectly?" the detective said, leaning forward ever so little.

"It was a cause of grief and despair," I told him. "It was the thing that destroyed their marriage."

The younger detective, who did not have a wedding band on his hand, seemed less interested in these vagaries. "You don't know where the woman is, you really have no idea?"

His insistence alarmed me; I wondered if they suspected that Dolores had shot Hector.

"Look, I wish she would come back," I finally offered. "I didn't *want* them to leave. I'd give anything for them to come back."

The older detective glanced at the younger one and nodded his head forward an inch.

"Okay," the other one said, "all right. Now, you got some kind of explanation for what this Hector did, seeing as how the only other witnesses are gone?"

"I thought Dolores gave a statement to the cop who was there."

"She did but it was very sketchy-like." He lifted his eyes from his clipboard. "She was upset."

"Right."

"So?"

"My only explanation is that he did it out of despair."

"You a shrink?"

"No."

And so on. I answered every question, I told them everything. My lengthy and confusing explanation of my affair with Dolores seemed only to confound their conclusions, but in the following days, as I sat in my house and spoke to no one and let the newspapers pile up outside the front door among the leaves and Chinese restaurant fliers and the grime of the city, the long shadows of the Corporation's legal representation silently moved in without my bidding, not to protect me but to protect the good name of the Corporation, and the police let the matter rest.

The cops did not ask the hardest questions, of course; the hardest questions were the ones I pondered with tortuous irresolution, such as what went through Hector's mind in those minutes that he quietly moved about the house while Dolores and Maria and I were in the garden. It haunted me to know all that he had *seen*—the bathtub, with Maria's bright plastic toys in it; the bedroom, its intimately rumpled sheets, a folded stack of Dolores's new underwear on the dresser, my socks and shoes and ties evident. Did Hector stop, his chest surging, and stoop closely to the bed to see the long strands of Dolores's hair on the pillow? Did he fling open the closet and see her new clothes? The spring dresses and new shoes? Yes, of course he did. Any man would. Every closet in the house was open, I later noticed, every one. He saw everything—he saw that I had the world available to me, as he did not, and even so, I had insisted on keeping his wife and child apart from him. And at some point he entered my office. I know this because the door was open and I always kept it shut to discourage Maria from rummaging around. On my desk, kept in eight or nine folders, were papers relating to different elements of the Volkman-Sakura deal, clipped together and left set in a perfect row. One folder was labeled WORLD CABLE OPERATIONS and when I returned to my office, it was lying atop another file at an angle. There was nothing in those papers that would mean much to Hector, in particular, but the *fact* of them, the brute reduction of the place where he worked, testified as to his smallness in the big web of things. Perhaps he even flipped through the papers, wondering if his name was there, which of course it was not. He would see that Big Apple Cable merited no special attention and that it was merely one of the Corporation's eighty-six local operations spread around the country.

But the worst thing that Hector saw in those fevered minutes was something else. Maria's bedroom—that bower of childhood—must have been the most devastating sight of all. The walls were recently adorned with a border of ABC's. And there was the low bed from Macy's children's department with its bright sheets and the toy chest with dolls and blocks and coloring books spilling from it, and I know that it was altogether too much for Hector to bear—that his child was being taken from him, seemingly *bought* from him, with such ease and effectiveness. There were a good five fist marks in the wall, slight depressions where the old horsehair plaster had been crushed against the wooden lathing underneath. I see now, more clearly, the pain of this. While we never own our children, we quite clearly mean to possess them.

And then there was that singular question—why did Hector shoot himself and not me? After all, it could have gone that way so easily. I'd kept his wife and child from him. Perhaps he knew instinctively that killing me instead of himself would not end his torment and would only push Dolores further from him. He understood what her reaction would be, her revulsion and anger. Above all, to the end, he wanted her love, and that may have been the thing that saved me. Or maybe he wanted to be sure that she and I did not stay together. But if he killed me, Dolores might mourn me. Perhaps he knew that if he killed himself he would kill whatever chance Dolores and I might have had.

Maybe. I've gone over those last minutes at least a thousand times, arranging the four of us on the square of garden bricks like the few remaining figures on a chessboard, and I have come to realize that Hector may have turned his gun on himself and not me for another reason, too. In the moment when his despairing impulse toward destruction was strongest, he looked at me and saw that I was holding Maria in my arms. If he had been thinking rationally, he would have told me to put Maria down—and I would have done it, given that he held a gun—but he was not thinking rationally, he was possessed by a deranged, sorrowful desire to prove his incontrovertible love for Dolores and to end his own humiliation. When he looked at me, he saw Maria too, and he would not shoot in her direction in an attempt to kill me. It could have been as simple as that.

♦ ♦ ♦

Only by accident did I figure out how Hector had found the address of my house in Park Slope. That information, after all, was exactly what I didn't want him to discover. The people at New York Telephone examined their records and said that although my phone number had unaccountably been changed, at no time did my street address pass into the province of the directory information operators. In the week after Hector's suicide I assumed Dolores had told one of her girlfriends. How else, I thought, could it have happened? The answer came after a drenching rain one evening, when finally I picked up Hector's coat from the bricks and carried it inside. Soaked, it must have weighed twenty pounds. In the clammy pockets, which had attracted some slugs, I found a crumpled, half-eaten bag of potato chips, a set of car keys, and a stub from the cheap seats of a Yankees game back in April. I realized that the keys might correspond to an unfamiliar old Buick parked down the block whose windshield was littered with parking tickets. A few minutes later, I inspected the car for a car alarm sticker, found none, then tried the keys in the driver's door. The second one fit. I slipped into the seat. Baby shoes hung from the windshield mirror—Maria's or little Hector's. I tried the ignition. The car started right up. Hector was the kind of man who kept his car tuned. I sat a moment with my leg out the door on the street and listened to the engine, staring at the long damp traffic tickets wedged under the windshield wipers.

Then I turned off the engine and inspected the inside of the car. Among the empty oil cans and old copies of the *New York Post*, I found a supervisor's training manual from Big Apple Cable, which Hector, no doubt, had received when he was promoted, thanks to me. I flipped idly through it and found the pertinent paragraph that explained the perfect irony of the timing of Hector's location of my house, why he had struggled to find Dolores and Maria for weeks and yet had succeeded almost immediately after being promoted at Big Apple Cable. Yes, the irony hit me like a baseball bat. The cup of my stupidity runneth over. When insisting to Janklow at Big Apple Cable that Hector be promoted, I should have remembered that the same wire of information that ran through the Corporation from Hector to me *also ran from me back to him.* When Hector was promoted, he'd received the cable installer's supervisor's manual. He dutifully took it home to study, and no doubt was jolted to attention when he read the same short paragraph now on the page before me, the paragraph that explained that "all top-level Corporation executives living in the New York metropolitan area/Big Apple Cable subscriber region receive full cable service completely free of charge" and that "supervisors are to be attentive that these accounts are serviced quickly and correctly." Once Hector knew this, all he had to do to get my address was look my name up on the subscriber computer system. The supervisor's manual explained how to do that, too.

Disgusted with myself, I tossed the manual back on the seat and got out of the car with the keys. Closed the door, wondered what to do. I opened the trunk. Next to a tangle of tools and jumper cables was a box full of beach stuff: tiny cheap shovels and pails, plastic sandals for walking on hot sand, a little inflatable raft, perfect for Maria, perfect for a Saturday afternoon at Atlantic City. Everything was new, still had the packaging and price stickers. Here I was discovering the doomed dreams of a dead man. I shut the trunk.

I decided to return to my house, but, giving the car a final look, I noticed a crumpled brown bag in the backseat, and to satisfy my curiosity, I unlocked the driver's door again, reached over the seat, and retrieved it. Inside the bag was a woman's shoe with the heel missing, some of Maria's clothing, and a handful of Crayola crayons, some broken. I stared at these items, waiting to remember why I knew exactly why they were in a bag together, why they were familiar to me — and then, in the suddenness of certainty, I *knew:* the broken shoe and clothing and crayons were the very same items that Ahmed had returned to Hector those many weeks prior when Hector had gone to Ahmed's building in his search for Dolores and Maria. I carefully picked all of Maria's crayons out of the bag. These were the ones she'd been coloring with on the subway, on the night I'd first seen the two of them. I remembered that the crayon that had rolled across the floor had been a certain dark red. Yes, here it was. For the second time I held it in my hand and this time I kept it, slipping it into my pocket.

Back in my house I hung Hector's wet, black coat over the head of my shower and it dripped for almost a day. When it was reasonably dry I put it outside my house on the fence. Within ten minutes it was gone. And the following day the city towed away Hector's car, probably to be sold at auction to a stranger.

As for the other questions, the less important ones, I meant to ask the Chairman whether he had played the whole game knowingly from the start or had changed his strategy as conditions themselves changed. It could have been either possibility. Lying back craftily for months, he'd seemed the epitome of the ruined monarch tottering on collapse; yet at other times, he moved with great speed and surety. Could one man play the game so adeptly? He knew just who I was from the beginning, he had been scanning the field, hidden in his booze and smoke, waiting for the messenger, waiting for the game to begin, feeling the reins tighten. The game included Morrison and all of us. The game is always bigger than all of us.

Also, I wanted to explain to the Chairman what had happened. I figured I owed him that. When I finally called, Mrs. Marsh asked hadn't I been reading the papers? Hadn't I heard? There was a tone in her voice. No, I said. She told me that the Chairman had a series of strokes one night while he was watching the news, and I was given to understand that his mind blew out like an engine throwing one piston after another. There had been no protracted decline, no confused ebbing of function. One day he was the Chairman and the next he was a seventy-one-year-old man being taught how to use a straw. All of it — the forty-five–odd years with the Corporation, his three wives and dozen or so mistresses, the names of his parents and children, the purposes of such things as music, bicycles, and light bulbs — gone.

I drove out to his mansion on Long Island that same day and talked my way in past Mr. Warren to find the Chairman dressed in yellow flannel pajamas, sitting on the sun porch. Though he'd lost perhaps fifteen pounds and the skin had fallen slack under his jaw, his blue eyes were bright with wonderment. His wife, the third one, sat in a room nearby, chatting happily on the telephone. The nurse tried to distract the Chairman with the television but he couldn't operate the remote control. He had no idea what it was, and clicked indiscriminately through forty or fifty channels, the light of the screen playing across his blank, amazed face as his blue eyes looked with rapt amusement at something beyond the images. I shook his hand gently and gave him a squeeze on the shoulder before leaving. Later I heard he regained a certain animal vigor and has taken up collecting golf balls. Instead of playing a regular round at Palm Beach or up in Newport at his club, he and his old caddy walk the greens relentlessly, the Chairman shuffling a bit lopsidedly, picking up discarded Truflites, Wilsons, and Titleists, and then he is driven home. Apparently there are a dozen or so buckets of old, nicked balls in his greenhouse.

♦ ♦ ♦

A police sergeant called a week later to say that Dolores had never showed up to claim Hector's body and did I know how to reach his family? It disturbed me to hear this and immediately I worried about Dolores and Maria. I told the policeman what I knew, where to inquire, including the employment forms on record at the Corporation, but the next day he called back to say that Hector's mother had died six months ago in Puerto Rico and they couldn't find a family at all. The neighbors in Hector's apartment building didn't know anybody, not real family members, and neither did anyone at St. Michael's Roman Catholic Church. There was no one to take responsibility. Did I know anybody at all?

When I told him I did not, he asked politely if they could release the body to me, because room in the hospital morgue was very tight, and otherwise the body would go to a pauper's grave, where unclaimed bodies of homeless people and abandoned infants are buried. and so I agreed and the Methodist Hospital morgue released the body to me. I had a funeral home in Sunset Park pick it up. I asked the funeral director to arrange for a Catholic service and to let the neighborhood know of it. Whatever was customary, I told him, the priest, the casket, flowers, everything. I paid him in full and explained that I would not be at the service or the burial, which I wanted him to oversee. I drove out to the Greenwood Cemetery and arranged for Hector to be buried in the plot next to his son. The cemetery official didn't understand who I was, since I was not a family member, but I paid for the plot and stone with cash and he seemed satisfied. My only consolation in doing these things is that Dolores may visit her son's grave and thus discover that her husband was properly attended to. Maybe she already has visited, I don't know.

I thought all these matters were finished but last October while I was watching the World Series on television, one of the Corporation's lawyers called to inform me that the Corporation was suing me for all of my retirement benefits in order to indemnify itself should one of Hector's family members, such as Dolores, surface and decide to sue the Corporation for Hector's death. When I protested, he pointed out that certain "abuses," as he called them, had allowed for the chain of circumstances. It could be argued by a plaintiff, the lawyer said, that I had maliciously caused mental anguish to Hector in my position of power in the Corporation. The lawyer and his "team" who had reviewed the possibility that Dolores could sue the Corporation thought she might be able to make a viable case. Thus I could sign a piece of paper or countersue the Corporation. I signed. I signed it all away. Of course, to this day, Dolores has never made a claim.

All of this happened just last year and it's changed me. The only thing that isn't different is my acid problem, which is still this burning crud, this bile, rising like blame or vengeance for everything I've ever done wrong. I went to my internist and he asked about the catching sensation in the throat. He was surpised to hear how much Maalox I was knocking back. This is not optimal, he said. There was a test he could do, in which I would swallow barium and get strapped down to a table that tilted my feet up to get an X-ray to see what was going on in there. It sounded like "Barrett's esophagus" to him. We'll do an endoscopy. Would I have to undergo a Nissen's plication? I asked. He was noncommittal. Let's increase your medication and watch it. He'd seen a number of cases such as mine, he said, and it could go on like this.

I'm living on my savings, but sooner or later I'll have to find work. I had to rent out my house to cover the monthly payments and it was taken by a young family with three children. The couple seemed glad to find it. The father, a big, hearty guy who reminded me of Harry McCaw, pumped my hand. I'm living now in a small, cheap apartment in one of the farther neighborhoods in Brooklyn. As I mentioned before I've been wandering through the city lately, moving around with no real purpose. The days go on forever. I'm quite neat in my appearance, shaving most mornings, and generally they let me sit at the window in restaurants. I'm that guy staring out through the glass with a stupid, far look on his face. I keep wondering what the way back is.

Sooner or later I'll get going. I'm sure of it. No doubt about it, actually. But right now I'm still caught up in the mystery of how it is that I live while Hector is dead, how it is that I once held Dolores and Maria tightly in my bed and they are gone and where I don't know. That, finally, is the inscrutable aspect of it. We passed through each other's lives with such mysterious velocity. She broke me, she remade me. I see now that I was foolish about her, overly sentimental. This is an old flaw in my nature, but in the case of Dolores Salcines, I should have been smarter, not so eager to get caught up in the idea of it. Dolores, after all, was hardly blameless. She was a woman who cheated on her husband with at least four men, then left him without telling him. She had lied to me from the start. And she seemed to have made no effort to talk it out with Hector; she forced his panic. Could it have ever worked out between us? I wonder what I was thinking.

And I see now, I guess, that Dolores's affections for me did not run deep enough that she would ever think lovingly of me. I know this, I know it in my heart, and it is only right. I am no more than some man whom Dolores happened to live with for a short time. Just some guy. A body. It could have been Jack Whitman, it could have been someone else just as easily. In the end, I was of little or no consequence to the heart of Dolores Salcines.

But knowing these things doesn't settle it for me. Last night I found myself staring at the swell and stir of the curtain as the air came in my apartment window, and for a moment then I am thinking I see Dolores behind that veil. I hear Maria's sweet little laugh. I love them, in that grieving, useless way. I test myself, to see if I remember their faces. Yes, I can. And then I think that they are somewhere here in the city, riding underground in the dark subways. Do they have a place to live, do they have any money? Such thoughts are sickening to me and I force them away.

So I keep moving. Or walking, rather. Just yesterday, I passed a big movieplex on the East Side, with eight or nine movies playing, a handful of them Corporation movies, one of them likely to gross nearly half a billion dollars worldwide this year, and I saw the crowds outside standing in line. They were excited by the prospect of being entertained, but there was also, it seemed, a fatigued, obligatory look in their eyes. If they wanted something else, I could not say what it was.

At lunch I remembered how much Liz loved french fries and so I stopped in a fast-food joint. Inside, a cardboard floor display explained that if you bought a hamburger or shake, you received a little rubber toy monkey, which happened to be a licensing spin-off from one of the Corporation's cartoon properties. Everybody has seen this figure. Maria has seen it, I'm sure. The Corporation has the injection-molded toys manufactured by the hundred-thousand gross in China, where they're produced cheaply by prison laborers. The monkey has very high product-recognition levels and goes back to the original celluloid film shorts produced by the Corporation in the 1940s. In fact, along with other of its cartoon characters and Hollywood memorabilia, the Corporation has opened up a national chain of stores—328 in all, mostly in suburban malls—where shoppers can also buy Corporation products: books, tapes, and clothes, movie posters, you name it. That little monkey now appears in Saturday morning cartoons on cable, in the classic full-length animation feature, in a child's videocassette series, in the Corporation's theme parks, and in other tie-ins, licensing agreements—watches, T-shirts, all kinds of stuff. Yearly gross is somewhere around forty million. The monkey is starting to appear in all the new entertainment technologies, too. He lives on as we the living do not. In the restaurant, a sign explained that you'd get one of the videocassettes if you spent above a certain amount on your food. A couple of burgers, maybe. Standing before me stood a little girl with blond hair and blue eyes and she beseeched her mother to buy her the videocassette. Such great desire, such passion. I'm not sure I understand it, really. But then again, I don't feel that I understand much of anything these days, except that I quietly went bad after Liz died.

In front of me, the mother did what her daughter wanted. I was glad, too. I've seen these cartoons; they're delightful and beguiling.

But of course the Corporation, the new Corporation, has many delightful and beguiling products on the way, and with the merger now completed it's completely global, well poised for the future; it will prosper as it lies astride the countries of the world, adept and canny, unkillable, offering even greater percentages of humanity the various entertainments. This is the magic of the Corporation. We live now to be entertained by arrangements of sound waves and light transmissions. And more is on the way, a tidal wave of new entertainments. It seems odd to me now that I ever would have cared so much about this. But always there will be the Corporation—already it has outlived nations. Some say the new Corporation is yet another harbinger of the twenty-first century, now nearly upon us.

I am sure that on the thirty-ninth floor that I was discussed and then forgotten. The Chairman is gone, too, and the new, expanded board quickly hired one of the big Hollywood studio heads to fill his position. The surface of things closed over like a gap on a calm lake, leaving no sign I had ever been there. The new management on the thirty-ninth floor has other things to worry about—the markets, the strategies, the numbers. That is the way of things in the Corporation, when you take the long view. Few are important for very long, almost no one in fact. Samantha is doing well, of course. And there is now a clever young guy who was quickly promoted to my place. His name is not known to me, but no doubt he is quite ambitious.